Alex strode to her and cupped her chin in his hand. "I have never known a more passionate woman or one who tried so hard to deny it." He gently pulled her fisted hands away from her dressing gown. "Hold me, Giana. Men enjoy being held as much as women."

She closed her hands around his back and rose to her tiptoes. "You are so big," she said.

He held her tightly against him for a moment, forcing his hands to be still. "I want to make love to you, Giana," he said quietly.

"Since I am already a fallen woman, I do want to know what the falling is like."

MORE FASCINATING ROMANCES BY CATHERINE COULTER

from **TOPAZ**

Rebel Bride   (404327—$5.99)
Lord Harry   (405919—$5.99)
The Duke   (406176—$6.99)

CONTEMPORARY ROMANCES from **ONYX**

Beyond Eden   (403398—$5.99)
False Pretenses   (401271—$5.99)
Impulse   (402502—$5.99)

Evening Star

Catherine Coulter

A TOPAZ BOOK

TOPAZ
Published by the Penguin Group
Penguin Books USA Inc., 375 Hudson Street,
New York, New York 10014, U.S.A.
Penguin Books Ltd, 27 Wrights Lane,
London W8 5TZ, England
Penguin Books Australia Ltd, Ringwood,
Victoria, Australia
Penguin Books Canada Ltd, 10 Alcorn Avenue
Toronto, Ontario, Canada M4V 3B2
Penguin Books (N.Z.) Ltd, 182-190 Wairau Road,
Auckland 10, New Zealand

Penguin Books Ltd, Registered Offices:
Harmondsworth, Middlesex, England

Published by Topaz, an imprint of Dutton Signet,
a division of Penguin Books USA Inc.
Previously appeared in an Onyx edition
under the title *Sweet Surrender*.

First Topaz Printing, May 1996
10 9 8 7 6 5 4 3 2 1

 REGISTERED TRADEMARK—MARCA REGISTRADA

Printed in the United States of America

To Hilary Ross,
with sincere thanks and appreciation

Chapter 1

Geneva, 1846

"Giana, I must fix that bow in your hair, it's hanging over your ear! And do hold still. We don't want to be late. Charles will be here soon and we cannot keep my future husband waiting for his dinner!"

Giana stood obediently quiet, eyeing herself in the long Derber mirror as Derry patted the blue velvet bow at the back of her head and tugged at the cluster of black curls over her ears.

Derry stood back and nodded approvingly, admiring her handiwork from several angles. "You are lovely, Giana," she said. But Giana was staring blankly at her in the mirror, paying no attention to her matching blue velvet gown.

"Derry," Giana said, turning to gaze up at her. "You have told me often enough how dashing Charles is, and that he loves you. But does he truly love you more than anything? Will he love you forever?"

Derry Fairmount regarded her seventeen-year-old friend Georgiana Van Cleve with the indulgent air of a girl who was a year older and engaged to be wed.

"Of course he loves me, you silly girl! And besides all that, he's everything I could wish for in a husband—he is ever so handsome and distinguished, and he is quite wealthy. It's true he lives in New

York, though," she added with a thoughtful frown. "My father is a dreadful snob, as only a Bostonian can be. But you've heard me tell you that often enough! Well, he saw last summer that dear Charles finds me quite to his liking, and has been busy, I can tell you, with all the marriage contracts and agreements. Boring stuff, but I suppose everything must be worked out before I return home."

"He will never leave you alone, Derry? He will stay with you always, and you'll never have to worry, about anything?"

Derry's happy smile stayed firmly in place, but she quickly hugged her friend. She knew Giana would miss her. And she knew that Giana, raised by nannies and governesses, looked to marriage for a sense of security, and of belonging, that she had never felt. Derry had visited Giana and her mother in London two years before, and although Mrs. Van Cleve was charming and beautiful, Derry had seen that her young friend was like a guest in her mother's house, feted, but somehow separate and apart from her. "No, love," she said gently, "married to Charles, I'll never have to be alone, nor will I ever worry. Someday, soon, Giana, you will have a husband and family of your own."

"I cannot imagine that," Giana said. She wished more than anything that Derry were younger, and not about to leave her. She cocked her head to one side, watching Derry buff her nails, and said, "but, Derry, isn't your Charles terribly *old*?"

Derry gave a trilling laugh, full-bodied and abounding with life, a laugh that Madame Orlie and her minions had failed to contain.

"Old? Well, he is forty-something-or-other, which is not at all old for a husband, especially one as rich as dear Charles! Did I tell you that his only child by his first wife, a daughter, Jennifer, is only two years younger than I? Of course I did! I'm rattling on like a chirper! Think of the fun she and I will have, just as you and I do!"

But I don't want you to have fun with her! "But what if she doesn't like you, Derry?" Giana pursued, keeping her eyes away from Derry's gaze.

"Really, Giana, why ever should Jennifer not like me? I am not an ogre, or a wicked stepmother!" The gay laughter bubbled over again. "Me, a *stepmother*! That concerns my mother, you know, and I must admit, it does give me pause, sometimes. But Jennifer, after all, is a daughter, not a wife, and the two are quite different. She will have no cause to dislike me."

"Yes, I suppose you are right," Giana said. "But if one believes all the romantic novels, the stepdaughter must hate the new mother."

"Bosh," Derry said. "Those books were dreadfully silly, but"—she rolled her eyes—"so very informative. At least I think they are," she added, blushing slightly. Derry's face took on a dreamy look, and slowly she began to dance around their room. "Boston was so beautiful that summer, and Charles so enjoyed waltzing with me."

Yes, Giana thought, feeling tears prick her eyelids, any man would want to waltz with Derry. She didn't want to feel envious of Derry, truly she didn't, but the thought of loving and being loved in return, of belonging to someone and never having to be alone again, was like a magical dream, a dream that had come true for Derry.

"You are awfully quiet all of a sudden, Miss Van Cleve," Derry said, drawing her imaginary waltz to a close.

"I was just thinking," Giana said guiltily.

Derry merely laughed. "Remember when we first

met, goodness, it was over three years ago. My ever-so-snobbish parents dumped me here in Geneva at Madame Orlie's exclusive young ladies' seminary to finish me off properly." Her eyes twinkled. "They will be so disappointed. After all your good influence, I still haven't achieved your clipped, starchy accent. You English—I think you are born speaking that way!"

Giana's twinge of envy dissolved under Derry's gay banter. She lowered her head and whispered, "You will leave in but three days, Derry, and I will be alone again."

"Nonsense, Giana," Derry said in a bracing voice. "You will not have to put up with another colonial like me. Next week you will have a new roommate, a nice English girl, who, from what she told us in her very nice English letter, is blessed with a handsome brother." Derry shrugged elaborately. "Who knows, perhaps he will be a prince charming."

"Unlikely," Giana said roughly, knowing that Derry was merely trying to cheer her up, and hating it. "There will be no one to tell you what to do," she said suddenly. "You will have servants, and do just as you please."

"Yes, and eat cream puffs for dinner, if I like. Old Maevis would have a fit, I know, the dear old dragon." Derry pursed her mouth tightly together and hunched her shoulders, doing a credible imitation of Maevis Danforth, their deportment teacher. "Like she sucks lemons," Derry giggled.

Giana smiled at her antics, as always, but the hated tears were still there, waiting for naught in particular to send them streaming down her face.

"Come, Giana, whatever are you daydreaming about now? You really must stop that, you know. I've told you often enough that people will think you're myopic, and we both know you've the eyes of an eagle."

"I will miss you, Derry," Giana said.

"Pooh!" Derry said severely, pressing her wadded handkerchief into Giana's hand. "New York is not the end of the earth, Giana. And it is not as if you were a poor little orphan. When Madame Orlie considers you fit to leave her poshy school, in . . . what, a mere six more months?" She paused a moment, gazing about their dimity-curtained room that gave onto the magnificent prospect of Lake Geneva, then shrugged her elegant shoulders with studied indifference. "Well, your dear mama can send you to New York to visit me. It is only fair, after all, for I visited you two years ago in London. And I'm sure I can convince dear Charles to bring me to London, next year, say. There are dozens of banks in London, and Charles loves banks above all things. Now, Giana, you must smile, and be happy for me. Look, your bow has come loose again. Quickly, my love. Madame Orlie should be greeting Charles and Jennifer anytime now, and I wish us to be ready when she calls for us."

As Derry's nimble fingers firmly pinned down the heavy bow, she saw Giana's eyes drop over her figure in the mirror. "How I wish that I were tall and had your beautiful blond hair, Derry. Look at me, I'm short and my hair is a stupid black. I don't even have a bosom," she added in disgust.

"I have told you before that in another year or so, you will become a veritable ship's figurehead!" She was pleased to see Giana smiling again, albeit tremulously. "If you get too big," she whispered wickedly near Giana's ear, "the gentlemen will stare at you rudely, and make you blush!" Derry thought of how

Charles occasionally swept his gaze over her, and it was she who blushed back at herself in the mirror.

"There, you look quite acceptable, Miss Giana," Derry announced. She stepped back to regard her friend. She saw her budding beauty, and knew that Giana saw nothing but an insecure little girl staring back at her. "One must never admit defeat at anything, Miss Van Cleve, nor give in to the doldrums. Now, my girl, straighten your shoulders, I hear Lisette coming. Charles has doubtless arrived."

Their greetings were stilted in Madame Orlie's severely formal drawing room, but no sooner were they tucked warmly into a carriage and on their way to the renowned Golden Lion than Derry was chattering gaily, gesticulating with only one hand, for the other was safely held by Mr. Charles Lattimer.

Giana stared shyly at Mr. Lattimer whenever he wasn't looking at her. He appeared to be everything Derry had rhapsodized about, and more. He was a tall man, slender and elegantly attired, with soft wheat-colored hair that was just beginning to gray at the temples—ever so distinguished—and light blue eyes that seemed aloof and cold until he smiled, which he did a great deal that evening. He was, Giana recognized, old enough to be her father, and Derry's as well, but with his elegance, his gentle yet polished manners, Giana soon came to believe that an older man such as he would only cherish his wife all the more. When he addressed an amusing remark to Derry, or lightly caressed her hand, Giana saw him as superb, the epitome of what a husband should be.

When they arrived at the Golden Lion, Charles gracefully assisted the three young ladies from the carriage. He had procured a private dining room, and after settling them around an immaculately set dinner table, he beckoned the waiter and ordered champagne in flawless French.

"Scandalous, sir!" Derry chided him, laughing.

"Ah," Charles Lattimer said, smiling down at his fiancée, "but we must celebrate, my dear."

"Champagne gives me a headache," Jennifer said, the longest string of words she had yet spoken.

"It makes Giana sneeze," Derry said.

"A toast," Charles Lattimer said, raising his glass. "To my beautiful bride." His blue eyes seemed to caress each of them, and his smile widened. "I appear to be blessed with a veritable harem this evening. Never have I enjoyed the company of three such lovely ladies."

"I will see that you don't in the future, Charles," Derry said, quirking a blond brow at him.

"My father always does just as he should," Jennifer said. "And besides, you are too young to tell him what to do."

There was a brief, tense moment of silence, during which Giana would have liked to give a swift, painful tug to Jennifer Lattimer's chestnut ringlets for her rudeness.

To Giana's relief, Charles Lattimer leaned back in his chair and said lightly, "A wife, my dear Jennifer, particularly one as young and lovely as Derry, can always tell her husband what to do. He is the most malleable of creatures, I assure you."

Giana took a drink of her champagne, and quickly sneezed. "I hope I am not leading to your moral downfall, my dear Miss Van Cleve," Charles said, thumping her lightly on her shoulders.

"Oh no, sir," Giana said, feeling her face go warm beneath his amused eyes.

"We once sneaked in some champagne," Derry said. "The gardener's boy bought it for us. I must agree with Jennifer. After half a bottle, the both of us had splitting heads the next day. Madame Orlie thought we had both come down with the influenza and sent us back to bed."

Giana's eyes rested on the sloe-eyed Jennifer to see her reaction, but there was none. She was playing with her food, her mouth sullen. Jennifer must, Giana thought, taking a ladylike bite of her creamed artichokes, resemble her dead mother, with those distant gray eyes of hers, so unlike her father's.

"My dear Derry," Charles said, "you are telling me that two such well-brought-up girls indulge in such wickedness?"

"Ah, our conversations were much more wicked, sir!"

Giana shivered suddenly, not from any draft, for the parlor with its blazing fire was cozily warm against the cold winter night.

"I hope you are not cold, my dear," Charles Lattimer said, leaning forward in his gilt-armed chair.

"Oh no, sir," Giana managed, blushing.

"I do not believe," Charles Lattimer continued, addressing the table at large, "that I should like to spend the winter in Switzerland. Much more snow than we suffer in New York, and the winds of the lake penetrate the thickest coat." He turned caressing eyes toward Derry. "My dear Derry, since we will be married right after Christmas, I will tell you that I have already done some refurbishing of your wardrobe. I trust you will approve the sable-lined cloak."

"How absolutely decadent, Charles!" Derry said, her chocolate-brown eyes twinkling.

"And how devastating on you, my dear," he murmured, lifting Derry's hand to his lips. He leaned closer to her and whispered something that neither Jennifer nor Giana could hear.

To Giana's surprise, Derry, always so clever and so sure of herself, stammered and blushed.

"I do feel a draft, Father," Jennifer said suddenly. "And everything is drowned in thick sauces."

"You must become more worldly in your tastes," Charles Lattimer said easily, leaning back in his chair. "I dislike provincialism."

"Would you like my shawl, Jennifer?" Derry asked her future stepdaughter.

"No, thank you, Miss Fairmount," Jennifer said. "If you caught a chill, Father would never forgive me."

"I trust I am not so heartless, Jennifer," Charles Lattimer said smoothly, "but I would dislike having to postpone our wedding."

"No need for you to worry, Charles," Derry said. "I never catch chills. You'll find that I have a most loathsomely healthy constitution. My dear Giana," she continued without pause, "you have scarce eaten a bite." Her eyes twinkled wickedly, falling for but a moment to Giana's bosom. "You will never grow unless you eat."

Giana blushed and cast a darkling glance toward Derry, but nonetheless quickly forked a bite of stuffed veal into her mouth.

Chapter 2

London, 1847

Aurora Van Cleve stared out of the bowed front windows that gave onto Belgrave Square. She watched the nannies in their starched gray uniforms gossiping quietly, their vigilant eyes on their young charges who romped in the lush green grass, some tossing a brightly colored ball around a circle to each other. Every couple of years, the young faces changed as the children grew too old to be taken to the park by their nannies, and new ones took their places. Odd that the nannies never seemed to change, save for the graying of their hair beneath their caps.

She looked down at her elegant slender hand and muttered at herself, for she had teased and fussed with a fingernail until it was a jagged wreck. Millie would be aghast when she saw it. The prissy old dear would likely scold Aurora as if she were still a child, and not a widow of forty.

Dear God, what am I to do? Aurora turned away from the bowed windows and gazed about her library, the only really comforting room in her twenty-two-room barn of a house. She had seldom been allowed into the library until Morton died, and on these rare occasions when she had been commanded by her husband to appear, it had been to heighten his vanity by exhibiting his young and beautiful wife to his business cronies, as if reminding them that he, a man of the merchant class, had succeeded in aligning himself with the aristocracy. She had been his prize purchase, his most brilliant possession. *How your colorless eyes used to stare at me, Morton, continually examining me for my worth to you.* It had taken her months after he died to step into this dark paneled room with his musty books creeping up three walls, its heavy mahogany-and-leather furniture still permeated then with the smell of his pipe. Aurora looked about the room and smiled, shaking off her memories of her husband, their bitterness dulled with time. Even his library, his man's domain, had been hers for twelve years, and it was no longer the starkly masculine library of a man of vast business interests, but a warm, feminine room, her room.

She gazed at the portrait of her and Giana over the fireplace, painted when Giana was but six years old. It had long ago replaced his portrait, buried now among discarded furniture and boxes in the attic. Giana looked a glowing miniature of her mother, even then. This beautiful child, her only child, had returned from her exclusive young ladies' seminary in Switzerland a beautiful young lady, and a stranger to her. How could she have been so blind as to believe that Giana would grow up as she had always imagined?

Aurora walked slowly to her delicate French desk and eased herself into a frivolous Louis XV chair with graceful gold-gilt curving arms, a chair that Morton would have despised. She looked down at a sheaf of papers that required her attention, but she soon pushed them aside. *I can never forgive myself for what I did to her.* There, she had admitted it, accepted the fact that it was she who was responsible for Giana's frivolity and her young girl's romantic foolishness. Aurora rested her head upon her hands and stared blankly before her, thinking yet again about the talk she had had with her daughter but two hours before.

Giana had gazed at her sullenly, her pretty eyes narrowed. "Really, Mama, I have no interest in all of this," she had said, waving her hand negligently toward the neat stacks of papers on Aurora's desk. "You tell me you want me to become like you, to immerse myself in business, and spend my days dickering over money."

Aurora ignored the insult, and kept her voice gentle. "It is all new to you, Giana, as it was to me twelve years ago after your father's death." *Never tell her that Morton would have carved out my heart if he had guessed that his fortune would fall into my hands.* "You are my heir, Giana, my only child."

"It is a pity that John died, for then you would not bother worrying me with all this, would you?"

Stay calm, Aurora. "Perhaps, Giana, but your brother did die. The Van Cleve business interests are now in my hands, and if you will agree to learn, someday it will be you who is in control." Aurora saw an excited glint in her daughter's dark blue eyes. *My eyes looking back at me.* Perhaps, she thought, she had finally gained Giana's attention and interest. "You are intelligent, Giana, I have known that since you were a child. You are really much like me, you know."

Giana interrupted her in a suddenly accusing voice. "If you believed me so intelligent, so much like you, Mama, why did you send me away?"

Aurora drew a steadying breath against the pain of her daughter's condemnation, unable for the moment to meet Giana's eyes. She rose slowly, her palms flat against her desktop. "There were two reasons, Giana," she said finally. "I wanted you to have everything that I did not have growing up. I wanted you to know the security that only wealth can bring." She lowered her eyes a moment. "And I wanted you to have the education that would prepare you to ..." She ground to an abrupt halt. *The truth, Aurora, you are not telling her the truth.*

"To what, Mama? To become a spinster who enjoys lording it over men and giving them orders? Your orders for *me*, Mama, were followed to the letter. I am quite proficient at mathematics, for example, just as you insisted. And I suppose I am intelligent, though that commodity is little valued. I won't be like you, Mama, and I have no intention of being alone. I will not be an oddity!"

"An oddity, Giana? Is it your wish then to be like every other petted lady in England? Do you want to deny that you have a mind and be a frivolous, empty-headed girl who will do nothing more with her life than become an equally frivolous, empty-headed woman?"

"Is it so odd, Mama, to want a husband and a family, to spend one's life loved and protected and cherished? Just because you weren't lucky enough to gain that, you condemn me!"

"Giana, I was possibly mistaken in sending you to Switzerland. Perhaps I should have kept you here with me, to learn with me, to see how life can be when you have some say in how you live it." Aurora shrugged helplessly. "If you would but try to understand. There was so much for me to learn, so many decisions, so many people depending on me." Aurora saw Giana's eyes resting with cold condemnation on her face. "Listen to me, Giana! Can you forgive me? I had too little time for you then!"

"And now you fancy that you do. It is not a matter of forgiving you, Mama. I am a grown woman now, and I have no wish for your precious plans for my future. I will decide my own future." Giana sensed that she had gone too far, and splayed her hands in front of her in an attitude of compromise. "Mama, the past is past. I will try to understand you, if you will but understand me." She smiled, suddenly radiant and self-satisfied. "Mama, I am in love!"

Aurora stared at her stupidly. "You are seventeen years old."

"You married Papa when you were seventeen."

No, I was sold to Morton when I was seventeen.

"You have just returned from Switzerland. You have been home for but a fortnight."

Giana's voice dropped to a rapt whisper. "I met him in Switzerland. He was traveling with a friend on business. His younger sister, Patricia, was my roommate after Derry left, and I got to know him quite well. I love him, Mama, and he loves me."

"Love! By God, Giana, you have no more concept of what love is than a moth flying toward a tantalizing flame!" She saw Giana's face pale with anger and she started at her own stupidity. "Who is he, Giana?" she asked quickly.

"Yes, he is tantalizing," Giana said, raising her chin defiantly. "His name is Randall Bennett, and he is as respectable as any mother could wish. His father is the second son of Viscount Gilroy. You should approve him, for he is interested in business, just as you are."

"Is he in London?"

"Oh yes. In fact, I saw . . ." Giana gasped at the awful slip she had made. She straightened her slender shoulders and hurried on before her mother could interrupt her. "Randall wants to meet you, Mama. It is I who have not allowed it, so you must not blame him. He wants your first meeting with him to be perfect. He has heard of you and thinks very highly of you. And I have told him all about you. I want to marry him, Mama, as soon as summer comes. I want to wed him in June."

Aurora was thankful she had learned over the years how to keep her emotions from showing on her face. She was at first taken aback at the sudden show of naive pride in her daughter's voice, and then she felt sudden consuming fury. Was she to lose her only child without ever having had the chance to know her? "He sounds like a paragon. Since the young man wants my meeting with him to be perfect, why do you not invite him to dine with us tomorrow night?"

Giana looked at her warily. Although she did not know her mother well, it did not seem quite right that she should suddenly become so reasonable. She gave in to a rush of excitement, glorying in what seemed to be a victory.

"I will see—write him an invitation, Mama. May I be excused now?"

"Of course, child." Giana fairly danced from the room, without a trace of her sullen, defiant anger.

Aurora looked up at a light knock on the library door. "Come in," she called in a taut voice.

"Mr. Hardesty is here, madam."

Aurora nodded to Lanson, a slight smile raising the corners of her mouth. Poor Lanson was so very battered-looking with his nose off to one side, the result of his last boxing match six years before. He made an unlikely-looking butler, but Aurora, as a woman living alone, was thankful for the talents he had learned in his former profession.

"Show him in, if you please, Lanson."

Thomas Hardesty stood a moment in the doorway, watching Aurora rise from her desk. Even in the harsh daylight, she looked exquisite, no telltale shadows or lines on her face, no gray streaking her ink-black hair.

"Your message sounded urgent, my dear. I had feared you were perhaps ill." His thin lips parted into a smile. "But seeing you as radiant as ever blasts that notion." Indeed, he thought, she had hardly changed in the twelve years he had worked as her partner. Such a pity that a woman as beautiful as she had no intention of ever marrying again—not even him, who admired her slender beauty almost as much as her vast fortune. He remembered how shocked he had been when she first told him she fully intended to take her husband's place. But he had quickly enough come to rely on her judgment and to admire her quickness of mind and her ability to discern the most subtle of problems. He strode forward to take her outstretched hand.

"Radiant? Hardly! But no, I am not at all ill, Thomas. I thank you for coming so quickly." Aurora turned away from him for a moment, and then said in a strained voice, "It is Giana. The foolish child fancies herself in love."

"You should rather say young lady, Aurora. I would imagine that Giana is the image of you when you were her age."

"And you doubt that I was ever a child."

Thomas' first memories of her were as the silent young wife of Morton Van Cleve, the exquisite gem he saw only on occasion. The image reminded him of the endless stream of mistresses that Morton took without a care to discretion. He had flaunted them like a string of second-rate nags before a thoroughbred.

"Now, Aurora," he said, grinning, "would I ever be guilty of such rudeness? No, you needn't answer that. Now, who is this gentleman Giana wishes to wed?"

"All I know is that he has the lineage of a gentleman. His name is Randall Bennett and his grandfather is Viscount Gilroy. I assume that he must be attractive, from Giana's besotted descriptions."

"And you want to know more?"

For the first time, Aurora smiled. "You read my thoughts too well, Thomas. Yes, I must know all about him. Giana is inviting him to dine with us tomorrow evening. When I meet him, I would like to know more about him than just his name and the fact that he has met my daughter clandestinely both in Switzerland and here in London."

Thomas whistled softly. "Giana is very young," he said, "and very innocent."

"And very foolish and romantic."

"Not unlike other young ladies of her age and background."

Aurora stiffened, and he said quickly, sensitive to her distress, "Do not fret about it, my dear. We will see. Will you come to your office tomorrow?"

Aurora nodded. "Certainly. Thank you, Thomas."

"Your wish, my dear lady," he said, proffering her a mock bow, "is my command. I will find out the name of the nurse who diapered our young gentleman. Incidentally, have you had an opportunity to review the option papers on the railroad stocks?"

"I have tried, but to be honest about it, I haven't been able to concentrate on them. Drew will be back shortly. I'm sure he'll be able to force my nose to the grindstone."

"At least Giana hasn't fallen in love with your secretary."

"She thinks Drew is imperfect because he wears glasses and does not spend hours on his waistcoats."

She added bitterly, unable to help herself, "And of course he is less than a man because he takes orders from a woman."

"Don't be sarcastic, Aurora, and cease your fretting. Giana is not the first seventeen-year-old girl to be infatuated. Now, I must be off if I am to discover all the skeletons in Randall Bennett's closet."

"I pray that it is a very large closet!"

Giana paced restlessly up and down the well-trod footpath at the south end of Hyde Park. She had sent Randall an urgent appeal to meet her, and he was late. She felt a gnawing apprehensiveness, and moved her feet to and fro, in pace with her thoughts.

"You will wear holes in your slippers with all that pacing," Randall Bennett said softly into her ear.

Giana jumped. "Oh, Randall, you startled me!" She turned swiftly, her heart thumping, her face flushed and excited. "I was worried you would not come!"

"My foolish little love," he said softly, raising her gloved hand to his lips. He felt a slight trembling in her slender hand as he held it overlong, and smiled.

"Whatever is the matter, my love? Your message was a mystery."

"My mother wants to meet you, Randall, tomorrow evening."

A worried frown creased his wide forehead as he released her hand. His smile became charmingly rueful, his voice uncertain. "You're certain that it is her wish, Giana? She is not . . . angry?"

Giana's excitement dimmed a moment. "No," she said finally, "I do not believe she is angry. But she is disappointed." At his faint questioning look, she added, almost apologetically, "You see, she intended that I would, well, follow in her path, learn all about the Van Cleve interests, and work with her."

Randall threw back his handsome blond head and laughed heartily. "What an insane thought! My God, my little Giana doing a man's work!"

"That is what I told her," Giana said in ready agreement, but for an instant she felt a surge of rebellion. She wasn't stupid, after all. She smiled, knowing that Randall hadn't meant to insult her. "I looked at her desk. So many documents, so many contracts and options. She has talked of little else in the fortnight I've been home."

Randall said in a voice of polite tolerance, "You and your mother are nothing alike, Giana. I grant that she has accomplished more than many men in her position, but to do so, she has sacrificed all her woman's gentleness. What man would want to cherish her, protect her, as I do you?"

To his momentary chagrin, Georgiana laughed. "You have never met my mother, Randall."

He managed to say lightly enough, "Indeed, my love. But still, she did place business above a home and family. You are different from her, beloved. Where she wishes to conquer, you wish to love, to share, to be a wife and a mother. And I value you for it. Value you above all women."

He saw that her lovely eyes were glistening with pleasure at his description of her, as he thought they would. "Has your mother agreed to our marriage?"

Giana chewed at her lower lip. "Not precisely, but I told her that I want to marry you in June. You will convince her tomorrow evening, my love, that you will make her a perfect son-in-law."

Randall gave her a merry smile, an easy movement of muscles and devastatingly attractive. He had never before kissed the beautiful girl standing so worshipfully before him. He deemed it time.

"Giana," he said on a groan, and lightly brushed

his lips to hers. He felt her start in surprise at his touch, and then felt a flutter of response. He moved quickly away from her, preening inwardly at the dull light of disappointment in her eyes. If the mighty Aurora Van Cleve proved difficult, or immune to his beguiling charm, he had no doubt that Georgiana would agree to elope with him.

"You will make me the perfect wife, my love. I must go now, I do not want any untoward gossip reaching your mother's ears."

"Yes, Randall," she said docilely, her heart still thumping erratically from the feel of his lips against hers. She stood watching him stride confidently down the path away from her. She felt a warm glow of pride at his tall, athletic frame, and the memory of his warm gray eyes resting upon her. Giana's step was light when she rejoined her maid, Daisy.

"Such a handsome gentleman, Miss Giana! And so polite and gallant."

"Yes," Giana said, delighted to find such slavish agreement so readily at hand. "He is all that is perfect, is he not?"

"Oh, yes, miss," Daisy said fervently, though she wondered if it was improper for the handsome gentleman to be meeting her young mistress without her mother's knowledge. Still, the gentleman's intentions were clearly honorable and the light in her mistress's eyes was a joy to see.

Aurora rose to stand beside Giana when Lanson appeared to announce Randall Bennett. As he strode into the room, Aurora saw his eyes flicker toward the elegant furnishings and rest for a long, hungry moment at the two Rembrandts that hung beside the fireplace. He was everything she expected of him. He was a handsome, sophisticated man nearing thirty who exuded confidence and wore a rueful, boyish expression on his face designed to melt a woman's heart. She felt her daughter's slender frame tense. *Tread carefully, Aurora. There is as much to lose as there is to gain.*

"Mr. Bennett," she said pleasantly as she stepped forward, her hand extended. "I am delighted to finally meet you."

Randall took her hand in a less firm grip than he had intended, but he was so startled that for a moment he could but stare. He had expected a stern-faced woman, likely a strident dowd, not this exquisite creature, as slender as a girl, gowned in the most feminine of confections. His eyes fell to her white shoulders that rose invitingly from the froth of white lace at her bosom, and lingered a moment on the delicately wrought diamond–and-ruby necklace that encircled her throat.

"I had wondered where Giana got all her beauty," he said at last. "Now my question is answered, Mrs. Van Cleve. You are strikingly alike."

"I trust we are more alike than you imagine, Mr. Bennett."

Randall smiled uncomfortably, for although her voice was perfectly pleasant, he sensed inflexibility beneath her beautiful exterior.

"I am so glad you have come, Randall," Giana said, relief in her voice at the warm greeting her mother had bestowed. "Would you care for a glass of sherry? Dinner is not served until eight o'clock and we have time to enjoy ourselves and become acquainted."

"Your tongue is running on railroad tracks, Giana," Randall said in a chiding, affectionate tone one would use with a charming child. "I would much enjoy a glass of sherry."

Giana blushed and smiled shyly as she flitted to the sideboard, her petticoats rustling in her haste.

Dear God, he is more dangerous than I thought. "Do sit down, Mr. Bennett."

Randall waited for Aurora to select a chair, and eased himself gracefully down opposite her. He held himself tall, his muscled chest shown to good advantage under his white brocade waistcoat.

"I understand from Georgiana that your grandfather was Viscount Gilroy. If I recall aright, the Randalls hail from Yorkshire. Your uncle, James Delmain Bennett, is the current viscount, is he not?"

Randall had expected her to know of his noble antecedents, for she too came of the aristocracy, and he replied readily, "That's right, ma'am. My uncle's home estate is called Gilcrest Manor. I spent much of my time there when I was a boy. It is a grand old house, but so very drafty."

That's right, Mr. Bennett, become expansive.

"I do so look forward to meeting your Uncle James, Randall," Giana said brightly as she handed her mother and then Randall a glass of sherry. "You have not told me much about him. And Gilcrest Manor, what a romantic name! I would like to visit all of your family."

Randall started only slightly. He said vaguely, "My uncle, unfortunately, has become somewhat of a recluse over the years."

"How odd," Aurora mused aloud. "I met your uncle about three years ago when I was visiting friends in Thirsk. He seemed a most convivial gentleman who much enjoyed the waltz. And his three sons were most pleasant and well-mannered."

It was a lie, of course, but Aurora saw she had hit the mark. *Thank you, Thomas,* she said silently, *for your information.*

"How marvelous!" Giana exclaimed. "You have three cousins! Are there any girls?"

"Yes," Randall said, "there is one girl. She is the youngest, but fourteen years old now, I believe. Rather lumpy, though, poor girl, takes after her mother. Not at all like you, Giana, or your gracious mother."

It was a compliment, but one at the expense of another. Giana looked at Randall uncertainly, then smiled. He was nervous, and rightly so, and anxious to please her mother. She said quietly, "I was very skinny when I was fourteen, which is just as bad as lumpy, I think. Everyone changes, Randall."

"Of course, Giana. Mrs. Van Cleve, the sherry is excellent. Your late husband must have stocked a fine cellar."

"Not really, Mr. Bennett. It is I who have seen to the quality of the wines and sherries. The sherry you are drinking is, of course, from Spain, near Pamplona, the Valdez vineyards. I am also a partner in the Blanchard vineyards in Bordeaux, and am thus able to secure the finest."

Two vineyards, in Spain and in France! Was there any end to the Van Cleve holdings?

Aurora saw the almost imperceptible glint in Randall Bennett's heavily lashed gray eyes. Such beguiling eyes they were until they flickered with greed.

"Are you interested in fine wines, Mr. Bennett?"

"My friends seem to trust my palate, Mrs. Van Cleve. But, of course, it is not simply the final product that I appreciate. I have a great interest in the science of the grape."

"You never before told me that, Randall," Giana said with naive enthusiasm. She felt inordinately pleased. "Randall shares so many of your interests, Mother."

"It would appear so, Giana."

"Dinner is served, madam," Lanson said from the doorway.

Randall rose quickly and looked ruefully from Georgiana to her mother. "How am I ever to make a decision with two such beautiful women?"

"You have two arms, Mr. Bennett."

"A Solomon's solution, ma'am," he said and offered each lady an arm.

Aurora smiled as Randall gracefully seated her in the tall-backed heavy mahogany chair at the head of the table. She saw his eyes widen at the richness of the room, its golden-papered walls covered with fine paintings, and was pleased. When his eyes fell to the table, her smile widened. Cook had been surprised to hear that Aurora wished to have dinner served in the large, formal dining room, for only three people. And the silver dinner service was fit for royalty. *Open your eyes, Giana! He does not love you, you foolish child! He loves only what you can bring him.*

"Tell me, Mr. Bennett," Aurora said with gracious interest over the first course of carrot soup, and turbot with shrimp sauce, "what are your interests?"

Randall sent a loving smile toward Giana, then gave Aurora a boyish grin. "Even though my uncle is of the aristocracy, ma'am, and thus takes little interest in worldly affairs, I fear that I am cut from a different cloth. As I have told your daughter, I am very much a modern man, and wish to make my mark in the business world."

"What business were you embarked upon when you visited Geneva, Mr. Bennett?"

"My visit was primarily a family matter. As Giana has probably told you, my half-sister, Patricia, attended Madame Orlie's seminary. I wished to assure myself that Patricia was happy and content."

"Did you manage to ascertain if she was happy and content, Mr. Bennett?"

Giana giggled. "I fear, Mama, that Randall had little time for Patricia once he met me." At Aurora's arched brow, Giana added quickly, "Oh, it was all my fault, Mama. Once I got to know Randall, I fear that I was loath to share his company, even with his half-sister."

"And your friend Mr. Joseph Stanyon, what was he about whilst you were becoming acquainted with my daughter?"

Giana's mouth dropped open. She had never told her mother the name of Randall's business friend. She had not liked the man, with his smug smile and thick lips, nor the way he had eyed her in an openly assessing way.

"Ah, Mr. Stanyon and I no longer are associates, ma'am. I regret to say that his . . . morals were not quite what a gentleman would approve." He gave Aurora a deprecating smile. "At the moment, I am studying various business possibilities."

"Randall is most interested in shipping, Mama. He has told me on several occasions that he wished he could have stowed away as a cabin boy."

"It is a very risky business, as I am certain you know, Mr. Bennett. The Van Cleve shipyards have been most fortunate."

"They have had the benefit of your excellent management, ma'am."

Aurora nodded graciously. "I understand that your father, Mr. George Bennett, has been ill for quite some time now."

Giana cocked her head at her mother, pleased that she was showing such interest in Randall, but perplexed as to how she knew so much about him and his family. Randall had always sidestepped her ques-

tions about his father. She was distressed to see him
lower his head a moment, as if in silent argument
with himself. She wished she could tell him that
nothing about his family mattered to her.

Randall slowly raised his head, and Aurora was
vexed beyond reason at the liquid sadness in his
eyes. He said slowly, "I have never wanted to upset
Giana with the miserable truth about my father,
ma'am, but since you insist upon knowing, I must
tell you that his illness is the result of strong drink.
My poor stepmother has had much to bear. It is only
because of my uncle's kindness that my half-sister,
Patricia, is receiving her education in Switzerland."

"Oh, Randall, how terrible for you!" Giana sent a
reproachful glance toward her mother. "We will
speak of it no more."

Randall smiled wanly. "Your dear mother has every right to know about my family, Giana, and of my
father's problems. You are her daughter, and I respect her for seeking to protect you from a gentleman
who could possibly be after your . . . fortune."

*Well done, Mr. Bennett, well done! Lunge headlong into
the crux of the matter! Show Giana your tearful sorrow,
tout your honor!*

"Well," Giana said, smiling now, "since we love
each other, Randall, she will never have to worry
herself with protecting me again."

"Allow a mother her concerns, my dear," Aurora
said. "If Mr. Bennett does not mind, surely you
should not quibble."

Lanson served a lavish second course of stewed
kidneys, roast saddle of lamb, boiled turkey, knuckle
of ham, mashed and brown potatoes, stewed onions,
rissoles, and macaroni. Giana's eyes widened at the
array of dishes, and she cast a questioning look toward her mother. She knew that her mother rarely

partook of traditional heavy English fare, preferring instead the lighter, more delicate French cuisine. She was on the point of making a small jest about it when she chanced to see Randall's eyes resting fondly upon each dish.

That's right, Giana. He is all English and inordinately impressed with this culinary display. He will likely run to fat before he is thirty-five. But by then he hopes to have a comfortable wife and a fortune at his disposal.

"I was admiring your waistcoat, Mr. Bennett. The design is most elegant."

"Thank you, ma'am. I designed it myself."

"I trust you paid your tailor, Mr. Dicks, an ample amount for his excellent skills."

Giana glanced at her mother warily, wondering at her odd conversation. "How do you know who his tailor is, Mama?"

Aurora cursed silently at Giana's untimely interruption, for the color had faded from Randall Bennett's cheeks.

She said lightly, "My business partner, Thomas Hardesty, enjoys Mr. Dicks's fine services. I am used to seeing his artful craftsmanship."

The bite of roast saddle of lamb tasted like ashes in Randall's mouth. Bitch, he wanted to shout at her. He knew now that he had underestimated her and that she had learned everything about him. She had but toyed with him earlier, forcing him to tell Giana that his father was a drunken sot. Ah, but he had handled that well, much to the dismay of the wily Mrs. Van Cleve. Now her thrusts were becoming direct, only slightly honeyed, barely enough that her daughter not yet understand. She had told him quite clearly that she knew him to be in debt and that Mr. Dicks was but one of the tradesmen to whom he owed money.

"You see how much you have in common with Randall, Mama," Georgiana announced ingenuously. "You even approve his attire."

"Of course, my dear child. More wine, Mr. Bennett? It is rather a heavy wine, but a fine vintage, I think you'll find.

"Where do you reside, Mr. Bennett?" Aurora continued smoothly, allowing no uncomfortable pauses.

"On Delmain Street."

Aurora parted her lips in an incredulous smile.

"I know it is not an elegant address, Mrs. Van Cleve, but I am alone—at least for the moment," he said with a caressing look toward Giana, "and have no need to squander money on myself."

"Randall is concerned for the future," Giana said.

"That certainly appears to be true," Aurora said easily. "He has, after all, spent a great deal of energy and time preparing himself."

Giana looked at her mother uncertainly, but Aurora merely smiled at her and motioned for Lanson to bring the dessert.

"I love cabinet pudding," Giana said, for want of anything better.

"And I prefer the blancmange and cream myself. I trust one of the two please you, Mr. Bennett?"

"Indeed, ma'am," he said. He was thinking that his only hope lay in convincing Giana to elope with him. He remembered her trembling lips when he kissed her. She was of a very different cut from her elegant, cold bitch of a mother.

They drank their coffee in the drawing room. Giana, fluttering between her mother and Randall with offers of sugar and cream, begged Randall to talk of his travels in Europe. This he did with great circumspection until the hour of ten.

"It has been a great pleasure spending this time in

your charming company, Mrs. Van Cleve," he said, not meeting her eyes.

"It has been most enlightening, Mr. Bennett," Aurora said, "for both my daughter and myself."

Aurora waited in stiff silence while Giana escorted Randall Bennett from the mansion.

"Well, Mother?" Giana demanded the moment she entered the drawing room.

"Mr. Bennett," Aurora said, choosing her words carefully, "is a most talented man. When his words are taken at face value, he appears most charming."

"I saw no other way to take his conversation, Mama. He is ever charming."

"Giana, my love, come sit beside me for a little while." After her daughter had obliged her, Aurora lightly clasped Giana's hand in hers.

"You appeared to know a great deal about Randall, Mother."

"Of course. Would you not expect me, as your mother and someone who cares very much about you, to look into what kind of man he is?"

"He has not had a particularly happy life, I know," Giana said. "To have to endure such a father!"

"I suppose that would be somewhat daunting," Aurora agreed, thankful that Giana had very little memory of her own cold father. "There are things you should know, my love," she said after a moment.

Giana looked guarded, but Aurora forged ahead. "His uncle, Viscount Gilroy, refused to have anything more to do with his nephew some five years ago. It appears that Mr. Bennett lost a good deal of money gambling and stole money from his uncle to cover his debt."

"That cannot be true!" Giana cried, pulling away from her mother.

"I fear that it is, Giana, and there is more. Mr.

Bennett is sunk in debt. His only hope of saving himself is to wed a girl with money. I believe that when his half-sister, Patricia, wrote to him about you, he saw his opportunity. Do you really believe that a gentleman, Giana, would meet a girl clandestinely, without the knowledge or approval of her mother?"

"But he met me quite by accident! It was I who fell in love with him first. Indeed, he was most concerned that what we were doing was not proper. As to his being in debt, I imagine that he spends a great deal of his money on his poor father."

"No, he does not. He hasn't seen his father in over a year."

Giana rose unsteadily to her feet. "It appears, Mother, that you have no faith at all in my judgment. Did Mr. Hardesty dig up all these vile accusations?"

"Thomas certainly did as I asked." She gentled her voice. "My love, there is no doubt that Mr. Bennett is indeed a fortune hunter. He is the kind of man who must perforce be charming, for it is his stock-in-trade."

"So you are telling me that the man I love doesn't love me, only the Van Cleve money! Is it hard for you to imagine that I can attract a man who could possibly care for me?"

"I am sorry, Giana, but what I've said about Mr. Bennett is true. There are many other men you will meet, men who are honorable and honest."

"Do you think me so ill-favored, Mama, that Randall could not care for me?"

"Of course not. I did not say that."

"I think, Mother, that you have said enough." Her voice rose coldly. "You wanted Randall here only to insult him and make thinly veiled threats. It was not well done of you, Mother. I see now that every word you uttered was meant to wound him. You must have believed me a simpleton not to see through it."

"I have never thought you a simpleton, Giana. For the moment, you are merely blinded by your infatuation and do not see him as clearly as do I."

"Even though I am but seventeen years old, Mother, I am not blind! Perhaps it is you who do not wish to see the truth."

"Giana, please," Aurora said, raising her hand.

"I am going to bed, Mother. Good night." Giana swept from the drawing room without a backward glance, her slender shoulders drawn stiffly back, her chin held high.

"Damn," Aurora said under her breath. Blind child!

She realized with a sense of dread that she must now move very carefully, else Giana would bolt and she would lose her daughter. But what was she to do now? Lock Giana in her room? Perhaps, she thought finally, there was a way, though not through Giana, to be sure. She could likely show Giana a signed confession and it would not sway her. But Randall Bennett was a man who knew his interests. She must convince him that they did not lie with the Van Cleves.

Chapter 3

"The Chartists are sniffing about the shipyards, Aurora. They got wind of the new hauling machine we are installing."

"I know, Thomas. What really worries me is the support they're receiving from the less savory elements in society." Aurora rose suddenly from her chair and splayed her hands on the desktop. "I cannot understand why men wish to destroy what will, in the long term, make their lives easier! Thank God we do not own any mills. Did you hear that Morris Clipton, one of the Chartists in Yorkshire, led a machine-smashing foray into Robert Holmes's cotton mill?"

"Yes. I have heard the damage estimates at well over ten thousand pounds."

Aurora sighed, and touched an ink-stained fingertip to her temple. "Poor Robert was screeching like a wounded pig! Not that I care for him or his methods much, mind you, Thomas, but the fact of the matter is—was—that the new looms would have meant that children would have been spared twelve hours of work a day!"

"Ah, Aurora, you are misunderstanding, on purpose, I think. Many of the Chartists don't want their children freed by machines to be educated. In many instances, the money the children earn helps to feed the family."

"Enough, Thomas. I know it is a complicated question, and one that we will not easily resolve. But one thing I do know: machines are here to stay. There is little we can do about men who abuse their workers, but the Van Cleve shipyards will not install machines only to boot the workers out to starve. When the new machinery is in place, I want every man displaced to be assigned another job."

"You are being quite a humanitarian, Aurora," Thomas said.

"It is simply good business, Thomas. We have several contracts that can't afford to be held up because our workers are malcontented."

"I will travel to Portsmouth to the shipyard and see to it personally."

"You can leave tomorrow, Thomas."

Drew Mortesson, Aurora's secretary, stepped quietly into the massive office. He knew that Mrs. Van Cleve's morning hadn't been altogether pleasant, what with the Chartists making threats at shipyard owners, and her spoiled little twit of a daughter but adding to her problems. He smiled at the thought of Randall Bennett kicking up his heels in Drew's outer office. With Mrs. Van Cleve's mood, the man's arrogance would soon be dashed. Drew waited patiently for Aurora to recognize his presence. She did quickly, smiling toward him ruefully. "Ah, Drew, you have come to rescue me."

"I think not, ma'am."

"Mr. Bennett is here, I take it?"

Drew nodded. "I have kept him waiting fifteen minutes."

Thomas Hardesty grinned. "A fine ploy, Aurora. He is likely gnawing at his fingernails by now. Let us just hope that you can send the blackguard about his business without much further ado."

Her eyes flashed at the thought of the impending interview, and Thomas smiled, wishing he could be present. Randall Bennett was a fool to tangle with Aurora Van Cleve, and likely he would discover that fact just as many other men had over the years, much to their surprise and chagrin.

"If you will excuse me now, Thomas. Drew, do show Mr. Bennett in, poor fellow! How vexatious that he has had to wait!"

Aurora was seated in her high-backed leather chair when Drew ushered Randall Bennett into her office.

She nodded pleasantly. "Do come in, Mr. Bennett. I am terribly sorry that I have kept you waiting, but there was rather urgent business that required my attention."

Randall bowed solemnly. "I quite understand the demands of business, Mrs. Van Cleve, and someday, soon perhaps, hope to help lift its heavy burden from your fragile shoulders."

He has the bravado of a man who knows he has but to click his fingers, and all will fall into his lap, Aurora thought. He has spoken again to Giana, seduced her again with his honeyed words.

"What a kind and noble thought, Mr. Bennett," she said, her fury hidden from her face. She rose slowly and walked around the huge oak desk. "No, stay seated, Mr. Bennett. You thought, perhaps, that I invited you here today to show you the domain that you hope will one day be yours."

He smiled at her winsomely, but said nothing.

"Actually, Mr. Bennett, I asked you here to clarify what I believe to be a misunderstanding on your part. Look about you, sir, for this is the last time you

will ever again be allowed into my office or onto Van
Cleve property."

"I hope that that will not be the case, Mrs. Van
Cleve," Randall said smoothly. He flickered a spot of
lint from his black sleeve.

"You are very sure of yourself, Mr. Bennett. Unfortunately, your certainty derives, I imagine, from my
daughter's rapt avowals of eternal love and devotion
to you."

"You have no other heirs, ma'am," Randall said
quietly. "Giana will marry me, despite anything you
have said or will say to the contrary. Come, Mrs. Van
Cleve, you have taken me in unworthy dislike. Can
you not understand a young man who happens just
once, when he is very young, to do something foolish? You must believe that I love your daughter and
will do everything in my power to make her the hap-
piest of women."

"I have rewritten my will, Mr. Bennett."

He raised a thick blond brow.

"If you manage to marry my daughter without my
permission, you will not see a sou until Giana is
thirty years old. Think about it, Mr. Bennett. You are
already halfway down the River Tick, your creditors
hounding your steps even now. Do you honestly believe that they will be content to wait for thirteen
more years?"

"You would not let your daughter starve."

"Indeed not," Aurora said coolly. "I will provide
her with gowns, two servants, and a pleasant place
to live, but that is all. You, Mr. Bennett, will have
nothing from me. I doubt that you could possibly
keep your true face from Giana for very long. She
will grow up, you know."

"And your grandchildren, Mrs. Van Cleve? Will
they also suffer from your ridiculous dislike of me?

Your daughter is a very . . . responsive girl, ma'am. I only hope that I can keep her from falling into my bed until we are safely wed. I would expect a son or daughter very shortly thereafter, I assure you."

Aurora felt a flash of fury that he had the gall to flaunt Giana's loose behavior in front of her, smirking all the while.

"You will have to find another chicken for the plucking, Mr. Bennett," she said only.

Randall rose gracefully to his feet. "Dear lady, that is hardly a complimentary analogy. Believe me, ma'am, there is no other woman I want."

She chanced to look him straight in the eye in an unguarded instant and recoiled from the cold ruthlessness she sensed in him. It occurred to her that such a man would not hesitate to remove anyone he thought in his way. She could not help herself, and took a step back. She said slowly, hating to so demean herself, "Mr. Bennett, I will give you ten thousand pounds to leave my daughter alone."

"Ah, my dear Mrs. Van Cleve, you finally admit to yourself that I have won. Surely if I were the fortune hunter you believe me to be, I would not be so stupid as to accept such a paltry sum when one day soon I could enjoy all the benefits of having you for a mother-in-law."

"On the contrary, sir, I believe you to be quite stupid. I will not see you again, Mr. Bennett. I bid you good day."

"Good day, dear lady," he said, bowing, and strolled negligently from the room, whistling softly under his breath.

His insufferable confidence shook her. *I should have Lanson beat him to a bloody pulp!* On the heels of that pleasing thought, she envisioned Giana rushing to him, and cursing her, never forgiving her.

* * *

"Giana, my love, how very charming you look! The rose silk is most becoming."

"Thank you, Mama," Giana said, eyeing her mother warily. "Did you wish to speak to me?"

"Yes, child, I did." Aurora gathered her thoughts together. "I talked to Randall Bennett today, at my office in the city."

"I know, he told me."

Aurora sagged where she stood. She had hoped to tell Giana before Bennett did.

Giana continued in a contemptuous voice, "I don't need your gowns, your servants, or even a place you would so graciously provide me to live, Mama. I will have Randall, and he is all that I will ever want. Neither of us care if you disinherit me. He told me that you offered him money never to see me again. He was dreadfully upset that you could treat him so badly. Oh, Mama, don't you see that Randall and I love each other? How could you, Mama!"

Aurora lost her calm and whirled on her daughter. "Yes, Giana, I did offer him ten thousand pounds, but he informed me it was a paltry sum he would not consider since he thinks he will eventually own everything that is ours." She paused a moment, looking hopefully into her daughter's face, but she saw only a wall of absolute distrust.

"For God's sake, my dear daughter, why do you think I met with him without your knowledge? I will tell you, Giana. I know I have rarely been so sure of anything, that Randall Bennett is the lowest kind of man, a fortune hunter. I love you. How can you imagine that I will sit by and let that immoral creature do as he wishes with you?"

"You love me, Mama? When did you decide that, pray tell? It has certainly been a recent discovery for you, since I have been out of your sight and mind nearly all my life! Why, Mama? Have you decided that you want me in your business and find Randall Bennett a nuisance?"

"Listen to me, Giana. It is true that I want you to join me in our business. I believe you are well-suited to it. I believe you would find satisfaction being your own woman, in charge of your own life. That in no way discounts a husband. It only discounts scum like Randall Bennett."

"I doubt that you have ever been in love, Mama. You do not know what it is like to know that a man loves you in return, wants to cherish you, wants to make you the very center of his life."

"What you are spouting is romantic drivel! No, I have never been in love, as you phrase it. Perhaps I am not the kind of person to ever become so involved. But, Giana, Randall Bennett will give you none of the things you want. You must believe me."

Georgiana drew herself up to her full height. "And you must believe me, Mama. I do not want a life alone. I want marriage and a family. I want Randall Bennett."

Aurora said suddenly, beyond constraint, "What would you think if I were to die after your marriage?"

"Mama, I don't understand you. Wait, what do you mean? What in God's name are you implying?"

"You know what I am saying, Giana. He merely taunted me when I informed him that you would not inherit until you were thirty years old. I sensed in him an utter ruthlessness against anything or anyone who stands in the way of his gaining our wealth."

Giana rushed away from her mother, toward the door to her bedchamber. She clutched the knob, whirled about, and screamed. "You are willing to say anything to ruin my life! Even accuse the man I love of planning to murder you! Dear God, do you hate me so much that you wish to destroy me?"

Aurora raised her hand in silent supplication, but Giana did not wait for a reply. She rushed from the room, her sobs ringing in Aurora's ears. Aurora stared blindly about Giana's frilly, feminine bedchamber. It is over now, she thought, and I have lost.

"Aurora! *Cara!* Behold, I am here not three days after I received your message in Paris."

Aurora leapt to her feet. "Daniele," she cried, and flung open the doors of the library. She threw herself into his arms, ignoring Lanson's startled stare.

Daniele adjusted his eyes to the dim light in the library. "By all that's holy, Aurora, what is this? Have you finally consented to lend me the thirty thousand pounds I need?"

Aurora drew back and smiled up at Daniele Cippolo, her business associate in Rome, and a longtime friend. If anyone could help her, it would be Daniele. Only he, she had thought as she penned her letter to him, was cunning enough to devise a means to foil Randall Bennett.

"I need your help, Daniele," she said without preamble. "Would you care for a glass of sherry?"

Daniele nodded and followed her graceful figure to the sideboard with his eyes. "If you did not request my visit to London, *cara*, to lend me money, you must indeed have a problem of infinite ... complexity." As she handed him his glass, he said, "There are shadows beneath your lovely eyes, Aurora. I cannot believe that the famous Aurora Van Cleve is betwixt and between."

"You phrase it so nicely, Daniele!" As he sipped at his sherry, Aurora took a restless turn about the room. "I do have a problem for which there seems to be no solution. It is Giana."

"Little Giana?" He struck his hand to his forehead. "How the years fly by! The girl is home from her fancy seminary in Switzerland?"

"Yes, she is, for a long three weeks now. Home and determined to marry a miserable bounder, a fortune hunter. She is all of seventeen years old," she added in a bitter voice.

"I had hoped that you would present me with a problem worthy of my abilities, Aurora." Daniele shrugged. "Truss the fellow up in a sack and send him off to India in one of your ships."

"The idea did occur to me, but 'twill not serve in this case." She gazed up at her longtime friend, feeling herself grow more steady and confident. Daniele had always had a calming influence on her, despite his occasional lapses into grand hyperbole. His clear gray eyes, set deep beneath bushy gray brows, were either serene or glinting with suppressed excitement. He was brilliant, a financial wizard, unlike his poor brother who had killed himself several years before. Once, some five years before, she had considered him as a lover, and, to her chagrin and subsequent amusement, it had been he who had refused. "One never mixes business with delight, *cara*," he had told her. "You are too valuable to waste time in an old man's bed." Thus it was that she told him everything, omitting nothing. She could see the intricacy of his thoughts as he inserted questions here and there.

"So that is how everything now sits," she concluded. "I have scarce spoken to Giana, since she accused me two days ago of ruining her life."

Daniele shifted slightly in his chair, and readjusted his exquisite pearl-gray waistcoat over his narrow chest. He was quiet for a long time, for such a long time that Aurora could not stay seated. She bounded to her feet and began pacing, clasping her hands in front of her.

"Stop playing Lady Macbeth, *cara*. It would appear that your Giana has forgotten that she is Aurora Van Cleve's daughter."

"How could she be so stupidly foolish and naive?" Aurora wailed, disregarding him and resuming her frantic pacing. "How can I make her realize that she will be nothing but a pet possession—and that for only a short time! How can I make her understand that to really experience life, she must be in charge of her own destiny and not hand herself over lock, stock, and body to a husband, particularly a husband like Randall Bennett?"

"Calm yourself, Aurora," Daniele said, holding up a silencing hand. "Not all men, you know, are like Morton Van Cleve—cold and rapacious."

"Oh, I know that," she snapped, whirling about to face him. "But still, the temptation is well-nigh impossible to withstand, even for the best of men. After all, in our just and proud land, a woman is naught but a brood mare, raised to view herself as an addle-headed, worthless ... Oh, I don't know, Daniele! I know that I'm not making much sense, but it is so angering that my own daughter would willingly wish to imprison herself, to stay a child, and never know anything of the world, the real world, the world that men possess."

"Your world, *cara*."

"Yes, my world! I was nothing but an empty husk until Morton died! God, the freedom, the knowledge that what I say and what I think mean something!"

"Have you said this to Giana?"

"Oh yes, but she merely stares at me like I'm some kind of oddity. She cannot see beyond her nose or hear anything but Randall Bennett's charming soliloquies! She is too young to begin to understand how very arid her life could be, and our fortune hunter has smothered her in romantic illusion."

Daniele said quietly, "Most women could not conceive of the world as you experience it, Aurora."

"That is because their brains have been rotted by the time they are twenty!"

"Perhaps," he said. He added thoughtfully, "I trust that you did not accuse the man of having designs on your life in front of Giana. Surely he would not go that far, *cara*."

Aurora drew a ragged breath. "Yes, I did tell her that he was, I thought, utterly ruthless. Would he remove me, her mother, were I to continue to thwart him?" She shrugged her shoulders angrily. "I do not know, Daniele. At the time I did think he was capable of such a thing. Now, well . . . it does seem rather melodramatic."

Daniele waved a dismissing hand, and rose abruptly to pace thoughtfully along the path she had trod. "It was wise of you to send for me, *cara*. *Si*, I can see that this problem requires . . . an unusual solution to resolve itself appropriately." He paused a moment, and asked her quietly, "Is Giana truly your daughter, Aurora? Are you certain that she would not be quite happy with a husband to master her, and her belly filled yearly with child?"

"I refuse to believe that. I see the intelligence in her eyes, Daniele, and flashes of pride, that is, when she is not acting the giddy chit. If Randall Bennett were not the cad I know him to be, I would allow her to lie in the bed of her own making. But, hear me, Daniele, I would be the most despicable of women were I to allow my daughter to wed such as him."

"It is a problem of the most profound sort,"

Daniele said. "I must ponder, *cara*. I beg you to stop wearing a hole in your Axminster carpet."

Aurora obligingly sat down on the sofa, and watched his brow pucker and his gray eyes narrow in thought. She was beginning to believe that this problem was beyond even Daniele's cunning, when he suddenly smiled and slapped his hands to his thighs.

"A most original solution, Aurora, and most daring," he said modestly. "Are you a prude, *cara*?"

"A prude?" she repeated, cocking her head at him. "I do not believe so, Daniele. Why do you ask?"

"Because, my dear," he said slowly, "our solution to Giana's infatuation is not one a mother would readily accept."

"Explain yourself, Daniele."

"I will, *cara*, but first you must agree not to interrupt me until I have finished."

She nodded, unconsciously leaning toward him.

He paused a moment, his eyes gentle upon her face. "You know, Aurora, before I tell you of my plan, it seems to me that you must yourself face the truth. It is not only Randall Bennett who distresses you, it is any man who would take Giana to wife."

"Of course it is," she said, drawing a deep breath. "At least until she is a woman grown, and has the sense and perspective to wed a man who would accept her for what she is, a man who would be content, if she wished it, to let her control her own money, to direct her own affairs."

"Such a man would be a rare find."

She nodded, sadly.

"Then what Giana needs, and quickly, is a strong dose of life, and from a vantage point that would leave no doubts in her mind. I would imagine that ladies in Rome are not at all different from your English ladies. And men, well, they are universally the same, are they not?"

At her nod, he said, "Well, then, I shall proceed."

He did, at great length, much to Aurora's astonishment.

"It all sounds so fantastic, so . . ."

"Immoral?"

"No, not really that. Risky. Giana is so very young. Such an experience as you paint would catapult her into a world that I myself have never seen, only guessed at."

He smiled, and gently mocked her. "Do you wish to be a pupil also, *cara*?

"I must think, Daniele," she said, disregarding his words. "God, were I to allow you to let her meet such . . . people, surely I would be a most unnatural mother."

"Now it is your own morality that eats at you, your concern at how you would view yourself. It would appear, Aurora, that you have little choice. You are wise enough, I think, to know what is best for your daughter, and how to deal with yourself and your own feelings."

"I can scarce envision such a burden."

"You will think about it, *cara*. Yes, you will think about it."

Aurora arose earlier the next morning than was her usual habit. When she emerged from her bedchamber, she saw Giana's maid, Daisy, clutching an envelope to her breast. Another assignation with Randall Bennett, of that she was certain. That, or Giana was prepared to elope with him. It was the sight of that envelope that decided her. She was on the point of marching into Giana's bedchamber, when she drew up, shaking her head. No, this would be a formal agreement between them; it would be conducted in the library.

"You wished to see me, Mother?" Giana stood in the doorway, hesitant to enter, Aurora knew, certain of another confrontation.

"Yes, Giana," she said as pleasantly as she could. "Do come in and sit down, my dear. I believe it is time we came to an agreement." How lovely she looks this morning, she thought, watching her graceful figure as she hesitantly seated herself on the edge of a papier-mâché chair. Lovely save for her sullen, pouting mouth.

"An agreement?"

"Today is the first of June. I will consent to your marriage to Randall Bennett on the first day of September if you will return to Rome with your Uncle Daniele and stay the summer with him."

Aurora could see the distrust in her daughter's eyes, the questions leaping about in her mind.

"When I say consent, Giana, I mean it. You will have as fine a wedding as you wish, with my full support and agreement. Randall Bennett, as my son-in-law, will be able, if he wishes, to enter the business."

"You think, Mother, that I will forget the only man I will ever love over the space of three short months?"

"No, Giana, that is not what I think." Aurora looked down at her hands, and saw her knuckles were white from clutching her chair back. She supposed it was Giana's scoffing voice that decided her irrevocably. "I have tried to tell you, Giana, that women, for the most part, lose all their choices once they wed, lose their freedom, and become only what their husbands wish them to be. No, don't interrupt me yet. I am not speaking specifically of Randall

Bennett, though I have no doubt that he would, once you were his wife and his property, treat you no differently. You would be trotted out on social occasions to be seen and admired as his possession, then quickly retired to your children and to the endless society of other women exactly like you. The most important decisions you would ever make would be what to have Cook serve for dinner, not the wines, certainly, for that is a man's domain. You would decide which nanny you wished for your girl children and would have a choice of dressmakers. Your husband, you would find, would soon take a mistress. He would conduct his affairs discreetly only if he felt any liking for you at all."

Giana could not help herself, and cried angrily, "Enough, Mother! Randall would not be like that . . . he loves me. He would cherish me, protect me, always! Never would he leave me to take a . . . mistress!"

She will not listen, Aurora. You have no choice, no choice at all!

"Very well, Giana, that is what you believe. Are you prepared to spend the three months with your Uncle Daniele in order to gain my support? It is really a very short period of time."

Three months without Randall! It seemed like an eternity. Giana gazed suspiciously at her mother, not understanding why Aurora could be so foolish as to think she would cease to love Randall, even if Aurora sent her to faraway China. She was tempted to tell her mother that she cared not a whit for her permission, when she remembered Randall's saddened voice. "Oh, my little Giana, if only you—we—could persuade your mother to approve of our love and marriage. Life for us would be so much more pleasant. It distressed me, my darling, that you would be torn between your mother and me."

"Very well, Mother, I will go with Uncle Daniele to Rome, but only for three months, mind you. But there is an agreement I demand from you in return. You must promise me that you will in no way try to remove Randall from my life while I am gone. If I return to find him changed in any way toward me, I shall never forgive you. Never."

"Very well, Giana. I agree to that. But before you agree, I must tell you what will be required of you in order to gain my approval. While you are in Rome, you will do exactly as Daniele tells you. You will meet ladies, married ladies of Daniele's choice, and see exactly how they live, how they think, what they talk about. Then—"

Giana scoffed, "Lord, Mother, I can do that in London!"

"Then you will see the other side of the coin. You will meet . . . women whom these same ladies' husbands spend their time with. You will talk to these women and learn from them how men use them, how, in fact, they scorn them and their wives."

"You mean . . . mistresses?" Giana's eyes were wide with astonishment. "You want me to become . . . become acquainted with . . . loose women?"

"No, not mistresses, for they are with just one man, usually for a period of time. The women I speak of are prostitutes. You will not, of course, become like them, but you will see both sides of life, Giana, and when you return in September, and if you still want to wed—"

"You mean, Mother," Giana said quietly, "*when* I return and *still* wish to wed Randall, not *if*."

"It will be your decision entirely, Giana. I swear

that I will not interfere. But you must do exactly as Daniele tells you to do, else our agreement is null."

"What a marvelously . . . unusual summer! I have never before met a bad woman," she added naively.

But you have certainly met a very bad man. "You do understand what I am asking of you?"

"Yes, Mother. You wish me to become intimate with both ladies and harlots!" Giana giggled. "But think of all the dreadfully wicked things I shall learn!"

"It will not be a summer holiday, Giana, I can promise you that." She saw that Giana had little notion of what it would mean to be confronted with the women who sold their bodies to men, and for a moment she doubted the wisdom of Daniele's idea, and she doubted herself. The picture she had painted of men and women was, she knew, strongly tempered by her own wretched life with Morton Van Cleve and the stream of fortune hunters who had flocked about her after his death. There were men, she knew, who loved their wives, who were good and loyal, but Randall Bennett was not one of them.

Aurora looked up to see Giana gazing at her oddly, unaware that her thoughts had danced across her face, creating grim shadows.

"Have you always hated men?"

Aurora started at the pity in Giana's voice, and it needled her. "I do not hate men, Giana. But they have power, physical power far greater than ours, and the power of the laws that they created for themselves. I am wary of them."

"But you wield power, Mother, and you are not a man."

The truth, Aurora. Tell her at least some of it. "It was never your father's intention that it would happen thus. If your brother had not died, I would be relegated to my embroidery, and endless days of emptiness."

"You hated Father."

"Without him, I could have never had you, child. And I love you more than anything or anyone else in this world."

"I cannot force you to answer me directly, Mother. I would that you begin to realize that I am no longer a little girl."

Aurora expelled her breath slowly. She said finally, very quietly, "Morton Van Cleve was a man such as I have described to you."

"So you wish to punish me for your own . . . bitterness, your own disappointment."

"No, I wish merely to protect you. I realize, Giana, that Randall Bennett has so filled your head with visions of romance and eternal devotion that you will not heed me. But, daughter, I know that if you were not an heiress, he would never have concerned himself with you. My wealth—our wealth—is both a blessing and a curse, for people, men and women, will try to cloak their true intentions in hope of gain. It is for that reason that you must learn to see the world as it actually is, so that when you finally find a man who truly cares for you, you will know it and be content."

"I have found such a man, Mother. It is you who refuse to be content. Randall cares not a rap for my money. Surely you cannot truly believe that this charade you have planned for me will change my mind or my feelings for him."

Aurora forced herself to swallow the knot of frustration that rose in her throat like bitter bile.

"If that is so, Giana, I will bow to your judgment in September. I know that you will wish to see Randall Bennett before you leave." *And I know that I can-*

not stop you. "You must promise me that you will tell
him only that you have agreed to spend the summer
with your uncle in Italy in order to prove to your
mother that your affection for him will endure for
three months. Do you agree?"

"Of course, Mother. I cannot believe that Randall
would approve of his future wife enjoying comfortable cozes with harlots, no matter what the gain."
She gave her mother a sunny smile and left the library.

Chapter 4

Rome, 1847

Daniele Cippolo's driver turned the open carriage about in the huge Piazza San Pietro, careful of the nasty-looking bay drawing the carriage to his left, and directed his gray in a wide arc out of the bright sunlight of the square into the shade cast by Bernini's imposing colonnades.

Giana drew a delighted breath and waved her hand toward Alexander VII's fountain in the center of the square. "I had forgotten, Uncle Daniele, how very impressive everything is. The fountain is truly lovely. May we ride down the Via della Conciliazione to the Tiber?"

Daniele smiled at her excitement. To him, the square was simply a place that was filled with too many tourists during the summer.

"Certainly, Giana." He gave rapid instructions to his driver, Marco, and the carriage skirted the vast colonnades and drew back into the harrowing traffic.

"I had also forgotten how very warm it is here in the summer, and so many people," Giana said, fanning herself. "I even had trouble sleeping last night."

"But I do not find it at all warm, my dear. It is your English summers that are intolerable. All that fog and damp! If you will but look more closely at all those people, Giana, you will see that many of them are your countrymen, here on holiday. The railroad is making Rome too crowded for everyone."

"Can you blame them? Rome is so very romantic! I wish that Ran . . ." She bit her tongue, and looked at him warily from the corner of her eye.

But Daniele only smiled, a tolerant smile that made Giana grit her teeth. He had seen Randall Bennett, had gone out of his way to have the young man pointed out to him. He had wanted, if possible, to assure himself that Aurora was indeed correct about his character, or lack thereof. To his delight, he had managed to engage the young man in a friendly conversation, indeed, had shared a glass of sherry with him at Boodle's on St. James Street, the result being that he itched to remove Giana as quickly as possible from London and Randall Bennett's influence. Conceited, arrogant puppy! As to his being as ruthless as Aurora had painted him, Daniele wasn't certain, but during the last two weeks he had spent in Giana's company, he had become more than impressed at how well the young man had succeeded in his duplicity, and to suspect that more was at stake here than just saving a young girl from a disastrous marriage. The young man had bragged, with Daniele's gentle guidance, of his noble connections and his forthcoming marriage to the daughter of a wealthy family. Which wealthy family? Daniele had inquired. Actually, Randall had confided, there was but a mother, a raving bitch of a woman who tried to deal in the business world with men. Daniele had allowed an incredulous expression, and Randall had sneered his disdain, assuring the foreign gentleman that he would soon have the lady well in hand.

In an effort to keep the smile on his face, Daniele shaded his eyes and gazed toward the Castel Sant'Angelo, the ancient ruin, once the Emperor

Hadrian's mausoleum, that stood stark and gray on a cliff overlooking the Tiber. It was a sight that never failed to make him thankful he was a Roman, and not a cold-blooded Englishman.

"So you still enjoy Roma, Giana? I recall that three years ago, I nearly succumbed to exhaustion squiring you about."

For a moment, she looked uncertain, wondering if she had demanded too much of him during her visit to Rome.

He leaned over and patted her gloved hand. "Perhaps, my dear, we will have time for you to return to Hadrian's Villa and frolic as you did so charmingly then, amongst the olive groves and cypresses."

Giana was silent for a long moment. She stared at the rows of colorful flower stalls along the Campo dei Fiori, scarcely aware of the bawling of the street vendors, the loud voices of haggling customers, and the racket of the traffic. Her Uncle Daniele had been a part of her life for as long as she could remember; he had always warmed her with his attention. But now she was with him at her mother's behest, not her own, and she felt dreadfully uncertain, even frightened, about what would happen to her.

Daniele watched her, in some part understanding her feelings. She was too young, he thought, and too caught up in her own little drama to understand what was in his mind. He had come to know Giana again during their journey to Rome, had learned that she had her mother's great stubbornness and singleness of mind, but none of her tempering wisdom. To think that what he had planned for Giana would in any way sway her! And she was still a child, without an adult's capacity to understand dissimulation and guile, a child who believed that Randall Bennett would provide her with love and security. He had

been just as much a fool as Aurora. Meeting prostitutes would probably provide her only with naughty
enjoyment and a stock of deliciously wicked memories, nothing more. No, Giana must experience the
hypocrisy directly, must feel for herself the humiliation many men of her class forced upon women.

It had taken him two weeks to resolve the unease
he felt at throwing Giana into the situations he envisioned now. He glanced at her sideways, her lovely
face open and filled with pleasure at her surroundings. He wondered if she would grow old hating him
for what he was planning to do. He knew he had the
guile and art of persuasion to convince her, if he
wished, without even telling her mother.

"Giana," he said, drawing her eyes to his face. "I
truly wish that we could spend another holiday together like we did then. But it cannot be. I will tell
you again that I agree with your mother about your
Mr. Bennett. You are giving us no choice, Giana, but
to give you a strong dose of life during this short
summer. I am afraid you have to grow up, and much
more quickly than I would like."

"I am grown up, Uncle," Giana said stiffly. "It is
only you and Mother who refuse to believe that my
love for Randall will survive a summer!"

"Perhaps, my child. But you must allow me the
hope that it will not last. There are grim realities in
this world, Giana, and I fear that Randall Bennett is
one of them."

"You are wrong, Uncle, quite wrong."

"Well, in any case, the both of us have said what
we feel. Your mother told you, my dear, that you
would be seeing all sides of life, not only the married
ladies of your own class, but also women of the other
side of the coin."

"Yes, Uncle. Prostitutes."

Her voice was light, almost insultingly so. It is all a wicked game to her, he thought. "Your mother," Daniele said with careful condescension, "has been much protected during her life. I doubt if she would recognize a prostitute if she saw one."

"Yes, Mother is quite the lady, in that respect."

"But you, on the other hand, wish to taste life, do you not, Giana? To understand and experience life so that you may more fully appreciate your position in it?"

"Of course," she said indignantly. "I have no wish to hide my head in the sand like some people do!"

"Ah. Do I take it, my dear, that actually *dealing* with, say, prostitutes, not just meeting them for a little chat over tea, would appeal to your sense of adventure, your thirst to understand this life we live?"

Giana stared at him, her blue eyes darkening in interest nearly to black. "What are you saying, Uncle?"

Daniele started to speak, then shrugged his shoulders. "Nothing, my dear. I had thought that perhaps you would wish to prove to me and to yourself, but no—it is too much to ask of one so young and . . . innocent."

"Dash it, Uncle! In September I shall marry. As a married lady, I shall do just as I wish!"

He looked still hesitant, even as she tugged at his sleeve. "No," he said finally. "Young ladies of your stamp and upbringing could not survive a taste of the world as it really is. It was foolish of me to even raise the issue!"

"Uncle," Giana said impatiently, "I do not know what you mean by my *stamp*, but I am certainly capable of seeing your so-called world!"

"In all its sordid splendor?"

She made a disdainful gesture with her hand. "You jest, Uncle. There is nothing you could make me see that would make me succumb to die-away airs!" She added, a gleam of understanding in her eyes, "And there is nothing, Uncle, that would make me give up Randall."

"You are so certain, my dear," he murmured, "for one so young, so untried, so sublimely ignorant. You have no more notion of life than a . . . well, it is not in my mind to insult you." He watched a myriad of emotions play over her expressive face before it settled into anger at his condescension.

"And I, my dear child," he continued in a gently taunting voice, "am equally certain that if we agreed to, say, a wager between the two of us, you would quickly renege, and rant to me of my wickedness, like the gentle young lady that you are."

"I assure you that I would not!" She paused a moment, eyeing him closely. "This wager, Uncle—if I agree to it and you lose, what is my prize?"

"Ten thousand pounds, Giana, a wedding present to you and your Randall Bennett."

"Ten thousand pounds!" she breathed, taken aback. She could picture Randall's excitement at such a gift, especially a gift she herself had earned. "And if I lose?" she asked with a shrill little laugh.

"If you lose, Giana, I will see you free of Randall Bennett."

"I accept!"

"Just a moment, child. I wish to tell you the terms of our . . . agreement."

She waved an impatient hand, but he said sternly, "No, Giana, I want your understanding, for I will not accept you playing the affronted little miss once we have begun."

"Very well, Uncle, if it will please you to shock me—for that is what you intend, is it not?"

"You will not just meet prostitutes, Giana. You will

play the whore, in a brothel. You will be treated like a whore, look like a whore. You will witness things your mother could not even imagine. However, I promise you that you will not be touched. You will remain a virgin. Do you still accept?"

Giana looked away from him, her hands nervously clasping in her lap. "I have never been to a brothel, Uncle Daniele," she said finally. "Indeed, I am not quite certain what one does at such places."

Daniele gazed at her profile thoughtfully. There would be no more euphemisms, he thought, no more words tempered for an innocent young lady's ears. "Brothels are houses of pleasure, Giana, places where men go to gratify their sexual desires."

He saw a blush of pained embarrassment creep over her cheeks. He stilled his nagging uncertainty and continued evenly, "Do you know what men and women do together, Giana? When they are not talking?"

She said shyly, flushing. "Randall has kissed me, on my mouth, several times. It felt most exhilarating."

"That is all?"

Giana remembered Randall caressing her back once, when they were alone for a moment in Hyde Park. His touch had frightened her, and she had drawn back. He had begged her pardon, his beguiling eyes pleading for her forgiveness.

"He touched my back once," she admitted, her eyes lowered to her lap.

"Ah. Have you ever wondered, Giana, why girls are kept so confoundedly ignorant until their wedding night?"

"Good girls, Uncle," she said in a prim and starchy voice, "are not supposed to know of such things until . . . until they marry."

"I see. I assume that you would also expect your husband to be equally ignorant of the physical side of life? Equally pure?"

She cocked her head to one side. "I had not thought about it. I had always assumed that men know everything . . . about that."

"And just how do you think they learn about sex?"

She flushed again at the naked, stark word, a word she had heard only Linette, a French girl, use to scandalize her friends at Madame Orlie's. "From . . . loose girls, bad girls."

"If this pool of girls is loose, bad, does it not follow that the men who use them are equally loose and bad?"

"I . . . I don't know. Men are different, at least that's what people seem to think. Derry, my roommate, and I would lie in bed some nights and discuss what we knew, you know, what we had heard."

He heard the naive innocence in her voice, and winced. For a moment Daniele felt a stab of anger at Aurora. Aurora, of all women, to keep her daughter in prudish ignorance. Perhaps, he thought, stroking his thick gray mustache, it was to the good that Giana was such an innocent.

"And just what did you decide from these discussions?"

"Well, the other girls used to say that we should . . . ignore that part of men's natures." She remembered her moment of pleasure when Randall had kissed her and her start of fright when she had felt his hand stroke down her back. "I don't think it is part of love."

You are too young to think like that, he thought. He wondered briefly if Aurora had ever discovered a woman's pleasure in a lover's arms. Her marriage to

Morton Van Cleve had certainly been a barren desert for her.

"There are so many brothels in Rome that I have lost count of them," he said. "Have you ever thought it curious that there are no brothels for women to go to, for their pleasure?"

Incomprehension held her expression blank. "Oh! Most women do not enjoy that sort of thing! Really, Uncle, you are being outrageous, and I don't want to talk any more about . . . *it*!"

"*It*? You mean sex? Intercourse? Mating? My dear child, lovemaking should be a joy, for women as well as men. It is as natural a part of life as eating and sleeping, at least it should be." He paused a moment, then allowed his voice to border on insult. "Now, have we discussed everything to your satisfaction? Have you more questions?" He was gratified at the result.

Giana said stiffly, her chin high, "Yes, I understand. I . . . I accept our agreement, Uncle."

"Be very certain, Giana."

"I am certain. Yes," she said again, "I am certain."

"I will trust you," Daniele said lightly, "to keep to your word, Giana." He sat forward in the open carriage and spoke quietly to Marco. When he leaned back against the black leather squabs, he said, "You do understand that our agreement is that you will do exactly as I bid you, do you not, Giana? You are never to refuse what I tell you to do?"

She nodded, remembering Randall's appeal at their last furtive meeting. "Please, my little love," he had whispered urgently, clutching her fingers so tightly that she had winced, "spend the three months with your uncle as your mother wishes. Our happiness and our future depend upon it. Do not disappoint me, Giana."

"You are going to become the most knowledgeable virgin in all of Europe and England, my dear . . . the most knowledgeable chaste virgin, that is."

The carriage rolled over the Ponte Umberto I. "Do you go to brothels, Uncle Daniele?"

He started at the timid question, and his eyes twinkled. "Yes, Giana. Not so often now that I am an old man, but yes, occasionally."

"Did your wife mind?"

"I never told her." Silent, cold Elana. Of course she had known, known about all his mistresses. But she hadn't cared . . . it kept him from her bed. She had been a proper wife, a proper lady.

She was silent again, chewing over this piece of information.

"Randall would never do that," she announced.

Daniele answered her only with an incredulous look, and straightened his white brocade waistcoat as the horse drew to a halt along a quiet, elegant side street.

He stepped down from the carriage. "You will stay here, Giana. I will return soon."

Giana was feeling wilted from the heat when Daniele returned some thirty minutes later.

"Come, Giana," he said, offering her his hand, "we have a short walk before us."

She accepted his outstretched hand and skipped lightly down to the sidewalk. "Where are we going?"

"To a brothel, my dear. I do not wish my driver to know where I am taking you, thus the walk."

Giana felt a curious sort of excitement. Now she would see what all this botheration was about.

"Giana, before we begin your . . . lessons, I want you to know that I care very much about you. I always have, ever since you were a little girl. Our time spent together over the years has brought me great pleasure. But I also want you to know that I do expect complete obedience from you this summer. Whatever I ask you to do, I ask for a reason. I will always ensure that you are not touched, but otherwise, I will show you a bit of life, as both a man's wife and his harlot live it. Some of what I will require of you will not be pleasant. Your introduction to a brothel is the first step."

"I care about you too, Uncle, though I care not one whit for all your elaborate charades!"

"You will trust me and obey me, without question?"

"You must know that I gave my word. You needn't continue asking me!"

"Very well."

Madame Lucienne Rostand, French by name and birth, waved a languid greeting to her generous friend, Daniele Cippolo. She felt a bubble of laughter at the sight of the openmouthed girl at his side. So this stiff little chit was to be in her charge!

"*Buon giorno*", she said in her heavily accented Italian. "Do come in. A glass of sherry, my dear Daniele?"

"*Grazie*, Lucienne. Sherry is fine."

"Shall I offer the child a glass of lemonade?" she said in rapid Italian, laughter sounding in her voice.

Daniele quelled a frown. He had brought Giana to this world, and it was ridiculous of him to go stiff and disapproving. "Would you like a glass of sherry, Giana?"

"No, Uncle," she replied in her starchy Italian, a legacy from her Swiss seminary, "I am not thirsty."

When Lucienne handed him his sherry, Daniele performed the introductions. "Giana, Madame

Lucienne runs the most exclusive brothel in all of Rome."

"It is most ... impressive," Giana said. She ogled the statues of plaster and marble men and women, stark white and stark naked, and bent in most unusual positions. She didn't know precisely what she had expected, perhaps an overabundance of crimson, for that was vulgar, she knew. The huge drawing room was furnished opulently, with many sofas and high-backed chairs, all in delicate shades of blue and white. Even the thick Axminster carpets were light blue swirls against pure white. There was no crimson. The heavy draperies were of royal-blue brocade with heavy gold tassels. She looked for a moment at Madame Lucienne, as opulent as the vast room, her flaming auburn hair piled high atop her head, her rich apricot silk gown cut fashionably, snug at the waist with billowing petticoats beneath, and draped off her sloping white shoulders. She could not begin to tell her age. Uncertain of what she should do, Giana tentatively held out her hand.

Lucienne laughed heartily, and shook the small mittened fingers. "A pleasure to meet you, Georgiana Van Cleve."

"Giana."

"Yes, well, Giana. A charming name. When you have looked your fill, my girl, we will get on with it."

Get on with what? Giana wondered uncomfortably. She sat herself stiffly on the edge of a delicate gilt-armed chair.

"I have looked my fill, madame," Giana said, a pique of rebellious anger in her voice at the woman's mocking tone.

"Ah, so there is something beneath those starchy petticoats! Very well, girl, this is a brothel. Wrapped up in clean linen, to be sure, but a brothel nonetheless. Our clients are all wealthy, the cream of Roman and European society. But, of course, they are still men, and the variety of their needs remains the same."

Variety of needs? Whatever was the woman talking about?

Daniele intervened. "Giana, Madame Lucienne will be your mentor, so to speak. You will spend some of your evenings here, watching and learning."

"Watching exactly what, Uncle Daniele?" Giana asked.

Lucienne dissolved once again into laughter. "Why, my girl, watching the wealthy gentlemen plow my girls, of course!" She downed the remainder of her sherry and thwacked the glass down upon a lace-covered side table. "Enough talk. It's time the girl began to learn." Lucienne rose to her full height, shook out her apricot skirts, and said in an imperious voice, "To be a successful wife, you must appear pretty and helpless and appealing to men, and of course be able to bear children until your breasts sag to your waist. To be a successful whore, you must be equally appealing, both in face and body, and learn what pleases men, not in the drawing room, but in the bedroom. Your uncle tells me that you have a handsome, virile young man awaiting you in London. If you wish to have the slightest chance of keeping him out of brothels like mine, my girl, you have to be both the lady and the whore. Now, stand up and let me have a look at you."

Giana sent a confused glance toward Daniele, and he nodded at her, his face impassive. She stood up awkwardly.

Lucienne walked majestically over to her and closed her fingers about Giana's chin, lifting her face upward. "A lovely face, no doubt about that. The sea-blue eyes and the black hair are a striking combination. And the creamy white skin, quite unusual here in Italy." She ran her fingertip lightly over Giana's cheek. "No need to be shy, girl." She stood back, her full lips pursed, and swept her green eyes over Giana's body. "My dear Daniele, she looks like a little girl on her way to church in that ridiculous white frock!" She turned back to Giana, not waiting for a reply from Daniele. "Take off the gown, girl, and let us see if your body is as lovely as your face."

"*What?*" Giana stood frozen, gaping at the woman.

"Take off your clothes," Lucienne repeated, more imperiously this time.

"But I . . ." She turned frantic eyes to Daniele. "Sir! I don't understand . . ."

Daniele said gently, "I told you, Giana, that some things required of you would not be particularly pleasant. You will please do as Lucienne says."

"Unrobe in front of *you?*"

He ignored the horror in her voice, and nodded.

"Of course, my girl. Daniele is a man of exquisite taste, and it is a man's judgment I need to assure myself that you are lovely enough for my gentlemen."

"This is ridiculous! *I will do no such thing!* I have never taken off my clothes in front of anyone, even Mother!" Giana turned on her heel, gathered up her skirt, and raced toward the door.

She drew to a skittering halt at Daniele's harsh voice. "Giana! So this is how you treat our agreement? I knew that you would grow pale and sputter like a little girl! But remember our wager, Giana, for I will hold you to it. If you do not come back here and do as you're bid, you will return tomorrow to London, and the agreement with your mother will be null!"

Giana suddenly remembered standing in front of her mother, listening to her in childish excitement when she mentioned prostitutes, remembered all her confidence and disdain such a short time before when Daniele had told her what he would do. Her face drained of color. She had not imagined this. But if she ran, it would be all over, and she would be returned to London to face her mother and Randall again.

"Whores, like wives," Lucienne said, "do as men wish them to, my fine little lady. If they balk, the gentlemen complain. The primary difference is that whores can grow rich, wives do not. That is the way of the world, and it is time you realized that."

Giana stood as still as the marble statues. Randall would not want her to be so demeaned, so humiliated! If he but knew what she was being asked to do, surely he would take back all his appeals to her to appease her mother. But she remembered the intensity of his gaze and the urgency of his voice when she saw him last.

She heard Daniele's vice, oddly implacable. "Do as you're told, Giana, else you will prove that you are a prideless child who strews her promises about like so many fallen leaves!"

But I am a lady ... not a harlot!

Slowly, her steps clumsy and awkward, Giana walked back to where Madame Lucienne stood, tapping her foot, her arms crossed over her massive bosom.

"I shall go through with your charade, Uncle Daniele, but know that no matter what you make me do, I shall have Randall."

"We shall see, Giana. It is a risk that I will take."

Giana found quickly that the reality was different from her show of bravado. Eyes downcast, her fingers trembling, she slowly began to unfasten the small buttons over the bodice of her frock.

"At the rate you're going, my girl, your gentleman's ardor will have evaporated! You must remember that men do not like to wait." Lucienne stepped forward and lightly slapped Giana's hands away. The rest of the small buttons slipped open quickly, and her frock fell to her waist.

"Good," Lucienne said as her fingers busily unfastened the layers of petticoats. "I am glad to see that your tiny waist isn't the result of corseting."

Giana felt her petticoats rustle down into a pile at her feet. Her lovely white muslin gown fell haphazardly over the stiff crinolines. When Lucienne's hands touched the straps of her shift, Giana closed her eyes.

She grimaced as cold air touched her naked flesh, and tried to cover herself with her splayed hands.

"Kick off your shoes."

Giana did as she was bid. Lucienne's hands pulled down the white garters from her thighs and rolled down her silk stockings. She wanted to scream for this to stop, but knew that she could not. She gritted her teeth and tried to push all thought from her mind, to be apart from what was happening, to feel nothing, to be like the statues.

Daniele could not help but stare at her. She was a beautiful girl, all white-fleshed, with but a curling triangle of midnight black hair between her slender thighs. Her breasts were high and round, the nipples a flushed pink. Her waist was narrow and supple above her flat smooth belly.

"She is acceptable, I think," Lucienne said to Daniele after a studied moment.

"Nice long legs," Lucienne continued at Daniele's nod. "Men like long slender legs, girl. I suppose your breasts will grow . . . after all, you're still quite young. Now turn around and let me see your back. Round and dimpled. Quite charming."

Giana jumped when Madame Lucienne lightly ran her hands over her buttocks.

"You needn't act like I'm going to shoot you, my dear. Our clients like to be enticed, it flatters their vanity and makes them all the hotter. You must learn to hold yourself erect, and at the same time, sway your little fanny to best advantage. If you don't, they might as well stay in their wives' cold beds, and lord knows, none of the fine gentlemen want that!"

Madame Lucienne paused a moment, then touched her finger lightly to the small birthmark in the center of Giana's left buttock. "It looks like a tiny flying bird! The gentlemen would much enjoy that, Daniele. Would you like to have a closer look?"

"No, Lucienne," Daniele said.

"You can dress now, my girl."

Giana bent down and clutched her discarded clothes against her. She looked wildly about for a place to hide . . . but Lucienne and Daniele were paying her no further attention.

"You will bring her back this evening, *caro*?"

Daniele shook his head, looking at Giana from the corner of his eye. He had been right, he thought, to plunge her immediately into the fray. Had he waited, moved more slowly with her, he might well have lost her. She was shaking, could scarcely manage to roll up her stockings. She was fighting to pull her shift over her head when there was a sound of giggling outside the room.

"Wait a moment, Miss Georgiana," Lucienne ordered. "Let us see what my ladies think of you."

Lucienne swept to the door and flung it open.

Giana saw three girls, none of them much older than she, craning their necks to see past Lucienne.

"So all of you have been peeking, have you! Well, come in, Lucia, Margot, Emilie.

"Three of my loveliest girls," Lucienne said proudly, lining them up, still giggling, in front of Giana. Giana was aware of auburn, blond, and chestnut beauty. One girl reached out and touched Giana's loose hair.

"Very lovely, madame," Emilie said.

Giana jerked away before Emilie could release her hair, and winced at the sharp pain in her scalp.

"The gentlemen will adore her, madame," Lucia announced wisely, her black eyes laughing. "We saw how very white she is! And that little patch of black hair covering her secrets!"

Daniele saw that Giana was white with humiliation, her eyes vague with shock. He said to Margot, a French girl with thick honey-blond hair, "Help Giana to dress, Margot. She is tired."

Margot nodded, her amber eyes serious. "*Viens, petite*," she said gently, and led Giana by the hand to a corner of the room.

Lucienne shooed the other two girls away. "All of you rest now. You must be at your best tonight!"

She turned slowly and smiled at Daniele. "A first lesson is always the most painful, is it not, *caro*?"

Daniele was gnawing his lower lip and did not answer her. He rose slowly, his eyes going toward Giana. "I will not bring her back this evening, Lucienne. Luigi del Conde and his strident wife are giving a dinner party tonight, and for the most part, the gentlemen and ladies who will be present are a fine selection. Let her meet all the gentlemen in their social setting before she meets them here. And their wives, of course."

"You believe, *caro*, that the child is old enough to understand the hypocrisy of it all?"

"She will understand," Daniele said, and rose. "Eventually." He shrugged and looked toward Giana. She was standing perfectly still, staring blindly in front of her as Margot fastened the tiny buttons over her bodice.

Daniele led Giana from the elegant three-story house on the Via Crispi and hailed a hansom cab. After he had given instructions to the driver to his sprawling villa off the Piazza di Pellicceria, he turned to his still-silent companion.

To his surprise, Giana whipped her head about to face him before he could say anything, and said in a trembling low voice, "Do not ask me to feel sorry for the plight of your precious Madame Lucienne, Uncle, or those other terrible girls, or try to make me believe that it is men who have forced them there! It is they who are the temptresses, they who throw themselves at men, not the other way around! They are without any tenderness, any goodness, without any feeling a woman should have. They are despicable! How dare that . . . *woman* compare whores to wives and ladies!"

Perhaps it was a mistake, Daniele thought, to take her to such a charmingly elegant brothel. But he knew that he could not expose her to the lower houses, where girls were held in practical servitude by their masters, abused and degraded until they were old at twenty-five and riddled with disease. He pulled at the corners of his mustache, but said only, "We will see."

But Giana wasn't through. She felt such humiliating anger that she threatened to choke on it. "How could you make me do that? How could you make me stand like a block of wood, naked, in front of that leering harridan . . . and in front of you?"

"Because, Giana," he said slowly, locking his gaze to hers, "that is exactly how a whore is treated. She is to have no feelings, no modesty. Her only worth lies in how well she will please the men who decide to take her. Madame Lucienne was but doing her job. Surely you see that she would not be so successful in her business if she failed to provide all her gentlemen clients with lovely young girls who were eager to please them."

Giana answered in a coldly vicious voice. "And does she please you, Uncle Daniele! Did I please you?"

"I did not look upon you as would a man who wished to enjoy your body. But I will tell you what such a man would say of you. Such a man would have been delighted with you. He would also have likely agreed with Madame. You are young yet and your lovely breasts will become fuller. It is said that a woman's breasts become softer and larger the more they are fondled. Did you not notice Margot's fully rounded bosom?"

A great shudder passed through her slender frame. Daniele wondered what Aurora would say if she knew he had forced her daughter to strip naked in front of him and be examined as if she were a painting in an art gallery. It was odd, he thought, how very innocent of the world Aurora actually was. Her virgin daughter, if she remained in Rome, would return to England far more worldly than her sophisticated mother. *Ah, Aurora, I pray you will forgive me if you ever learn of this!*

Giana's thoughts continued in tumbled confusion, with no direction or conclusion, save that the woman Lucienne was a beast, the kind of woman no lady should ever have to meet. Perhaps it was true that some men, men who had been disappointed in love, sought solace at such places. But Randall would not have to! She knew she was certainly not a cold woman, and she would always love Randall. He would not be disappointed in love!

"The watered silk is lovely, my dear. It makes you look as fresh as a rose."

"Thank you, ma'am," Giana said to Mirabella del Conde, her hostess. The dinner had been a long one, with many courses and removes, and Giana, as the newcomer and the center of attention, had felt woefully tongue-tied in the company of the ladies and gentlemen.

"She is so very young," Mirabella said, her words intended for none of the other ladies in particular. She sighed as she sat down and picked up her embroidery frame.

Giana sat stiffly on the edge of her chair, wishing that the gentlemen would not take long over their port. She felt so out of place, her Italian, though reasonably fluent, stiff and wretchedly accented.

Luciana Salvado, the wife of a wealthy Italian railroad investor, a tall, willowy woman whose hair was as inky black as Giana's, said loudly, "Do you enjoy needlework, Miss Van Cleve?"

"Please call me Giana, ma'am. I would wish to improve, of course."

"Well, you have a lifetime to learn. Perhaps if you become tired of too much sightseeing, you shall come to my house for a light collation. Many of us meet there. You see, we are embroidering an altar cloth for—what did you say the name of the church was, Mirabella?"

"Saint John."

"Ah, yes, Saint John."

"My children were confirmed there, Luciana," said

Signora Camilla Palli, a thin, pinched-looking woman whose nervous fingers continually plucked at the skirt of her plum taffeta gown. "My little girls were so lovely in their white gowns. And Father Pietro was so very pleasant and attentive."

"*Si*, and he is so enthusiastic about the altar cloth. Mirabella has the greatest skill—she has designed the pattern, with the aid of Father Pietro, of course."

Camilla continued in an undertone, a certain snideness in her voice, "It is because Mirabella is so much alone that she achieves such skill."

Luciana said, "I hope to travel with my husband to your country one day, Giana. My husband tells me that your Prince Albert is planning a great exhibition."

"Yes, ma'am. I understand that the committee is still deciding upon the architect."

"Now, Luciana, you know that Carlo will never allow you to accompany him," said Camilla.

"It is to be an exciting event," Giana said. "I think all of you would enjoy it."

She noticed several startled glances. "Ladies," Mirabella said, "do not travel such distances."

"But why, ma'am?" Giana asked, equally startled.

Camilla Palli said in a superior voice that was beginning to grate on Giana's ear, "Really, Miss Van Cleve, I wonder at such a question from you. A lady's sensibilities would surely forbid such strenuous travel, and there are, of course, the children to be considered."

"Yes, I suppose there are many considerations," Giana said.

"Of course Camilla is right," Mirabella said, glancing toward the clock just to the left of the mantelpiece. "Can you imagine being jostled by all the common people?" She shuddered delicately. "I wonder what the gentlemen can be doing?"

"Smoking their vile cigars and drinking port," Luciana said matter-of-factly.

"Oh dear," Mirabella said, stabbing her needle into the swatch of material, "I just missed a stitch."

"How is your precious little baby, Angela?" Luciana said, disregarding Mirabella. "Angela has been married but a year and a half, my dear," she explained to Giana. "A little girl this time, but she isn't repining. I myself had three girls before I gave my husband a boy."

"Maria can hold her head up now," Signora Angela Cavour said. "But surely, Luciana, we shouldn't talk of such things. Miss Van Cleve— Giana—is not yet married."

"I will be, in September."

"How marvelous for you," Mirabella said, her eyes darting again toward the clock. "Oh dear, the gentlemen are taking a long time, aren't they?"

"Your fiancé is English?" Angela asked in a soft, shy voice.

"Yes, ma'am. He will likely enter my mother's business."

"Your mother in business! Surely you are jesting, Giana!" Mirabella's hand was poised over the tambor frame in awful silence.

"Yes," Giana said stiffly. "She is quite good— indeed, since my father died, she has increased the Van Cleve holdings substantially."

"How very odd," Luciana said, a thick black brow arched.

"A pity she did not marry again," Camilla said in her pontificating voice. "Imagine a lady involving herself in all that ... drudgery."

Giana flushed at the repetition of her own words to her mother. Somehow Camilla made them sound so priggish and offensive.

"She has had many offers, ma'am," Giana said quietly. "She prefers making her own decisions."

Luciana's thin dark brows remained arched. "A lady entirely on her own—I vow it is something I should not like to contemplate. At least she had the good sense to protect you, Giana."

"What kind of business?" Angela asked quietly.

"The Van Cleve interests are varied, ma'am. Shipping, vineyards, the railroad." Giana realized she did not know many of the Van Cleve interests. She had never bothered to ask. "Perhaps," she said tentatively to Luciana, wanting to impress, "Signore Salvado will meet with my mother on railroad business if he goes to London for the exhibition."

"Carlo meeting with a lady on business! I am afraid not, my dear child. I am afraid my Carlo would as soon meet with the monkeys at the zoo! I am sorry, but he has strong opinions on such things."

"I wish the gentlemen would finish with their port," Mirabella said, glancing again at the clock.

"They are likely discussing the political situation," Camilla said. "Did I tell you, Signorina Van Cleve, that my darling daughter is also to wed? Such an amiable young man, and the scion of an old and distinguished Roman family."

The fragile Angela said hesitantly, "I have heard it said, Camilla, that Vittorio Cavelli is a rather wild young man."

"What young man does not enjoy himself before he is wed?" Camilla shrugged. "My dear Cametta has met him, and thinks that her father and I have made a fine choice. He is quite a handsome boy, and well-spoken."

"Cametta does not known him well, ma'am?" Giana asked, surprised.

"Our daughters are raised a little differently in Italy, child. Clemetta emerged from the convent but three months ago. Her father and I arranged the match for her."

A little differently! Certainly Giana had been well chaperoned at Madame Orlie's, but a convent!

"We protect our daughters, Giana," Luciana said, her lips drawn in a prim line. "Even your visit with your Uncle Daniele must be seen as a bit unusual."

"You have no chaperon, Signorina Van Cleve?" Camilla asked.

Chaperon? Uncle Daniele is all of sixty years old!

"No, ma'am," Giana said, "but I can hardly see that it matters. After all, Uncle Daniele has known me since I was a small child." *And he saw me strip naked in a brothel today.*

Mirabella's fingers worried over her tambor frame, and she said, without looking up, "The English are not as careful with their daughters as we are."

Angela said softly, patting Giana's hand, "Your Uncle Daniele is a fine gentleman. I believe that my husband has some dealings with his banks, but of course, I know little of it."

"Ah," Mirabella said, "the gentlemen."

The gentlemen, Giana saw with some relief, were filing into the drawing room. Save for the lilting Italian, they could just as easily have been Englishmen. Signore Conde, their host, a tall, gaunt-featured man whose dark eyes seemed to dart everywhere. Signore Cavour, plump and good-natured, the fragile Angela's husband. Signore Salvado, the gentleman who would sooner meet with monkeys than with her mother, a handsome man, though a little stocky, with a bushy black mustache and thick side whiskers. His dark eyes seemed to probe when they rested upon Giana. And Signore Palli, the superior Camilla's heavy-jowled husband. She looked toward Uncle

Daniele, distinguished in his severe black evening clothes. He met her eyes and arched his thick black brows in silent question. About what? Giana wondered. She suspected that the gentlemen had been drinking heavily, for their laughter was easy and their conversation loud.

She started at Signore Salvado's husky voice. "My sweet child, Daniele tells me that your famous mother is now in charge of a railroad."

Aurora would give him the brunt of her tongue, Giana thought, if she heard the sneering condescension in his voice. She said stiffly, "My mother, *signore*, is active in many areas."

"Actually," Daniele said, "Signora Van Cleve is working with a Mr. Cook, the idea being to provide cheap rail fares for people who could not otherwise afford such travel."

Giana felt herself flushing. If Uncle Daniele had not been present, she would not have been able to say anything specific about her mother's plans. She tried frantically to remember any scrap of conversation about it. She brightened, saying, "I believe it is a fine idea, *signore*. So few people can afford to visit the sea, for example."

"The common people are like our dear ladies in one respect," Signore Cavour said, laughing. "They must have our guidance and not forget what God intended them to be."

Daniele cast a quick glance at Giana and said blandly, "And just what did God intend our ladies to be, gentlemen?"

"The delight of our lives," Signore Cavour said, giving Angela a gentle smile.

Signore Conde, Mirabella's husband, rolled his eyes, saying. "A drain on our purses!"

"And our patience!"

"Surely you are too harsh, Carlo," Daniele said to Signore Salvado, Luciana's husband.

Carlo smiled cryptically at his wife. "A wife is to be a loving creature, her aim to please her husband and bear his children."

"I daresay that all of us would agree," Luciana said, smiling toward the thin-lipped Carlo.

"What do you think, Giana?" Daniele asked.

"I . . . I believe that a lady should be protected and cherished by her husband, and respected for her gentleness and wisdom."

"Wisdom! She sees a new ribbon, and so much for wisdom!"

"If a man sees a . . . new cravat, Signore Palli, he is also considered to have lost his wisdom?"

"A young lady with a sharp tongue, *signorina*," Signore Cavour laughed. "It is said that such a combination bodes ill for a happy union."

"I am certain that Giana meant nothing by it," Angela said, smiling hesitantly.

Giana kept an uneasy silence, her eyes upon the toes of her white satin slippers. Why had she simply not kept her mouth shut, like the other ladies? She looked up and was taken aback to see Luciana and Mirabella regarding her with open disapproval. Camilla was gazing at her questioningly. Only Angela Cavour was smiling. Giana tried to return her smile, but she saw Angela raise her soft eyes to her husband's face, and quickly dropped her eyes to her toes. Had they not been even slightly angered by Signore Palli's joke at their expense?

"Mirabella," Daniele said easily, breaking the momentary silence, "a glass of your excellent sherry, if you please."

* * *

"Well, my dear Giana," Daniele asked during their ride back to his villa, "did you enjoy your evening?"

"Yes, of course," she said, forcing brightness to her voice. She paused a moment, then added, "Do you think Italian ladies are like English ladies, Uncle?"

"In large measure. Did you enjoy their company?"

"Signora Luciana asked me to join them in embroidering an altar cloth."

"How very interesting, to be sure."

Giana heard the gentle contempt in his voice, and avoided his eyes.

"As my ersatz niece, and a young English lady of impeccable breeding, you were obviously accepted into their ranks." As Giana made no reply, Daniele sat back against the squabs and stroked his mustache. He had to remember to ensure that Giana would not be recognized by any of the gentlemen as his niece. A wig, he decided, a blond one, perhaps.

Daniele turned his gaze back to his silent niece. Her evening had not proved to be an entirely pleasant experience. Bless her heart, she must have been profoundly bored, at least he hoped so. She was her mother's daughter, and her snapping retort had come naturally.

"I liked Angela Cavour," Giana said, gazing at the darkened stalls that lined the Via di Fiore.

"She is near your age. Such a timid little mouse. But so appealing, is she not? You will undoubtedly see her again. That particular group of ladies is often together. I daresay that you will enjoy many hours in their company. Of course, in the near future you will have more in common with them."

Giana listened for a moment to the clopping of the horses' hooves on the cobblestones. "Tell me, Uncle Daniele," she said, "what are Mother's plans with Mr. Cook?"

Chapter 5

Giana touched her fingers lightly to the blond curls that fell lazily over her forehead and stared unblinking at the image of a stranger.

"Hold still, *signorina*," the maid, Rosana, said in her wheezing voice. She was a plump older woman, dressed always in severe black, wool in winter and cotton in summer, whose upper lip was shadowed with a clump of soft dark hairs. "You have large eyes, and now they are even larger with the kohl. A bit of powder, some pink rouge on your lips, and you are ready."

"I am hungry," Giana said with a touch of belligerence when Rosana allowed her to rise.

"Your supper will be taken with the gentlemen," the maid responded placidly. "It is just as well that your belly is empty when I lace your waist."

Giana groaned as Rosana jerked on the corset laces. She clutched the armoire door to steady herself, sucked in her breath, and held it. She did not again look into the long mirror until Rosana stood back, obviously pleased with her handiwork.

There was the stranger again. The blond wig was a mass of soft curls framing her face, a face that seemed all eyes. Her soft yellow chiffon gown was tight about her slender waist and fell from her shoulders in layers of pale cream lace. Giana stared at the

white expanse of bosom the corset pushed upward,
her face scarlet beneath the white powder.

She felt Rosana's hands close about her waist and
jerked away in embarrassment. "*Bene, bene, signorina*," Rosana said complacently. "Your waist is so
narrow I can nearly span you."

Madame Lucienne pushed open the door of the
bedchamber and stood studying her charge with a ju-
dicious eye. If not for the terror in the girl's huge
eyes, she would have looked as lovely a harlot as one
would wish. Lucienne supposed that once she had
felt just as Giana did, but it was too long ago for her
to capture the elusive feeling. For a moment she was
somehow sad that this girl would keep her maidenhead, yet lose her innocence. She quickly quelled her
moment of weakness, for after all, business was business. She nourished a feeling of impatience and, she
admitted to herself, envy for this English girl whose
mother was rich enough to provide her everything.
Here she was playing nursemaid to a girl who was
so stupid as to want to throw away everything on a
man, and a fortune hunter at that! Well, the little twit
was in for a shock.

"You look passable, Giana," she said at last.
"Come, some gentlemen have already arrived."

Giana ran her tongue over her painted lips. They
felt slippery and tasted of ripe cherries. "But how am
I to behave, madame?"

"Flirt with the gentlemen just as you do with your
young Englishman. If any of them wish to bed you,
I shall simply tell them that your . . . services have already been secured for the night. Daniele will be arriving shortly to take you in hand. You will
remember, my girl, that you are not to stand around
like a stick. I expect you to be as charming and enter-
taining as the rest of my girls, else Daniele will be

told." Better not to tell her the rest of it, Lucienne thought, looking at the huge, still-frightened eyes.

She patted her full dark blue brocade skirt, regarded her own bountiful bosom in the mirror, and said, "Come, girl. Gentlemen like to be entertained, and they are never to be kept waiting. Mind, now, you are to mix your English with liberal French and Italian. Daniele does not want to take the chance that you will be recognized as his well-bred English niece."

Giana followed in Lucienne's imposing wake through the wide carpeted corridor that gave onto each of the girls' rooms, and down the winding staircase. She saw a man's appraising eyes upon her before they even reached the bottom steps. He had just entered the front door, and was standing next to Fusco, Lucienne's majordomo. He was quite fat and old enough to be her father, with huge side whiskers and wide-spaced dark eyes.

"Ah, my dear Lucienne," he said, strolling over to them. "If all of your girls are like this lovely chit, you will end up with more *lire* in the bank than most of your customers."

"Ah, but I already have, Alfredo," Lucienne said with light laughter in her voice. She tapped his coat sleeve. "This is my little . . . Helen. Come, Helen, welcome Señor Alfredo Albano. He is visiting Rome from Seville."

Giana shrank back against Lucienne, so frightened that she could not speak. At last she managed a jerky nod.

"A virgin?" Alfredo asked, his eyes resting upon her breasts.

Giana blinked at his bald question, but Lucienne laughed delicately. "I fear not, my dear Alfredo."

Señor Alfredo sighed heavily. "I fear that the only

virgins left in the world are so ugly that only a blind
man could enjoy himself." He paused a moment,
darting his pink tongue over his thick lower lip. "I'll
take her in any case, Lucienne. She is a beauty, and
what a lovely mouth. A skilled mouth, I trust."

Facing a man who wanted to buy her body, a man
who was quite open about it in fact, as if he were
purchasing a bottle of wine, made her want to disap-
pear into the thick carpet beneath her feet.

Lucienne laughed again. "I fear you can only enjoy
her charming company, Alfredo. Her services have
been bespoken."

"Such a pity. She is so young and fresh-looking.
Well, little Helen," he continued to Giana, "perhaps
some other night I can possess you."

Giana kept her eyes downcast, and felt Lucienne's
elbow against her ribs. "You are in Rome long, sir?"

"Not long enough, I fear," Señor Alfredo said.
"Where do you come from, Helen?"

"From . . . Paris," Giana said.

"Ah, then you must have a beautifully skilled
mouth."

Giana looked up at him with incomprehension.
"Thank you, señor."

"You are quite right, Alfredo, and I know that is of
particular interest to you, isn't it, my friend? Come,
let us have a glass of champagne."

Giana dutifully followed in Lucienne's wake toward the sound of men and women laughing in the
drawing room. She wondered what that leering old
man had meant about her mouth.

She felt his hand on her bare arm, and felt goose-
flesh rise where his fingers caressed her. She was on
the point of slapping him away, but she saw
Lucienne's narrowed eyes. She lowered her head and
allowed him to lead her into the main salon.

"You like my touch, little one?" Alfredo asked her, grinning.

No! I hate your slimy fingers and I hate you, you toad!

"I am thirsty," she managed in halting Spanish.

"Ah, she speaks, and in my tongue! How very delightful. Have you ... visited Spain, Helen?"

"No," she said so numb with humiliation that she did not at first see Signore Salvado.

"What have you here, Alfredo? Ah, the new girl Lucienne was telling me about."

Giana felt Alfredo's fingers tighten possessively about her arm. "Are you the one who has bespoken her services for the night, Carlo?"

Giana looked up at him in astonishment. Luciana's husband ... here, and quite at his ease in a brothel! She felt a moment of terror that he would see through her disguise, but when she forced herself to meet his hungry eyes, she saw no recognition in them. She thought of Luciana, his wife, not terribly attractive, to be sure, but nonetheless his wife.

She heard Signore Salvado say, "No, I am not the lucky man. But look around you, Alfredo, at all the lovely ladies. Come, my friend, with all the negotiations we conduct during the day, you mustn't be downcast because you cannot have your first choice at night!"

Alfredo was looking at her as a dog would a prize bone. "She even speaks a little Spanish," he grumbled.

Signore Salvado grinned, and before Giana could react, he reached out his hand and rubbed his open palm over her breasts. "*Dio*," he said, "I would not care if she were deaf and dumb."

She shrank back, unable to help herself. Carlo Salvado frowned. "Mind your manners, girl," he said, a glint of anger in his dark eyes.

"I am thirsty," Giana said again, this time in Italian.

"A pity that she is not hungry," Carlo said. "What I would give her to eat!"

"I must go," Giana said.

Lucienne watched Giana lurch back and saw Carlo Salvado's lips tighten. She swayed gracefully toward them, her servant, Draco, close behind her with a tray of drinks. She said in a coquettish voice to Carlo, "You are such a mouthful, signore, that all of my girls become limp with pleasure at the thought of you. But look, gentlemen, Emilie and Jeannette are most interested in what you have to offer them."

Carlo Salvado took one last, lingering look at Giana's breasts, shrugged, and walked away, Señor Alfredo with him. "Perhaps another night, Helen," Alfredo called over his shoulder.

"Little ninny!" Lucienne hissed at her. "A whore, or a wife for that matter, must not show disgust! If the gentlemen want to touch you a bit, you will smile and pretend that you enjoy it. Do you understand me?"

"It . . . He was disgusting," Giana whispered, still trembling.

"Don't be a fool! Do you think gentlemen come here only for conversation?" She saw that Giana would still protest, and said sharply, "Do you see that gentleman over there? The one with his arm about Lucia? Go stand near them and listen to Lucia. Perhaps you will learn how to hold your tongue and behave. Here," she added, grabbing a glass of champagne from Draco's silver tray, "drink this. It will help relax you."

Giana clutched the slender glass stem between her fingers as she walked over to the davenport where Lucia sat. There was a marble statue of a naked woman behind the davenport, and she slipped quietly behind it. She saw the man openly fondling Lucia's ripe breasts, and Lucia was giggling and pressing herself toward his hands. The man gave a quick yank at the material over her breasts, and a large dusky nipple popped out. To Giana's horror, the man leaned over and closed his mouth over it. She saw his tongue circling the nipple, his teeth nipping.

Giana was so surprised that she stared.

She heard Lucia say in a drawling, intimate voice, "Now, signore, you cannot take me here. Let us go upstairs."

The man gave a groan, but rose quickly. Giana saw Lucia's hand lightly brush over the bulge in his trousers.

She tossed down the champagne, scarcely tasting it. *Oh God, what have I done!*

She managed to stay hidden behind the statue as they walked from the salon, their bodies pressing against each other. "Well, Giana," she heard Daniele say softly to her, "what do you think of our house of pleasure?"

"Why, it is charming, to be sure," she said with vicious brightness.

"It pleases me that you have not lost your sense of humor."

She looked at him as if she would have liked to wring his neck, but he only smiled.

He continued easily, "It took me a while to recognize you. The blond wig makes quite a difference, as does all the makeup. Have you spoken to Signore Salvado?"

"Oh yes." She sneered. "He was all that is gracious! He touched me, Uncle. Here!"

He saw her hand steal protectively over her

bosom. "Signore Salvado is usually quite generous with girls who please him. Did he ask for you?"

"I said I was thirsty, and he said it was a pity that I wasn't hungry, then laughed with that other man."

"He also thinks himself a wit. I trust you laughed."

"It is difficult to laugh, Uncle, when one doesn't understand the joke."

"Well, it is only your first evening, is it not? Doubtless understanding will come in good time. Lucienne provides most pleasant surroundings, don't you think? All her girls are lovely, well dressed, and skilled. Come now, my dear, it is time that you learn what goes on upstairs."

Giana allowed him to take her arm, and walked stiffly beside him as he led her from the room. She heard Signore Salvado call after them, over the laughing conversation, "You old devil, Daniele! So it is you who will enjoy the little blond morsel!"

Daniele merely smiled and waved a languid hand.

"For those gentlemen who do not wish to ... partake of Lucienne's girls, there are other pleasures." He walked beside her down the long upstairs hallway, past the closed doors, to a narrow door at the end of the corridor, hidden behind a purple velvet drapery. He shoved the drapery aside, opened the door, and nudged Giana ahead of him.

The room was small, with but one sofa and two papier-mâché chairs, both set on a kind of dais, facing the far wall. There was a ceiling-to-floor brocade tapestry covering the wall, displaying nude figures at a Roman banquet.

"Come sit down, my dear," Daniele said, waving her to one of the chairs. "I selected Lucienne's house for several reasons, one of them this room." He pulled a golden brocade cord and the tapestry parted in the middle. Giana found herself staring through a wide glass into the next room.

"This is the Golden Chamber. The gentlemen within know that they are being viewed, of course. From inside the room, this glass appears only as a mirror. One of science's marvels."

Giana forced her eyes to focus into the room. She saw that its walls were covered with heavy gold brocade draperies, the huge bed in the center of the room with heavy golden coverlets. Even the carpeting was a deep lush gold. She drew in her breath when Señor Alfredo suddenly came into view. The fat old man was naked, and beside him, smiling sweetly up at him, was an equally naked Emilie. Giana had never before seen a naked man, and her revulsion brought bitter bile into her throat. Her eyes fell from his huge belly to the limp shaft of flesh at his groin, surrounded by thick black hair.

"He is not a particularly sterling specimen of manhood," Daniele said dryly, "but not unlike many men who grow older and have a taste for their food."

"I cannot stand it!" Giana cried, lurching up from her chair. "It is disgusting!"

Daniele grabbed her shoulders and gently pushed her back down into her chair. "You will please sit down, Giana, and watch. Emilie is most skilled with a man such as Señor Alfredo. And open your eyes, child!"

When Giana saw Emilie again, she had moved from the bed and was kneeling in front of Señor Alfredo. She was smiling up at him, caressing his fat legs lightly, her slender hands moving slowly upward until they stroked the flesh at his groin. To Giana's horror, Señor Alfredo pressed his hands against Emilie's head and began to slowly sway his hips toward her in a rocking motion. Giana watched,

mesmerized with shock. That was what he had
meant about her mouth! Giana gagged, unable to believe that Emilie did not. She could see Señor
Alfredo's face turning florid, his mouth splitting over
his clenched teeth. He tensed suddenly, and she
could hear him cry out through the nearly soundless
wall.

"She has killed him!"

"Only for the moment," Daniele said, grinning.
"She has brought him to orgasm, the point of the
whole business."

He released Emilie and she fell back on her
haunches, her lips covered with a white liquid.

"What is that? What is wrong with her?" Giana
cried.

Daniele was appalled at her ignorance. "It is his
seme, Giana, his man's seed. Usually," he added, "it is
what a man plants in a woman's body, but of course,
a woman's mouth is also a delightful receptacle, as
you see."

"Please, Uncle Daniele, can we not leave now?"
She turned away from the sight of Señor Alfredo
running his hand contentedly over his now limp
flesh. "Please, it is so horrible . . . so—"

"No! It is life. The act you just witnessed is one
that your Randall will expect of you, unless of course
you faint at the suggestion. Then you can be certain
he will take himself to a skilled vixen like our
Emilie."

"No!" she cried. "He would not! He is not like that
disgusting fat old man!"

"Well, he is certainly not old or fat, but for the
rest . . ." Daniele shrugged. "He is a man."

Giana watched Señor Alfredo casually embrace
Emilie, his fat arms squeezing her slender ribs. She
was momentarily fascinated by the soft whiteness of

Emilie's body. Her breasts were full and rounded, just as were her hips, and her long hair trailed down her slender back. Emilie embraced Señor Alfredo and kissed him full on his mouth, her hands still fondling that limp shaft of flesh at his groin. Giana turned vague, empty eyes to Daniele, then jerked up from her chair, her hands clamped over her mouth. She could not stop the racking sobs that broke from her throat.

Daniele did not touch her. He stood quietly beside her until she was silent. He handed her a glass of wine. "Drink this, Giana. Perhaps you have . . . learned enough for your first evening."

"How delightful to see you again, Giana. I had hoped you could come to dine last evening, but Daniele told Teodoro that you were otherwise occupied. Do let Bela take your shawl." Angela Cavour fluttered about as she spoke, and then drew Giana's arm through hers. She led her into a small solarium that gave onto a flower-filled balcony. "This is my favorite room," Angela said, waving her hand before her. "The hills are so green and lush during the early summer. Do sit down and tell me what you have been doing. Enjoying all of our marvelous sights, no doubt."

Giana could not help but laugh. There was an irony in the sound that made Angela regard her with widened, worried eyes. "My dear Giana, are you all right? It has been terribly warm of late. Have you been too much in the sun?"

Giana took hold of herself, and stared at Angela Cavour. Fragile, gentle Angela. Did her husband do unspeakable things to her? Surely not, it was impossible.

"Thank you for inviting me, Angela," she said at last, bringing her voice to calm.

"It is my pleasure, Giana. I do not have many friends my age. I thought we could have lunch here on the balcony. Perhaps later, you would like to see my little Maria. Unfortunately, I do not think Teodoro will be able to join us. He is so busy of late, so very involved in his business. Ah, here is Bela with our lunch. I try to eat very lightly during the day," Angela confided. "Teodoro does not like me to be at all heavy."

Giana pictured Teodoro Cavour, a smiling young man, but one whose stomach stretched his trousers. "But Signore Cavour is heavy," she said.

Angela shrugged and smiled slightly. "Nonetheless, I wish to please him."

"You are so small, Angela," Giana blurted out, "so light."

"Now I am, but when I was carrying my baby, I looked so grotesque, as if I were hauling about a mountain! Teodoro did not like it at all, and I could not blame him." Angela flushed and quickly said, "Do forgive me, Giana, I should not speak so bluntly. You are so young and as yet unwed."

"Not much younger than you, Angela." *And not so very innocent after last night!*

"I am turned nineteen just last month, Giana. But an old married lady now. Do tell me about England. How I long to visit your country."

Giana tasted a bit of the mixed fruit salad before she replied. "It is much cooler than Italy, but you know that. The closest thing we have to the Piazza San Pietro is Trafalgar Square, not nearly so impressive, I assure you. Eston Station is new, only ten years old, and imposing with its Doric colonnade.

But surely, Angela, you can visit England, perhaps when the exhibition opens."

"Oh, that is not possible," Angela said slowly. "You are a most unusual young lady to be able to travel without a chaperon or your mother to such a faraway place."

"My mother," said Giana, "does not want me to be . . . ignorant of things."

"Perhaps Signora Van Cleve is right," Angela said in her soft voice. "I have never traveled abroad. Teodoro is even worried that I will get lost when I leave the house. He wants always to be with me when I go out."

"You are not stupid, Angela."

Angela merely smiled and played about with the tiny fresh shrimp on her plate. "I think Luciana would much like to visit England. She has already confided in me that she wants to accompany Carlo on his next business trip. Whether he will allow her to, I don't know."

Giana chewed on a succulent slice of orange, suddenly angry. "Have her threaten her husband with a lover," she blurted out, "if he does not take her."

"Giana! Oh, you mustn't talk like that!" Angela gasped Then, to Giana's surprise, she giggled. "She would, if she had the idea, I suppose. Luciana is most strong-willed, you know. Her daughters are all terrified of her." She frowned and pushed her half-filled plate away. "No, it is impossible. If she were to do such a thing, Carlo could lock her away in a convent and take away her children."

"That is terrible! Surely he could not be such a monster!"

Angela shrugged, a faint pitying smile on her lips. "Of course he could, dear Giana. And he wouldn't be a monster."

But surely Luciana's precious Carlo had mistresses!

"But why do you just . . . accept that? It isn't right, truly."

Angela reached over and patted Giana's hand. Giana followed her gaze toward an old woman in a starched gray gown and white cap who was walking toward them carrying a frilly pink bundle in her arms.

"Ah, my dear Giana. This is my baby, Maria." Angela held out her thin arms and took the infant on her lap.

"Not too long, signora," the woman said in a chiding voice. "The master does not wish you to tire yourself."

"Oh, Teodoro," Angela said, smiling fondly at the mention of her absent husband, "he always fusses so. He believes me so delicate, and in truth, I am not. Look, Giana, she is smiling at you."

Giana looked at the baby's tiny face, and indeed, the little girl's mouth was curved upward. She let the baby clutch her finger and pulled gently against her grip. Suddenly before her was the image of Alfredo's seed glistening on Emilie's lips. *That* made this exquisite child? She shuddered, unable to help herself.

"Angela," Giana said after the woman had taken Maria away, "exactly how are babies made?"

Angela turned a dull shade of red and looked quickly away from Giana, her hands fluttering nervously in her lap.

"I . . . I am sorry. I do not mean to embarrass you. It is just that I am not certain exactly how it is done."

"I know," Angela said finally, her voice barely above a whisper. "I also wanted to know before I was married. I think it is better if one does not know. It is best that one's husband shows what is necessary."

Giana saw her flush again, and tilted her head questioningly. "Does it . . . hurt?"

"Only at first, then not at all. Teodoro is a very kind man, and very considerate."

What does kindness have to do with anything!

"I see," Giana said.

"No, of course you do not, but your husband will show you what is expected, dear Giana. He will be gentle, I am certain. It is not something to dread, indeed, I find that I sometimes . . ." Angela stopped in mid-sentence, still flushing. "And the result can be a lovely baby." She rose suddenly and her voice became brusque. "Now, my friend, this is most improper talk! Let me show you my roses and azaleas. They are among the most beautiful in all of Rome, even more lovely, I think, than those at the Piazza di Spagna. Have you walked up the Spanish Steps to the Piazza della Trinità di Monte? I can scarce climb twenty of those steep steps without feeling faint! But Teodoro's arm is always there to steady me."

Elvira, a tall, long-legged girl with flowing thick black hair, lay on her back on the golden coverlet, her white legs parted. A young, pale-skinned man, hairless and as soft-looking as Elvira, stood over her, running his long fingers along the inside of her thigh.

"It appears this gentleman will proceed in a more . . . routine fashion," Daniele said dryly. "This, my dear Giana, is how most wives are taken."

The man straddled Elvira's legs and pushed himself against her, his white buttocks in the air.

"I do believe Elvira is enjoying this," Daniele said indifferently, "else she's a fine actress. Probably the latter."

Elvira wrapped her long legs about his thrusting buttocks and looked up at him, her face contorted.

"He is hurting her."

"Oh no, my dear. Elvira's studied expressions encourage her partner to believe that he is the only man in the world and that she is experiencing great passion."

Elvira and the man were rocking against each other on the bed, his arms rocking Elvira's shoulders and her hands stroking his white back. The man suddenly tensed and threw back his head.

"Elvira is quite talented," Daniele observed as the man collapsed on top of her. "She had to spend very little time and not a great deal of effort."

But Giana's eyes were closed. That was how babies were made, that was what Teodoro did with Angela. *That is what you will do with Randall!* Somehow, she could not now remember the pleasure she had felt when Randall had touched his lips to hers. She felt only fear and revulsion and shame.

"Could Elvira have a baby?"

"Whores do not have babies, Giana, only wives." At her look of incomprehension, he sighed and said, "There are ways to prevent conception, and a girl who beds several men a night must use them. You may ask Lucienne if you are interested in specifics."

Giana shrugged indifferently. "Since I will never be a whore," she said coldly, "I have no need to know."

Giana took up her post behind the naked statue, thankful she had hidden herself from the longing glances of Señor Alfredo. She gazed about the brightly lit salon and rested her eyes indifferently upon Elvira, whose hand nestled comfortably upon a gentleman's thigh. Laughing, brash Elvira, only twenty years old, a whore since she was fifteen. "*Sí,* little Helen," she would say in her bright, lisping voice, "I am everything you are not, but what you are, I cannot understand. *Non capisco*! Men," she would say, "are such simpletons! One has but to toss them a smile, caress them ever so gently, and part one's legs. And the money they will pay!" She would roll her glinting dark eyes. "So much easier than being married to some poor *macellaio*, how you say, ah, butcher, and cooking and having babies every year!"

"Do you ever *feel* anything?" Giana had asked her once.

Elvira had raised her lovely thin black brows. "My poor Helen—this is my *occupazione*, my business! My pleasure will be one day with a man I choose!"

Elvira, the temptress, the seductress, the user of men.

Giana started at the touch of Lucia's hand upon her arm. "Look, *cara*," Lucia whispered. "Is he not the most beautiful man you have ever seen?"

Giana followed Lucia's pointing finger. A man stood in the doorway of the salon in the company of Signore Travola, a wealthy shipowner. He was handsome, Giana admitted, tall, broad-shouldered, and narrow-waisted. He rested his topper against his double-breasted black dress coat, set over straight black trousers. His waistcoat was pearl-gray silk, his shirt and cravat snowy white. She judged him to be in his late twenties, very dark, with thick black hair and nearly black eyes. He was much too large a man to be Italian, and he was clean-shaven, without the fashionable bushy side whiskers. He was doubtless a foreigner, but what nationality, she could not guess. He smiled at something Signore Travola said, displaying even white teeth. "*Sí*," she said, "he is attractive, I suppose."

Lucia sighed. "I hope he chooses me. He has an air about him . . . a man who knows women and enjoys them." She gave a delicious shudder.

"He is still a man . . . and a client."

"Ah, *cara*, you are so funny! If you met him at one of your fancy dinners or at a ball, wouldn't you be drawn to him? Want him to take you in his strong arms?"

"No."

"You are such a child! A little moth, afraid of the blazing flame! Wish me luck. I would certainly prefer him to that plump little Mario Galviani who sweats all over me." Lucia danced away, her eyes bright, her full hips swaying provocatively. She took a glass of champagne in her hand and struck a pose against a high-backed chair, one meant, Giana saw, for the beautiful young man.

Giana watched him as he gazed about the salon. Though he seemed to laugh easily when his companion spoke, she thought he looked bored. He smiled perfunctorily toward Lucia, but made no move toward her. His dark eyes found Giana's for a brief instant, and she quickly drew back into the shadow of the statue. She found, to her surprise, that she was shaking. He was too large, too overpowering, and he frightened her.

Alexander Saxton raised a thick black brow as he studied a tall honey-haired girl.

"*Dio*, Alex, you have the look of Satan himself," Signore Travola said, grinning over the wide space between his front teeth. He followed Alex's gaze. "That is Margot, my friend. From what Madame Lucienne tells me, Margot arrived on her doorstep some five months ago, after the bloody French had killed her sister in the February riots in Paris."

"Rome's gain, undoubtedly."

"She has the saddest eyes and the softest mouth, so I have heard. She is just the medicine I would prescribe for a man who has the look you do."

Alex said dryly, "Medicine, Santelo? I do not particularly care for a medicine that has already been taken by so many men."

Santelo laughed heartily. "Always so fastidious, Alex. Since this is your last night in Rome for a month, you can hardly find a virgin and set her up as your mistress before you leave. That would be a waste in any case. And you are mixing pleasure with business on this trip, are you not?"

"*Si*," Alex said, his dark eyes on the girl Margot again. He admired the graceful curve of her long neck, and her sloping white shoulders. Her waist appeared tiny in the huge bell-shaped gown. He sighed, and said more to himself than to Santelo, "I do have the need, and the girl is tempting enough." His gaze swept the now crowded room. "Who is that other blond girl? The one who seems to be hiding behind the statue?"

Santelo shrugged and shook his finger. "You had better hurry, Alex. I see another gentleman interested in your Margot. Your obvious preference for blond-haired girls can prove a problem in Rome."

Alex raised a sardonic brow again. "It is not particularly a preference, Santelo, it is just that I enjoy discovering if all the hair is blond. Now, my friend, if you will excuse me, I think it is time I took my medicine. I will doubtless see you in the morning before I leave for Milan."

Signore Travola watched his American business associate wend his way toward Margot, his stride graceful for so large a man. He was not particularly surprised to see Margot's amber-colored eyes light up in genuine pleasure. Most women responded to the handsome American like that. He wondered what it was Americans ate that made them grow so large. He watched Alex take Margot's arm and guide her from the salon. As they passed him, he winked broadly at Alex. "Do not forget that lovely mouth," he mocked softly.

"Who is that beautiful man, *caro*?" Lucienne asked, handing Santelo a glass of champagne. "So large he is. A foreigner?"

"*Si*, an American, Lucienne, a businessman from New York."

"He has the look of a wealthy man."

"His shipping empire grows by the day."

"And yet he is young."

"And in need of the tonic your Margot will provide. He lost his wife last year. He works like a demon ... perhaps to forget."

"He will forget tonight," Lucienne said complacently. "Now, you must please yourself, *caro*." She beckoned Lucia, and turned away to greet Daniele.

Santelo eyed the sloe-eyed Lucia, and knew he was not in the mood tonight to be smothered between her huge breasts. He tossed down his champagne, shook his head at Lucia, and bade good night to Lucienne. He took his leave, wondering as he walked out into the warm night if Alex was enjoying himself.

"Good evening, Lucienne," Daniele greeted her. "I see my chick is hiding again behind her statue."

"Ah, *caro*, that is because Señor Alfredo is here again tonight. He vows not to leave Rome until he has tasted her charms. Even with the skills she has learned to keep my gentlemen at arm's length, she fears Alfredo will simply haul her over his shoulder and carry her upstairs."

"So she has learned some of your skills, Lucienne?" Daniele asked with great interest.

"The child has learned a thing or two, I think. Before you arrived on Tuesday evening, she chatted most skillfully with several gentlemen. They adored

her, but she told them with a practiced *moue* of disappointment that she was already engaged for the evening. She had them eating out of her small hands,
thankful they had the chance to speak to her! At least
she no longer plays the terrified little girl I remember
clutching my arm three weeks ago."

Although Daniele appeared pleased with Lucienne's description, he felt a tug of sorrow. He had
noticed himself that her beautiful eyes no longer
shone with a young girl's sparkle.

"She talks to my girls quite a bit, just as you
wished. Margot was complaining to me that she
never runs out of questions!"

"No, I don't suspect that she would." Daniele
paused a moment and sipped his champagne. "I am
conducting something in the nature of an experiment
next week. Giana will spend the day with girls and
boys near her own age. Indeed, one of the young
men—" Daniele paused at the sound of a man's
shouting voice. He saw Draco make his way unob-
trusively toward the man, and Lucienne's attention
followed him.

"The fool has drunk too much," Lucienne muttered. "I will talk to you later, Daniele."

Draco escorted the gentleman gently from the salon,
and within a couple of minutes the gay conversations
resumed. Daniele made his way to Giana.

"Good evening, my dear," he said.

"Uncle, who was that loud fool?"

Daniele shrugged. "Someone new to Lucienne's es-
tablishment. He will not be allowed entrance again.
Are you ready to accompany me upstairs?"

"For another lesson?"

"Yes."

"I would as soon not, Uncle. There is nothing you
can show me that I haven't already seen."

He heard indifference in her young voice, and was not sure if she feigned it. "Nonetheless," he said, offering her his arm.

Giana sucked in her breath when Daniele opened the curtain to the Golden Chamber. It was the young man Lucia had pointed out, with Margot. His dark eyes were resting upon the wedge of thick blond hair between Margot's plump thighs.

"I am pleased with you," Alex said, and drew her to him.

Daniele observed the couple on the golden bed with the objectivity of a connoisseur. Margot was astride, her white hands splayed on his wide chest, her head thrown back above her arched back.

"It is one of the few times a man allows the woman the upper hand, so to speak," he said to Giana. He saw that Giana had lost her negligent pose and had grown taut and silent beside him.

Giana watched the man's huge hands as they stroked through Margot's hair and down her back to knead her full hips. There was both gentleness and power in his hands. He swung Margot onto her back in an easy graceful motion, and knelt above her. Giana wanted to look away, but she couldn't seem to move her eyes away from him. She had never seen a man's body so perfectly proportioned, so severely elegant. His massive chest was covered with a mat of curling dark hair, and his waist and belly were lean and sculptured with muscle. She drew in her breath sharply as he gently raised Margot's legs to his shoulders. She saw him meet Margot's wide eyes before he smiled and lifted her hips to his mouth.

Giana felt her blood rush to her face. She felt oddly warm, especially in her belly, and her lips were suddenly dry. "What is he doing, Uncle?"

Daniele smiled in genuine pleasure. "It appears

that you haven't seen everything yet, Giana. He is giving Margot a woman's pleasure, something one rarely sees in a brothel. And from her response, my dear Giana, I would say he is doing it admirably well."

Margot was trembling, breathing in short gasps. She tried to pull him over her, to give him his pleasure, but he held her tightly to him. He was a master, this one, she thought vaguely.

"Relax, Margot," he said to her, raising his head. "I want no playacting from you. I want to feel your pleasure."

"No, signore," she panted, her body aching with sensation. "I am not important . . . it is you—" A great shudder coursed through her body, and she clenched her teeth to keep from crying out, but a groan tore from her throat. He moved astride her and gently parted her with his fingers, his eyes on her dazed face. She tasted herself on his lips as he plunged inside her. She felt her body stiffen and let her cries fill the room. It had been so long, so very long since she had felt such pleasure.

Giana couldn't seem to breathe easily as she stared at the heaving couple. The heat in her belly seemed like a fire in a hot desert. She shook her head, trying to clear her mind, but she felt herself shudder when Margot shuddered, felt herself flush as Margot writhed beneath him, her face contorted, her hips thrusting upward frantically, almost desperately. What was happening to her! Giana had never seen a woman so abandoned, only the men. To be certain, the girls groaned and moved about when the men took them, but Giana knew that they were pretending, nothing more.

Giana saw the sweat glistening on Margot's white flanks. The man's huge body was still pressed against her. He seemed to be devouring her, consuming her. She was suddenly terrified at the answering response in her own body. "Please, Uncle," she cried, her voice hoarse, clutching at Daniele's sleeve, "I want to go home! Please!"

"You have learned something tonight, Giana." He gazed at her flushed face, his eyes searching hers. "You have seen something I had not expected you to see. Imagine giving a whore pleasure."

Giana's throat suddenly seemed clogged, and she turned her face away. The man had made Margot like a crazed animal, while he controlled her, caressed her with his gleaming dark eyes. And she, just watching him, had trembled, as if it were she he was touching. She pressed her back against the chair, wanting only to escape him. Giana felt herself clammy with sweat, and she wanted to bathe, to cleanse her body and her mind. Her eyes went back to them again, and she saw Margot sprawled limply on her back, the man beside her, kissing her face and her tumbled hair. She shuddered at the sight of his manhood thrusting out from the thick black hair at his groin, still pressed against Margot's thigh.

Giana tilted her frilled parasol to shadow her face from the blistering sun and gazed back through the magnificent terraced garden toward the vast Villa d'Este. For a moment she let the sound of the tinkling water from the hundreds of fountains drown out Cametta Palli's bright chatter. She had thought to enjoy herself today, for she hadn't been in the company of people her own age since she had left Switzerland. But she felt oddly annoyed with their incessant chatter, and was not quite sure why.

"Come, Giana," Cametta cried gaily, "let's walk to the Temple of Vesta."

Giana nodded, thinking it the most sensible thing Cametta had said all afternoon. Although her half-dozen petticoats were heavy and cumbersome, and her corset pinched her ribs, she did not want to sit again and listen to Cametta prattling to her fiancé, Vittorio Cavelli.

"But I am too tired," Bianca Salvado cried. "I want to rest." She cast an imploring glance toward Vittorio Cavelli, her pink lips pouting.

You mean flirt, Giana thought on a sigh. She felt bored, bored with all the talk of how many flounces looked best on the girls' dresses, and of all the plans of the young gentlemen who had accompanied them on their outing to Tivoli to see the Villa d'Este.

The five girls were all unwed, as were the young men in their party. A manservant had accompanied them to serve their refreshments, and Signora Palli stayed a discreet distance from the group.

Vittorio Cavelli, Cametta Palli's fiancé, smiled gaily and gave Giana a mock, teasing bow. "Our English visitor has the stamina of a mountain goat."

"But you are too serious, Giana," Cametta said severely. "I have not heard you laugh once, and Vittorio is so amusing!" She lowered her voice and added on a sly whisper, "And so is Bruno. Don't you think he looks romantic with his dark hair falling over his forehead? His eyes grow so languid when he looks at you!"

Vittorio was not at all amusing, but Giana forced a pained smile to her lips. He talked only nonsense, flattering the girls with his oily charm. What did Cametta see in him? As for Bruno Barbinelli, all he needed was to fake a club foot to complete his attempt at being Lord Byron. The several times she had seen him before, he had appeared content to keep his distance and simply gaze at her—with a penetrating stare he seemed to be practicing.

They rested, as Bianca Salvado wished. The young men spread blankets upon the ground and helped the girls display themselves to their best advantage. Glasses of lemonade were passed about by Signora Palli's stolid, silent manservant.

"I do wish," Cametta whispered to Giana, "that Vittorio and I could be alone. Do not tell Mama, but I have met him on several occasions at the Piazza del Popolo. But of course my maid was with me." She sighed soulfully, her soft brown eyes resting adoringly upon the slender Vittorio.

Giana looked at her oddly.

"Ah, do not say that you disapprove! You know what parents are! They forget that they were once young and in love."

"Yes, I suppose they do."

"We will be marrying in but two months! They are so stuffy!"

Giana gazed over at Signora Palli, who was complacently drinking her lemonade, one benign eye on her daughter.

"Do you love Vittorio?" Giana asked suddenly.

Cametta cocked her dark head, bouncing her tight curls over her ears. "Of course! Who would not? He is so handsome, so gallant." She shuddered delicately.

"But do you *know* him?"

"Giana, how foolish you are! I know him enough to let him . . . kiss me." She rolled her eyes. "His mouth is so firm, and yet so gentle. I much enjoy it. Of course, he apologizes for being so forward."

Bianca Salvado said, "What secrets are you two tattling?" She did not wait for a reply. "Vittorio," she trilled, touching her fingers to the young man's immaculate blue sleeve to gain his attention, "I believe Cametta is telling Giana all about you!"

"I trust you are being kind, little pigeon," Vittorio said, a charming smile indenting the creases beside his mouth.

"Pigeons are such nasty birds, Vittorio! I vow I would prefer another fowl."

But his smile didn't quite reach his eyes, Giana saw. My God, she thought, staring at him, he is bored! How strange, she thought, studying him from beneath her lashes; the way he gestured with his hands when he spoke, his palms up and his fingers spread, somehow reminded her of Randall. Don't be a fool, Giana! she chided herself, angry at her thought. Randall was not a vain fop, and he was never bored in her company.

Bruno Barbinelli, a dark, brooding young man, an image he was at pains to project, rose and proffered Giana an elaborate bow. "Would you care to stroll through the gardens, signorina? We will not, of course, be out of Signora Palli's watchful sight."

Giana paused for only a moment. She wanted to walk about the beautiful gardens, no matter who her escort. She looked a question toward Signora Palli, and at the lady's gentle nod, she allowed Bruno to help her rise, and tucked her hand through his arm.

"Do not go far, you two!" Cametta called out, and dissolved into an affected giggle.

"You mustn't tease him, Giana! His eyebrows are already drawn together!" Bianca looked toward Bruno's twin sisters and tittered loudly until they joined her.

"It is a beautiful day," Bruno said.

"Yes."

"Are you enjoying your stay in Rome?"

"It . . . has been most unusual."

Giana stopped in front of a fountain, pulled off her glove, and glided her fingers through the cool water.

"You speak Italian quite well."

"I am learning."

"Your eyes are beautiful."

Giana started at the bland compliment. *"Grazie,"* she said, and walked on. Was he going to start reciting poetry?

"My sisters tell me that you are engaged. Such a pity."

Giana chanced to be looking at his eyes at that moment, and she saw an assessing gleam in their brooding depths. "Why is it a pity?"

"Because this Englishman met you first."

"Yes, I suppose that he did."

"I could make you forget him, you know."

Giana felt a sudden urge to laugh. He spoke with such passion, his dark eyes filled with limpid sincerity. It was so very trite, and he was so very young. She suppressed the laugh, feeling suddenly very ancient.

"I don't think so, signore."

"You are so small, so delicate, Giana," he continued, his voice becoming deep and more impassioned. "This Englishman cannot deserve one of your poise, your sensibility."

One of your wealth!

"Undoubtedly you are quite right, Bruno," she said with a brilliant smile. She bit back a grin as he blinked rapidly at her.

"What else have your sisters told you about my . . . fiancé?"

Bruno shrugged, palpably relieved at her neutral question. "That he will join your family's business."

"Actually, it is my mother. She is my only family."

There was a look of incredulity on his smooth-cheeked face. "I . . . I did not know that your mother was a . . . businessman."

"I assure you she is not. She is a businesswoman."

There was an appraising look in his eyes again, and a question, but she did not enlighten him. She knew all about Bruno Barbinelli, and his twin sisters, and his father, who was searching for an heiress to marry his only son.

She felt his fingers tighten about her arm. "I have wanted for the past two weeks, ever since I met you, to be alone with you. You are so exquisite, Giana, a small, innocent little bird who wants to be loved . . . and tamed."

"How about a dove, Bruno? I have always had a liking for doves. They are small and innocent, would you not agree?"

"You do not take me seriously," Bruno said in an aggrieved voice.

"You are very young."

Startled, he exclaimed, "Young! I am twenty-three years old!"

"Odd, you seem younger . . . much younger."

He flushed angrily, but his voice rang with passionate sincerity. "You are toying with me, signorina, but I like a girl with spirit. You take my gentleness and my desire to please you as a sign of an immature man."

He clasped her shoulders and jerked her toward him. It was too much and Giana could not help herself. She burst into merry laughter. He released her so suddenly that she stumbled backward.

"You need to be tamed," he snarled, his dark face now truly flushed with anger, his studied passion forgotten.

"Why?"

"Why what?" he growled, staring at her with open dislike.

"Why would you say that I need to be tamed, when I simply find you funny?"

"Funny!"

"Well, amusing then."

"You are supposed to be a proper young lady, not an outspoken, insulting . . ."

"Bitch?" she supplied kindly.

"*Dio*, I would not marry you, even if you are . . ." He broke off, and clamped his teeth over his lower lip.

"Even if I am wealthy. Now that you have spoken your mind, Bruno, perhaps we can stop this elaborate charade. I think you are probably quite nice. You prefer poetry to girls anyway, do you not?"

He said stiffly, drawing himself to his full height, "The day is very warm. I wish to have another glass of lemonade."

"I think that is a fine idea, Bruno." *And the most palatable thing you've said.*

As they walked back to their party, Bruno maintaining an angry silence, Giana wondered at herself. She did not understand why she had been so very impolite to Bruno, despite his motives. She had, she saw, wounded his vanity deeply. She realized suddenly, a flush splaying over her cheeks, that she would have felt flattered and would undoubtedly have preened at his ardent attentions but a month ago.

It was a galling insight, and she felt ashamed that it was true. But he had been so obvious with her, had made her want to laugh. She touched her fingertips to her cheeks. She must remember that she was in Rome, and people were different here, despite what Uncle Daniele said. They were different, not she!

But the sight of the River Anio and the Temple of Vesta that afternoon brought only a trite compliment to her lips. She could not seem to pay much attention to either the scenery or her companions. Signora Palli asked her once if she was feeling ill, and Vittorio gazed at her oddly from his elegantly arched brows. Bruno maintained a brooding silence and the girls were left to flirt with the other young gentlemen, whose names refused to come to Giana's mind.

She shared a quiet dinner that evening with Daniele. Over a game of chess he said, "This is the first time in Rome you have been with people your own age for an entire day. You have not remarked upon it."

Giana moved her queen's bishop to a diagonal bearing down upon his white king. She shrugged, not raising her head. "It was not particularly remarkable, although I did enjoy visiting Tivoli. There are five hundred fountains in the gardens at the Villa d'Este. I read it in a guidebook. Is that not interesting?"

"What did you think of Vittorio Cavelli?"

She had expected him to question her about Bruno, for she had the inescapable feeling that he knew of the young man's interest in her. She raised her head and regarded him with some surprise.

"He is all right, I suppose. Attentive to Cametta, says all the right things, but I do not particularly like him. He is not sincere, perhaps."

"As you know, Vittorio is the heir of an aristocratic family," Daniele said smoothly, moving his knight to attack her bishop. "It is as true in Italy as in England that the aristocracy still wield much influence and control much wealth. But the rest of us, Giana—and you are one of us, despite your mother's titled antecedents—are becoming a force they must reckon with.

Year by year, we grow stronger, are more wealthy. Year by year, the aristocracy become more degenerate and more impoverished. Vittorio's marriage to Cametta Palli is quite understandable. She becomes a countess and Vittorio can continue his idle existence in comfort. Her dowry is quite monstrous."

Giana's fingers were poised over her bishop. "What are you saying, Uncle?"

"Noting of any importance, I suppose." He shrugged. "It is most unusual that Randall Bennett wishes to soil his aristocratic hands with business."

"I told you that he is different," she said. "Check, Uncle."

"How odd that you should have your father's skill," he remarked, staring down at the board. "With all your mother's remarkable intelligence, she could never grasp the intricacies of the game."

"And mate."

"Most delightfully unfeminine of you, my dear."

Chapter 6

It was a scorching, humid day, as only a day in August could be in Rome. Giana wished for nothing more than a tub of cold water she could sink into and sleep. Her layers of petticoats felt like a dead-weight, and her damp underclothes chafed against her skin. She gingerly wiped a drop of perspiration from her lip before it could fall on the swatch of white embroidered linen she held. Many wealthy Roman families had weeks before escaped the heat and journeyed with their households to the cool mountains to the north. They had all gone except for the Pallis, the Salvados, and the Condes, and even they had packed their children off. It had been with a sigh of relief that Giana had bid good-bye to Cametta Palli and Bianca Salvado. It was only Angela Cavour, who had been gone for three weeks now, that Giana missed. Soft-spoken, gentle Angela. Giana, of course, could not go with her. Brothels were always open, even in August.

Giana let out a sigh of boredom and jerked her needle again through the linen. She was aware that Mirabella del Conde had stirred herself to watch her again, and as luck would have it, the needle was well laced and the light brown silk thread pulled through easily.

"Nice even stitches," Mirabella said in her flat

voice. "I like the shades of brown. They will make lovely seat covers for the solarium chairs."

Giana merely nodded, so bored with the eternal embroidery and their endless conversations that she wanted to scream. *There has to be more to life than this!* Once the thought had finally spoken itself in her mind, the reply was not long in coming. *There is more to life . . . and your mother has found it.*

Giana shook away the thought. She was simply out of sorts with the ghastly heat. *And the ghastly boring company of these ladies.* Giana realized that Camilla Palli was speaking to her. "Yes, ma'am?"

"I was saying, my dear child, that Cametta much enjoyed the outing with you last month to the Villa d'Este. She wished that you could have accompanied her to the mountains."

"It was . . . most interesting, ma'am. On a day like today, I wish I were splashing in a fountain somewhere."

"One becomes accustomed to the warmer weather," Luciana Salvado said. She lowered her eyes to her embroidery and continued in a reproachful voice, "I only wish you had enjoyed all the young people on your outing."

"But I did," Giana said quickly.

"That is not what Bianca told me," Mirabella said. "She said that you left poor Bruno sadly cast down."

"I sincerely trust not, ma'am. He is very pleasant. It is just that I found his attentions rather . . . awkward. He is rather immature, I think."

Camilla Palli tittered, a sound very much like her daughter, Cametta, made, and just as grating. "You, dear child, are only seventeen! I daresay he would make a fine husband."

"You forget, ma'am," Giana said, jutting out her chin, "that my fiancé awaits me in England."

"Dear Bruno is related to me," Camilla explained. "His mother is my cousin."

Ah, Giana thought, and you are piqued because I can't be nabbed!

"Englishmen are so cold, I have heard," Mirabella said to no one in particular, threading her needle.

"The climate in England is cooler than it is here," Giana said blandly.

"That is not what Mirabella meant," Luciana said sharply.

When Mirabella's eyes went to the clock, Giana's gaze followed hers, and with a relieved smile she rose. "It is time for me to meet my uncle," she said.

"But you have not yet finished the chair cover," Mirabella said.

"I fear it will have to wait, ma'am. Uncle Daniele will not." Even the thought of spending the evening at Madame Lucienne's brothel seemed preferable to this.

"Your gown looks quite limp, Giana," Luciana said. "You should lace your corset more tightly. It prevents wrinkles."

"I fear I would faint if I did, ma'am. It is so warm."

"Still," Camilla pursued in Luciana's wake, "a lady should always appear immaculate. I am certain your dear mother would give you the same advice."

"Perhaps," Giana said, inching toward the door of the salon.

"Let me ring for a servant," Mirabella said finally, seeing that Giana was set upon leaving. "Where has the time gone?" she said brightly. "It is already four o'clock! My dear husband does not work so late now in August. I expect him home soon, yes, quite soon now."

* * *

Daniele settled back against the leather squabs of the carriage, enjoying the stirring of a slight evening breeze against his skin. Giana sat silently beside him in the open carriage, staring toward the Tiber, sluggish and muddy in late summer.

"You were always such a chatterer, Giana. Has the Roman heat tired your tongue?"

"I suppose so, Uncle Daniele."

But Daniele knew it was not the heat. Giana had fallen into brooding, thoughtful silences more and more as the weeks passed. He decided to test the waters.

"You will be returning to England in two weeks."

"Yes," she said. "I hope it will be cooler in London."

Not an auspicious beginning, he thought, tugging on his mustache. "Your mother writes that she misses you."

"Yes, I saw her letter." She paused a long moment, then looked squarely at Daniele and said, "I look forward to seeing those I love again."

Damnation! What could he do to convince the stupid girl? He grinned to himself, but only briefly, remembering his encouragement of Signore Barbinelli and his favored son, Bruno. Giana, by all accounts he had heard, had seen through his flowery blandishments and sent him about his business. He wondered if Bruno was less skilled than Randall Bennett. Evidently so. That, or Giana, at an eight-hundred-mile distance, had preserved Randall's image, perfecting it with a kind of nauseating piety.

He grew suddenly angry, both with the endless situations he had created for Giana and with her for clinging like a drowning person to a man who had no more substance than a dream. And she had grown seemingly indifferent lately to the scenes she witnessed in the Golden Chamber. He glanced at her set profile. There was steel in her, and a core of stubbornness. He would have to write to Aurora and tell her there was more of her father in Giana than she suspected. But for now, Morton Van Cleve's heritage was his problem.

"Go to Madame Lucienne's room, Giana," he said when they arrived at the brothel, "but do not bother to change your clothes or put on your blond wig. Stay there until I come to fetch you."

"Why?" she asked him shortly.

"You will see soon enough," he told her.

She quirked a black brow at him and smiled mirthlessly. "So the gentlemen are to be deprived of my charming conversation this evening?"

"I believe they will survive their disappointment."

She asked him again what he had planned for her amusement this evening, when he returned to fetch her. He glanced at her sharply, for her voice sounded bored, as if she were inquiring about the weather.

"It is rather . . . difficult to describe, my dear," he said finally as he took her by the arm and led her down the long corridor toward the small door that gave onto the Golden Chamber. She stopped at it, but he waved her forward, and pulled open the door that led to the fourth floor.

"Are those not the servants' quarters?"

"Some of them are. Come."

She followed him silently up the narrow stairs until they were at the top of the house, with tilting eaves overhead. He ushered her into a small room that was very different from the other one. There was only a small table and two chairs set in the middle of the room, and the walls were papered in stark dark blue.

"Sit down, Giana. We will have supper here. The . . . entertainment will begin a bit later."

It was very warm in the small room, and Giana tugged at her high-necked collar. She felt drained and tired. Despite Daniele's air of secrecy, Giana supposed that her entertainment was to be another evening of watching a man, ridiculous-looking in his naked, sweating lust, heaving and grunting over a girl. She no longer found them disgusting; indeed, they no longer intruded in her conscious thoughts. She had set herself apart from them, had retreated for many weeks now from the nightly spectacles. They no longer touched her.

A light dinner of fresh shrimp, fruit, and cool white wine was brought in by a servant soon after they were settled. Giana ate sparingly, for every bite she swallowed made her corset press that much tighter against her sweat-damp shift. They ate in silence, and Giana sensed that Daniele was not particularly pleased with her tonight. She thrust her chin forward aggressively. Let him sulk in his failure, she thought. I have kept my end of the bargain. It was odd though that Randall's face was no longer clear in her mind. What was clear, and what was precious to her, was his remembered gentleness and his trust in her. She had known weeks ago she would not let him down; he was her lifeline. Her eyes clouded as she wondered if her face was as blurred to him as his was to her. She became aware that Daniele was speaking to her, and lifted her eyes from her plate. She smiled, hearing his words, for he was speaking about business, a carefully neutral topic that would raise no arguments between them.

"Forgive me, Uncle, what did you say?"

"I was telling you about the business venture I am considering with your mother. It involves some speculation, admittedly, but with the unrest plaguing Europe, I fancy there is little risk in banking on still more immigration to America. And the poor souls will need ships to travel on, ships that will not dump them below with cargo, to risk dying before they arrive in New York."

"You are providing the capital, Uncle?"

"Yes, and your mother will have the ships constructed in the Van Cleve shipyards."

"They cannot be simple cargo ships, then. Nor can they be constructed like the passenger liners, because the souls immigrating to America will not have the money to pay." She tilted her head, and her voice became grim. "After all, if the Irish must leave Ireland because of the terrible potato famine, it cannot be expected that they will have two sous to rub together for a voyage to America."

"True. Design is the crux of the problem. Aurora has several of her designers working on a solution: how to make ships equally suitable for cargo and for families without compromising either the safety of the cargo or the lives of the passengers."

"I trust you will not pour your capital into the project until there is a solution."

"I have no intention of living out my old age as a pauper," he said, grinning at her.

A light rap sounded on the door, but Daniele did not move to open it. He walked instead to the golden cord beside the thick blue velvet drapery and pulled it open.

The room was more stark than the Golden Chamber, Giana saw, without the lush furnishings. But the sweating naked man on the bed with the buxom Lucia astride him, her position unusual in that her back was to him, was but more of the same. Giana could hear the man groaning as Lucia raised and lowered her body, splaying her hands sensuously over his legs. Giana could not prevent a shudder at the animallike sounds he was making.

Suddenly the door to the chamber burst open, and another man flung inside, fully dressed.

"Now for our own special commedia dell'arte," Daniele said softly. "All well rehearsed, with everyone knowing his part."

Giana stared at Vittorio Cavelli. He was dressed in a full-sleeved white shirt, tight trousers, and black riding boots. He was slapping a riding crop against his thigh, his smooth young face mottled with fury.

"What is this!" he yelled. "You miserable unfaithful bitch, you offer yourself to my best friend the moment I leave you alone!"

Lucia drew herself off the naked man and cowered away from Vittorio, covering her bountiful breasts with shaking hands. "No," she cried, "it was he who seduced me! I swear it! He forced me to submit!"

"Liar! Deceitful whore! You were riding him like a wild mare! Well, did you seduce my wife, force her?" he angrily demanded of the naked man, who now sat on the edge of the bed.

The man, as young as Vittorio, olive-skinned and slender, broke into loud, scornful laughter. "She tore my clothes off," he said, pointing toward the trembling Lucia. "She is a whore, and unworthy of you, Vittorio. She will spread her legs for any man who wants her."

Giana darted a confused glance toward Daniele, but his face was impassive. Her fingers clutched the arms of her chair so tightly the knuckles showed white.

"No, no!" Lucia cried. "It is not true, my dear husband! Never would I betray you willingly! The fiend forced me!"

"Shut up, harlot! I will teach you that I am your master!"

Vittorio raised the riding crop and brought it down over Lucia's white shoulders. Lucia shrieked and fell to her knees in front of Vittorio, clawing at his riding boots.

"No, my husband, no more, I beg of you!"

"The unfaithful whore must be taught a lesson," Vittorio snarled to the other man. "Bind her."

Giana lurched forward in her chair, a cry on her lips. She felt Daniele's hand grasping her arm, pulling her back. "Hush," he hissed. "Do not intrude on their charming charade."

She watched numbly as the man pulled Lucia to her feet and bound her wrists together with a silk scarf that Vittorio tossed to him. He pulled her long hair from her back and held her against him, stretching her upward until she stood on her tiptoes.

"No, my husband," Lucia wailed, "do not do this!"

Vittorio walked slowly toward Lucia. "Whore," he spat, and brought the riding crop down across her white buttocks.

"Stop it, Uncle! By God, you must stop this!"

"Shut up, Giana. Lucia would not thank you, you know. She earns a good deal of money playing these games."

"It is Vittorio Cavelli."

"Yes, I know. A most . . . winsome young gentleman."

The other man held the straining Lucia tight against him. "Again, Vittorio, again! I want to hear her scream!"

The riding crop descended again and again, and Lucia yelled, tossing her mane of black hair, writhing frantically to escape the whip.

"Give me her belly!" Vittorio cried suddenly. He

ripped open his trousers as the other man whirled Lucia about to face him, and drove his thigh between her legs to spread them. Vittorio lashed her once again with the riding crop, and slammed into her. His yells of sexual pleasure mixed with Lucia's screams. He fell away from her onto the bed, and watched as the other man quickly untied Lucia's wrists and flung her to the floor.

"Take the bitch! Cram the unfaithful little whore!" Vittorio cried.

Giana said not a word as the man drove into Lucia's belly. White-faced, she rose and walked from the room.

Daniele loosened his collar and set his empty brandy snifter upon the sideboard. He thought he heard a noise, and turned to walk from the library onto the balcony. He drew up at the sight of Giana, dressed only in her white cambric nightgown, leaning over the railing, staring at the magnificent sprawling city. She had tied her heavy black hair in a ribbon off her neck, and lazy curls framed her face.

"You could not sleep my dear?"

"No, it was too hot," she said, not turning to face him.

"There is some breeze here."

"Uncle Daniele?"

"*Si?*"

"Will Vittorio do . . . that to Cametta when they are married?"

"It is unlikely. Her family would be most displeased were he to tie her up, beat her, and share her with another man. If she had no family, it would be another matter entirely."

"He is unnatural."

"He is wild and young and quite degenerate. At

least Cametta will be a countess. With the money she will bring him, he will be able to indulge all his elaborate charades. Given his tastes, I venture to guess that Cametta will not have to suffer much of him in her bed."

"Cametta loves him."

"She is infatuated with him, and has less sense than a child. She will be perfectly happy, I assure you. Vittorio will give her a child, and then she can lead the kind of life for which she has been raised."

He saw Giana shudder.

"Are you cold, my dear?"

She shook her head. "No, I am ... sad."

"Don't be," he said sharply. "It is life."

"But she will be his wife!"

Daniele sighed. "Giana do you still not understand? Being a man's wife is all the girl can aspire to, but it is not much. A wife holds a place somewhat higher than a man's servant and somewhat lower than his dog. She is his chattel, by law. If he wants to beat her, he can, unless, as in Cametta's case, her family holds the purse strings. Then, I venture to say, it would not be excessively wise. But even if the man's pleasures are somewhat perverted, like Vittorio's, any court in Italy, or England for that matter, would uphold his right to do whatever he wished. A wife must submit. It is her duty." Daniele was silent for a moment. "I recall a story about the famous French author Victor Hugo. You may know he is reputed to be quite a lady's man. He married some eighteen years ago. It is said that his wife protested his excessive sexual appetites, claiming that he had forced her nine times on their wedding night. The judge, as of course any man would, reproved her sharply and returned her to her husband."

Giana felt her throat close over angry words. Her

gaze remained fastened toward the darkened city. *Why can I not see Randall's face? Why can I not imagine what he would say at such a story?*

"Did you know that a woman in England cannot even sign a contract? Your mother, to transact her business, must have Thomas Hardesty, her partner, affix his noble signature for it to be legal. I find it odd that your Queen Victoria not only encourages such things but also has actually backed laws to further subjugate women."

Daniele laid his hand on Giana's arm and was surprised to find her rigid beneath his fingers.

"What are you thinking, my dear?"

Giana drew a deep breath. "I was thinking," she said quietly, knowing that she wasn't speaking precisely the truth, "that with all the injustice in the world, it is fortunate for me that I will have Randall to protect me."

Daniele's intake of breath sounded like a hiss. "Bennett protect you? Has it never occurred to you, Giana, that you should want to protect yourself?"

She waved away his words, and her voice was softly sad. "I don't know if I could bear leaving Randall, Uncle."

"Randall, my child, or what you still imagine him to be?"

"Good night, Uncle," Giana said stiffly, shaking off his hand. "It is cooler now. I believe I will be able to sleep."

Chapter 7

"The Flower Auction," Daniele explained to Giana, "is a touted Roman tradition."

"What an unusual name. What is it, Uncle?"

"When a girl is a virgin, as you are, my dear, she is considered a prize until the first man takes her maidenhead, or deflowers her. Hence the name Flower Auction. Attendance is carefully controlled, with only very wealthy, selected gentlemen admitted. I have seen the list of gentlemen who will be present. Several of them unfortunately have seen you at Madame Lucienne's, and so, my dear, to safeguard your shady reputation, you will wear an auburn wig."

"You want me to be one of the girls at the auction?"

"Yes. I have already spoken to Signora Lamponni, the directress, so to speak, of the event. I have paid her a fee, and she will allow you to take part. Only the most beautiful girls have been selected, all trained harlots, but their virginity has been carefully guarded in anticipation of this night. The sums of money sometimes paid for their maidenheads is truly astounding."

"You go too far with this, Uncle!" She shook her head vigorously, her lips tightly compressed.

"You will not have to worry, Giana, for I shall be

the man who buys you, and I promise I shall close the bidding before you are naked on the dais."

"Naked!"

Her eyes were huge with outrage, but he ignored her, and continued smoothly, "Yes. You see, the gentlemen bid for them. They remove their clothing, slowly and enticingly, to let the gentlemen's lust raise the sum bid for them all the higher. They disrobe until the bidding has stopped and a man has bought their services for the night. But it frequently happens that the gentlemen draw out the bidding just to see the girls standing naked before them. Then if the man who has purchased a girl wishes, he can examine her himself, in front of all the other gentlemen, to assure himself that she is indeed a virgin."

"It is despicable! I will not be part of such a disgusting, perverted display!"

"Oh yes you will, Giana. Yes you will. You are so close to fulfilling both your agreements; to your mother and to me. To refuse to cooperate with me now would mean that all you have done would go for naught."

"Mother would be frantic if she knew what you were making me do!"

Daniele shrugged. "That, Giana, is beside the point. Your mother placed you in my care; and you, my dear, agreed to undertake whatever I wish. Do not flout me now, Giana. Think of the prize you will have in such a short time."

He hooked his thumb under her chin, forcing her to look up at him. Her beautiful eyes were still filled with shock, her expression mutinous.

"Please, Uncle," Giana whispered, "do not make me do this. I beg of you."

He hesitated but an instant, then said firmly, "Don't worry, my dear, I will buy you before you have to remove your gown." He saw that she would protest further. "Listen to me, Giana. All you have done this summer is observe passively. You have no idea of what it feels like to be the object of a man's desire. No, you will neither plead nor argue with me further. At least at the Flower Auction you will feel what it is like to be put up for sale, like a horse."

Giana drew back from him, her body taut. But two more weeks, she thought, but two more weeks. But she felt afraid, more afraid than she had felt that first night at Madame Lucienne's when Signore Salvado had casually caressed her breasts. She raised her face and looked at him. "Not a horse, Uncle," she said coldly. "A mare."

"Good. You have regained your perspective, I see."

A welcome thunderstorm blew through the heat-baked city, and took the heat with it. Giana found she even needed a shawl over her demure white silk gown. There was not a bit of makeup on her face to spoil the innocence of the tender young flower in her virginal white gown, waiting to be plucked. Only the curling auburn wig with its fluffy tendrils falling over her forehead served to disguise her.

The villa Daniele directed his driver to was off the Via Merulana. It was a tall red-brick building set behind a thick wall of trees and a high black iron fence. A servant in black livery opened the grating gate upon seeing Daniele's elegant invitation. Giana started forward at the sound of dogs snarling near the carriage.

"No need to worry, they are chained, Giana. Signora Lamponni likes her privacy. I will shortly leave you in her hand. You will join the other girls before you make your entrance into the grand salon to mix with the gentlemen. The auction begins promptly at eight o'clock." Daniele leaned over in the carriage, took Giana's chin in his hand, and said gently, "I urge you to look about you, Giana, and to listen. It is true that all the girls, save you, are quite willing to be auctioned off tonight, for they will earn a great deal of money in the process. But the fact remains that it is men and their desires who have made the Flower Auction a fact. It is they who have placed such value on a girl's virginity, and they who will pay to take that innocence. It is, I suppose, a reaffirmation of their power, of their manhood."

"You are a man, Uncle."

"Yes, but an old one. I find I become quite the philosopher as my own desires fade. I don't want you to become a victim, Giana, it's really as simple as that. That is your mother's wish also, I might add."

"But is there still no caring? Do not some men love their wives faithfully? Surely they cannot all be animals. What of Angela's husband, Signore Cavour?"

"Yes, he is faithful to his young wife, so far as I know. She is lovely, quite submissive, and worships him. He is a god to her, a role he undoubtedly relishes. But even with his love, she is smothered in stupid tradition that dooms her to a life that is appallingly restricted, while he . . ." Daniele shrugged. It was odd, he thought, that he should be condemning a quite workable system, one that he himself never questioned, had in fact found most comfortable, until he had met Aurora.

"Signore Cavour is fat," Giana said, "and Angela starves herself to please him."

Daniele laughed. "She is wise for one so young. Perhaps she will keep him faithful. Who knows?"

Giana shrugged, but her lips were drawn into a thin line. He leaned over and patted her gloved hand.

"Do not despair, Giana. Someday you will find a man who will be your equal, and be all things to you, as you will be to him." Daniele waited for Giana to throw Randall Bennett in his face as the paragon of all virtues, but she remained silent.

She was shown by a stone-faced woman servant into a small antechamber where five young girls were chatting gaily. They looked up, watching her as she entered, and she felt for an instant as if she were back at Madame Orlie's seminary, joining the other girls for afternoon tea, until she saw their eyes. They were assessing her value, just as might a competitor. They were all quite young, pretty, and dressed in soft pastel colors. With their full skirts pressed together, they looked like a vivid rainbow.

"Ah, you are finally here, signorina. Come, I wish to speak to all of you before you join the gentlemen."

Signora Lamponni was an immense woman, tall and large-boned, with striking sable-colored hair and wide brown eyes. She was dressed in severe black silk, like a respectable middle-aged matron, and not a procurer of young virgins. The five young faces were staring at her, drinking in her words. Giana shook her head, realizing that she was not listening.

"You will drink with the gentlemen, if they wish it, and converse pleasantly with them. Do not let any of them monopolize you. The more gentlemen who see what delights you have to offer, the more money they will bid, and more money will be yours. They are not to fondle you, for it is against the rules. As all of you know, there are only very wealthy gentlemen present. If you are truly skilled, it is possible that the man who buys you will wish to keep you for his mistress."

There was a low buzz of excited speculation among the girls. Dear God, Giana thought, they want this. All of them. But they were so very young, as if they had just emerged from a classroom.

"Remember," Signora Lamponni continued, "when it is your turn on the dais, you may remove your clothing seductively, or play the innocent. You are all virgins, despite your varied skills, and it is that fact that makes you so valuable. When you are alone with your gentleman, you will, of course, behave in whatever manner he wishes. You are all trained well enough to know what to do."

"What a pity that one cannot grow a maidenhead every day," one of the girls said.

"We would all be rich in a month!" another added, laughing.

Signora Lamponni clapped her hands. "Enough chatter! It is time for your debut, ladies."

Giana trailed slowly after the girls into a large salon, brightly lit with candle chandeliers. It was a magnificent room, with high vaulted ceilings adorned with classical scenes, and beautiful marble fireplaces set at each end. Rich crimson velvet curtains covered the long windows, and lush carpets were scattered over the inlaid parquet floors. Everything smelled of beeswax and lemon. The furniture was light and delicate, in the French style. At the far end of the salon was a square dais. About thirty men, all dressed in elegant black evening wear, were seated about the room in small groups, some smoking and drinking, all conversing with their friends, as if they were spending a relaxing evening at home. When the girls filed in, a hush fell over the room.

Giana head a sudden laugh, and a burst of renewed conversation. The girls appeared to study the gentlemen, as if deciding who pleased them most. Giana watched them preen proudly and swish their wide skirts as they walked toward the men, engaging smiles on their lips.

Giana's hands were clammy and cold, and she rubbed them on the skirt of her gown. She could not imagine displaying herself to these strange men, inviting them to assess her charms, inviting them to buy her! She saw Daniele, but when she started toward him, he frowned and shook his head. Giana knew she could not continue standing like a rigid puppet, doing nothing. She felt fear bubble up within her. She was being a fool, she told herself, thrusting the fear away. These men could do nothing to her; she had but to speak to them as she did at Madame Lucienne's. It would all be over soon.

Alexander Saxton motioned to a servant and took a glass of sherry. He sipped the smooth wine and watched with indolent amusement as the bevy of girls giggled and pranced among the men, their faces alight with anticipation. Anticipation of earning a good deal of money, he thought with sudden annoyance, stubbing out his cigar. Why in the name of heaven he had agreed to come to this ridiculous display of Roman decadence was beyond him.

"Now, there's a little sprite," Santelo Travola remarked to him, pointing toward a raven-haired girl whose full breasts pressed impudently against the high-necked white gown she wore. "The bidding on that little beauty will be strung out, you may be certain. None of the gentlemen would want to deprive the others of seeing her lovely body."

"She already looks like a whore," Alex said.

"You are too severe, my friend. Ah, one of the girls is coming this way. I beg you to be civilized. Alex."

Giana stopped suddenly and sucked in her breath in consternation. She recognized him as the man she had seen at Madame Lucienne's with Margot, the one who had made her feel as though it were she beneath him. Her face flushed scarlet at the memory. He looked up and caught her eyes with a frankly uninterested gaze. Then he smiled, a lazy, mocking smile, and cocked his forefinger toward her.

Giana looked about wildly, but Daniele was speaking to another gentleman and paying her no heed. She looked back at him, and saw his black brow arch, frankly assessing, as he watched her hesitate.

A gentleman spoke to her, but she paid him no heed. She knew she had to do something, talk to one of them. She squared her shoulders, drew to an uncertain halt in front of him and gazed into his dark eyes. There was something about him, a barely leashed savagery that warred with the elegance of his dress. He was too large, too overpowering.

"What is your name?" he asked, negligently sipping his sherry.

"My name is . . . Helen."

"I suppose it is as good as any."

He changed suddenly from Italian to English. "Do you wish a glass of sherry?"

Giana shook her head.

"You are not trying terribly hard to please me . . . Helen."

She said sharply in English, without thinking, "I do not care if I please you, sir."

"Ah, the wench has claws. Beware, Alex. This one does not seem impressed with your charms."

"Or my money, it would appear, Santelo," Alex said, his eyes sweeping over Giana. "You are English," he said, his eyes studying her face.

Giana reeled back, realizing too late that she was being stupid. She answered swiftly in French, her voice curt, *"Non, monsieur, je suis française. Il faut . . . excusez-moi, s'il vous plaît."*

"No, I will not excuse you," he said in English. "I wish to speak with you, Helen. Sit down, here, beside me."

She looked at his outstretched hand, bent her trembling legs, and sat down.

"Now, what is an English girl, an English virgin, doing selling her wares in Rome?"

"What are you, an American, doing in Rome?" she shot back in her clipped English, realizing it was useless to pretend.

"Unlike you, my dear, I am buying, not selling," he said in a mocking drawl. "You recognize my accent, I see."

Giana saw his dark eyes were glittering with interest; he was beginning to enjoy himself. She realized she had no experience with a man like this—he made her feel uncertain, even frightened. She fanned her hands in front of her and prepared to rise. After all, he couldn't touch her, it was against the rules. "If you will excuse me, sir."

"We have already been through that, Helen. You will stay. I wish it. What color is your real hair?"

Her eyes flew to his face, and in an unconscious gesture she touched her fingers to the soft auburn curls over her ear.

"So it is a wig. I thought as much. Somehow the blue eyes don't quite fit with the auburn hair, and there is not one freckle to mar your beautiful white skin." He leaned toward her, as if he were going to touch her hair, and she jerked back, terrified. He frowned at her suddenly pale face, his black brows rising upward over his impaling eyes.

"I applaud your approach," he said slowly. "It is quite refreshing, like a trapped, innocent little doe, or perhaps Santelo is right, you're a little kitten, with claws."

"I am certainly not an animal," she said, "and I have no approach," she added, running her tongue over her dry lips. She was quite unaware it was a very sensual gesture.

He laughed. "Do you not, my dear? It was you who pretended interest in me, if you will recall. When I saw you wished to make me the object of your, ah, desire, I decided to be polite."

"I do not like you," Giana said in a grating tone, unable to keep her tongue still in her mouth. She spoke in a low voice that only Alex heard.

"You become more fascinating with each insult." He paused a moment, and studied her flushed face. "How old are you, Helen?"

"I am seventeen, and you, I daresay, are quite old."

"Twenty-eight. Ancient, I suppose, to one of your tender years. But look about you, Helen. I am one of the youngest men here. Would you not prefer losing your prized, quite expensive maidenhead to me rather than one of these other paunchy gentlemen?"

He can't touch me, she thought wildly, and I am safe, for Daniele will buy me! *But what would I feel if he touched me?* She felt color rise to her cheeks and dropped her eyes. He believed her a whore, and though he seemed to be drawn to her, she sensed he disliked her, and it angered as well as shamed her. She struck out at him. "You, sir, are vulgar, but I suppose it is to be expected, you being an American. Yes, I am English, but of course you know that already."

"And you, Helen, play the part of the outraged well-bred young English lady to perfection. I applaud your acting talents."

"Careful, Alex, the girl likely has spikes on her maidenhead!"

Giana glared at the Italian who was siting forward in his chair beside them.

"She appears not to like you either, Santelo," Alex said. He sat back in his chair and crossed his long legs. He tapped his fingertips together and regarded her with great interest. He decided she intrigued him.

"To show I'm a good sport, I'll offer one *lira* for her," Santelo said, grinning widely to show a space between his two front teeth.

Giana could not seem to tear her eyes away from his tapping fingertips, the same blunt-ended fingers that had caressed Margot's white body. He leaned toward her, and she jerked back, nearly unbalancing herself. She saw one of the girls, a chestnut-haired, green-eyed beauty, touch Santelo's arm, drawing his attention.

"Now we can have a little privacy," Alex said. He sat back again, and watched her with ease. "Somehow you don't look like a Helen. What is your real name? Molly? Daisy?"

"That is right," she said in a cold, clear voice. "My name is Molly. Most astute of you."

His white teeth flashed through his grin. "You have an agile tongue. Let us hope that your tongue and your lovely mouth are as skilled in other areas as in speech."

Giana drew back as if he had struck her, her face paling.

"Ah, our lack of innocence is finally revealed. Tell me, Helen or Molly, do you enjoy pleasuring men in that way?"

She shook her head, mute.

"What do you enjoy?"

"I enjoy embroidering altar cloths."

Alex stared at her, his head cocked to one side. This one was a minx, smart-tongued and saucy. He itched suddenly to touch her, to find out what it would be like to bend her to his will, to make her cry out for him. He heard the girl beside Santelo giggle loudly at one of his friend's inane jests and was pleased that this girl, Helen or Molly or whatever her name was, had sought him out. She was a challenge and he enjoyed challenges. He was beginning to regret that he had to leave for Paris in the morning.

"Tell me, my dear, once you have lost your most prized possession, what will you do?"

For a moment Giana did not know what he was talking about. Alex watched her eyes widen, ever so innocently, he thought, congratulating her silently. To his surprise, she stiffened, and he saw understanding in her eyes, and something else, something like pain.

"That is none of your business," Giana snapped, drawing herself up. She thought she heard him chuckle, and wished she could strike that smug, confident smile from his face.

"Perhaps you would like to come to Paris with me? I am most generous, if you please me, and would buy you pretty gowns and the like."

Please you! "I would be delighted to see you off to hell. You would likely feel quite at home there, in the company of other lechers."

He drew back, momentarily annoyed at her blatant rudeness. The hunter in him rose to the fore, and he laughed, and taunted her. "I do not think that whores ascend to the heavens, Helen. After all, if it were not for whores, there would be no need for lechers."

"On the contrary, if there were no lechers, there would be no need for whores. It is men who make the rules, not women."

He reached out suddenly and grasped her wrist in his fingers. She gasped in fear and tried to pull away from him. "You can't touch me," she hissed as his fingers tightened. "Let me go!"

"You are right, of course," he said, releasing her. "The merchandise is not to be handled, save by the buyer."

Giana scrambled to her feet. "I am not an animal and I am not merchandise! I ... I do not wish to speak with you anymore!" Before he could stop her, she turned and fled, her wide skirts swishing between the chairs.

Santelo whistled. "What did you say to the girl, Alex? Never have I seen such an ill-mannered chit at the Flower Auction."

Alex stared after her thoughtfully. She had managed to skirt the rest of the gentlemen and was standing with her back pressed tight against one of the marble fireplaces.

"She dished out insults faster than I could return them. She wants taming, and manners."

"Perhaps Signore Cippolo will buy her," Santelo said, pointing toward a heavy older gentleman whose attention had veered toward her.

Alex looked closely at the man's dissipated face and felt a knot of distaste in his belly. Cippolo would hurt her; Alex could see it in his eyes.

"Ah," Santelo said, "the auction begins."

Signora Lamponni stood on the dais, a tall hat in her hand, shaking it gently.

"The girls will draw numbers, to determine their order," Santelo explained softly to Alex.

Alex watched Helen reach into the hat with the other girls and pull out her number. He thought her hand was shaking. Alex shook his head. Dammit, the chit couldn't be frightened. All the girls were here because they wanted to be.

"And now, the little doves will leave us," Signora Lamponni announced in her deep voice, waving the girls out of the saloon, "until their numbers are called. I hope, gentlemen, that you approve this season's offerings."

There was a murmur of approval.

"We will now begin the bidding. Number one is Claudia, a delightful ... well, delight, from Milan."

Claudia pranced onto the dais and curtsied to the gentlemen.

"Isn't she lovely, gentlemen? What is my bid for this charming little virgin?"

Someone called out a hundred *lire.* There was some laughter, then another bid. Claudia slowly pulled off one of her long gloves. She grinned and tossed it to a gentleman who sat near the dais.

Giana watched Claudia from behind the curtain. She was the center of attention, and seemed to be enjoying herself immensely. She heard bids in *francs, lire,* and pounds.

She looked down at her number—four. What would Daniele do, she thought wildly, if she simply refused to take her turn on the dias? What could he do? She tried to picture Randall in her mind, as she had many times before when she was frightened, but somehow his image would not weave itself together, and she could feel nothing but uncertainty. She felt a tear trickle down her cheek.

Claudia was standing only in her petticoats and chemise. There were raucous cheers from the men, and the bidding slowed. The men knew the game, and none would end it until Claudia was naked.

Claudia's petticoats dropped to the floor, one after the other. Soon she was standing only in her chemise, a lacy affair that reached just to her knees. Her silk stockings were held up by frilly black garters.

There was another bid, in *lire,* and Giana quickly reckoned how much it was in English currency. Two hundred pounds!

Giana's face went perfectly white when Claudia at last stood naked. Her hands rested enticingly on her hips, her shoulders pressed forward to push her breasts closer together. She was running her tongue over her pouting lips.

"Two hundred and fifty pounds!" someone yelled, to more applause and laughter.

"Do you wish to assure yourself that the lovely Claudia is a virgin, signore?" Signora Lamponnia asked.

"Why not?" the man cried out amid the applause. He heaved himself onto the dais.

Now Giana understood why there was a sofa. Claudia walked to it, her hips swaying provocatively, and lay down on her back. The man waved his hand in the air and drew a curtain between him and the audience.

Giana turned away, clutching at her stomach. Nauseating bile rose in her throat.

"*Dio*," the man shouted, pushing the curtain aside, "she's ready for me and a virgin!"

The man paid Signora Lamponni while Claudia's clothing was gathered up by a servant. They left together through a small door behind the dais.

"Number two," Signora Lamponni called out. The girl next to Giana giggled and winked, and walked seductively onto the dais.

Giana turned away and sank into a chair. She lowered her head and stared down at the tips of her white leather slippers. It seemed but a few moments had passed when she noticed the two remaining girls were staring at her. "Who is number four? It is you," the girl said to Giana. "Quickly, the gentlemen are growing restless!"

"Number four," Signora Lamponni called out again, her voice more strident.

Giana felt someone take her arm and pull her up from the chair. She felt a hand in the small of her back, shoving her toward the dais. She walked forward in a daze, her eyes fastened to the floor in front of her.

"Ah, there is the little wildcat!"

"Watch out for this one, she's a hellion!"

"This is Helen," Signora Lamponni said. "She is French, a delightful addition to this season's offerings."

"So delightful that she'll scratch your eyes out!" Santelo shouted out, enjoying himself.

"I'll take her," Signore Cippolo called out. "One thousand *lire!*"

"Take her with what, a whip?"

Giana stood frozen as the man laughed, her eyes still on the floor. She heard Signora Lamponni hiss, "Take off your glove, you stupid girl!"

Giana raised her eyes and met Daniele's impassive gaze. Slowly she drew off her right glove.

Alex watched her, frowning. If he didn't know better, he would have thought she was frightened out of her wits. She looked like a puppet, all stiff and wooden, her movements awkward and graceless.

Lazily he called out, "Three hundred dollars."

"The American is used to taming savages!" someone shouted.

Signore Cippolo eyed the American from beneath his heavily hooded eyes. "Four hundred!"

Giana heard Signora Lamponni cursing under her breath. "The other glove, you witless child!"

Giana sent an agonized glance toward Daniele as the other glove fell to the floor in front of her.

"Five hundred!"

"The little wench is shy!"

"It is a good act!"

"Take off your gown!" Signora Lamponni growled. *Dio*, the little fool could ruin her reputation!

Giana's fingers moved numbly toward the fastenings on the bodice of her white gown, and stopped.

Daniele knew that she would not be pushed further. He had to take his chance, now. In a loud, commanding voice, he shouted, "One thousand dollars!"

An astounded silence followed Daniele's bid. Giana dropped her arms to her sides, relief flooding her.

Alex gazed over at the old man. A man old enough to be her grandfather would take her. He shifted his gaze back to the dais and saw her standing perfectly still, as if she were somehow apart from the proceedings.

Signora Lamponni was ready to close the bidding. He heard himself shout, "Two thousand dollars!"

Daniele reeled. Jesus Christ! What was the bloody American doing? He looked at Giana, and saw her weave where she stood.

In a quite calm voice he shouted back, "Four thousand dollars!"

Signora Lamponni quickly said, "It is done. Four thousand dollars."

Daniele rose quickly, but Alex was quicker. He walked toward the dais and said quietly, "It is the procedure, is it not, that the buyer pay you the full price, signora?"

Signora Lamponni nodded helplessly.

Alex peeled off two thousand dollars in bills from his wallet. "I request to see this gentleman's four thousand dollars," he said politely.

"Are you calling me a liar?" Daniele tried, schooling his features into his haughtiest look.

"No, sir. I merely wish to assure myself that you have the four thousand dollars."

Daniele carried no more than five hundred dollars. He made a last effort. "The signora knows that my credit is sound. I will return shortly with the money."

"But the price must be paid upon the close of the bidding, is that not the procedure, signora?"

Signora Lamponni shot Daniele a helpless look. "That is true, signore."

"Uncle," Giana whispered, taking a jerking step.

Daniele knew he could do no more here. He caught Giana's dazed eyes and gave her an encouraging smile.

He turned to the American and said stiffly, "The girl is yours, sir." He turned on his heel and strode from the salon.

"The American gets her!"

"For two thousand dollars, she'd better have two maidenheads!"

After Alex had given Signora Lamponni the two thousand dollars, she asked him, "Do you wish to examine her?"

"It would be difficult, since she is fully dressed," he said dryly, gazing toward her. Her shoulders were squared defiantly, and she stared back at him, her chin high in the air.

To Signora Lamponni's great relief, he shook his head. "It is not necessary."

He stepped to Giana and said, "Pick up your gloves, Helen."

She made no move.

He sighed, and took her arm. "Then we will leave them."

"Number five," Signora Lamponni called out quickly.

Alex felt her tugging against him. He said in a low, angry voice, "Enough acting, little harlot, else I'll have you stripped right here!"

Giana went limp against his arm, and he led her from the salon into a small room dimly lit by gaslights. He took her shoulders in his hands and regarded her silently for a moment.

"You can stop your playacting now, Helen or Molly. How does it feel to be the most expensive virgin in all of Rome? You had better be worth it."

She stared at him, her eyes dark and wide. He was so large, huge and terrifying, and he believed her a whore. Where was Uncle Daniele?

"Let me go," she whispered, her voice wispy and thin in her fright.

"I think not, little one. I shan't let you go until the sun rises, and perhaps not even then." Alex pulled her roughly against his chest and forced her chin up. He covered her mouth with his and pressed his tongue against her tightly sealed lips. He felt her tremble, and forced himself to slow. He eased his hold and let his hands rove gently down her slender back.

Giana felt the change in him. His hands held the back of her neck, but he was not pushing her against him. She parted her lips to beg him to leave her alone, and felt his tongue slip inside her mouth, touching hers. She felt a shock of unwanted pleasure course through her, and she gasped, horrified at herself.

Alex felt her respond to him. He lowered his hand to caress her hips through all her damned petticoats. He felt her shuddering against him, then, suddenly, she was fighting him, struggling wildly against him with all her strength, her small fists striking his chest and shoulders.

Giana felt the auburn wig slip to one side She gasped and threw up a hand to right it.

Alex laughed, and jerked the wig off. "So, my

sweet, you've black hair. It is quite lovely. Why did you wish to hide it? After all, I would have known the moment I had you naked."

"You will get your two thousand dollars back," Giana babbled. "I swear it. It is a mistake. Please, you must let me go!"

His dark eyes narrowed dangerously. "Stop this nonsense, girl! I am no longer in the mood for your coy acting." He gentled his voice, not really understanding why. "I will be easy with you, have no fear, little one. I felt you respond to my kiss. I will make you feel more, much more." He heard her gasp, as if in outrage, and said in a hard voice, "I have always wanted to give a harlot her fist lessons. Enough now."

"No!" she shrieked. She threw herself at him, clawing at his face.

Alex felt her fingernails draw blood. "You damned little wildcat!" He grabbed her wrists to protect himself, but she ducked her head down and bit him. She was kicking wildly at his shins. He drew back his fist in fury and slammed it into her jaw. She crumpled where she stood.

He drew out his handkerchief and gingerly wiped away the few drops of blood on his cheek. He stared down at her for a moment. Her thick black hair, come loose from its confining pins, was spilled down her back.

"I must be a half-witted fool," he said aloud. Jesus, he thought as he picked her up, how was he to carry an unconscious female in his arms through the lobby of his hotel? He held her in one arm and pressed his fingers over her jaw. She would have a bruise, but thankfully, he hadn't broken anything. The little fool! Why the devil had she attacked him?

He found himself admiring her creamy English

complexion and the thick black lashes that fanned against her cheeks. His eyes fell to her slender neck and to the bodice of her gown, ripped open in their struggle. To his surprise, the torn chemise beneath was plain white linen, with not a frill or a row of lace.

Her firm young breasts rose and fell. His fingers rested against them before he drew the chemise over her. He carried her through the side entrance of the huge house, nodding to a servant to fetch his carriage. He felt a drizzling rain against his cheek. He cursed softly, shrugged out of his coat, and covered her with it.

As he waited, he found himself wondering if she had prized herself so highly she did not expect to have to strip. He held her tightly against his chest, protecting her from the rain. He heard a sudden noise and whipped about. But he was too late. He felt a crash of pain in his head.

"Giana! Giana! Child, are you all right?"

Daniele shoved Alexander Saxton's inert body away and pulled Giana into his arms, shaking her.

Giana felt an instant of terror and lashed out at him.

"Stop it, Giana, it is I, Daniele!"

"Oh, thank God!" she gasped, struggling to her knees. "Why? I don't understand—"

"I will explain everything to you, Giana. Come, let us get out of here."

"Did you kill him?"

"No, child, he will just have a sore head on the morrow. Quickly, Giana."

Alex heard the name through the veil of pain that clouded his mind. Giana. What an odd name, he thought.

Chapter 8

Giana took in a deep breath of fresh September morning air. She delighted in its crisp coolness, though she shivered in her summer cloak. She allowed the coachman, Abel, to assist her from the brougham, and stood quietly for a moment beneath a full-branched oak tree on the west side of Hyde Park. She watched the few elegantly dressed gentlemen and ladies who were promenading along the walkways. How delightful it was that every word she heard was English! She tilted her face up to catch a sliver of sun that broke through the blanket of leaves above her.

"Giana!"

A tight smile spread across her face as she turned to gaze at Randall Bennett striding toward her. He was, she thought, as devastatingly handsome as she remembered, exquisite in smartly tailored buff riding clothes and black riding boots. She wondered vaguely where he had left his horse, or if there was no horse, and he had simply decided that he appeared to best advantage in riding clothes.

"Ah, my little dove, you are home at last. God, the days have been endless without you!" He grasped her mittened hands in his and squeezed them.

"Hello, Randall," she said.

"How beautiful you look, my love. That is a new bonnet?"

"Yes, I bought it in Paris."

Randall Bennett laughed and pulled her against his chest. "We are talking nonsense. What I really want to do is hold you in my arms." She felt his hands stroke her back, and she slowly pulled away from him.

"You are looking well, Randall."

"Since you are with me again, my love, it cannot but be so. Come, Giana, sit down with me, I've so much to tell you."

She placed her hand on his arm and strolled with him to the small circular pond that lay beneath a green web of leaves, and sat down on a narrow stone bench. She spread her skirts gracefully about her and allowed him to lace his fingers through hers.

"It is a pity we have no bread crumbs for the ducks," Giana said.

"My little dove," Randall said, his eyes bright with excitement, "I have found the most perfect setting for your beauty."

"You mean I look well surrounded by quacking ducks?"

"Silly girl," he said, laughing. The engaging dimple on the right side of his mouth deepened. "No, my love, it is a charming manor house, called Horsham Hall, but an hour by train from London. The owner, poor fellow, is all done up and has to sell. When we return from our honeymoon, it will be our country home. The gardens are exquisite, and of course there will be servants to see to all your needs."

"My needs?"

Randall dropped his voice to an intimate whisper.

"Do you not want your husband to be successful in business, Giana?"

"I suppose it is rather inescapable, given that I am a Van Cleve."

He raised her hand to his lips and kissed her fingers one by one. "Alas, my love, to be worthy of you, it seems that I will have to spend much of my time in the workaday world. But soon, very soon, Giana, you will have a child, my child." His voice caressed her and his eyes swept down her slender figure.

"You have not asked me, Randall, about my summer in Italy."

He looked charmingly rueful. "Forgive me, Giana. My excitement in seeing you finally . . . I seem to be able to think only of the future, and our life together. Did the time pass as slowly for you as it did for me?"

"Yes, it passed very slowly."

It occurred to him suddenly that her voice sounded curiously flat. She could not have heard about the opera dancer—he had been so careful! Even her bitch of a mother had steered clear of him during the summer.

He studied her face, but all that struck him was that she looked so very lovely, so unspoiled. "Time will never pass slowly again, my love," he said softly.

"You are doubtless right. Let me understand you, Randall. You have found this manor house in the country, and you wish me to live there whilst you are gaining fame and fortune here in London. Or rather," she added, her eyes roving past him to rest upon a preening duck beside the pond, "just fame. The fortune, of course, is already there."

"If it pleases you, my darling, we can also purchase a house here in the city," he said carefully, wondering again at the curious flatness in her voice.

But her upturned face was clear, her vivid eyes guileless. "I want only your happiness."

"I am glad to hear you say that."

He arched an elegant brow. "Could I want anything else?"

Giana smiled, but her eyes held a strange glitter.

"Giana, has something happened? You seem somehow different, my love. Your mother is prepared to stand by her bargain, is she not?"

"Oh yes," she said, shrugging. She watched him take a deep relieved breath. "Randall, are you a good lover?"

He started at her question, utterly shocked that she would wonder such a thing, much less ask bluntly about it. He saw that she was perfectly serious, and decided not to chuck her on the chin and call her a naughty puss. Perhaps she had heard something. He laughed softly, intimately, thinking that it behooved him to tread warily. "Giana, my little love, you will have your answer the night of our wedding. I will do my best not to disappoint you."

"I know that I will not."

"Not what?"

"Ever be disappointed by your prowess as a lover, Randall."

He preened, taking her words at face value. He managed to say in a severe voice, "You mustn't talk like that, love, it is not at all proper, and you tempt me beyond reason."

"You don't look tempted beyond reason."

He laughed. "If there were not people strolling close by, I would forget myself and let you understand me."

"The problem is, Randall," she said, each word distinct, "that I do understand. Did you know that a woman cannot divorce her husband for adultery?

She has not the right. The husband, on the other hand, can do whatever pleases him, and if his wife is unfortunate enough to take a lover, the husband can not only divorce her, he has the right to keep her children and all her money. In short, if a wife does anything to displease her husband, she can end up in the street without a penny to her name."

He eyed her carefully, wondering what the devil was on her mind. "The laws are perhaps unfair," he said, "but I assure you, Giana, that such a circumstance would never apply to us." He tried to laugh heartily. "I trust it is not your intention to ever take a lover, my darling."

"Oh no, never would I do that. I simply wondered if you were well-versed in a husband's rights."

He shrugged elaborately. "I know only that it is a husband's responsibility to care for his wife, to protect her and keep her pure and unsullied by the mundane concerns of life. And, of course, to love her with all his heart."

"I see," she said, frowning thoughtfully.

"It is nothing for you to be concerned about, sweetheart. I have decided our wedding can be held in early October. Earlier, if you wish it. And for our honeymoon, I had thought of Greece. We could hire a yacht and sail the islands."

"It sounds like a costly proposition."

So that was it! Her damned mother had convinced her that he wanted only her money! "Giana, believe me," he said with passionate sincerity, clutching her hands tightly, "I love you, only you. I would not care if we stayed in my rooms for our honeymoon, so long as we were together. It is all I have ever wanted and all I will ever want. I will work hard to support you, my love. Your mother will discover that I am no lackadaisical fellow to hang on her bounty." He patted her hand fondly as one would a precocious child's. "And even though you tell me that you understand about a man's needs ... well, you will find out on our wedding night how much I need and desire you, Giana."

"You are fluent, Randall, terribly fluent."

"I do not know what you mean."

"You say all the right things, and so very well, as if you had rehearsed them in front of the mirror."

His jaw tightened in anger. "What is this, Giana? Why are you speaking nonsense? Are your affections so easily engaged that you found another in Italy? Do you no longer love me?"

"I never loved you, Randall."

He rose quickly and strode jerkily back and forth in front of her, slapping his riding crop against his boot. She saw Vittorio Cavelli for an awful instant, raising his riding crop, his face mottled with fury as he stood over the cowering Lucia. "You lie! You are trifling with me, madam, a man who sincerely loves you!"

She shook her head clear of the memory, and forced herself to look up at Randall. Odd, she thought, how his face lost much of its beauty twisted with anger. She admitted to a moment of fear of him and his riding crop, but shook it off. "Do you use the crop on women, Randall, when you are making love to them?"

"Ah, now you would accuse me of being a wife beater?"

"No, I did not say that. After all, you have never been married."

Randall managed to gain control of his temper. She had heard of the opera dancer, he must face it. Her damned mother must have had him followed, and now the little chit was toying with him, wanting him to confess all and beg her pardon, likely on his knees. But what was this nonsense about his riding crop? He dropped the offending crop to the ground and sat down beside her again. "Giana," he said softly, his gray eyes clouding with pain as they held hers, "there is no other woman, save you. A man . . . well, a man sometimes has needs, before he is married, of course. I do not know what your mother told you, but I saw the girl because I was so very lonely for you. She is nothing to me, Giana, and I sent her away long before you returned to England. You are the only woman I will ever want or love."

Giana wanted to giggle. The vain, strutting peacock thought she had found out about a tawdry affair!

"Do not apologize, Randall. I understand about men's needs, truly I do. What I do not understand is why only men are allowed to have them."

Why was she pushing him, he wondered frantically, and speaking openly about sex, and a woman's needs, for God's sake!

"As I told you," he said hoarsely, "when we are wed I will teach you about pleasure, yours and mine. You must believe me, my love. After you are my wife, I will never have need of another woman."

She wanted to tell him that what he had said made not a whit of sense, but she knew that to continue on was needless, in fact cruel of her. But it was he who was the cruel one, the one who had purposefully sought her out, played on her dreams. Dear God, he hadn't even had the good sense to stay out of another girl's bed until he had her safely wed to him! She rose swiftly to her feet and looked down at him.

"Randall," she said, her voice clear and cool as the morning air, "I have no intention of wedding you. Indeed, I doubt that I will ever marry any man, so you cannot accuse me of betraying you with another. I understand that Norman Carl Fletcher, the very wealthy banker, has an unwed daughter. She is not terribly pretty, but of course, that doesn't really matter, does it?"

Randall Bennett rose shakily to his feet. She was looking down her nose at him as if he were some sort of insignificant bug. He gazed at her white throat above a delicate row of lace, and wanted for one long moment to strangle her until she was on her knees before him, begging him.

"You cannot do this to me," he snarled, so beside himself with anger and disappointment that he could think of nothing else to say.

Giana shrugged and drew her cloak about her shoulders. "Good-bye, Randall."

As she turned to go, he grabbed her arm and whirled her about to face him. "No woman casts me off, particularly a spoiled, vain little bitch like you!"

"Let me go, Randall."

"Let the lady go, sir."

Randall dropped his hands out of sheer surprise. He whipped about to see the Van Cleve coachman.

"Thank you, Abel," Giana said quietly. "I am ready to leave now."

"You will pay for this!" Randall Bennett shouted after her.

When Abel assisted her into the brougham, she turned and asked him, "How did you know that I might need you?"

" 'Twas not me, Miss Giana, 'twas your mother. Said to me, she did, that even though Mr. Bennett was all smiles and oozing charm, he had the look of a man could turn nasty."

Giana stared at him. She had not told her mother what she intended to do about Randall—perhaps, she thought now, to punish her. But her mother had known anyway, and had protected her. She said dryly to Abel, "Let us go home. I want to ask my mother if she is ever wrong about anything."

"You do not look happy, Giana," Aurora said carefully as she handed her daughter a cup of tea.

"No? Well, I suppose that I'm not. Seeing the man one believed a prince of men for the first time as he really is is not a particularly happy experience." She sighed. "But I am relieved, Mother, very relieved that it's all over."

There was silence between them, an uncomfortable silence. Giana said suddenly, "The medicine was bitter, Mama, so bitter that I still believe I may choke on it."

"I . . . I am sorry, Giana," Aurora began.

"Mother," Giana said, interrupting her with a raised hand, "my . . . bitterness, such as it is, has nothing to do with you."

What in God's name did Daniele do? "Will you tell me what happened, Giana?"

Giana did not want her mother to know that her valued friend, her trusted friend, had done everything to her daughter save stake her to a bed. "I cannot, Mother, really," she said at last, shaking her head. "I wish only to forget and to carry on with my life, such as it is now."

Aurora searched her daughter's face. "The . . . prostitutes you met and spoke with—what did they . . . that is, were they so very awful?"

To her surprise, Giana smiled. "No, they were not awful."

"Please try to understand, and forgive me, Giana. I could think of nothing else that would allow you to see Randall Bennett as he really is, no way to make you understand that marrying him would be the worst mistake of your life. I intended merely that you see with your own eyes the . . . underside of people, the kind of men who use their wives, and condemn them and their daughters to unutterably empty lives."

"I know, Mother." She wondered whether Daniele had told her mother anything of what occurred, then realized that it would be ridiculous to imagine him doing such a thing. No, what had happened had been between the two of them. She devoutly prayed that she would never see Daniele again, for just to see him would bring it all back.

"It is odd, you know," Giana continued to still her mother's questions, "but now I can see my father quite clearly as one of those men. And I can see you, Mother, how you must have suffered under his negligent cruelty." She remembered a paunchy, mustached man from Germany who had not been content with one of Madame Lucienne's girls. No, he had demanded to be pleasured by three. A pig of a man.

Aurora struggled with her startling words, and suddenly gaped at her. Giana's eyes were clouded, as if there were too many unhappy images, too many painful memories vying for possession. They still held innocence, but it wasn't the innocence of a young girl's romantic dreams, it was a dark innocence. She said slowly, "I made the decision after your father's death that I wanted no more of living with a man. That is not to say I have not had men become dear friends. Nor must you think, my love, that you will not meet a man who will be much more to you, a man you can trust, and respect, and love."

Giana gave her mother a twisted smile. "I think, Mother, that after Rome, I cannot imagine ever trusting a man like that." Before Aurora could contradict her, Giana rushed on. "I was really quite good in mathematics, you know, despite all my letters to the contrary. And though I am abominably ignorant of ... finance and commerce, I do not think I am precisely stupid. Will you teach me, Mother?"

Aurora looked at her daughter sadly. What price had Giana paid for her victory? If only, she thought, she had not shut her out, had not left her to governesses, and to that ridiculous girls' seminary.

"Yes," she said quietly, "I will teach you, Giana."

"Excellent." Giana rose from her chair and twitched out the wrinkles from her gown. "You see before you a pupil who intends to excel."

"Giana, will you not tell me about ... Rome?"

"No, Mother, I will not." She smiled. "It is best forgotten, by both of us."

Chapter 9

London, 1851

Russell Street was nearly bare of shoppers in the late afternoon. Aurora glanced only cursorily about before dropping her eyes to the cobblestones and lifting her heavy taffeta shirts to cross the street to the colorful display window of Mademoiselle Blanchette's, the fashionable milliner's in London. She was thinking about the cargo hold of the *Orion*, picturing it empty of its wooden crates and fitted with temporary bunks and dividers for human cargo. She and Daniele had outfitted four ships in the past three years to carry passengers to America, and now even more were needed for the exodus to the newly discovered gold fields in California. She did not hear the rumbling carriage wheels until the wild snorting of a horse caught her horrified attention. She jerked about to see a huge bay stallion pulling a smart brougham bearing down on her. *Stupid fool!* she thought to herself. The horse veered miraculously to the side, nearly tipping the brougham before the driver brought him to a jolting halt.

Aurora, her heart in her throat, could only stare stupidly at the passenger who jumped down from his seat and strode over to her, yelling toward his liveried driver to hold the horse steady.

"Madam," the man bellowed at her, "what the devil are you doing woolgathering in the middle of the street!" He grasped her arms to steady her, and pulled her to the sidewalk. He did not release his hold on her, guessing aright that her legs were weak as water from the shock.

"I am sorry," Aurora managed, leaning limply against him

"Are you all right?" he asked her, not bellowing this time.

"It was stupid of me," Aurora said apologetically. She forced her legs to support her and looked up into the face of an uncommonly handsome man. He was tall and slender, and dressed in the height of fashion. His black frock coat was molded nicely to his shoulders over a waistcoat of rich maroon silk, and his broad-stripped trousers were elegantly tapered over his long legs. No man of business, she thought inconsequentially. His eyes were a pale gray, nearly silver, heavily hooded with the longest black lashes she had ever seen, and his hair, black as her own, was winged with white at his temples.

"You have the most beautiful eyelashes," she said stupidly.

His silver eyes twinkled at her.

"I am sorry," she repeated, shaking her head at her foolishness. "You are quite right to be angry, for I wasn't paying attention. Thank you for not hitting me."

The strong hands on her arms eased. "Are you married?" the man asked.

Aurora blinked up at him.

"Are you married?" he repeated smoothly.

She shook her head. "I am a widow."

"Excellent," he said. She felt his long fingers touch her cheeks as he straightened her *capote* hat. "What is your name?"

"Aurora."

He grinned down at her as he retied the blue taffeta bow under her chin. "What a relief that is. I am delighted that it is not Mary or Prudence, names I cannot abide."

"Why ever not?" she asked, looking up at him with a bemused eye.

"The names of my nurses when I was a tot. Dragons, the both of them. If you were endowed with a name like that, it would try my soul, I assure you, ma'am."

Aurora laughed; she couldn't seem to help herself. "And what is your name, sir?"

"I am Arlington, you know," he said. "All Arlingtons have long eyelashes. I say, Aurora, where do you live?"

"Belgrave Square," she said, aware that his slender hands had somehow moved from her bow to her elbows.

"Nice area, that," he said. "Come along, Aurora, I will take you home now. You've had a nasty shock, bad for your nerves, and mine."

"But I—"

He gave her that engaging grin again, and despite herself, the corners of her mouth curved up in answer.

"Good girl."

"I am not a girl, Mr. Arlington! I am forty-four years old!"

"Then you should be mortified, my dear. A lady of your advanced years standing in the middle of the street, her mind filled with daydreams." She wanted to protest that there was rarely a daydream in her mind, but he was already pulling her toward the waiting brougham.

"Incidentally," he said as he handed her up, "you may call me Damien. I've never been a 'mister.' "

"Then what are you?"

"My dear girl, I am the gentleman who it taking you to lunch tomorrow."

"Lunch?" Aurora repeated faintly, wondering where her wits had gone begging. He was a total stranger, and here he was calling her, Aurora Van Cleve, by her first name and ever so confidently settling her in his brougham.

"Yes, my dear, Should you like that?"

She should have told him that he was impertinent, but instead, she nodded. "Yes," she said, "I should like that."

"Excellent. I will come for you at precisely ten o'clock tomorrow morning."

"Ten o'clock . . . for lunch?"

He gazed at her, a black brow winging up in surprise. "Why, yes, Aurora. You see, my dear girl, my favorite restaurant, the Iron Horse, is in Windsor." He lightly patted her hand, told his driver their direction, and settled back beside her.

"But I did not buy my bonnet," she said, pointing helplessly toward Mademoiselle Blanchette's shop.

Damien Arlington turned to smile at her. "We will buy any number of bonnets, after we return from Windsor tomorrow. I have excellent taste, you know."

"But I don't even *know* you!"

"We must begin to remedy that tomorrow at lunch, my dear. I am quite a respectable fellow, you need have no worry for your virtue or your reputation. I say, you aren't thinking of bringing a chaperon, are you? That would be a deuced nuisance."

"Her name is Faith," Aurora said demurely.

"I knew you were a clever minx." Damien smiled and patted her hand again.

"Surely, sir," Aurora essayed, "you have better

things to do with your time than help me buy bonnets!"

"Well, of course," he said, "but that must wait until we know each other a bit better."

Aurora flushed angrily. "I am not a . . . a loose female, sir!"

His silver eyes glinted down at her. "Neither am I a loose gentleman, Aurora. Now hush, my dear. Although Ned is an excellent driver, I like to keep my eye on old Spartan here—he is not terribly fond of city traffic."

Aurora settled back against the soft leather squabs, unable in any case to think of anything further to say to him.

When they arrived at Belgrave Square, she directed him to the Van Cleve mansion. It was on the tip of her tongue to inform this impossible man that she was occupied on the morrow, but his hands were suddenly strong about her waist, lifting her down to the flagway.

"How very beautiful you are, Aurora," he said, his silver eyes locked on her upturned face. To her horror, Aurora blushed like a silly schoolgirl. He touched the tips of his long fingers to her cheek. "You go inside now, my dear, and rest. You are doubtless possessed of an exquisite calm, and I wish you to regain it." He took her arm and walked with her to the deep steps at the front door.

"Until tomorrow morning, Aurora," he said. He turned about and strode away from her, his step jaunty.

Aurora gazed after him. He waved to her as the brougham turned down the street, and without precisely deciding to, she raised her arm in answer.

"Madam," Lanson said as she stepped into the entrance hall, "Miss Giana awaits you in the salon."

Aurora murmured a faint thank-you to Lanson and passed into the drawing room.

"Mother," Giana said, picking up the silver teapot, "we have time for a cup of tea before we meet Thomas and Drew. Mother?"

"Yes, love?"

"Are you all right?"

Aurora walked toward the front windows, pulled aside the heavy draperies, and stared out. "I hope it doesn't rain tomorrow," she said.

"It does not look like rain," Giana said, eyeing her mother askance. "Why does it matter in any case?"

"I am going to Windsor for lunch," Aurora said, and walked past her daughter out of the drawing room, her tea unnoticed.

"To lunch? With whom?"

Aurora turned at the foot of the stairs. "With Damien," she said.

Giana stared after her mother, too confounded to question her further. She turned an astonished eye toward Lanson. "Who is Damien?"

"A gentleman who drives a very smart brougham, Miss Giana."

"Mother," Giana called after Aurora. "We must leave in an hour!"

Giana cocked her head to one side and tugged on her left earlobe, as she always did when she was concentrating. Drew smoothed his bushy side whiskers, the one extravagance he allowed himself as the head assistant to Mrs. Van Cleve, and waited for her reply to Thomas Hardesty, her mother's partner. "I do not understand, Thomas," Giana said, frowning down at the stack of papers in front of her, "why you are not even considering the proposal from Pierre LeClerc. Believe me, I can answer any questions you may have. I've had the wretched offer under my nose for nearly a week now—even under my pillow!"

"You have prepared a most thorough assessment of his proposal, Giana, and I agree that the numbers look more than gratifying. But have you discovered anything about LeClerc's reputation and business practices?"

"So far I know only what his business representatives say of him here in London, and that, of course, is positive. I have assigned Draber to check into his financial position, and Draber is reporting that he is worth a great deal of money."

"Do you remember that French ship *Alliance* that sank in a storm off Ceylon last year?" Aurora asked her daughter.

"Yes, of course. It is in my report."

"All hands were lost, and the two dozen passengers whose misfortune it was to be on the ship," Thomas continued for her. "It was insured to the hilt through Lloyd's. In fact, Oran Dinwitty handled it. He discovered that the *Alliance* was a solid ship and the storm that sank her was not all that severe. He suspected mischief, but could not prove anything."

"Certainly Oran Dinwitty knows what he's about," Giana mused aloud.

"There is more," Aurora said. "We discovered through our Captain Mareaux, who was in Colombo at the time the Alliance was in port, that she had already dropped her cargo, contrary to what LeClerc purported, and money had changed hands, money that was probably not on the *Alliance* when she was lost, but snug on an English ship."

"There was one survivor, the second mate," Thomas said. "A man called Jacques Lambeau. Oddly enough, he was found murdered some six months ago in Marseilles. His style of living until his death was rather splendid, from what Captain Mareaux could find out from a former crew member in France."

"You mean," Giana said, gazing from her mother to Thomas Hardesty, "that LeClerc paid this Jacques Lambeau to sink the *Alliance* with everyone aboard? And then had the man killed?"

"It would appear so," Thomas said. "Unfortunately, there isn't proof, but suffice it to say that Lloyd's will not touch another LeClerc ship. That is why LeClerc has made us such a grand proposal for a share of the Van Cleve shipping line. His aim is to merge with us as a silent partner, throwing all his ships under the Van Cleve umbrella and name. As a partner, he would have the good name of Van Cleve to cover him, and the right to retain his own crews. And he would be a partner in one of the largest shipping lines in Europe."

Aurora shrugged. "Doubtless LeClerc believed we wouldn't find out about his troubles with Lloyd's. But we have found out. Were we to accept LeClerc's offer, we would likely find ourselves as uninsurable as he is."

"Then there is certainly no profit to be made there," Giana said dryly.

"No indeed," Thomas agreed. "Now, if you two agree, I will see to it that LeClerc is informed that we have no interest in pursuing any business relation with him. As to the additional evidence we have uncovered . . ." He turned to Drew. "Would you see to it, Drew, that the French authorities are informed? There is nothing very substantial, but perhaps it will interest them."

Giana sat back for moment in her tall leather-backed chair, a wry smile about her mouth. She had just learned a valuable lesson, one, obviously, that her mother and Thomas had prepared for her. "Now that you two have left me spinning in the wind, I presume you have an alternative to LeClerc."

Thomas grinned at her and picked up a sheaf of papers. "Indeed we do, Giana. We've received a proposal we think worthy of serious consideration. It comes to us from America—New York, to be precise—from a wealthy shipbuilder, Alexander Saxton. You will see that his offer emcompasses far more than does LeClerc's."

"But first, Thomas," Giana said, amusement in her voice, "you must tell me all about Mr. Saxton's cook. Have you discovered that she has a fondness for poisoned mushrooms?"

"Well, I don't know about the cook or the mushrooms, but Saxton is third-generation shipping. His grandfather, George Saxton, founded a small shipyard in Boston before the turn of the century, and his grandson learned the business from him and from his own father, Nicholas, from the time he could walk. Mrs. Amelia Saxton, his mother, died when he was fourteen, his father some four years later. He has one younger brother, Delaney Saxton, something of a dark horse. All we know about him is that he is somewhere in California, caught up in the gold rush. It appears the elder Saxton is possessed of several qualities his father did not have: he is extraordinarily ambitious and he has both cunning and imagination. When he was twenty-two, he married Laura Nielson, the daughter of Franklin Nielson, a Quaker gentleman who owned one of the largest whaler yards in northeastern America. With one stroke, Saxton gained a good deal of capital from his early marriage, and used it to expand his father's shipyard."

"He sounds rather mercenary to me," Giana said, "married for money when he was but twenty-two."

"The word is 'ambitious,' Giana," Aurora said.

"When his wife's father died some seven years ago," Thomas continued, "Saxton sold the Nielson shipyard in Boston and moved the entire operation to New York. Since that time, he has made a series of risky, but very imaginative moves—"

"Like what, Thomas?" Giana asked.

"Well, he managed—how, I do not know—to gain a stake in the ferry business controlled by Vanderbilt. It has brought him a goodly income without much outlay. Today Saxton, as the age of thirty-two, is one of the wealthiest shipbuilders in New York, and one of the ablest. Certainly he is possessed of the Americans' peculiar breed of arrogance and brashness, but his judgement seems sound enough."

"He sounds like a boy marvel," Giana said dryly. "What does he want from us, Thomas?"

"He wants a merger with Van Cleve. He proposes to build six new ships for the Van Cleve line—at a savings for us, because he also owns very productive lumber and steel mills—so that we can take better advantage of the increasing demand for cargo shipping to India."

Giana interrupted him. "But why does he need us, Thomas? If he builds the ships, why does he not just create his own shipping line?"

"It seems some years ago he directly involved some of his own ships in the India trade. Write it up to his youth, I suppose. In any case, he had great hopes, only to discover that the existing British trade agreements, including our own, did not allow for interlopers. By allying himself to an established shipping line that already has guaranteed contracts, he is removing a good deal of the risk to himself." Thomas paused a moment before continuing. "Of course, to realize his profit, Saxton must buy into us. He wants fifty percent ownership, making us the Van Cleve/ Saxton ship lines."

Aurora herself answered Giana's outraged gasp. "Saxton undoubtedly knows that the Van Cleve shipyards in Plymouth are not what they were twenty years ago. Profits are low because we must compete with the Americans' abundant raw materials and labor, and we ourselves haven't the capital needed to bring the shipyards up to snuff. Saxton would bring us quite a sum, and build the ships we need more quickly than we ourselves can. He knows the loss of the *Constant* hurt us badly, and that we are in danger of losing some of our most profitable trade contracts. The truth is that we need Saxton more than he needs us, and he knows it. Thus his outrageous demand for equal ownership."

"You believe he knows how much the loss of the *Constant* hurt us?" Giana asked.

"Certainly he knows. A man of his acumen would not have less information about our business than we do about him. He doubtless is quite aware of all our commitments, commitments that will not be met if he or someone else isn't brought in quickly to rescue our hides."

"How I wish we could divert funds from our other holdings, and tell all these ... vultures to go to the devil!"

"As much as we all would like that, Giana," Thomas said, "we must reserve our capital for Aurora's partnership with Mr. Cook. With the masses of people who are traveling by rail as part of Mr. Cook's tours, from all parts of England to the exhibition, that is likely to be our proverbial golden goose."

"Would you like to study Mr. Saxton's proposal in detail now, Giana?" Aurora asked.

"I suppose so," Giana said, taking the sheaf of papers from Drew. "I just wish we didn't have to bring in an outsider, and an American of all people. This Mr. Saxton sounds dangerous."

Thomas laughed heartily. "It will be our job to remove his teeth. You and your mother will probably enjoy just that, since our Mr. Saxton is reputed to be something of a ladies' man."

"A lecher?" Giana asked.

"Not that, Giana. His wife died some five years ago, supposedly in a boating accident at the Saxton summer estate in Connecticut. He has one daughter from his marriage, Leah, a houseful of servants, and a young man's need for pleasure. He cuts a wide swath with the ladies, so I hear."

Giana snorted. "Why did you say 'supposedly,' Thomas? You are not hinting that he did away with his wife, are you?"

"Certainly not. The American newspapermen are a sensational lot, and with Saxton being young and quite wealthy, and his wife something of a recluse, they blew the tragedy out of all proportion. No, our Mr. Saxton is not a man to murder his wife. He appears to enjoy his work and his ladies. No harm in that, certainly,"

"None at all," Aurora agreed, standing. "Giana, my dear," she continued to her daughter, "I understand that you and Drew are going to the exhibition again today."

Giana nodded, her eyes brightening. "I promise you, Mother, it's worth being squeezed by all the crowds."

Drew said dryly, "To be honest, Mrs. Van Cleve, there aren't too terribly many people interested in McCormick's mechanical reaper, besides Giana. She shows little interest in the other thirteen thousand, nine hundred and ninety-nine exhibits."

"Strive for a bit more enthusiasm, Drew, if you please! There is money to be made with his invention. I understand he has moved his company to Chicago, and is beginning production of his reaper on a grand scale." She smiled slyly and added, "Drew has told me of an expert machinist here in London. Perhaps we could consider sending the man to America to learn how to build the reaper, then patent the process ourselves here in England."

Aurora chuckled and said to Thomas Hardesty, "I cannot imagine where Giana got this unscrupulous streak."

"Come, Mother, you know that I am jesting ... I think. At least we could consider marketing his reaper here in England."

"Perhaps Mr. Saxton would have something to offer you in such a proposition," Thomas mused.

"Maybe so, Thomas. Mr. Saxton will come to London for the negotiations, will he not?"

"We shall insist upon it." Thomas shot Aurora a droll look. "His London business associate, Hammett Engles, would perhaps be a bit ... apprehensive about dealing with Aurora by himself again."

Giana gave a crow of laughter. "I remember Mr. Engles and his shipping stocks! Such a conceited man!"

"Perhaps he is," Aurora agreed in a mild voice. "Getting him to sell short to a buffleheaded female like me was most gratifying." What she did not mention was that Mr. Hammett Engles was no longer an adversary, but rather, she supposed, something in the nature of a suitor. She found, perversely, that she enjoyed his boundless conceit, if only for one evening a month at the opera.

Drew consulted his watch. "A Mr. Claybourn is due here shortly, ma'am."

"Ah, yes," Aurora said, rising to shake out her skirts. "He is Daniele Cippolo's English representative. Daniele, I fear, with all the political debacles in Italy, has found himself short of capital. The *Orion* will likely have to be our project, and ours alone."

At precisely ten o'clock the following morning—a sunny morning, Aurora saw from her bedroom window—there came a stalwart rap on the front door. Lanson, his eyes all curiosity above his crooked nose, answered the door.

"I am here to see Mrs. Van Cleve," Damien said, not bothering to hand his hat and cane to Lanson.

"I will ascertain, sir—"

"Good morning," Aurora said in a ridiculously high voice as she swept down the staircase. She wore a vivid green silk gown fitted snugly at her slender waist and billowing out over half a dozen petticoats.

"How beautiful you look, my dear," Damien said, his gaze following her descent. "And punctual. I see that I was right about you, Aurora. You are as calm as a placid lake."

Giana appeared, as if on cue, in the doorway of the library, her eyes darting from her mother's becomingly flushed face to the tall gentleman who was turning leisurely toward her.

"You are Aurora's daughter? Quite beautiful, my child, but your mother stole a march on you. What is your name?"

"Georgiana Van Cleve, sir!"

"Not, I assure you," Aurora said, "Mary or Prudence!"

"No," Damien said, smiling down at her, "I knew you would never be guilty of anything less than perfect taste. Let us go, my dear. Georgiana, you may or may not see your mother for dinner this evening."

"But, who are you, sir?" Giana prodded.

"Why, I am Damien Arlington, of course."

"What is your business, sir?" Giana perservered.

Damien looked at her, clearly puzzled. "Business, my dear child? If you really wish to know, I shall ask my man about it."

Giana looked at him, nonplussed.

"Perhaps this evening, Georgiana," Damien said. "Come, Aurora."

She heard her mother's laughter, and turned to Lanson. "I think I will see Mr. Hardesty this morning."

Aurora was still laughing when Damien assisted her into an open carriage. She saw a coat of arms painted on the door, and realized for the first time that the driver, Ned, was liveried.

"What is so amusing, Aurora?"

"My daughter," she said, her eyes twinkling. "I expect you may be receiving a formal dinner invitation from her soon."

"She is a lovely girl. I will look forward to it."

Aurora shook her head, still smiling. "That remains to be seen, sir. Who are you, Damien?" she asked. "I saw a coat of arms on your carriage."

"You want all of my names, my love? Very well. I am Damien Ives St. Clair Arlington, eighth Duke of Graffton."

"Oh dear," Aurora gasped. "You have made a mistake, sir—your grace!"

"Ned, keep a smart pace!" his grace called to his driver. "A mistake, Aurora?" he said, tucking her nerveless hand over his arm.

"I am Aurora Van Cleve. I am in trade . . . *business*!"

"Of course you are, my dear. I have never been able to abide stupid women, and I knew you for a remarkable woman the moment I saw you. I do wish though that you would not make it a habit to stand in the middle of the street."

"I . . . I was thinking how we could fit the cargo hold of the *Orion* for passengers to America."

"Poor brutes, the Irish. What with the famine, they haven't much reason to stay, have they? And did you solve the problem, Aurora?"

She shook her head, incurably honest. "No, I fear that I was thinking about you."

"Most appropriate, for you were rarely out of my thoughts last night."

She realized suddenly that he had not been at all surprised by her announcement. "You know who I am?"

He appeared genuinely amused. "Indeed. Do you not think that I would wish to know all about the lady I am going to marry?"

"*Marry!*"

"My son, Edward, Lord Dunstable—a dull fellow, but stalwart in his duty—told me that your thankfully dead husband was something of a rotter. Appalling the way your father sold you to the fellow, and you only seventeen."

Aurora stared at him in astonishment. "Perhaps Morton Van Cleve was a rotter," she said, remembering the pain. "I do know that if he had any notion that his fortune would fall into my hands, he would have paid the devil himself to blight me with fire. As to my father selling me, well, he was a gambler, you know, his blue baronet's blood could not save him, only me. My husband made a very generous settlement. Yes, he was a rotter. We never loved each other. He merely wished another possession." She halted abruptly. Why had she confided any of her bitterness to a stranger?

"Well, it is over now, my love," his grace assured her, patting her gloved hand. "You will enjoy being married to me."

"But it has been over for many years, and I have been my own woman. I don't know what made me prose on about it, really! And marriage to you, your grace ... I begin to believe you mad!"

He eyed her with tolerant amusement. "Mad? To love you? Really, Aurora, do not insult yourself, I do not like it." His incredible silver eyes swept over her, lingering for just a moment at the cream Valenciennes lace at her throat. "I fear we are a bit too old to have children, but Edward, my heir, is hale and hearty, as are his two younger brothers and three sisters."

"I ... I would like to enjoy the lovely scenery for a while, your grace." Obligingly he fell silent, content to watch her.

The Iron Horse Inn, situated on a quaint cobblestoned corner in Windsor, boasted a view of the castle from the windows in its private dining room. Aurora was tenderly assisted into her chair, while the waiter, a young man with a pointed beard, hovered over the duke, awaiting his pleasure. She held her tongue until Damien had ordered and the waiter had withdrawn from their private dining room.

"I have been a widow for many years, your gr—"

"Damien, if you please, Aurora. I trust you will like the chicken? Their bechamel sauce is renowned."

"Damien, I am not some sort of addlepated female! You ... well, you took me quite by surprise, but I am a very responsible woman, usually. I am quite used to making my own decisions and doing things just as I like. I have not found gentlemen to be ... overly gratified at my occupation. Gentlemen do not like women with brains."

"I pray you will not insult me again, Aurora. Never, I repeat, never, compare me to other gentlemen."

The waiter returned with the wine, which the duke did not bother to taste. He merely waved him away again.

"Now, try the wine, it is a light, dry Bordeaux."

"I own vineyards in Bordeaux," she said desperately.

"Then you can advise me on our cellar," he said serenely. "To us, Aurora, and our future together."

Aurora sipped her wine. "I own Van Cleve enterprises, Damien, and I ..."—she took on a militant look—"and I control all my businesses myself, with my daughter's help."

"Excellent, my love."

"I am very wealthy, Damien. I vowed long ago never to wed again and let a man control my fortune."

"Whatever would I do with another fortune?" he asked her with some surprise. "If you wish it, I will let you manage mine as well. I really have no head for business matters."

Aurora regarded him helplessly. "A duke does not marry a woman of the merchant class, Damien, even if she is a baronet's daughter."

"I trust," his grace continued serenely, "that you do not dislike men, after your rotter of a husband. I am an excellent lover, so I have been told."

"This is plain speaking indeed!"

He gazed at her for a long moment, a question in his eyes. "You are woman of sense, my love—why should I not speak plainly? My first wife, now happily in the hereafter, was a silly woman, vain and demanding, and an earl's daughter. I abided her because she did, albeit begrudgingly, give me children. I vowed that my second wife, if I ever found a lady to my liking, would be the woman of my heart. I have been looking for some ten years now. I am thankful I did not run you down yesterday."

"You know nothing about me! You—"

"Learning all about you would likely take more years than I have left to me. I am forty-seven, Aurora. Will you have me?"

The ever-lingering waiter appeared again with their lunch. Damien shot him a frustrated look and waved him away. "Stay gone this time, Cranshaw," he shouted after him.

Aurora looked down at her chicken breast bathed in bechamel sauce, and giggled. "The wine is making me light-headed," she said. She clasped her hands in front of her. "I am not a lady to sit about dispensing tea, Damien. Indeed, I am a woman of strong character, and I cannot abide the useless lives ladies of fashion lead."

"A railroad line is being completed to Bradford, a small village just to the west of Graffton Manor. I am thinking of purchasing my own private car. Will you advise me?"

Aurora shook her head, not at him, but at herself. "Yes," she said, "I will advise you."

"And will you kiss me? I cannot think of my lunch looking at your beautiful mouth." He rose from his chair, cupped her chin in his long fingers, and raised her face to him.

"You are the woman of my heart," he said softly.

Chapter 10

It was a struggle to see through the thick gray veil of early-morning London fog. Alexander Saxton turned down Court Street, thankful he could make out the sign above the fog line. He regretted he hadn't taken a hansom cab to the Van Cleve building on Grayson Lane from his hotel. Jesus, how could these people stand to be shivering in the middle of July! A man nearly ran into him as he rushed by, likely a clerk on his way to work, and late at that. Not so very different from New York, he thought. As he crossed the street, he heard an offended yell. "Eh, gov'nor, mind where yer going!" A cart filled with beer kegs rumbled by, the driver shaking his head at Alex. No, Alex thought, not much different at all from New York.

He rehearsed the coming meeting in his mind, reviewing the points on which he planned to give and those on which he would not bend. Why his London associate, Hammett Engles, could not have handled the early negotiations was beyond him. He had insisted that Alex come to London and conduct the entire matter himself, writing that Aurora Van Cleve was not a woman to be taken lightly. Still, he would have sent Anesley O'Leary, his assistant in New York, had not his London solicitor, Raymond Ffalkes, agreed that he himself should be in London for the duration. Although Alex hadn't much cared for the pompous Ffalkes when he dined with him and Hammett the night before, the man appeared to know his business. Alex needed a holiday, and he had never visited London. He did look forward to seeing the exhibition in Paxton's incredible Crystal Palace and partaking of London's other pleasures. He would deal with the wily Mrs. Van Cleve in his spare time and take himself to Paris by the end of the week.

He stopped in front of a three-story gray brick building and looked up at the finely scrolled lettering above its double doors. VAN CLEVE ENTERPRISES and below: *11 Grayson Lane*.

A young man approached him in a tomblike lobby that echoed his footsteps. He was directed to the second floor. Everything was old in London, he thought as he climbed the wide marble stairs, old and stolid, fairly reeking of English respectability. He pushed open a double set of thick oak doors and found himself in an elegantly appointed outer office. A young man, this one with bushy side whiskers and glasses, rose to greet him.

"Mr. Saxton?"

At Alex's nod, the young man said, "My name is Drew Mortesson, Mrs. Van Cleve's assistant. Welcome to London, sir. Mr. Ffalkes, your solicitor, Mr. Hardesty, Mrs. Van Cleve's partner, and Mr. Hammett Engles, your London associate, are in the conference room. If you will follow me, sir."

"And Mrs. Van Cleve?" Alex inquired, arching a thick black brow. From all he had heard, the lady dragon always saw to her own business.

Drew paused but an instant before replying, "Unfortunately, Mrs. Van Cleve has fallen ill with the influenza. Her daughter, Georgiana Van Cleve, will be conducting the meeting."

Not another woman! Although he knew a good

deal about the mother, Alex hadn't bothered to check up on the daughter. He must have betrayed his thoughts, because Drew Mortesson said quietly, "I believe you will find Miss Van Cleve to be as capable as her mother. Although she is young, she has been completely involved in all the Van Cleve interests for the past four years, and is qualified to discuss every aspect of the proposed merger."

"I am certain that she is," Alex said with ill-disguised sarcasm. Now he was to do business with a damned girl, or perhaps a spinster of uncertain years. He supposed, in all fairness, that he would have been equally put off if it were Aurora Van Cleve's son. He had endured quite enough of puffed-up sons in their father's businesses.

A bell sounded, and Drew cast a harried look back toward his office. "If you will excuse me for a moment, sir," he said, and hurried away.

Alex strolled down a thickly carpeted corridor that swallowed the sound of his steps. Stolid and depressingly quiet, he thought, like a well-kept mausoleum. He much preferred the chaotic activity of South Street, with its tightly packed row of tall-masted ships, and their passengers mingling with porters, carmen, and drays, and, of course, the frenetic high-hatted clerks from the offices across the street. He had torn down a large countinghouse that had dominated South Street in the 1820's, and built in its stead a stately three-story edifice. Because he had had fond feelings for his deceased father-in-law, he had named the building A. Saxton & F. Nielson. His huge office occupied half the top floor, and whenever he wished, he could swivel about in his chair and gaze out the huge glass windows onto the bustling street.

He paused a moment to study the row of paintings on the corridor walls above the rich wainscoting. Por-

traits of ships under full sail with their names in gold
script. The *Netherlands*, the *Cornucopia*, the *Alaistair*, all
famous ships built in the early years of the century.
There were later pictures, daguerreotypes, showing
several Van Cleve ships in the Plymouth shipyard. The
Hunter, a huge cargo vessal with enough white canvas
rigging to cover a building, had docked in New York
the week before he had left, carrying cases of wine
from the Van Cleve vineyards in Bordeaux.

On the opposite wall were more paintings and daguerreotypes, these depicting the history of the locomotive. The first was drawn by the primitive *Novelty*
locomotive, with an attached omnibus and owner's
coaches. Next was the *North Star* with its train of
early carriages. And finally, a daguerreotype of the
single-wheeler locomotive built about six years before that ran on eight huge wheels. His attention was
captured by another drawing. It was Henson's famous design for an "Aerial Steam Carriage," publi-
cized even in America. He smiled, shaking his head
at such foolishness.

Alex continued down the corridor toward a richly
carved set of double doors that looked to be the
thickness of his forearm. He looked to see if Drew
Mortesson was coming, but he was nowhere in sight.
He shrugged and opened the doors. He strode into
another antechamber, impressively furnished with
heavy mahogany chairs and a black leather Benting-
ton sofa, this one, he supposed, the waiting room
outside Aurora Van Cleve's throne room.

To his surprise, he saw a curtained glass window
on the far wall that gave into the next room. He wondered if he would be able to see whom he was to do
business with, without he himself having to undergo
their scrutiny. He stepped quietly to the window and
drew the curtain. It was a splendidly decorated

room, every inch of it showing subdued good taste.
At the far end, set near the floor-to-ceiling windows,
was a huge mahogany desk. He wondered somewhat
cynically why the heavy velvet draperies were open,
for there was nothing to see save thick fog. A long
oak table with heavy comfortable chairs around it
was set in the middle of the room. A decanter on a
silver tray with crystal glasses grouped about it was
readied at its center. He saw Mr. Ffalkes, standing by
the window, looking like a plump fop, mopping his
wide brow with a handkerchief. His business associate, Hammett Engles, was seated near the desk, looking somewhat like a mournful undertaker in his stark
black, shuffling papers in his lap. He supposed the
other man was Thomas Hardesty, Aurora Van
Cleve's partner. He was pouring himself a cup of tea,
Alex suspected, from a pot on the edge of the desk.
His thin mouth had a look of bored amusement, and
his gray eyes seemed vague. He was not, Alex decided, a man to underestimate. Perhaps Aurora Van
Cleve's success was the work of that mild-looking,
likely very astute man. He saw a woman standing
with her back to the men, facing the window. She
was dressed fashionably enough, but her silk gown
was a subdued gray, and the corset she undoubtedly
wore managed quite well to conceal any curves beneath her bodice. Her hair was inky black and coiled
into a thick chignon at the nape of her slender neck.
She turned at something Ffalkes said, laughing
lightly, and he saw a very young profile, not at all
unpleasing. Thomas Hardesty walked toward the
long table and she turned to follow him. When he
saw her full face, he felt an instant of vague puzzle-
ment, and then a blighting shock of recognition. He
had to be mistaken! He felt a knot of fury clutch his
belly as he studied her. It was she—he would never

forget that face. The vivid dark blue eyes, the elegant arched brows, the raven-black hair. But it made no sense! Helen, Molly, Georgiana Van Cleve ... *Giana*, the odd name he remembered hearing that night four years ago in Rome. Georgiana Van Cleve, the famous Aurora Van Cleve's daughter, had played a cheap little harlot to bilk him of two thousand dollars, and arranged to have him bashed over the head for good measure! He had been insane to buy her in the first place, but what had truly galled him, galled him still, was that he had been played for a fool, an utter ass, who had rushed headlong into the trap she had set. He remembered quite clearly how she had sought him out in the room of gentlemen at Signora Lamponni's Flower Auction, how she had managed to gain his interest and ignite his desire for her. A marvelous actress, that one. He had tried to find the little bitch, even postponed his trip to Paris, but with no success. She seemed to have vanished, and that stiff-lipped madam, Signora Lamponni, had told him that all she knew about the girl was that she had come from Paris, highly recommended, of course. He had known she was lying, but there was no changing her story. She quickly offered to refund his two thousand dollars, but he had slammed out of her presence, so infuriated that he could scarcely think straight. He supposed it was best that he hadn't found the little slut, for if he had, he might have strangled her.

Dammit! How could this girl be Aurora Van Cleve's daughter ... the harlot he had bought as a virgin in Rome four years ago? Virgin. That was a laugh. He intended to find out. But first he would show her she was playing in his world now.

Drew Mortesson appeared at his elbow. "Excuse

me, Mr. Saxton, for leaving you. If you will accompany me, sir, we can proceed."

Alex nodded at him, drew in his breath, and schooled his features. He followed Drew into the conference room, which was suddenly quiet at his entrance. He purposefully set his gaze away from Georgiana Van Cleve.

"Gentlemen," he said, acknowledging Ffalkes's and Engles' presence. "You, sir," he continued, proffering his hand, "must be Thomas Hardesty. It is a pleasure."

"I assure you, Mr. Saxton, that it is also our pleasure," Thomas said. "It is gratifying to have a bit of migration to this side of the world, even though it is for but a short time. I suppose that Drew has told you of Mrs. Van Cleve's indisposition," he continued smoothly. "Her daughter, however, is most worthy to take her place. Miss Van Cleve, sir."

Alex turned dark mocking eyes toward the girl. As he had listened gravely to Mr. Hardesty's greeting, he had thought he heard a small gasp. Now he saw that her eyes were wide upon him, her face as pale as the white lace on her gown. He was immensely pleased that she recognized him. The little rich girl who had played out her games in Rome knew well who he was.

Giana felt her heart plummet to her toes. She saw his dark eyes sweep over her, just as they had that long-ago night—confident, even insolent—and now, taunting. She felt a shock of remembered terror and humiliation of that night. Her eyes were drawn to his hands, large with long blunt fingers, fingers that had caressed her. She remembered her nails raking over his face in her fear, and the black pain when he had smashed his fist against her jaw.

She wanted to run, but instead she sagged in her chair. Never, Aurora had preached to her, never let a

man rile you ... and believe me, Giana, some of
them will try! They will be condescending, arrogant,
even stupidly flattering. Men like that you must treat
like wooden sticks. You can laugh at them; it makes
their tongues stick to the roofs of their mouths. Or, if
you prefer, be indifferent; it makes them question
their manhood and their confidence. Even as Giana
remembered her mother's words, her mind screamed
at the man: what are you going to do? Will you accuse me of being a whore in front of all these men?
She knew that her complexion had turned sickly
white. She felt a morbid sense of the inevitable, but
she refused to let him gloat further at her discomfort.

She said from her chair in a creditably calm voice,
"You must be Mr. ..." She stumbled on his name.
"Saxton, is it not? How do you do?" She started to
offer him her hand, and quickly withdrew it when
she saw he did not move to take it.

A thick black brow rose a good inch at the calm indifference in her voice. His gaze held hers for a moment, and he admitted to being impressed with her
bravado.

"Forgive me for being somewhat late," he drawled
in an insolent tone. "I should leave that prerogative
to the ladies, who so richly deserve it."

Damn you, she cursed at him silently. So that was
the course he was going to follow, at least for the
time being. "Forgive me, Mr. Saxton, for forgetting
your name ... a fault that is certainly more grave
than being a mere ten minutes late. But men in
business ..." She shrugged elaborately. "You seem to
look so much alike ... it is difficult sometimes to
keep names and faces straight."

"Then I shall have to be sufficiently memorable so
that you won't forget my name again, won't I ...
Giana?"

God in heaven, where had he heard her nickname! The cold-blooded bastard!

Thomas Hardesty observed their interchange with blank incredulity. What kind of perverse game were they playing? And why was Saxton deliberately insulting her?

Hammett Engles was staring at Alex as if he had lost his mind. He turned nervously to Raymond Ffalkes, and motioned him to be seated. He said to Alex, his voice taut, "Please, Alex, sit down. It is time to get to business."

"Business?" Alex drawled, flicking his eyes toward Giana. "Certainly it is always pleasant to while away a morning with a lovely . . . lady, or an evening. But business, my dear fellow?"

Giana felt a rush of crimson flood her cheeks. He was clearly going to continue toying with her, hoping, undoubtedly, that her composure would shatter. Dammit, she would not give him the pleasure!

She saw that of all the gentlemen only Drew wasn't flustered. He was glaring at Alex Saxton with narrowed, assessing eyes.

Giana said quickly, "Do not, I beg you, be offended, Drew. Mr. Saxton is, after all, an American, and doubtless he is unused to dealing with women."

But quite used to dealing with harlots, Alex's narrowed eyes said to her. Surely, she thought wildly, she could explain everything to him, make him understand that it had all been a mistake, a ghastly mistake.

"Business it is," Alex said aloud. "I have no other plans for the morning." He eased his powerful body down into a chair, crossed his long legs, managing to look insolently bored. "Well," he barked toward Ffalkes, "let's get on with it, man!"

Raymond Ffalkes tugged briefly at his cravat, noticing crazily as he did so that Saxton was not wearing a cravat, but rather the thin black tie newly in fashion. "As you know, gentlemen, ma'am," he began in a pompous tone, "this merger will be of ultimate benefit to both parties, and a particular boon to the Van Cleve interests." Giana stiffened at his condescension, wishing she but had her mother's poise and her wit. But her tongue lay dead in her mouth.

"Under Mr. Saxton's direction, I have prepared a summary of the gains to be realized by Van Cleve, gains, I might add, that render Mr. Saxton's offer more than generous." He looked down at the papers in a neat stack on the table, and extracted one of them. "If you will allow me to enumerate the profitability projections, based upon the active control to be exercised by Mr. Saxton's management."

Thomas Hardesty interposed calmly, "It is, of course, a point of negotiation, Mr. Ffalkes, as to the control such a merger would bring to Mr. Saxton." He looked toward Giana, and to his relief, she seemed perfectly in control of herself again. She said in response to his look, "Please continue, Mr. Ffalkes, with your discourse. I am certain we will find it most enlightening."

Despite herself, Giana gazed warily toward Alex Saxton. She stiffened in anger, for he was regarding her flippantly, as if he expected nothing she could possibly say to be of any importance. We shall shortly see, she thought, forcing her eyes back toward Mr. Ffalkes. "Let poor Raymond have all the rope he wants," her mother had said. "It is you, Giana, who have all you need to spring the trapdoor when he has wrapped it about his neck."

Mr. Ffalkes beamed. He had let Hammett Engles convince him that Miss Van Cleve, the little chit, was as sharp as a tack. He thought of his wife, Lenore, commiserating with him but that morning, shaking her gray head. "My poor dear, to be forced to sit through a meeting with a young woman! It is unheard of, and quite improper. I but hope that you can flatter her enough to please Mr. Saxton."

Giana let him drone on, citing his figures.

". . . and with the stowage of the twelve Van Cleve ships, and of course, taking into consideration the loss of the *Constant,* it would appear that—"

"Excuse me, Mr. Ffalkes," Giana interposed. "You have not accounted the present total cargo stowage of the twelve Van Cleve ships, merely projected an increase to eight thousand tons. Would you please tell me how you developed that figure?"

Raymond Ffalkes was mildly annoyed. "Just a moment, Miss Van Cleve, and I will give you the information." He shuffled through the papers and withdrew the ledger a clerk had prepared for him the previous week. "The stowage is currently thirty-eight hundred tons."

"How very odd, Mr. Ffalkes," Giana continued, as if perplexed. "I find it most gratifying that with a simple change in management, and the eventual addition of six ships, cargo space can be so impressively increased. Perhaps Mr. Saxton has developed a special technique to stretch a ship's hold?"

"No, Miss Van Cleve," Ffalkes snapped. "There must be an error here, yes, I'm afraid there has been an error."

"We can deal with your error later, Mr. Ffalkes," Giana said sweetly. "Pray continue."

Raymond Ffalkes faltered a moment, but gathered confidence again when Miss Van Cleve did not interrupt him. ". . . and the projected profit increase, based upon the expanded trade routes, falls in the range of thirty percent, or roughly one hundred thousand pounds per annum."

"Excuse me, Mr. Ffalkes," Giana said. "It is our un-

derstanding that we can reasonably expect to expand
our current shipping to China, not the more profitable
India trade. I believe if you will but recheck your figures with that in mind, you will find that the projected
increase is closer to fifteen percent, or fifty thousand
pounds per annum, accounting, of course, for any im-
provements Mr. Saxton's management may make."

Raymond Ffalkes turned a mottled red. Thomas
Hardesty hid his smile behind a quickly pulled handkerchief, wishing Aurora were present to hear her
daughter carry out her part. A look of unholy glee lit
Drew's sensitive face.

"Indeed, Mr. Ffalkes, I believe that if we are to begin our negotiations in earnest," Giana continued,
laying her hands palm down on the table, "I must request that you work with Mr. Engles or Mr. Saxton to
correct your estimates. I suggest we adjourn until
you have amended your reports. I bid you good
morning, gentlemen."

"Miss Van Cleve."

Giana drew to a halt at the sound of Alex Saxton's
silky voice behind her. She turned to look at him, her
heart thumping loudly in her breast.

"I believe," Alex said in a voice loud enough for
everyone to hear, "that you and I should discuss this
merger over dinner this evening. I will fetch you at
eight o'clock."

To Drew and Thomas' absolute astonishment,
Giana nodded.

"Very astute of you, my dear," he said, drawing
close to her. "There is much, is there not, for us to
discuss?"

Chapter 11

Aurora set aside the afternoon edition of the *Times* and smiled a welcome to her daughter.

Giana forced a smile in return. "You look miraculously recovered, Mama," she said. She thought her mother looked stunning, in fact, in her tea gown of soft yellow silk, her long hair braided in a coronet atop her head.

"It is fortunate for us the influenza is so very unpredictable, isn't it, Giana?" Aurora laughed. "Sit down, my love, and tell me all about the meeting and Mr. Saxton."

Giana walked to a spindle French chair and clutched at its back. She gazed abstractedly for a moment at a vase of exquisite red roses, sent, she knew, by his grace earlier in the day, before looking back at her mother. "The light guns performed well, I think. Another meeting with me, and the gentlemen should be ready for your entrance."

Aurora frowned at Giana's subdued tone. Thomas had told her that Giana's performance had been sterling, and she had expected her to be elated with her success. She noticed Giana was pale, too pale, and her eyes were overly bright. "Did something happen to upset you, Giana?"

"Upset me, Mother? Why, no." *You need not know any of it, Mother, until I know what he wants.*

"Raymond Ffalkes hung himself with a bit of assistance from me, just as we knew he would. I adjourned the meeting with queenly scorn, much to Thomas and Drew's amusement."

"I would have liked to see Raymond's reaction to being bested by a twenty-one-year-old girl! And what of Mr. Saxton? What is he like?"

He is a bastard! He toyed with me like a snake with a field mouse. "I believe," she said carefully, "that he was rather peeved with Ffalkes, but he did not interfere when I adjourned. Actually, everything happened just as we planned, even down to the figures we knew Mr. Ffalkes would use." She raised wary eyes to her mother's face. "I . . . I am having dinner with Mr. Saxton this evening," she said.

"You are dining with him," Aurora repeated stupidly.

"Yes, Mother."

Aurora regarded her lovely daughter, uncertain how she should respond to her bald announcement. In the past four years, she had watched Giana blossom into a beautiful young lady—the picture of herself, she thought without conceit, when she had been her daughter's age. But she had refused any social entanglements at all with gentlemen, preferring older men, like Thomas, for her escorts.

"I see," she said at last. "You like Mr. Saxton, then."

"We are dining together to discuss . . . American commerce, that is all."

"I see," Aurora said, not seeing at all. "Where are you dining?"

"I don't know. We did not discuss it."

"You must have a care, then, Giana. Since Mr. Saxton is not familiar with London, why do you not recommend the Albion or London Taverns? It is ridiculous that a lady may not dine anywhere she pleases in the company of a gentleman, but so it is."

He is no gentleman! He would likely take her to Soho, Giana thought, paling. After all, he believed her a whore—why would he not treat her like one?

"I should like to meet Mr. Saxton when he comes for you this evening," Aurora continued.

But he might tell you all about Rome! "He is really nothing out of the ordinary, Mother. Somewhat boring, actually."

"Still, if you would not mind. I promise not to talk business." Her eyes twinkled. "In fact, I will have to arrange to appear a trifle pale. After all, am I not a victim of the influenza?" As Giana did not answer her, Aurora continued lightly, "I have found that much headway can be made in private, say, over a dinner. That is perhaps why Mr. Saxton has invited you. I know you will keep your wits about you, Giana. Remember, the Van Cleves must retain control. Our merger with Mr. Saxton can exceed no more than forty percent, total value."

"Yes, Mother, I know." Giana looked away from her mother again, at the vase of roses. She wanted nothing more than to escape her mother's penetrating eye, to be alone to think about what she was to do.

"They are from Damien's hothouse at Graffton Manor," Aurora said, following her daughter's eyes. "Lovely, are they not? The duke will be dining here this evening. He will be sorry to miss you."

"Yes, certainly." Giana fidgeted with the brocade on the chair back. She had been worried for weeks about her mother's flirtation with the duke, and now her unease about the coming evening fashioned itself into anger. "You have seen a great deal of the duke in the past weeks, Mother. You have not told me if you are planning to marry him."

Aurora rose from her chair and drew her daughter to her, hugging her gently. "You did not seem to wish to speak of it, my love. He has asked me. Perhaps I have been carried away by that impossible man. I never know what he will say next, but what he does say is invariably charming. Perhaps I am in my dotage. I feel like I've known him for years."

"I don't understand you, Mother. Surely you, of all women, would not give up all you have to marry again. He would be your husband . . . just as was my father. You cannot to it, knowing what you know about men and marriage."

"He is not at all like your father, Giana, of that I am certain. Have you ever . . . desired a man, Giana, physically?"

Images of men, grunting and heaving over the girls at Madame Lucienne's brothel, careened through Giana's mind. All of them were repellent, all save one. The man who had bought her at the Flower Auction. "Yes, Mama," she said finally, "one man. It was not Randall Bennett."

"A man in Rome?"

"Yes."

"Then you will understand me when I tell you that I desire Damien as a woman desires a man. I had not realized how inward I had become over the years. I want Damien's voice, his touch, his caring. I want those things, Giana, for myself."

Giana shook away the memory of Alex Saxton in Rome, the memory of wanting him even in her fear. It frightened her.

"How can you give up all you have gained in the past fifteen years, Mother, all because of a ridiculous man who makes you blush like a silly schoolgirl?"

"Giana, I have told you that I am certain about him. He is honorable and loving. I trust him."

"That is like trusting one of the lions at the exhibition! He may toy with you for a time, for his amusement, but when he tires of you, he can tear you apart. I grant you that the duke is charming, wiser, perhaps, than other gentlemen. But you cannot believe that he treated his first wife with anything like mutual respect! She was a brood mare, a possession, and you know it. Did she not breed five or six children for him?"

Aurora heard the anger behind her daughter's words, anger that suddenly seemed too strong, too wrenching. She said gently, "Giana, we are raised to believe certain things, behave in certain ways. It is unfortunate that the laws give men such power over women—"

"Men made the bloody laws!"

"My marriage to Damien would probably mean that I would work all the harder," Aurora said lightly. "Damien fully intends that I conduct his affairs. I expect his man of business will have a fit when he discovers how things will be after I become the Duchess of Grafton. I love you, Giana, more than anyone else in the world. We would continue to be close, continue to work together. The only difference would be Damien, and I know that he would add to our lives, not take anything from us."

"Obviously, Mother, I cannot call upon Daniele to carry you off to Rome."

"Nor do you need to, Giana. I am forty-four years old and know what I want." She lightly touched her fingers to her daughter's hand. "I hope you too will find such a man as he, a man who will not try to subjugate you or own you."

Alex Saxton's dark face rose before her. "Not I,

Mother," she said in a broken voice. *You are a fool!*
"Forgive me, Mama. I doubt there is such a man as
you describe for me. I do want you to be happy, you
must believe me." She managed a crooked smile. "If
the duke ever upsets you, I will run him through
with a rapier."

Aurora had seen the myriad expressions flit across
her daughter's face before she replied with such
forced lightness. She sensed they had nothing to do
with her marriage to the Duke of Graffton.

"I shall dutifully warn him."

"I pray, Mother," Giana said, keeping her voice
even, "that the duke will be what you want. And you
needn't worry about me. I must change now,
Mother."

"I too, my love. Giana . . ."

"Yes, Mother?"

Aurora shook her head. "Nothing, my love, it will
keep."

"Mr. Saxton, Miss Giana."

Giana rose quickly and stood with her back
pressed against the mantelpiece. Alexander Saxton,
dressed quite correctly in formal black evening wear,
strode into the drawing room. She had not realized
he was so large. Even Lanson, who was built like a
bruiser, seemed dwarfed beside him.

"Mr. Saxton," she said in a cool voice.

He walked slowly across the room to her, his lips
tightening as he took in her attire. She thrust up her
chin at him. If it was his intention to treat her like a
harlot, she had decided she would not give him the
satisfaction of seeing her dressed like anything but a
dowd. She felt her spectacles slip down on her nose,
and pushed them back up.

"Miss Van Cleve," Alex said, coming to a halt be-

fore her. "How delightful you look." His eyes swept
from the severe spinsterish chignon at the top of her
head, past the glasses perched on her nose, and
down the expanse of mustard-brown silk to the slippers that peeped from below her hem, the only fashionable piece of apparel she wore. But he saw her too
as she had looked four years before, her soft breasts
bared to his eyes, her sooty black lashes fanned
against her white cheeks.

Giana flinched despite herself at his intimate gaze.
"My mother has requested to meet you, Mr. Saxton,"
she said unsteadily. "Would you care to follow me?"

"In a moment, Miss Van Cleve." Before she knew
what he was about, he pulled the glasses from her
nose. He ignored her gasp, and raised them to his
eyes. "Clear glass," he said aloud, and calmly tossed
them through the grate into the fireplace. "I recall
well what you look like, Giana," he said, quite con-
versationally. "The memory is vivid, in fact. Now, I
will give you thirty minutes to take yourself upstairs,
gown yourself appropriately, and rid yourself of the
ridiculous hairdo."

"I will do no such thing, Mr. Saxton! How dare
you give me orders!"

"Ah, you approve your appearance, then? It fits
your image of yourself?"

"It is none of your affair, sir!"

"I beg to differ with you, Miss Van Cleve, but it is
very much my affair." He saw that she was rigid
with anger, and said in a voice of dangerous calm, "If
you do not do as I say, Giana, you will regret it, I
promise you."

Giana, her cheeks crimson, whirled about, grasped
her full skirts in her hands, and fled the salon.

"Thirty minutes. It would be unwise of you to
keep me waiting," he called after her.

When Giana appeared precisely half an hour later, Alex was seated quite at his ease, a snifter of brandy in his hand. "Ah," he said, "much better. How very innocent you look, my dear, every inch the young lady."

Abigail, Giana's maid, had expertly brushed out the thick chignon and braided her hair into a coronet atop her head. She had tugged wisps of curling black hair to fall over her forehead and tumble over her ears, a style, she had informed Giana tartly, that went with her young years. She had planted a diamond-and-emerald necklace about her neck, and fitted her with a gown of pale yellow taffeta that hugged her narrow waist and fell in graceful folds over her petticoats.

"Now, my dear, let us not keep your mother waiting longer. I trust she is feeling better?"

"Yes, much better." Giana felt herself pale under his insolent gaze. "You will not," she began, "that is—"

He cut her off. "Tell Mrs. Van Cleve that her charming, innocent daughter enjoys playing the harlot? I am relieved that she doesn't know. If you do as I tell you, there is no reason for you to worry."

He walked beside her up the wide staircase. "Or does your mother know all about your . . . little games? Perhaps she is even proud of you . . . or like you?"

Giana jerked around to face him and struck the flat of her hand against his cheek. He caught her wrist and bore it back to her side so roughly that she gasped aloud. "I will add that to your bill," he said.

One of the most imposing men Aurora had ever seen opened the door to her sitting room for her daughter. She quickly took in his broad shoulders beneath his elegant evening wear, the lithe grace of his hips and long, muscular legs. His black hair was as inky as Giana's, but his eyes were vivid and long-lashed, dark brown, almost black, and at the moment, regarding her as openly as she was him. Was this why Giana agreed to spend the evening with him? Was she taken with his masculine grace despite herself? But Giana had said he was nothing out of the ordinary, that he was boring, in fact.

"Mrs. Van Cleve," he said in a deep, pleasant voice.

"Pray come no closer, Mr. Saxton," Aurora said from her reclining pose on her daybed. "I would not want you to come down with my stupid complaint. Giana, my love, you look charming."

"Thank you, Mother," Giana said in a flat voice.

"Giana tells me, Mr. Saxton, that Raymond Ffalkes was somewhat remiss in his presentation at your meeting this morning. I have never believed it wise to leave such details to solicitors and accountants. They seem to ... underestimate people."

Alex's rich laughter made Aurora start. She glanced quickly at Giana. My Lord, she thought, he is a splendid animal.

"Yes, ma'am," Alex said, his dark eyes crinkled in amusement. "I have told him firmly that I do not pay him to think or to judge my business ... opponents, merely to provide accurate information. I trust you will find him more worthy at our next meeting. Indeed, ma'am, you look very nearly healthy. Perhaps you will be present?"

Aurora smiled pleasantly. "That remains to be seen. But surely you do not consider the Van Cleves opponents, sir! We both want the same things, I am sure. A merger that will benefit us all. This is your first trip to England, Mr. Saxton?"

"Indeed it is, ma'am. I hope to have our business

complete by the end of the week, and then enjoy myself."

"It will be up to your associates, I believe, to expedite our dealings. Is your daughter traveling with you, Mr. Saxton?"

"No, Mrs. Van Cleve, Leah is safely ensconced in New York with her governess. The child is too young as yet to appreciate the . . . delights of travel."

Aurora coughed, as if on cue, and Giana said suddenly, "You have had enough . . . tiring conversation for one evening, Mother."

"I trust," Alex said smoothly, "that you do not equate tiring with boring, Miss Van Cleve."

"My mother is ill, sir!"

"I begin to think myself the daughter being scolded by a fond mother," Aurora said, filling in the naked gap left by her daughter's outburst. "Where will you go to dinner?"

"To the Albion," Giana said, gazing stone-faced toward Alex.

"Indeed, I had decided upon the London Taverns, but no matter. It has been a pleasure meeting you, Mrs. Van Cleve. I hope for your speedy recovery."

"Thank you for your concern, Mr. Saxton. I hope you will not be too late, Giana. Tomorrow is a full day, is it not?"

"I am relieved you have dressed like a young lady," he said as he assisted Giana into the hired carriage outside. "I was half-afraid you would change into something more suited to your . . . profession." He ignored her gasp. "Or is business so good that you can play at being a lady with the gentlemen you deal with? There must be many men," he continued, as if musing loud, "to choose from in the world of business."

"You are an insufferable jackass! London will not miss your like when you take your leave."

"But I will be well remembered, Giana, you may count on that, at least by you."

He was answered with stark silence. He grinned into the darkness and sat back comfortably.

Dark rain clouds hung low in the sky and the air was damp and chilly. Giana hugged herself against the carriage door and concentrated on the clip-clop of the horse's hooves over the cobblestones until the carriage turned onto Great Russell Street and came to a halt before the elegantly facaded Albion.

"I was delighted at your selection of restaurants. I was rather afraid I would be thrust willy-nilly into the more unsavory side of London. There are so few places, are there not, where a lady may take a gentleman to dine without destroying his reputation?"

He assisted her to step down from the carriage, paid the driver, and escorted her, his hand cupping her elbow, into the Albion.

"Ah, Mr. Saxton," Henri, the maître d' said as he expertly divested Giana of her shawl and Alex of his hat and cane. "Mr. Engles told me to expect you, sir. Do follow me, *monsieur, mademoiselle,* I have arranged your private room, as you requested. And the turtle, it is divinity itself this evening."

"I thought you made plans at the London Taverns," Giana said through her teeth as they followed the debonair Henri into their magnificent private room.

"I told you that it mattered little to me, Giana. Are you disappointed that Henri dashed your hopes and accorded me a royal welcome? Wealth and power grant many privileges ... even to brash Americans."

Giana sat stiffly in her chair as Alexander Saxton ordered a claret, Château Margaux, 1844, from their waiter. When the claret arrived, Saxton described the full-bodied wine in fluent detail to the beaming waiter, all in flawless French.

"To our renewed . . . acquaintance," Alex said.

Giana glared at him, not touching her glass.

Alex ordered for both of them, without even asking her what she preferred, and sat back, regarding her thoughtfully. Giana waited until their waiter was at the door, and coolly called him back. "I do not care for the salmon Indienne, nor the new potatoes."

The waiter cast an uncertain eye toward Alex.

"What would you prefer, Miss Van Cleve?" Alex asked, smiling a bit at her show of defiance.

"The mutton soubise, if you please and the asparagus. The St. Cloud pudding and the sparking champagne, iced. I do not care for the claret. It is too heavy."

Alex nodded toward the harassed waiter, and sat back in his chair, crossing his arms over his broad chest.

"I was not aware you had even tasted the claret, but no matter. You did indeed make quite an ass of Ffalkes this morning. He thought it was premeditated, of course, called you a cold-blooded bitch and the like, which we both know is anything but the truth." He saw her blue eyes flash. "Had you been a man, he would of course have admired your cunning. I gather Mr. Ffalkes is not one of your customers."

Giana's eyes fell to her dinner knife, and she found herself clutching it like a weapon. He laughed dryly. "Do not, I beg you, stab me here. It is you who could not afford the scandal, Giana." He added thoughtfully, "It will be quite interesting to find out how you managed it. I even find myself wondering if your mother was really ill."

"I don't know what you mean."

"Really? The way Ffalkes was braying on, even I would not have grasped what he was saying and not saying if I had not had, shall we say, prior information. The others, Engles included, did not realize it. A clerk, I assume, who works for Mr. Ffalkes gave you a preview?"

Gina dropped the dinner knife. "Obviously I will not tell you, Mr. Saxton, any of my sources of information. As for my mother, I was glad to see how well she looked this evening." She looked as if she would have continued, but the waiter returned, bearing a tureen of turtle soup.

Giana stared down at the soup and felt her stomach knot in protest. She watched Alex eat heartily, a look of pure loathing on her face.

"If looks could kill, I most certainly would be dead meat by now," he said, grinning at her as he spooned up the last bit.

"Let up stop this ridiculous fencing, Mr. Saxton. It is obvious that it is your intent to blackmail me and my mother. What is your price? Do you hope the Van Cleve shipyards and ships will be turned over without a sou to you?"

He appeared to study her, turning her words over in his mind. "Do not deny me the upper hand, Miss Van Cleve," he said. "Allow me my fencing time with you. It is to your benefit, I assure you, for it lessens my anger at you. I have cursed myself so many times during the past four years, cursed myself for not examining you myself in front of all the other buyers, stripping you naked and thrusting my finger inside you. You can still blush. How very charming." He suddenly sat forward in his chair and tapped the tips of his fingers together thoughtfully. "Indeed, I was a fool, for likely I would have discovered that you were anything but a virgin even then. At fifteen years old, Giana?"

"I was seventeen!"

"Ah yes, I remember now your telling me that. You know, the only fact I bothered discovering about you, the famous Aurora Van Cleve's daughter, was that you were in an exclusive young ladies' seminary in Switzerland until you were seventeen. Surely you can imagine my surprise when I first saw you, the little harlot who had bested me. Was it your habit to travel to Rome during your holidays for your amusement? Rich young ladies, I suppose, do get bored and crave excitement. Your, shall we say, solution was most unusual. Perhaps you fell in with an . . . unusual lover in Rome, Giana. Was it that disgusting old man I saw eyeing you at the Flower Auction, the one who forced my hand by bidding that outrageous amount for your nonexistent maidenhead?"

Giana closed her eyes against his words. "You have insulted me enough, Mr. Saxton. Only one thing you have said is true. I did attend Madame Orlie's seminary in Geneva."

"Ah, and you were not in Rome playing the harlot that summer? Do you plan to deny that?"

"You must believe me, it was all a ghastly mistake. I am not, and never have been, what you think. What can I do to convince you that I am not a . . . harlot?"

"There is something," he said, "only one thing you can do."

Giana's eyes flew to his face, suddenly hopeful. "What?"

"You can give me your virginity," he said in a bored drawl.

She wanted to scream at him. Tears stung her eyes, and she resolutely blinked them away.

"Go ahead, Mr. Saxton," she said as calmly as she

could. "Vent your anger. Relieve your spleen, if you must, though I should prefer that you choke on it."

"You will cease your insults and your playacting, Giana, though in all honesty you are really quite good. Perhaps even now you could have convinced me, my dear, but you see, I remember." His voice became hard with cold anger. "It took me some time, but I finally remembered seeing you at Madame Lucienne's. You were standing in the shadows behind a marvelously nude statue and a potted fern. You were wearing a blond wig that time, and it was long before the Flower Auction. You see, I was drawn to you even then. I wondered if you visited the Flower Auction each time it was held to pick the likeliest stranger for your plucking. How well you read my attraction to you. You were even certain that I, unlike some of the other gentlemen there, would not demand to examine you for your valuable maidenhead. No, my dear, aghast expressions and trembling denials will not do. I looked for you, you see, you and that old bastard, but I gathered you realized I wasn't a man to take such blatant robbery quietly, and went into hiding. It was wise of you, for it would have given me great pleasure to thrash you within an inch of your life. There is much you owe me, Giana, and you may be certain that I will be paid in full."

"Two thousand dollars," Giana whispered. "I will repay you. You must believe me, it was not what you think. It was all a mistake." Alex gave a crack of rude laughter. "You will certainly pay, Miss Van Cleve, but I have no interest in the money."

"Stop it!" Giana cried, slapping her hands over her ears. She removed them quickly when the waiter appeared with their dinner.

She waited in silence until they were alone again.

"You will stop talking to me like this, Mr. Saxton. You are vicious and cruel and I will have no more of it. I have promised to repay you."

"As I told you, Miss Van Cleve, you will most certainly repay me. I am quite used to getting value for my money. And when an adversary breaks the rules, I react in kind. So save your mewling protests, my dear, you but anger me."

Giana stared down at her mutton, then raised a pale face and said unexpectedly, "You struck me. . . . I was struggling with you because I was terribly frightened, even though you refuse to believe me."

He did not reply immediately, seemingly intent on savoring the tender salmon. "It was then I discovered you have very lovely breasts, Giana," he said, his eyes falling to her heaving bosom. "If your accomplice hadn't been so efficient, I would have found out for myself that I held no virgin in my arms, but as it was, I discovered only that you were wearing undergarments. Such a nuisance to caress a woman wearing so damned many layers of clothes. But you have become even more beautiful in the years we have been apart. You have the body of a woman now. I have never preferred girls, no matter how skilled they are."

Giana lurched to her feet, clutching her reticule. "I want to go home now! I will not listen to you any longer!"

"Sit down and try at least to eat some of your dinner. You are too well known to attempt racing out of here without my escort. Besides, you would not have come unless you were curious about what it is I want. I have not yet told you."

Giana eased back down into her chair, eyeing him warily.

"I have come to a decision," he said presently, as if

discussing a business matter. "You asked me if I intended to blackmail you and your mother. I consider it a waste of my time, in general, to play at business with a girl, but your performance this morning piqued my curiosity. I will not blackmail you in our business dealings—indeed, I would find no amusement in that. I will tell you what I will expect of you tomorrow afternoon when you visit Kew Gardens with me. Do not again dress the dowd, Giana."

She knew what he wanted now. He was simply gloating, amusing himself with her. *Tell him the truth!* "Mr. Saxton," she said evenly, "I was in Rome four years ago, it is true, but not by my own choice! I did nothing, I swear it, nothing save . . . observe."

A thick black brow rose. "Ah, a young lady learning about sex by sitting in a brothel? An interesting finish to a girl's education."

"I did not wish to be there, you must believe me, and stop this nonsense."

"Giana," he said quietly, "I have told you there is but one way you can prove yourself to me, and your unbelievable story."

She forced herself to look him squarely in the eye. "I am a virgin, Mr. Saxton, no matter what you think."

"Excellent," he said, appearing to be much diverted. "I have not enjoyed a virgin in quite a long time. Indeed, I believe my last virgin was a charming young lass in Paris some two years ago. And she did not cost me two thousand dollars."

"Damn you, I did nothing! I was forced to attend the Flower Auction, just as I was forced to be in Madame Lucienne's brothel. I have told you that I will give you back your two thousand dollars! You may purchase as many virgins in London as you wish!"

"Oh no," he said easily, his fingers lightly caressing her arm, "I fancy a more skilled partner. Virgins can be a deuced nuisance. They know nothing of how to please a man, much less themselves. You, I know, will please me admirably."

She jerked her arm away, as if his warm fingers burned her flesh.

"Very well, Mr. Saxton," she said, drawing a calming breath. "You would not know the truth if it smashed you in your smug face. The Van Cleves are quite wealthy, sir, as I am certain you know. We are also possessed of some power. If you wish to spread it all about London that Georgiana Van Cleve is a harlot, I have decided that you should do so. In short, Mr. Saxton, you can go to hell. My reputation will survive. The wealthy and powerful always survive, but I am certain you know that from personal experience. Did you not survive the scandal caused by your wife's supposed accident?"

His face paled and he stared at her a moment, calming himself, she supposed. She felt a moment of elation. Then he smiled, a cruel smile.

"No," he said slowly, his eyes hard upon her face. "My wife, Laura, did not die accidentally."

"Ah, so your poor wife chanced to displease you, Mr. Saxton? Did she see you for the ruthless man you are? Or perhaps hated you because you were unfaithful to her? How many brothels did you visit, how many mistresses did you keep while she was alive? I would imagine it is not terribly difficult to arrange a boating accident."

"No," he said again, a brief glimmer of pain shadowing his eyes, "it would not be difficult. But, my dear, that is all ancient history, and none of your business."

He shook away the anger and pain the memory of

his wife still brought him, and said in a carefully controlled voice, "Let me say that your bravado about not fearing any scandal I might raise is very affecting. I do not doubt that if things were different, my announcement would do you little harm. But there is something else to consider, is there not? It is all over London that your beautiful mother is being courted by the Duke of Graffton. You cannot tell me that such a blue-blooded peer of her majesty's realm would stomach such scandal. Ah, I see that you at last understand. What would the dear duke say if he knew that his future wife and stepdaughter would never be received in his circle?" He smiled widely into her white face and drawled softly, "You know of course what I will demand. Make up your mind to it, my dear, for I will have you, and willingly, until I am tired of you. If you insult me further, I may even take you for my permanent mistress whenever I visit London."

It was odd, Giana thought, with almost blank disinterest, how the devil had come to claim his own. She thought of the angry words she had hurled at her mother that very afternoon, and flinched. She realized that whatever she did, she could not tell Aurora. Aurora Van Cleve would tell Saxton to hie himself to the devil, regardless of what his story would do to them. And there was the merger. Would Saxton risk that as well?

She said in a surprisingly calm voice, "Is your little revenge so important to you that you would risk the merger?"

"Our dealings have nothing to do with the merger," he said, still smiling. "Indeed, you know as well as I that the Van Cleves need this merger more than I do. If anything happens, Miss Van Cleve, it will be your doing, not mine." He shrugged. "Do not repine. It is likely that I will but improve your skills, and you will not find me a selfish lover. Would you prefer a man like Raymond Ffalkes, paunchy and short, a man who likely sweats like a pig in heat?"

"I hate you," she said in a weary voice. She looked down at the congealed mutton on her plate. "I am quite finished with my dinner, Mr. Saxton. I would like to leave now."

He tossed his napkin on the table and obligingly rose.

He knows he's won, Giana thought, damn him!

"I wish you luck in our merger negotiations, Miss Van Cleve," Alexander Saxton said smoothly as their carriage stopped in Belgrave Square. "It is your business wits against mine. But about our other business, you have until Friday." He shepherded her up the wide steps to the Van Cleve mansion. "Until tomorrow morning, then, my dear," he said.

She turned to face him, and Alex gazed for a moment into her wide midnight-blue eyes. He quickly cupped her chin between his thumb and forefinger and pressed his lips to hers. He suddenly released her, wincing at the pain in his shin.

"I know," she said harshly to him, wiping her hand across her mouth to erase the touch of him, "you will add that to my bill!"

He rubbed his kicked shin against his other calf. "You may be certain that I shall," he said, and turned away from her, whistling as he strode back toward his carriage.

Chapter 12

"Gentlemen," Alex said, rising from his chair, "you will excuse us now. Miss Van Cleve and I have made plans to visit Kew Gardens. My dear?"

Drew watched in astonishment as Giana docilely rose to stand beside him. "You will not then be accompanying me to the exhibition, Miss Van Cleve?" he asked.

"Perhaps next week, Drew," she said, having, in all truth, forgotten about the exhibition. "Mr. Saxton is a visitor to our country, and I feel it my duty to show him about a bit."

"I trust you will all have time to enjoy her . . . company after I've left England," Alex drawled.

As Drew watched Mr. Saxton escort Giana to the door, his hand lightly upon her back, he wondered if perhaps she was fascinated by his American bluntness. Odd to see her so pleasant to the man now when she had given him Dutch coin all morning.

Forty-five minutes later, Alex was handing Giana onto the cruise boat *Billy* that would ferry them up the Thames to Kew Gardens. He stared toward London Bridge for a moment, thankful for the occasional sunny day in the London summer, and turned mocking eyes to Giana.

"It has been quite an eventful day already, Giana. But don't you think you pushed a bit hard this morn-

ing? You need capital and my ships, and your shipyards in Portsmouth have fallen markedly in production since you invested so heavily in the Midlands
Railroad. It has also come to my attention that you
are having difficulty obtaining the lumber for building, and that, too, is a problem solved once we agree
to terms."

"You are repeating yourself, Mr. Saxton," Giana
said.

"Am I? You distress me, Miss Van Cleve. I would
like to charm you out of your sullens, if you would
know the truth."

"You are a blackguard, sir!"

"Actually, Giana," he drawled, giving her a caressing smile, "I have rarely felt so completely justified in
my actions. If you would but be honest with yourself
just once, you would cease spitting at me and draw
in your claws."

"I am honest with myself, Mr. Saxton. It is you
who refuse to believe the truth." She gazed at him
curiously. "Do I look like a harlot, sir?"

"Thank God, no. If you did, I likely wouldn't want
you."

It occurred to Giana that her protestations of innocence but whetted his appetite. She sighed. She could
not very well play the harlot now. It would only add
to his amusement.

"I would that you simply think of our coming together as payment, long overdue. Why not just think
about the pleasure we will share? I think I can make
you forget, at least for a while, how much you wish
to scratch my eyes out."

He touched his hand gently to her shoulder, and
she pulled away to the railing of the boat.

"You have no reason to fear me, Giana. It will not
hurt." He sighed soulfully, his eyes crinkling with

amusement. "Such a pity that I even now have to guess at the whiteness of your slender thighs and the beauty between them."

"Stop it! Damn you, stop it!"

"Ah, the virgin act again. Well, you may play at what you will for the next two days."

Giana turned on her heel, her face white beneath her straw bonnet. She jostled her way through the tourists chattering all about her to the far stern of the boat, and stared down into the churning, dirty water of the Thames.

She felt his hand close over her arm. Why did he make her feel so very warm? She asked coldly, wanting to distract him, "Why do you wish to visit Kew Gardens?"

"I grow flowers, and some of the most exotic in the world are tended there." He grinned down at her. "You find that so unusual, Miss Van Cleve? Actually, I have a particular affinity for the family *Orchidaceae.* The word is from the Greek *orchis,* which actually means 'testicle.' I see from your outraged expression that you did not know that. Well, in any case, you can relax in the knowledge that I will not try to make love to you all afternoon. Today, my dear, you are simply a delightful ornament for my arm. When you are with me, I know at least that you cannot plot dastardly schemes. I presume you are familiar with Kew Gardens so that I may count you as my guide?"

Giana was somewhat familiar with the famous gardens. At least she admired their lovely ponds with the graceful swans crisscrossing the water.

"That would be preferable, Mr. Saxton, to listening to your braying," she said acidly.

Alex answered her with ready laughter. "It delights me that you do not affect die-away airs, Giana. Indeed, you are a most amusing companion."

Doesn't he know how to take offense? she wondered. *Why should he bother himself when he knows he has won?*

"I trust your skill in bed rivals your wit."

His voice was caressingly soft. Despite herself, the stark image of him as he had looked with Margot rose to her mind. Margot, writhing and crying out in mewling whispers, as he thrust his hard-muscled belly and hips against her. *Margot enjoyed him . . . no act, that.*

"What troubles you, sweetheart? You look lost in a dream. I can but hope that I am in it with you."

"The only place I wish you to be, Mr. Saxton, is with the devil!"

But her cheeks flushed, telling him he had caught her in a lie. "As intimate as we will be, Giana, would you not begin to call me Alex? When you moan my name with pleasure, you'll find 'Mr. Saxton' won't do at all."

"You will find out soon enough, *Mr. Saxton*, what names I think appropriate for you."

As they strolled through the wide lanes that cut through the gardens, he held her hand tucked firmly in the crook of his arm. Giana discovered he was appallingly knowledgeable, spouting out Latin names as readily as he had French wines. He lost interest in her lessons when they reached the glassed hothouse where the orchids were tended. She felt somewhat put out when he struck up a long conversation with the gardener who cared for the delicate flowers, and spent nearly two hours reverently leaning over the blossoms, extolling their beauty more to himself than to anyone else present. They had to practically run to catch the last boat back to London.

"I hope you enjoyed yourself," she growled at him when they at last scrambled onto the boat.

"Indeed, my dear. In fact, I am tempted to leave business discussions to Raymond and Hammett tomorrow. Edward Blakeson, the gardener I was talking to, has agreed to show me more of his methods so I may improve my luck with my orchids in Connecticut. They are quite delicate, you know, more so than a woman. And of course their care is quite different." He paused a moment, grinning down into her stone-set face. "I hope that I may learn how to care for them as well as I care for women."

"Your . . . innuendos are not amusing, Mr. Saxton."

"You wish me to speak more bluntly, then? Surely you know that the thought of holding you in my arms, of kissing your soft mouth, Miss Van Cleve, makes me tense with anticipation."

"I would prefer you not to speak at all," she muttered, pulling her fingers away from his caressing hand. "You do not desire me, you want only your petty revenge!"

"You are really quite wrong. I will be pleased to prove that to you."

"I do not want you to prove anything, Mr. Saxton. I only want you to leave me alone and leave London."

He stroked his fingertips over her open palm. "Odd," he said thoughtfully, gazing into her eyes, "you seem to tremble when I touch you."

Giana snatched her hand away. "Please," she whispered.

"Please what, my dear? Dare I guess?"

"Go to the devil!"

"Perhaps I *am* the devil," he said, his eyes alight with laughter. "When next I kiss you, Giana, I would appreciate your leaving off the violence. My shin still aches. I suppose I should be grateful that you did not kick me elsewhere."

She frowned at him, helpless to dampen his good humor, and fell into a brooding silence. She was terribly aware of how close he was standing at casual ease beside her. *Who is there to know or care if I give my virginity to him? I am twenty-one, no longer a silly schoolgirl.* She started, aghast at herself. Damn him!

"I wish you would stop teasing me!" she blurted out. "And you are so damned big, I cannot see past you!"

He stepped behind her and gently drew her back against him. "Is this better?"

She imagined her naked hips pressed against his belly, and blanched at the shiver of pleasure it brought her. "It is not!" she nearly shouted at him. She turned crimson at the interested stares of their fellow passengers.

"Then you will have to tell me what you like, my dear," he said easily, letting her go. "A man's pleasure is very much bound to his woman's. Oh, I forgot to tell you. We will be leaving Friday by train to Folkestone. I have procured us a lovely house at the strand. Do make whatever arrangements you must with your dear mother."

To Giana's surprise, her mother was awaiting her downstairs, beautifully gowned. "The duke," she said, smiling, "is to join us again for dinner. He was disappointed you were not here last night, and insisted upon seeing you, *en famille.*"

"That is nice," Giana said, her voice abstracted.

Aurora watched her daughter jerk off her gloves and pace about like the tigers at the exhibition. "I trust you enjoyed your outing with Mr. Saxton," she said lightly. "Where did you go?"

"No, I did not, and it was Kew Gardens."

"Then why did you agree to see him again? And

why Kew Gardens? Surely there are more amusing places for a visitor in London, particularly a gentleman."

"He likes flowers," she said flatly. "When is the duke expected?"

"Soon. Incidentally, Giana, Thomas visited me this afternoon, filled with praises for you. He said he had never seen you so . . . engaged."

"The merger is important," Giana said. "And I have no intention of giving that man anything."

"Well, that is certainly good business."

"Mother, I have decided to leave London for a while. A school friend of mine has invited me to . . . Folkestone."

"I see," Aurora said, not seeing at all. "When do you intend to leave?"

"On Friday afternoon."

"And your return?"

"I . . . I am not quite certain."

"And your friend's name? In case I need to get in touch with you."

"Blakeson," Giana said, the gardener's name at Kew Gardens. "The Edward Blakesons. I will be met at the station in Folkestone and do not know their address."

"Do you wish Abigail to accompany you?"

"No! That is, it is not necessary. Susan Blakeson, my friend, will certainly share her maid with me."

"His grace, the Duke of Graffton, madam," Lanson announced from the doorway.

"It took a duke to make Lanson pretentious," Aurora said under her breath to Giana. She rose and shook out her skirts. "Show the duke in," she said.

The duke's eyes, Giana saw, were glued to her mother, alight with pleasure. The ruby signet ring on his third finger flashed brightly as he brought Aurora's hand to his lips.

"Must we really wait until our wedding night, my love?" he whispered against her ear.

"No," Aurora said.

"Little baggage," he murmured. He turned to Giana, who was fiddling awkwardly with a Sèvres figurine. "Forgive my abstraction with your beautiful mother, my child, But surely you cannot blame me."

"Good evening, sir," Giana said, taking in her mother's besotted gaze. "No, sir, I cannot blame you."

"We see eye to eye. Well, Giana, I understand you had quite a day."

" 'Twas but more of the same, sir," she said with sublime disregard for the truth. "Your days are always far more interesting."

The duke looked mournful. "Today I tried to tell that damned son of mine, Edward, you know, that you, dear Giana, are far too intelligent and much too discerning to have anything to do with a pompous oaf like him. He is persuaded you would make him a superb wife."

Giana started, then laughed, unable to help herself. "You are jesting, sir! Come, Edward is much enamored with Lady Arabella Lawton."

"True, I have been found out. But at least your face is now sunny, my dear. Life is far too short to take too many things seriously. If one cannot smile, one might as well cock up his toes."

"Smile in the face of overwhelming adversity. That is your advice, your philosophy, sir?"

"You may be certain, Giana, that now that I have found your mother, I shall die with a happy smile on my vacuous face. Now, ladies, I am famished. Is dinner to be served soon?"

"Dinner is already served, and you have two arms, your grace."

"To my profound relief, my dear."

Chapter 13

Euston Station was hot, a press of milling travelers, harried porters, and shouting hawkers. "Some things are the same everywhere," Alex said to Giana. "There's our train, I believe." Giana weaved where she stood. He grasped her elbow and she blinked away her dizziness, locking her knees beneath her.

"Should I take that as a compliment, Giana? Are you so overwhelmed that you are thinking of fainting on me?" At her angry gasp, he continued heartily, "Do wait, my dear, until I have you safely within. Ah, here is our porter."

"Your wife is ill, sir?" the porter asked.

"My wife? Just a bit faint from the heat." He gazed down at her, smiling widely. "She will feel much better presently."

Alex assisted her into their private car, made room for the porter to place their luggage on the racks above their seats, and settled himself comfortably down beside her.

He gave her an engaging grin. "Come, Giana, surely I am not such a bad bargain? I wish you would admit you are not so averse to our little adventure."

Little adventure? That was what he thought of it?

The whistle sounded shrilly, and the train jerked

slowly forward, its stacks billowing clouds of black soot.

Are you insane? "No!" she shouted, grasping frantically at the door handle. "I will not go with you!"

Alex grabbed her arm and pulled her, squirming, against him. "Hush," be said in a surprisingly gentle voice. "You are just nervous. It will pass."

"I hate you," she said against his shoulder.

"Do remember you said that when you are in my arms tonight. It will give me pleasure to remind you." He regarded her flushed face a moment, a thick black brow arched upward. His voice became a caressing drawl. "You want me, you know. Whenever I touch you I feel you respond to me. You tremble delightfully. And your bonnet is askew."

Giana pulled away from him and righted her plum-trimmed straw bonnet. She felt oddly weak and closed her eyes against a pain in her temple.

Alex watched her as she sat stiffly, staring straight in front of her, her cheeks flushed and her fists clenched in her lap. He could not for the life of him figure out why she was still acting the outraged maiden.

"It will be some years before you equal your mother," he said after a while. "Indeed," he continued thoughtfully, "I do believe I have given on more points to her than I had intended. A remarkable woman, your mother. But then, she has only Van Cleve interests to think about."

"She wishes to meet with you again on Monday."

"Then we will have only three nights together, my love. No matter, there will be other nights, and days too. I enjoy making love in the sunlight, though there doesn't ever appear to be any in London. Do you?"

"No," she said shortly, presenting him with her taut profile again.

"Yes, indeed," he mused aloud. "Aurora Van Cleve

is most remarkable. I see now why Raymond and Hammett were leery about dealing with her. You lack her charm, Giana, but perhaps I am not being fair. Are you exquisitely charming to other men?"

"No," she said.

"Your mother even laughs charmingly. I have yet to hear you laugh, Giana."

"You never will."

"I begin to believe that unless I wish to carry on a monologue all the way to Folkestone, I might as well take a nap and garner my strength. Do rouse me if you wish to become more communicative." He folded his arms over his chest, stretched out his long legs, and closed his eyes. Within minutes, he was snoring.

Giana refused to admit to herself until the porter announced Canterbury that she was ill. She pressed her palms against her cheeks and they were hot to the touch. Her throat felt scratchy and her headache was now a steady pounding. She wanted to laugh, but tears burned her eyes instead. She stared over at Alexander Saxton, peacefully sleeping. Wild thoughts careened through her mind. She could cosh him over the head with her valise. She could strangle him with one of her silk stockings and chuck his body from the moving train. At least it would stop his miserable snoring! *Insensitive clod!*

She was ill. Surely he would not want to make love to her if he knew. She reached a hand to his shoulder, then withdrew it. She could easily picture the unfeeling brute regarding her with amused disbelief if she told him she was sick. He would likely laugh and ask if she had any better tricks to try. She tried to focus her mind, but her head seemed to be spinning. She closed her eyes, and when next she was aware, the train was slowing. They were coming into Folkestone.

The porter rapped on their compartment door and opened it.

"Folkstone," he said, eyeing the slouched gentleman.

Alex gave him a wide smile. "Excellent. At last, my love!" He reached over and patted Giana's gloved hand intimately.

The porter gave him a disgusting answering grin, almost a leer.

"Forgive me, Giana, for being such a boring fellow and sleeping the whole journey. I promise that you will have my full attention for the next three days." He yawned and stretched his lithe body. "I allowed myself to see the more interesting side of London last night in Raymond's company."

"I hope that you have caught some vile disease."

"You will learn, Giana, that I am most fastidious. Indeed, that is the last fate you should wish for me," he added on a mocking grin. "Such vile diseases are catching, you know."

Giana allowed Alex to bundle her into a closed carriage and pull its worn wool rug over her legs. She stared out the carriage window as the horse clip-clopped through the quiet streets. She had always liked Folkestone, until now. She sat weakly against the moldering leather squabs, listening to the pounding in her head, and ignoring Alexander Saxton.

The carriage drew to a halt in front of a small whitewashed cottage surrounded by a low wooden fence. There was a slight misty drizzle, and Giana raised her face to it as Alex helped her down from the carriage. She suddenly realized that she was thirsty, terribly thirsty.

She said as much to Alex when he ushered her into the cozy front parlor of the cottage.

"I am too," he said somewhat ruefully. "First things first. Sit down, Giana, and I'll set the fire."

She could think of nothing else to do, and sank down onto a chintz sofa. There were light dimity curtains on the windows, and thick wool rugs scattered on the floor, held in place by the heavy mahogany legs of solid chairs and side tables. It was a comfortable room, and she did not want to leave it. She did not want to think about the bedroom.

"I'm hungry," she said hopefully.

Alex turned, his task completed, and said cheerfully, "I will give you the biggest supper you can hold, my dear, but not just yet. Think of how romantic it will be to drink champagne and eat a late supper before the fire. A very late supper."

Suddenly she wasn't hungry at all. She lurched to her feet and dashed her hand over her forehead. "I don't want any supper," she said stupidly.

"When it came down to it," he drawled, "somehow I did not think you would mind waiting for your dinner."

"That is not what I meant!" Her voice sounded slurred and low, completely unlike her. The fire was blazing brightly, and yet she felt herself shivering. She walked toward the welcoming fireplace to warm herself.

"Take off your cloak and bonnet, Giana."

She did so, her fingers clumsy and awkward. He helped he, tossing the garments to the sofa.

She felt his hands on her shoulders, and jumped. He was turning her toward him, molding her against his body. His hands were caressing her arms, and she felt a warmth in her body—whether because of him, she did not know. *Tell him again that you are a virgin. Tell him that you are ill.* But her only protest was a soft moan from deep in her throat. *No, do not tell him anything.*

Alex looked down into her glazed eyes. Her cheeks

were becomingly flushed, her lips slightly parted. He felt her hands pressing against his chest. "Relax, love," he said gently. Slowly he lowered his mouth to hers. She tasted warm, he thought crazily, delectably warm, the heat of her passion welling up to him. He felt her lips tremble, and when his tongue slipped into her mouth, he felt her start, as if surprised. He closed his arms tightly about her back and drew her against him, exploring her mouth with his tongue just as he would her warm belly. He left her mouth and kissed her eyes, her cheeks, her throat.

"Alex," she said uncertainly, trying to draw back from him. "I am thirsty. Please."

Alex was trembling, and did not heed her soft voice for a moment. He wanted her desperately, and it surprised him. He was mauling her like an untried boy.

"Yes," he said slowly, getting a hold on himself. "I am too. Champagne?"

She nodded. Perhaps champagne would clear her head.

Alex drew a bottle from his valise and popped the cork, spewing the warm champagne over the carpet. "I even had the foresight to bring glasses," he said, grinning at her. Why the hell was she staring at him so warily, as if he were some sort of untamed beast? "Here," he said gruffly, handing her a glass.

The champagne slid down her throat, cooling her mouth. She downed another glass and asked for a third. She was beginning to feel light-headed, not at all an unpleasant feeling, and the pounding at her temple was lessening.

"Can an experienced man always tell if a woman is a . . . virgin?" she asked.

He eyed her curiously for a moment. "I suppose so, usually. Did the first man you enjoyed not know you were a virgin?"

She ignored his gentle taut. "If a woman has led a very active life, horseback riding, and all that, is it possible he would not know she is a virgin?"

"It is possible, I suppose, but there would still be a bit of pain." He cocked his head at her. "You fascinate me, Giana. Why your interest?"

She shrugged. "I merely wondered, that is all." She held out her glass to him again.

"No more, Giana. I have no wish to have a drunk woman in my bed."

"I don't want to be in your bed, Mr. Saxton," she said stupidly.

"Then how about in front of the fire?" He took her glass and set it down on a small table, his movements deliberate and slow. He would go easy with her until she wanted him.

He gently caressed her face, and raised her chin to him with his fingers. When he touched his lips lightly to hers, she parted her mouth willingly. While his tongue caressed her mouth, his hands roved lightly down her back to cup her hips. He felt her stiffen, and then, to his immense pleasure, she rose to her tiptoes to fit herself against him.

"I hate all the damned clothes you women wear," he muttered against her ear.

She felt his fingers prodding at the tiny buttons over her breasts. He kissed her again, deeply, and pushed her gown from her shoulders. When she felt his hands against her bare flesh, she clung to him.

"Still more garments, Giana," he said, pulling open the ribbons of her chemise. She drew back, suddenly frightened, and tried to cover her breasts. She raised wide, confused eyes to his face.

Alex didn't notice. He gently pulled her hands away and gazed at her full breasts. His hands trembled as he gently cupped them. She was incredibly

white, her flesh like smooth silk, her nipples a pale
pink velvet. As he caressed her, he felt a bolt of anger
at the thought of other men touching her, delighting
in her as he was now. He leaned down and closed his
mouth over her.

Giana gasped, in surprise and in pleasure. She felt
her breath quicken, and arched her back to him.

Alex nuzzled the soft nipple of her upthrust breast
into tautness. He felt her quivering against him,
heard low, broken moans from deep in her throat. Jesus, he thought, there is such passion in her, such
openness and giving. And why not? Why would she
give her body to so many men if she did not enjoy it?

"Damn you," he growled. He jerked off her gown,
and with it, her many petticoats. She stood passively,
letting him roll down her silk stockings and pull off
her shoes. He stared up at her a moment, drawn into
the molten blue of her eyes.

"I . . . I don't understand," she whispered. Her
mind felt heavy and dull, and she shivered again, for
only her chemise covered her now.

With a low groan, he grasped the straps of her chemise and tore it from her.

Giana clutched at herself. She was naked and he
was staring at her. She tried to focus her mind on
what he had meant, but his mouth was covering her
face and throat with light, nipping kisses.

"I knew I was not wrong about you," he said.
"Your pulse is pounding, my love." His fingers
moved from the fluttering pulse in her throat, slowly
downward to her belly. When they probed through
the dark curls that hid her woman's mound and
found her, she fell forward against him.

He felt her soft woman's flesh moisten and swell
to his fingers, and he smiled as he kissed her trembling offered mouth. He eased his finger into her,

feeling the heat of her body, and the convulsive tightening of her muscles. Then he was beyond thought. He pulled away and ripped at his clothes.

She was cold again. Slowly she let herself fall to her knees, clutching her arms over her breasts. She heard him chuckle, and then she felt the warmth of his body over her, felt him gently pressing her onto her back.

"Loose your hair, Giana," she heard him say, but her arms were leaden at her sides, and she only stared up at him vaguely. He was naked, beautifully naked, and he was covering her, warming her. She arched upward, silently begging him, for she was too embarrassed to ask, and she saw him smile, even as his fingers closed over her again.

This must be passion, she thought. Her body felt taut, yet soft and open to him. His fingers left her and she moaned at the loss.

"Just a moment, Giana," he murmured. He pulled the pins from her hair and glided his fingers possessively through the loose, thick tresses down to her waist.

"You taste delicious," he said, his tongue lazy on her mouth.

His body was scalding hot, and she clung to him, welcoming him as he moved on top of her.

"Four years I've wanted you," he groaned.

Alex felt himself losing control. *Dammit, you must think about anything but her!* He reared up over her, and she cried out as his warm body left her. She tried to pull him back down, lurching upward, only to feel him press her back.

"A moment, love," she heard him say. He was gazing down at her belly, his dark eyes on his gently probing fingers. "But I cannot wait, my love." Pressing her thighs apart, he gasped in his need and thrust himself into her.

"No!" she shrieked suddenly. She felt searing pain as he drove into her, as if he were ripping her apart. She was shaking her head wildly, spilling her hair over her face and eyes. She clutched at him, and a shrill, thin wail tore from her mouth.

From a great distance, she heard him curse, his voice bewildered and angry. "Shit!"

She felt tears wetting the tangled tendrils of hair at her temples. She was pinioned beneath him, held like a captive butterfly, impaled by him. "I am a virgin," she whimpered.

"Jesus, Giana!" he roared. Suddenly his huge body was tense above her, and his hard flesh was throbbing deep within her. She felt him shudder and his seed spewing from him, filling her.

Alex was panting, cursing himself between rasping breaths for a rutting bastard. He rolled off her and rose, so angry with himself and with her that he cursed again, cursed until he could find no more words. He heard her sobbing, and turned back to her. He saw tears on her flushed cheeks, and streaks of blood on her thighs. She was shuddering, hugging her breasts with her arms. She opened her eyes and met his furious gaze.

"I am sick," she whispered.

"Sick," be repeated stupidly. "What the hell do you mean you're sick? You were a virgin, damn you, and that is not an illness!"

He clapped his palm over her forehead and felt the heat of her fever. "Damnation," he said, and without another word he hauled her to her feet and lifted her into his arms. "I am not an ogre, you little fool," he growled at her as he carried her down the short hallway into the bedroom. "You should have told me you were ill. Your mother's influenza?"

"My mother didn't have the influenza."

Alex felt the anger of a foolish man. "Of course not," he muttered. "That hardly explains why you didn't tell me you were feeling ill!"

"You would not have believed me."

Probably true, he thought. "Does your head hurt?" he asked sharply as he tucked the covers about her.

"Yes. It stopped for a bit with the champagne."

"You were a goddamned virgin! Jesus, I forced a goddamned virgin into bed with me! Why the hell didn't you tell me?" He cursed under his breath at his own question.

"I'm going to be sick," Giana said, lurching upward.

Alex grabbed the chamber pot just in time.

He fetched her water and held her head while she washed her mouth out and then drank greedily.

He tucked her in again and laid his palm on her forehead. He ran his fingers through his hair, and drew a deep breath. "You will need a doctor." He rose from the bed and stared down at her. "Damned little fool," he said. He shook his head. All he seemed capable of doing was spouting curses. What an incredible debacle!

"I will go fetch a doctor. The chamber pot is beside you if you need it while I am gone. For God's sake, Giana, keep covered up and stay warm!"

She heard him moving about in the parlor, then heard the front door slam. She sat up and gazed about the dim room. She was no longer cold. She felt blessedly numb, except for the throbbing pain between her thighs. It brought her a measure of reason. *You do not have to see a doctor, Giana. You can escape him. There are trains back to London.*

She tried to lurch out of the bed, struggling with the heavy blankets. She wriggled off the side and slipped to the floor. She staggered to the parlor and looked stupidly down at her petticoats, her stockings, shoes, and undergarments scattered about the floor. Her fingers seemed like someone else's, clumsy and stiff, as they forced the buttons of her gown to fasten.

To Alex's supreme relief, he found a doctor but four houses away from the cottage. It was eight o'clock at night, and Dr. Preston eyed the disheveled gentleman on his front step with a dire sigh.

"My . . . wife is ill," Alex said, his American accent never before so obvious. "You must come quickly. I have tucked her into bed, but I fear she is quite sick . . . with the influenza, I believe. She has fever, chills, and a headache."

Dr. Preston thought fondly of his pipe, waiting to be stuffed with his Jamaican tobacco. "Very well," he sighed. "I will be along shortly. Your name, sir?"

"Saxton. Alexander Saxton. We are in the rented cottage, the white one that backs onto the beach."

"I know it," Dr. Preston said. "You are American, sir." At Alex's abstracted nod, he relaxed a bit. "Don't worry, sir, your wife will be fine."

Alex walked quietly into the dim-lit bedroom. For a long moment he simply stared at the messed bed, refusing to believe that Giana was gone.

"Giana! Where are you?"

He strode into the parlor and saw with a glance that her gown was gone, and her cloak. Her reticule and shoes were on the floor with her undergarments. He was on the point of bursting out the front door when he felt a draft coming from behind him. He whirled about and dashed to the small kitchen, through the back door that stood ajar, and down the shallow back steps to the garden.

"Giana!" he shouted.

The garden gate was creaking in the wind on its rusted hinges. He pushed the gate open and found himself on the beach. A pale quarter-moon shone down on the water, silvering the gentle whitecaps.

"Giana!"

He saw a huddled splash of blue in the moonlight. She was lying on her side on the damp sand, her legs drawn to her chest, the softly hissing waves lapping gently over her bare feet. He ran to her side and fell to his knees beside her on the coarse sand. He lifted her into his arms, and she did not struggle against him, only gazed at him vaguely. He wanted to blister her ears with her stupidity, but he doubted she would understand him. He had barely time to strip off her cloak and gown and put her back into bed before a sharp rap on the front door announced Dr. Preston's arrival.

Dr. Preston sat beside her, surprised to find wet sand on her cheek. "She has been swimming?" he said sarcastically, casting a baleful eye toward Alex.

"I found her on the beach when I came back," Alex said. "I assume that she became delirious and wandered out."

"Mrs. Saxton," he said to her, gently shaking her shoulders.

"Hello," she said to the strange gentleman staring down at her.

Dr. Preston watched the young woman's eyes close, then pulled back the covers to listen to her heart. He saw she was naked, and snapped, "Bring her a nightgown. She must be kept warm."

He was in a biting humor when Alex reappeared, a flannel nightgown in his hands.

"This is your wedding night, I take it, sir!"

Alex stared at him.

"Blood, man! There's blood on her thighs! Damnation, could you not have waited to consummate your marriage until your bride was well again? Have you no sense at all, man?"

"Very little, it would appear," Alex said. "I will bathe her."

Dr. Preston snorted. The lady wasn't dangerously ill, in his opinion, but the influenza would keep her weak and fevered for at least two days. He wondered silently how the devil she could have been so out of her mind from the fever to want to set out for a stroll on the beach. Damned young people, anyway. Not a grain of sense in any of them.

"She's sleeping now, which is for the best. I'll leave a saline draft for her. Keep her in bed, sir, and you can keep away from her! She should be fit again in a couple of days. She's young and strong, but she can't withstand the influenza and your amorous attacks as well. Do you have a woman coming in to cook for you?"

Alex shook his head. He had intended the small cottage only for bedding Giana.

"Well, Mr. Saxton, then you will have to be nurse and cook."

Dr. Preston accepted his payment, snorted yet again, and took his leave, with the admonition that if Mrs. Saxton worsened, he would return.

Alex closed the front door and leaned against it for a moment. He returned to Giana, gently drew back the covers, and bathed the blood from her slender thighs. He found himself grinning reluctantly at the very virginal flannel nightgown as he smoothed it down over her hips. He buried her again under a pile of blankets, and gently wiped the beach sand from her face.

"I am sorry, Giana," he said.

Chapter 14

She sought him out during the night, drawn to his warm body like a moth to a flame. Alex molded her tightly against the length of him, though he himself was sweating from all the blankets. Gradually her trembling stilled and she sighed deeply, easing into a deep sleep. Alex resigned himself to a miserable night.

He slept only fitfully. His thoughts would not slow as the events of the past week jostled about helterskelter in his mind, leaving him angry one minute and smiling grimly at his own stupidity the next. She had been in Rome, dammit, and she had sought him out at the Flower Auction. She had behaved oddly, even insultingly, but she had been at Madame Lucienne's brothel, as well. He shook his head wearily. Only Giana would be able to provide him answers. She had told the truth, but certainly not all of it? Why? Was she protecting someone? Hadn't she wanted to protect her own innocence? He remembered her surprise, and her response to his lovemaking, despite her illness. Until he had hurt her. Damned rutting fool! A bloody virgin, and obviously a young lady, despite what he had believed, what he had seen! He found himself smiling grimly again. After what she had seen that summer, she was hardly an innocent young lady. Still, he had compromised her, and the thought made him tense with annoyance at himself.

He saw himself now as the unwilling bridegroom, the inevitable payment for his revenge and his desire. He, Alexander Saxton, who had vowed never to tie himself in marriage again. He felt a fleeting moment of pain at the thought of Laura, and quelled it resolutely.

Giana moaned softly into his shoulder, squirming against him as though he were her safe harbor from a bad dream. He shifted slightly to accommodate her. Dammit, he wasn't at all certain that he even liked her! She was headstrong, sharp-tongued, as independent as a damned man, and appallingly intelligent. She was also lovely, in face and figure. At that lapsing admission, he felt an unwanted surge of desire, for she was pressed closely against him, her belly but a flannel nightgown away from his suddenly interested member.

He finally fell back into a light sleep, knowing, even accepting now, that he would marry this Englishwoman. A man simply did not poach as he had on the upper-class preserve without accepting the consequences. His last thought was that his mother-in-law would be a damned duchess.

Giana did not become fully awake until the following evening. She remembered waking during the day and sipping a quite delicious soup that Mrs. Preston must have brought them. She was no longer feeling feverish, and her headache had lessened. She heard Alex coming down the hall and quickly closed her eyes. The last thing she wanted was to have to face him, knowing full well that he would have a dozen questions for her. She could feel him staring down at her. Unable to help herself, she sneezed.

"I thought you were awake," she heard him say. She opened one eye and glared up at him.

"Leave me alone," she said succinctly.

"I would like to, Giana, but I'm not such a villain. What's done is done, and the both of us will make the best of a bad situation. Don't get yourself into a lather, you'll only bring on your fever again."

"What do you mean?" she asked, opening her other eye.

"Well, there are, of course, quite a few questions I have for you, but not now. I will wait until you are well again. But regardless of your answers, we shall marry. You were a virgin, and I can think of no other reasonable course but to toe the line to the altar."

"The altar," she repeated stupidly. When she finally grasped his meaning, she gaped at him. "Marry you? Mr. Saxton, I would allow the human race to become extinct before I would accept you as a husband."

"You are feeling more yourself, I see," Alex said. Oddly, her outraged refusal made him angry, and he felt his control slipping. Little fool! Had she no sense at all? "We will discuss it tomorrow, when I don't have to fear you relapsing on me."

"We have nothing to discuss!" she said furiously. The pounding in her head suddenly sharpened, and she closed her eyes, turning her head away from him on her pillow. "I told you the truth from the beginning, but you chose, arrogantly, not to believe me."

"You told me only enough of the truth to sound completely unbelievable!" he growled. "Your stupid denials in the face of what I saw with my own eyes! You sounded like a silly, bleating sheep. Rather, ewe. That I find mightily interesting." He saw that her cheeks were becoming flushed. "Drink this lemonade and go back to sleep. Perhaps you'll be more reasonable on the morrow, though I doubt it."

Giana drank the lemonade obediently, though sleep was the last thing she wanted. She closed her eyes until he left the bedroom. Marry him! Was he out of his ridiculous American mind! Arrogant beast! She had wanted him, but it was dreadful! And her illness had nothing to do with that.

Odd how she had never considered that he would take this particular tack. Americans weren't gentlemen—she had always believed that—but faced with his angry decision, she had to revise her opinion of them. No, she would not. A gentleman would never have forced her to bed with him in the first place.

When she felt the bed give as he climbed in beside her, she forced herself not to move. Insufferable clod! Could he not at least leave her be and sleep on the sofa?

She knew he was stubborn, knew that once he had set his mind to something, he would be immovable. But she had paid her debt to him. And she was already feeling stronger. All she needed now was opportunity.

Her eyelashes fluttered when the bright sunlight spilled into the bedroom, giving her away.

"Open your eyes, Giana. I know you're awake. I've brought you some bread and more lemonade. While you eat, I'll go fetch us some food."

She felt her blood race in her veins. She nodded docilely, even smiling slightly as he helped her sit up in bed.

"Since I have no idea where to forage, I might be a while," he continued. "Stay in bed, and use the chamber pot if you need to. No trips to the outhouse in the back garden, and for God's sake, stay off the beach."

"Very well," she said, not looking up at him.

Had he known her better, a red light would have flashed at her ready compliance. He said over his shoulder when he reached the open doorway, "When I return, we will talk."

It was nearly noon before Alex, laden with packages of food and bottles of a light white wine, returned to the cottage. He stepped into the bedroom quietly, not wanting to disturb her if she slept, and clenched his jaw in anger. He knew that she wasn't wandering about outside. She had left, and taken her valise with her. He found a hastily scrawled note on her pillow. "Mr. Saxton," he read, "you may take yourself back to America with my best wishes, and with a clear conscience, at least where I am concerned. I trust that even you will now consider my debt paid in full. Though you will be tied now to the Van Cleves, you will not have to worry that anyone will ever know what happened, nor will you ever have to deal with me again. As you so kindly said, I have many years to go before I equal my mother. I will not even pray that your ship sinks on your crossing back to New York." She had signed with an insolent flourish: "Georgiana Van Cleve."

Lanson tugged at his ear as he said to Aurora, "The American gentleman, Mr. Alexander Saxton, ma'am, is asking to see Miss Giana. I informed him she has not yet returned from her holiday. He then insisted that he wishes to see you."

Aurora calmly put down the Sunday paper she was reading and rose. "Do show Mr. Saxton in, Lanson."

Alex glanced at the rich inset bookshelves that

lined two walls of her library, and admired her taste in the light French furniture that gave the room a cool airiness. "Mrs. Van Cleve," he said as he stepped toward her.

Aurora returned his cool greeting, offering her hand. "Mr. Saxton, I believe Lanson informed you that Giana has not yet returned."

Alex took a deep breath, and plunged forward. "It is because of your daughter that I have come, Mrs. Van Cleve."

An elegant black brow arched upward. "Indeed, sir? Pray sit down, Mr. Saxton. Would you care for a glass of sherry, perhaps?"

"Yes, thank you."

Alex watched her walk gracefully to the sideboard and pour the wine from a crystal decanter. He wondered, yet again, if he weren't being a total and complete ass. Giana could not have been more specific. She never wanted to see him again. She did not wish to marry him, and in her mind, she had released him from any obligation he might feel. But dammit, he had dishonored her, and she, stubborn little fool that she was, would simply have to realize that there was no choice for either of them. He accepted the glass from Mrs. Van Cleve and sipped at it.

"From your own vineyard, Mrs. Van Cleve?"

"Yes, Mr. Saxton. This particular sherry is from Pamplona."

Aurora seated herself opposite him and waited patiently for him to get to the point of his visit. When the silence lengthened, she said with cool impatience, "Giana is in Folkestone, visiting friends."

"No," he said baldly. "Giana was with me in Folkestone."

Aurora felt her stomach plummet to her toes, though she showed no outward sign of astonishment. "I see," she said carefully. "If that is so, Mr. Saxton, why aren't you with her now?"

"She . . . left me there. I had assumed that she would return here, indeed, that perhaps she had told your butler to lie to me."

"But I have told you Giana is not here." Her eyes held his gaze, and though her mind was racing, she continued calmly enough, "Perhaps, sir, you had best tell me what happened."

Alex rose restlessly from the sofa and paced the floor in front of her. He turned to face her suddenly and rapped out, "I was the man who bought Giana four years ago in Rome at the Flower Auction."

"The Flower Auction?" Aurora repeated blankly. "I do not know what you are saying, Mr. Saxton."

"The Flower Auction, Mrs. Van Cleve, is an event held for wealthy gentlemen every few months in Rome. I attended the function toward the end of the summer. Your daughter, ma'am, was one of the virgins who was to be auctioned off to the highest bidder. It was I who bought her. Unfortunately, or fortunately, depending on your point of view, I was struck over the head, and awoke in an alley. I searched for her the next day, and for the old man I believed struck me, but she had vanished. I did not see her again until we met in your conference room. I hope, Mrs. Van Cleve, that you can imagine my confusion and my ire."

Aurora paled before his eyes. Dear God, what had Daniele forced Giana to do! Sold at an auction! She raised appalled eyes to his face. "I would imagine, Mr. Saxton, that the old man was her uncle, Daniele Cippolo. He would have struck you to protect my daughter."

"This is beginning to sound like some ludicrous melodrama!"

"Mr. Saxton, what have you done to Giana! Where is she?"

"I don't know where she is at the moment," Alex said quietly, "but I must find her. I want her to marry me."

"Marry you!"

The self-assured Aurora Van Cleve was trembling and regarding him with bewilderment. "Mrs. Van Cleve," he said, sitting down beside her, "I see that I should tell you everything." He did, beginning with that night at the Flower Auction. He told her of his fury at seeing Giana again, the daughter of the famous Aurora Van Cleve. "So you see, ma'am, I threatened her into my bed. It was a debt she owed me, a debt I was determined she should pay. Please do not imagine a sordid seduction scene." For the first time, he smiled slightly, his features relaxing. "Giana came down with the influenza, but she didn't tell me—why, I still do not really know. I will not lie to you, ma'am. I took your daughter, and at first, she wanted me. Unfortunately, her illness and my . . . exuberance combined to make quite a farce of the evening." He stared down at his hands, clasped together between his knees. "You needn't worry about her illness now. She was feeling much better by the time she left this morning. She wrote me this note." Alex dug into his waistcoat pocket and handed the folded square of paper to Aurora.

Aurora read Giana's brief letter once quickly, then again, more slowly. When she raised her eyes to his face, he said, "Your daughter doesn't mince matters, does she, ma'am? But in this instance, she is being an irresponsible little fool. I am not pretending to be in any way the gift horse, Mrs. Van Cleve, it is just that I will not let another suffer for an ill I myself caused.

You must tell me where she is. I will convince her, you may be certain."

"You are telling me, sir, that you blackmailed my daughter into your bed, and now, with your man's pride, you blithely expect her to fall into your arms!" she shouted at him.

"Yes, ma'am," he said quietly. "That's about it, I expect."

Aurora took a deep breath to compose herself. Giana, she guessed, had escaped to Cornwall, to the small cottage near Penzance that had once belonged to Aurora's father. "No, Mr. Saxton," she said quietly, "I will not tell you where she is, though I do have a good notion of her destination. She seems, from her note, not to wish to have anything more to do with you. I will bow to her judgment."

"Judgment! The little chit has so little sense she deserves to be thrashed! Christ, Mrs. Van Cleve, she wasn't completely well when she left Folkestone this morning."

"You appear to nourish strong feelings toward my daughter, Mr. Saxton."

"I freely admit it, ma'am. I have no intention of being refused by a headstrong, silly girl who seems to have no idea of the consequences."

"Forgive me, Mr. Saxton, but Giana knows the consequences quite well. I have found myself wishing sometimes that she would be nothing more than a silly girl again, if but for a day."

Alex gazed at her thoughtfully for a moment. "You appear to know something about the summer I saw her in Rome. Giana refused to tell me much about it, merely chirped that it was all a mistake and that she had not been at fault. Nothing more."

"Yes, Mr. Saxton," Aurora said quietly. "I know

about Rome, at least I thought I did. I was responsible for her being there that summer."

"I am tired of games, Mrs. Van Cleve," Aléx said, his voice thick with impatience. "Are you saying that you sent your seventeen-year-old daughter to a brothel?"

Dear God, could that be true? "I suppose you deserve the truth, Mr. Saxton, at least the truth as I know it. Do drink your sherry; indeed, I think I will join you. This will take a while. . . .

". . . So you see," Aurora concluded some time later, "I . . . entrusted her to Daniele, but our agreement was that he was only to have her converse with . . . prostitutes, learn from them about the other side of life. Had I ever imagined such a thing as a Flower Auction, I might have thrown her into Randall Bennett's hungry arms. I am still not sure. She asked me never to look into the particulars of that summer. The changes in her were obvious. She has avoided any entanglements with younger men and has thrown her considerable energies into the business. What I do not understand is why she didn't tell me about you."

"She may have feared you would kick my American hide out of London and destroy the merger."

"Your hide is still in jeopardy, Mr. Saxton! Let me ask you a question. Would have attempted to ruin us if Giana had turned you down?"

"Why no, of course not. I wanted my revenge, and it seemed the way to ensure it. Of course, I tried to be quite persuasive with Giana." He paused a moment, frowning into his glass of sherry. "Your daughter can be every bit as ruthless as I, ma'am. I believe she never imagined that I would come here. If she had, she might have tried to stick a knife in my ribs. I am beginning to believe that she came with me to

Folkestone because she wanted to, and I gave her the perfect excuse. You must tell me where she is. I will ensure she comes to her senses."

Aurora remembered Giana telling her she had desired a man in Rome. It could not have been anyone but him. She had seen her daughter's eyes when she was with him. Giana felt something for him, of that Aurora had been certain from the first day he arrived. She could not escape the feeling that Giana would have a great deal to say to him if he had the chance to mull it out with her. But she could not betray her daughter, no matter what she thought. "I will not tell you. If Giana feels anything for you, she will come to you of her own accord. I will not pressure her to wed if there is no caring, if there is only that awful motive, duty. You are an American, Mr. Saxton. Giana is an Englishwoman to the tips of her fingers. And that would be the very least of your problems. No, Giana must do what she feel best. I will not interfere."

Alex rose. "Then I will find her myself, Mrs. Van Cleve," he said in a harsh voice.

Aurora watched him stride from the library, her brow furrowed in thought. "I wish you luck, Mr. Saxton," she said under her breath.

She chewed on a hapless fingernail for several minutes, for she knew that without her help, he would never find Giana, locked away in a corner of Cornwall, and his business concerns would soon call him back to New York. She rang for Lanson to bring Giana's maid, Abigail, to her, and crossed over to her desk to pen a letter to her daughter.

Chapter 15

"Do stop fretting, my dear girl."

Aurora gazed up at Damien, still clutching Giana's latest letter. "I suppose you are right. She does sound well and content." She still marveled at his aplomb. She had waited, weeks before, when she had first begun her recital to him of what had happened, for his toes to curl in his shoes at her story. But his silver eyes had remained soft, and he had leaned over and patted her hand. "You have behaved most admirably, my dear, yes, most admirably. Another woman would now be cursed with a malicious son-in-law and a wretchedly miserable daughter."

"But you cannot understand, Damien!"

"Hush, my dear. I wish to kiss you."

And so he had, and not a chaste kiss.

"I suppose it is time to ask her to come home for our wedding," Aurora said now, still troubled. "My people have told me that Alexander Saxton has given up his search and is off to Paris and then to New York."

"It occurs to me," Damien said, "that Giana's Mr. Saxton cannot be altogether motivated by chivalrous tomfoolery toward a destroyed virgin. He must feel something for the girl, else he would have given up long ago."

Aurora sighed. "I have given up thinking about his

motives. I know he has spent a good deal of money trying to find her. Indeed, I feared once that he would succeed. He nearly got his hands on one of my letters to Giana."

"Perhaps you should relent and tell him where she is. Let the two young people fight it out between them. Cornwall is a tomb of a place, and they could yell at each other to their hearts' content."

"Surely that would not be right, Damien! Giana has insisted in all her letters that she does not wish to see him."

"Silly chit," Damien said, his mouth curved in a grin. "I did not tell you, my love, but your Mr. Saxton tracked me down a while ago at White's, of all places. Tried to convince me to use my influence."

"No!"

"Ah, yes. A forceful man, Mr. Saxton. Giana could do much worse for a husband, I think."

Aurora thought of Drew and Thomas. She had told even them that Giana was on a well-deserved holiday. She had not been sure if they believed her. But if Mr. Saxton had approached even the duke, it was likely he had talked with both of them, though they had said nothing of it to her.

Aurora rose and shook out her silk skirts. "He is gone now, Damien. I hope our lives can be as they were again."

"Do you really, my dear? It wounds me that you have forgotten our marriage."

"That," Aurora said, laughing, "I did not mean!"

"Write to your daughter and bring her home, my love."

"Indeed I shall." Even Dolly had asked her that morning if Giana would be returning for her wedding.

"I trust so, Dolly," she had said carefully, looking up from her dressing table into Dolly's placid face.

"Well, now, hold still, my pet, and let me finish arranging your hair. The duke is likely pacing downstairs." Dolly chuckled as she deftly twisted her thick hair into a high chignon. "Your duke is as spanking anxious as a young bridegroom! And his brood of children have behaved very nicely, the lot of them. No trouble there. Just imagine you, my pet, a grace!"

Even the London weather, usually perverse in October, was blessedly warm and bright when the Duke and Duchess of Graffton emerged from St. Andrew's Church in Brussels Square. Their five hundred guests, peers of the realm and members of the business class, mingling tolerably well, this day at least, pressed them toward the duke's festively decorated open broughman, like a huge flock of brightly plumed peacocks, shouting their best wishes. Giana rode in a carriage with the duke's three daughters, all exquisitely gowned in peach silk, and kept her laughter bright on the day of her mother's wedding.

She gasped in surprise when they arrived at the duke's mansion on Grosvenor Square. The huge dining room was packed with white-linen-covered tables, groaning under the weight of more food than even she had ever seen. The duke had filled the mammoth ballroom, where the afternoon reception would blend into an evening ball, with pots of roses, carnations, violets, and jasmine from his hothouse at Graffton Manor. At least forty white-gloved footmen stood at attention, awaiting the onslaught of guests, under the watchful eye of Gordon, the duke's butler.

Giana smiled determinedly at her position in the reception line, greeting the endless stream of guests in a loud voice above the laughter and deafening conversation. She had no opportunity to speak to her mother and her new husband for nearly two hours.

She heard her mother say gaily to the duke, "I have been kissed by more gentlemen and patted on the hand by more ladies than I dreamed lived in all London!"

"The ladies only shake my hand," the duke mourned, smiling down at his wife.

Giana inched toward her mother, and stood a moment in front of her, a crooked smile on her lips. "The deed is done, Mother. You are still certain you want to stay with this *impossible* gentleman?"

Aurora hugged Giana, laughing joyfully. "It would quite ruin his reputation and standing were I to leave him now, my love!"

"My feet feel like they're a hundred years old," the duke said.

"Just wait for the dancing, sir!" Giana turned to hug her new papa. He smelled of tart shaving lotion and a hint of sweet tobacco. She felt tears spring to her eyes.

"I am the one to be teary-eyed, puss," the duke chided her. "After all, I have made my proverbial bed. At least," he continued, winking over Giana's head to Aurora, "my proverbial bed will no longer be empty."

"For shame, your grace!" Aurora whispered, flushing delightedly.

"You are both so happy, and I am happy for you."

"Thank you, my love," Aurora said softly.

"Ah, my dear boy, a hug for your old auntie!"

Giana stepped aside as the turbaned purple-gowned dowager Countess of Shrewsbury sailed like a ship under full speed into the duke's arms. She turned away, her destination the ladies' withdrawing room, when she heard the Countess of

Elderbridge proclaim in a loud nasal voice to her bosom friend, the Viscountess Charlberry, "The dear duke will not have to blush for the behavior of his new stepdaughter. A modest, well-behaved girl."

"But it is my understanding, my dear Aurelia, that the daughter is involved in business, along with her mother."

The countess snorted. "Likely Damien will do nothing about it, dear. I've never seen him so besotted! He is more vague than ever."

And he is sublimely happy, Giana thought, looking back from the two elderly ladies toward the duke. She thought she looked a pale copy of her mother, who had never looked more radiant in her soft ivory silk gown. Indeed, her mother seemed a happy continent away from her.

She mingled dutifully with the chattering guests who stood about the banquet tables, doing justice to the silver plates heaped with Russian caviar. She raised her glass of champagne for the toast to the bride and groom, made by the duke's cousin, Lord Elgin Brayton, a dapper little man dressed all in pearl-gray silk.

It seemed forever before the orchestra, alerted by Gordon, the duke's butler, tuned their instruments and opened with a waltz. Giana watched her mother and the duke, smiling whimsically at each other, glide gracefully around the dance floor before other couples joined them.

She saw the duke's youngest son, George, striding toward her. She was not up to his eager, youthful flirtation and slipped out of the ballroom down a long portrait-lined corridor that gave onto the gardens.

The evening was as splendid as the day had been, she thought, gazing up at the full moon. Music wafted from the mansion, drowning out the guests. I should be glad to be alone, she thought, quelling a knot of misery that threatened to build in her throat, and leaned over to sniff one of the last remaining blooms on a rosebush.

"I had hoped to dance with you, Giana, but you escaped me yet again."

Giana started at the sardonic voice behind her. She turned slowly to face Alexander Saxton, oddly breathless at hearing the voice that had haunted her, even in sleep, for nearly two wretched months. *Have some pride, Giana! For God's sake, don't let him see your ridiculous joy!* She drew back at his expression, etched in the shadows of the moonlight. He was blazingly angry. Damn him, what right did he have to be angry!

"You are supposed to be in Paris," she said, "or New York."

"I was in Paris, but as you see, I am now in London. I thought I would give your mother and the duke my congratulations, though I expect they will be rather taken aback at my appearance."

He was standing too close to her, and she took a step backward, nearly tripping on the train of her gown. He reached out his arms to her, steadying her. She shook herself free, furious with herself for taking pleasure in his touch. "What are you really doing here?"

"I did not want to leave our ... business unfinished, Giana. I was curious where you have been hiding for the past seven weeks."

"In Cornwall." She gazed up at him desperately. "Mr. Saxton, I have not changed my mind about anything. I do not understand how you can be so pigheaded about this."

"You are thin, Giana," he said, sweeping his eyes over her. "And your complexion is sallow, but that

might be the moonlight and the peach in your gown.
You should not wear pastels, my dear."

Giana clapped her hands over her ears. "For God's
sake, Mr. Saxton, leave me alone! Haven't you done
enough to me?"

"I have done . . . too much to you, Giana. I am sure
your lovely mother wrote you in her letters that she
spilled the whole story of why you were in Rome
four years ago."

She nodded, grimacing at the memory of her
mother's appalled letters. At least he no longer believed her a perverted rich girl who played games in
brothels. *It doesn't matter what he thinks of you, you
fool!*

"But she really knew very little, except that you
were innocent. And your Daniele appears to have
taken quite some liberties with your . . . education.
Odd that it took you four years to discover what it is
really like to bed with a man."

"You arrogant ass!" His words dug deep, and she
could not forgive him. Her hand flew toward his
cheek, but he caught her wrist and bore it back to her
side. "You hurt me!"

"When I took you in Folkestone, or now?"

"Why do you wish to torment me?" she whispered, a forlorn catch in her voice.

"I do not want to torment you, Giana," he said. "I
want you to become my wife."

Giana could not stop tears from welling in her
eyes. Even as they spilled onto her cheeks, she felt
her stomach turn. She wrenched away from him and
stumbled toward a line of thick ivy bushes. "I am
sick, damn you!" she cried.

"Not again," she heard him say wearily behind
her.

There was nothing in her stomach, for she had

been unable to eat that day. But she felt her body heave, and fell to her knees on the thick grass. She felt his hands on her shoulders, steadying her. When the nausea receded, he hauled her to her feet and carried her to a stone bench beneath an arbor of roses.

"I think I remember what comes next," he said, no amusement in his voice. "Sit still like a good girl, for once, and I'll fetch you some water. Thank God there is no beach about."

She rinsed out her mouth, not caring that he was watching her, and downed the rest of the water. In a spate of anger, she hurled the empty glass at him.

He ducked it handily, and said, as if nothing had happened, "You are not still ill from the influenza, are you?"

"Don't be stupid," she said.

"Then my unexpected presence brought you such mingled delight that you threw up?"

Giana returned his amused expression with a look of loathing. "Leave me alone," she muttered, "just leave me alone."

"Giana, we have bandied insults like a pair of duelists. I am weary of being the villain in this drama of yours, weary of wasting my time with a silly child who, for all her supposed brains, has not a whit of sense."

"Silly child!" She lurched to her feet. "Damn you, Saxton! I am not a silly child! You miserable bounder, children do not get pregnant!"

Her words hung naked between them. "I did not mean that!" she cried. "You make me so damned angry, and I wanted to get back at you!"

Under her appalled gaze, he began to smile, his eyes full of devilry.

"Don't you dare look so smug!" she raged at him. "I tell you, it is not true!"

"I am glad it's not what I've done . . . tonight that made you throw up," he said, his smile widening. They were the first words that came to him. He was glad he had them to speak, because in truth his mind was reeling at her revelation. He had planned to confront her tonight but one more time, as a sop to his conscience, perhaps. But now, in rapid succession, he was to be a husband and a father again.

He's right. You have not one whit of sense. All he needs to do is taunt you and you lose your stupid head! "It is not fair," she said more to herself than to him. "One time, one miserable time, and the result is that I cry when I don't want to, retch in my evening gown, say things I don't mean to say, and look sallow." She raised angry eyes to his face. "And you have the gall to stand there laughing at me! It is not funny, damn you! God, I should love to thrash you!"

"Then do it," he said coolly. He pulled open his evening coat and unbuttoned his waistcoat, baring his shirt to her.

She did. She slammed her fists against his belly, letting all her fury loose, until she had no more strength, and fell limply against him.

"Do you feel better now? After our child is born, I'll let you thrash me again. You'll doubtless be stronger then."

"I'll be strong again in but a few minutes," she growled against his shoulder.

He smiled over her head. "Everything will be all right now, Giana, I promise you." He meant what he said. This headstrong, delightfully stubborn English girl would become his wife. He would hear her out, counter all her foolish objections, and drag her to the altar.

"Nothing will ever be right again," she muttered. "One time. One stupid time."

"I know," he said. "It isn't fair, is it? You are almost two months pregnant now. We should be married as soon as possible."

"No," she said, "I will not marry you."

"When did you discover you are pregnant?"

"I've known for over a week."

"Ah. Then you must have spent those seven days thinking about every possible thing you might do. Did you decide to bear a bastard? Travel to the Continent, perhaps, to have your child in hiding? Will you give your child up, or pawn him off to society as a long-lost niece or nephew?"

"I thought perhaps he or she could be my mother's child. She is not too old to bear a child."

"I am certain your mother would have something to say about that," he said wryly. "Have you told her?"

"No, not until I decide what to do."

"The child is mine too, Giana, and you must grant half the decision to me. Do not make my child, our child a bastard. Marry me."

"I can't marry you! You're an American!"

"I am not that officious, am I? Did you in your machinations even consider telling me?"

"Yes, but I quickly dismissed it."

"Why?"

"I do not intend ever to marry."

He was not surprised, not really. Not after what Aurora Van Cleve had told him, and what Giana had seen in Rome. He could not very well bludgeon her into accepting him. "I know that you have seen first-hand how some husbands treat their wives. But marriage need not be like that, Giana. You have but to look at your mother. Do you think the duke would ever be unfaithful to her, or abuse her trust in any way?"

"He could if he wanted to," she said. "All the marriage contracts in the world would amount to nothing if he wished to control her and her fortune. It is the law."

"So you are afraid of marriage, then. Are you afraid that I would lock you in a back room and gamble away your fortune, bring a string of mistresses into my house, perhaps, and parade them in front of your nose?"

"It would be your right, and your words are very telling, Mr. Saxton. It would be *your* house." She straightened and rose from the bench. He let her go. There was a world-weariness in her eyes that made him want to hold her, make her forget what she had seen in Rome. "At least there are no more lies between us, Mr. Saxton. It is your child, but in my body. You are free to leave, and I want you to go. I will inform you of my plans when I have made them."

"I believe it is not just marriage you fear, Giana," he said, rising to tower over her. "I think you fear yourself, fear the passion you felt for me. As ill as you were that night in Folkestone, there was a part of you that wanted me, wanted to let you feel a woman's pleasure, though you scarce understood it."

He cannot know that! "Your loathsome male arrogance is showing again, Mr. Saxton. I pray I shall have a daughter and not a son."

"Prove it."

"Prove what?" she said, backing away from him.

"Prove that you are indifferent to me. If you truly are, I will withdraw from your life, just as you wish. You don't fear that your body will disagree with your ridiculous pronouncements, do you?"

She felt a tingle of fear. "You will leave me alone, then?" she whispered.

Lord help me, he thought. "Yes."

His dark eyes were caressing her face, and she could not seem to tear her gaze away. She thought crazily that he would savage her, bruise her in his attempts to arouse her.

"Am I now to do my worst?" he murmured, smiling as if he knew what was in her mind.

She did not deign to reply. Alex drew her toward him, as if he were her partner in a waltz, his left hand pressing at the small of her back, his right resting lightly on her shoulder. Her body was stiff, steeled against him. He kept his touch light and leaned down, not to kiss her mouth, but to nibble her ear. "When next we make love, Giana," he said softly, his warm breath filling her ear, "you will feel no pain. I will lie beside you and caress you, like this." His lips caressed her eyes and her cheeks, circling her mouth, without touching her lips. She felt his hands stroking her back and gliding around to her breasts.

"I remember how soft you are, Giana, when you want to be, how your breasts fill my hands. You will arch your hips to me, and we will move together, until you cry out for me."

She stiffened against him, but when he gently cupped her breasts, she felt her nipples grow hard, felt them ache. "No!" she gasped, her fists against his chest. "You will not seduce me with words, damn you!"

"No more words, then, love." His breath was hot against her lips, and she felt his tongue glide gently over them. He closed his fingers around her neck, drawing her closer to him. She felt him hard against her through her petticoats, and whimpered, unable to help herself.

"Damn you," she moaned. She parted her lips to

him, and when she felt his tongue touch hers, she wrapped her arms about his shoulders and pulled him down to her. He felt her shudder.

He kissed her deeply, and then drew back, studying her eyes, vague and dreamy in the moonlight.

"I am sorry, love," he said in a ragged whisper against her hair.

She pressed her head against his shoulder until the painful ache eased, and broke into furious sobs.

Alex gathered her in his arms, rocking her body against him. "Hush, Giana."

"God, I hate you," she said. She pulled away from him and he let her go.

"How can you want me to make love to you one moment, and hate me the next?"

She gave him a defeated, desolate look. "The duke loves my mother," she said. "You do not love me, nor do I love you. Just because my body shows the poor judgment to ... desire you, you expect me to forget all that you are, all that marriage entails, gaze at you with dewy eyes, and agree to anything you say."

"It would be a nice conclusion," he said, smiling, "but I know you well enough, Giana, to know that you will thwart that fond hope. Come now, I'm really not such a bad bargain, and you cannot think I am anything like your fortune-hunting Randall Bennett. I am even willing to overlook the fact that your new stepfather is a damned duke."

"I will not sew alter cloths! I will not be a brood mare and sit around with other ladies watching the damned clock, wondering where my husband is, and talking about servants, food, and children!"

"You are obviously quite ... fertile, Giana," he said, trying to repress his grin, "but you cannot be a brood mare without me. I have no wish to breed five or six children and have my wife pregnant until she is thirty. We could easily prevent conception, you know."

"Yes, I know. But wives are kept pregnant, and husbands, damn them, feel it their god-given right to go find their wretched pleasure with mistresses! I will not do it!"

"How do you know about contraception?"

"In Rome. I asked. I wondered how the girls at Madame Lucienne's kept from becoming pregnant."

"Ah, your unusual education again. So you see, if you are not pregnant all the time, I will have little need to go elsewhere for my ... wretched pleasures."

She felt color stain her cheeks. "That is not what I meant," she said in a taut voice. "Please, Mr. Saxton, you must listen to me, for I am quite serious. I will not marry you. I have plans for my life, and they do not include giving up my identity to a husband, pandering to his needs, or pleading for spending money?"

"It comes down to the fact that you don't trust me."

"Power corrupts, Mr. Saxton, and I have no intention of being its victim."

"It would appear we have reached an impasse. Tell me what you intend to do, Giana. Your position is rather untenable, you know."

He saw her shoulders slump. "I don't know yet," she said.

Dear God, he thought, he could not leave a twenty-one-year-old girl pregnant with his child. He drew a deep breath and said baldly, "I have a proposition for you, Giana."

"A proposition," she repeated, gazing at him warily.

"We will announce that we have been secretly married. You will come with me to New York, as my wife. If you find the trappings of married life with me offensive, you can return to England after our child is born and simply say that we were divorced. Then no one would question the legitimacy of our child. And you would not be bound to me, ever, legally."

"You mean live a lie, pretend that we are married. Lie to my mother, lie to everyone."

"You may tell your mother or not, as you wish. If, on the other hand, you discover that living with me is not the appalling degradation you envision, we could wed whenever you wished it. It would be up to you, Giana."

Giana pressed her hands to her cheeks. "I don't . . . what to say! I must think!"

He smiled at her tumbled speech. "Even you, Giana, would admit that there are some benefits to marriage. I offer you those benefits without any of the ills."

"Why, Mr. Saxton?"

"I can think of no other solution remotely acceptable to either of us. There is but one promise you must make me. If you decide to return to England, you must promise that I will be allowed to see my child, to have my role in his or her future."

"It is insane! All of it. You cannot mean it!"

"I mean every bloody word, dammit! You must decide, and quickly, before all London knows you are breeding. Surely you wish to avoid that kind of scandal."

"But you don't even like me!"

"I trust you will become more amiable once the sword of Damocles is no longer hanging over your head. I am even willing to wager that you have a sense of humor."

"But there is nothing in this for you. I know your

reputation in the business world, Mr. Saxton. This is completely unlike you. Why?"

He wondered why indeed. He supposed he did not like to be thwarted. No, it was more than that. He had wronged her, taken her innocence, and at the same time created a child. *And you desire her, more than she knows.*

"I do like you, Giana," he said. "It is true that I, like you, thought I would never again contemplate marriage. But the fact of our child remains. Will you agree?"

Giana gulped, but nodded. She raised her face to his and drew a deep breath. "I cannot think of any better result for the child, Mr. Saxton. I . . . do agree."

"Never have I had such difficulty convincing a woman not to be my wife. We will allow a couple of days to elapse, time enough for licenses to have been processed, inform the newspapers, and be on our way to New York by the end of next week."

Seven months with him, living with him intimately, as her husband. Seven months in America. She pressed her finger to her temples, imagining her mother's astonishment, after all she'd written to her about him. Aurora had played the devil's advocate with her at first. Would she be dismayed now? She brightened, thinking of Derry.

"You are smiling, Giana. What are you thinking now?"

She glanced up at him. "I was thinking about a friend of mine, Mr. Saxton, a dear friend whom I haven't seen in four years. She was full of all the romantic drivel young girls thrive on, then. She has been married four years now, and is likely miserable."

He silenced a sharp retort that was blistering his tongue. He said stiffly, "I believe you've made your-

self quite clear on your views, Giana. I think it wise
that you contain your cynicism, at least in front of
others. To the world, we will be a happily married
couple."

"Ah," she said. "Does that mean that I must hang
on your every word and gaze at you with limpid,
dewy eyes?"

He heard a quiver of laughter in her voice, and
smiled. She did have a sense of humor, thank God.
"Do so tonight at least. Now, Giana, let us return to
the ball. I think it wise that you introduce me to a
few people if our elopement is not to come as too
much of a shock."

He offered her his arm. Giana lightly laid her hand
on his black sleeve. "Do you think you could bring
yourself to call me Alex?"

"I think I can manage it, sir. I also think that first
I shall introduce you to the Duke and Duchess of
Graffton."

Chapter 16

Giana gazed down from the third-floor window of her room at the Royal George Inn at the fog-laden streets of Bristol. The raucous singing of a group of rum-happy sailors drifted up to her.

> 'E ain't the man to shout: Please, my dear!
> 'E's only the lout to shout: Bring me a beer!
> 'E's a bonny man wit' a bonny lass
> Who troves 'im a tippler right on 'is ass!
> And to hove and to trove, we go, me boys,
> We'll shout as we please till ship's ahoy!

A lump rose in her throat at the sharp cockney sounds. Tomorrow she would leave England aboard the American steamship *Halyon*. She left the window and nestled herself against the evening chill in the large, airy room by the glowing fire in the grate. She kept a wary eye on the door that adjoined her room to Alex's. He had assured her he had booked two rooms for them at the Royal George Inn. She simply not thought to ask him if there was a door connecting them. She had given up with the buttons at the back of her gown. Where was the maid he promised to send up to help her undress?

She remembered how her mother had recovered quickly, at least, at her wedding ball when she had seen Giana smiling up at Alexander Saxton, her hand nestled securely in his. She had told her mother the truth, two days later, all of it, adding with a sickly smile that Aurora must simply regard it as a seven-month holiday in America, with a grandchild as the joyous result. To Giana's surprise, her mother had succumbed more quickly than she had imagined. She had insisted they dine together, and Alex, seemingly perfectly at his ease, had lounged after dinner in the sitting room with the duke, smoking a smelly cigar. What had irked Giana was the smile her mother had given Alex before they left, an unspoken message passing between them. When she had taxed Alex with it, he had given her a lecherous grin. "She knows, my dear Giana, what pleasures await you."

"There will be none of that!" Giana had gasped. "We are not married, Mr. Saxton!"

Giana brushed out her hair. She was on the point of braiding it when there was a light knock on the adjoining door and Alex walked in wearing a burgundy velvet dressing gown.

"Where is the maid?" she managed, nervously kneading the back of an armchair.

"Damn," he said, "I knew there was something I forgot to do. No matter. I'll play your ladies' maid this evening."

"What is that in your hand?" she asked suspiciously.

He presented a bottle of champagne and two glasses. "I believe," he said blandly, "that it is customary for the loving bride and groom to toast each other on their wedding night."

"Is it some sort of fertility rite?" she asked acidly.

Alex threw back his head and laughed deeply. "In your case, Giana, it seems it worked wonders, even with you feeling ill. Not very romantic, though, I grant you. Would you like to undress now or drink a glass with me?"

"One glass, sir. I am tired and would like to retire."

Giana looked into the frothy bubbles and waited impatiently for Alex to make his toast.

"To my English bride," he said. "May she bring culture to the uncivilized savages of New York."

"Hear, hear," she said, "but for only a short time!"

When she had finished her glass, Alex poured her another. "It is your turn to make a toast, my dear. Tradition, you know."

She eyed him for a moment over the bubbling rim of her glass. "To a man who is too conceited for his own good."

"The man is willing to share his conceit."

"The man wears his conceit like suit of clothes. Without it, he would be like the naked emperor!"

"Hear, hear!"

"No, Mr. Saxton, no more," Giana said firmly, rising from her chair.

"Are you certain, Mrs. Saxton?"

She started. "Oh dear," she said ruefully, "I suppose that I must accustom myself to that."

"Yes, it would be most embarrassing to introduce you as my wife, 'Miss Van Cleve.' "

She smiled uncertainly and presented him her back. "The buttons please, Alex."

The tiny buttons parted quickly under his fingers. When her gown was loose to her waist, she felt his hands warm on her bare shoulders. She jumped at the tingling pleasure his touch gave her. She tried to pull away from him slowly, with dignity.

"What the hell is that?"

"What is what?"

"This thing you have laced up to your eyebrows!"

"It is a corset, sir. I suppose you will have to un-lace it too."

"You were not wearing that nonsense in Folke-stone."

"No," she said, "I wasn't." *I wasn't because I knew you would undress me!*

She breathed in deeply as the corset loosened. "Ah, that feels better," she said. She felt him pull it away from her, and saw him lean toward the fireplace from the corner of her eye. "What are you doing?"

"Destroying that piece of armor."

She watched the stiff material flame up. "The bon-ing won't burn," she said. "I would appreciate it, Alex, if you would not destroy any more of my clothes."

"No more corsets. Jesus, you're thin as a rail, and when you do fill out a bit, that wretched contraption could harm the baby."

"I hadn't thought of that."

"There are some other things you haven't thought of as well," he said obscurely.

"You can leave now, Alex," she said in a too-loud voice. "Thank you for helping me."

"Leave my bride on our wedding night? I would not be such a bounder, Giana."

She kept her eyes fastened on her toes. He knew, damn him, that she wanted him, and there he was, standing quite at his ease, but three feet from her, la-zily studying her.

"Haven't you anything better to do?" she snapped, still not looking at him.

"Indeed I do," he agreed amiably. "Making love to my bride is my sacred duty."

"I am not your bride!"

"Do you have any idea how adorable you look

with your gown falling about your hips and your hair loose?"

"You of all people know that I am not the least bit adorable! Please, Alex, just leave now. I don't want you to make sport of me anymore!"

His smile faded and he threw himself down in a chair with his back to her. "Get into your nightgown, Giana," he said abruptly.

She picked up her cotton nightgown and stalked behind the dressing screen. Her fingers were trembling. *Say something, Giana!* "What time does our ship sail tomorrow?"

"Nine o'clock in the morning. I've already seen to the stowing of your trunks. We shouldn't have to dash about."

Alex turned to her as she stepped from behind the screen, clutching her dressing gown about her. Her face was pale in the dancing firelight, and she looked for the world like a small, frightened child, save for her luminous eyes, which held his in silent question.

He strode over to her and cupped her chin in his hand. "I have never known a more passionate woman," he said softly, "nor one who tried so hard to deny it." He gently pulled her fisted hands away from her dressing gown. "Hold me, Giana. Men enjoy being held as much as women."

She closed her hands tentatively around his back, and rose to her tiptoes. "You are so big," she said.

He held her tightly against him for a moment, forcing his hands to be still. "I want to make love to you, Giana," he said quietly.

"Since I am already a fallen woman, I do want to know what the falling is like."

He dropped a light kiss on her nose, and smiled when he saw her brow furrowed in thought.

"What if I don't like it?"

"If you don't like it, Giana, you may personally divest me of my manhood," he said in great seriousness.

"I fancy I will not dislike it that much!"

He kissed her on her pursed lips and swept her into his arms. To Giana's befuddled surprise, he did not carry her to the bed, but eased down into an armchair in front of the fireplace, settling her comfortably on his lap.

"Promise me you won't wear a corset anymore."

He sounded perfectly serious. She was nestled against his shoulder, her body molded against his, and he was quizzing her about her wretched corset! "I promise," she said quickly.

"So agreeable already," he murmured. He eased her back against his arm and smiled down into her expectant face. "You look for the world like a child on Christmas morning."

His voice was a caress. She felt his fingers on her throat, resting for a moment over her pulse. The sash on her dressing gown fell open and she felt his fingers prodding the buttons of her nightgown. She closed her eyes in anticipation and embarrassment. She felt cool air on her shoulders and breasts, and opened her eyes again. He was staring down at her, his fingertips following his roving gaze. She drew in a sharp breath when his hand cupped her breast.

"I used to be flat-chested," she said absurdly.

"I used to have small hands." His hands left her breast and trailed deliciously down to her stomach. He pressed his palm against her belly, barely touching the triangle of hair that covered her woman's mound. To her consternation, he leaned his head back against the chair top and closed his eyes, his traitorous hand still on her—as if she were an armrest, she thought indignantly, as if he were bored! She tried to stiffen against him, but succeeded only in rearing up against his arm, sending his fingers lower.

Alex opened his eyes and lazily studied her flushed face. "I begin to believe that if there is any forcing to be done, it will be by my shy bride."

"Cad!" she growled at him. "If you are so uninterested, why don't you simply leave!"

He smiled, wondering if she could feel the urgent hardness of him beneath her hips. "Leave you, princess?" he asked in a husky whisper. "No, I won't do that again." His fingers were tangled in her nest of hair, searching for her, even as he spoke. They caressed her lightly, and left to glide over her thighs. Giana drew a shuddering breath and pulled herself up against his shoulders.

"There will be no guilt on the morrow, Giana, no regrets," he said, holding her still against him. "Even though you are not my wife, you are mine, now and tomorrow. Do you understand what I'm asking of you?"

Giana pulled her face from his cheek. "I am here, Alex," she said.

Alex would have said more, but it was not the time for talk. Her passion was unknown to her, a tantalizing unknown she would say anything to discover. He carried her to the bed, cradled in his arms, and pushed her open nightgown from her shoulders. She trembled as he stripped it away and gently lifted her naked onto her back.

"Are you cold?"

"A little," she said breathlessly.

"A moment, love," he said, shrugging off his dressing gown. He stood naked, his manhood thrust out from his body, giving her time to study him.

She followed the mat of black hair on his chest as

it narrowed to his belly and bushed out again at his groin. "You want me," she whispered.

He grinned. "Could you ever doubt it?" He climbed into bed beside her and balanced himself on one elbow, not touching her. "I have never understood why blonds are thought so alluring," he said. "Do you know how delectable you look, all silky white with those soft black curls?"

He laid his hand over her breast, delighting at her racing heartbeat. "Come to me, love," he whispered.

He pulled her against him and kissed her deeply, savoring the softness of her mouth and her tentative response to him. He held her against his arm and stroked her breasts, her hips, until she whimpered soft mewling cries into his mouth. He pressed her belly hard against his manhood and dipped his face down to suckle her breast.

"Alex, please . . . please help me," she whispered, her fingers digging at his shoulders.

He reared up over her, his lips following the trail of his hands, and eased himself between her thighs. "You are beautiful, Giana," he said, parting her flesh to his hungry eyes. "Delicate, like opening petals, pink and soft."

She lifted her hips against him. "Like one of your flowers?" she gasped.

She felt his strong hands grip her thighs and raise her to him until his warm mouth closed over her. She suddenly saw him in the Golden Chamber. "This is what you did to Margot," she panted.

Alex raised clouded eyes to her face. "Margot?"

Giana could not stop her hips from twisting against his hands. "Yes," she gasped. "I saw you, Alex!" she babbled. "I saw you in Rome, making love to Margot at Madame Lucienne's."

His mind cleared at her tumbling words. "What are you saying? How could you have seen me?"

She wanted to yell at him that it didn't matter, but his eyes were questioning on her face. "You were in the Golden Chamber. I was beyond the glass, watching you. I thought you knew."

"No, I did not know, Giana. What man would want to be observed coupling with a whore?"

"Many men did," she said, the absence of his mouth bringing her reason. "And they were all the same, except—"

"Except me," he finished quietly.

"Except you," she repeated. "You were different. I think you are too vain to allow a woman to fake passion with you."

He pulled himself up beside her again and watched her eyes darken with disappointment. "It is not just vanity. I enjoy bringing a woman to pleasure. It makes the experience more complete. Now, I have nothing more to say for the moment. Do you?"

"No," she whispered.

He smiled as he leaned down to kiss her. He would never have to worry about Giana faking anything with him.

He circled her slender waist in his hands, enjoying the silken feel of her, and trailed his tongue over her belly. He gently rubbed his palms over her nipples before his hands swept down to grasp her hips. Her beautiful, slender body was open to him, and he caressed her, pushed her beyond herself. He felt her legs stiffen and heard her cry out, tossing her head wildly on the pillow. He held her in her pleasure for another moment, then reared back, trembling, and thrust himself into her warm flesh.

"Giana," he whispered, and captured her mouth. She tasted herself, and the knowledge that he had known her so intimately fired her passion. She wrapped her legs about his hips, drawing him deeper, and moaned into his throat. She felt his huge body shudder and tense, and she kissed him wildly, boldly thrusting her tongue into his mouth, just as he was thrusting into her body.

Alex moaned and fell heavily on top of her, holding her languid beneath him.

"I think," Alex said at last, his voice teasing, "that the Van Cleves and the Saxtons have at last consummated their merger."

He felt her lips curve into a smile against his throat. He closed his hands under her back and pulled her against him.

"Well, Giana, is it to be the butcher knife?" He dropped a light kiss on the tip of her nose.

"Only if you leave me," she said.

She clasped her arms tightly about his chest and wriggled close against him, keeping him deep inside her.

"Women are supposed to want to talk after lovemaking," he whispered against her forehead.

"How odd," she said.

He felt her eyelashes sweep closed against his shoulder. He cast a jaundiced eye toward the lamps that were still lit in the room. Perhaps later, if she pulled away from him in sleep, he would douse them. He found himself thinking about the myth so many men chanted as gospel. Their wives, those paragons of purity who were too good, too beyond the cravings of the flesh, to do anything but their duty, silently and stoically, in the dark. He guessed that Giana could be that way, with another man. Perhaps that was vanity on his part, but then, he would be the only man ever to possess her. He fell asleep, a half-smile on his lips.

* * *

Alex started awake. A strand of hair was in his mouth and there was a warm, pliant body pressed against him. He cocked his eyes open, startled to see sunlight bursting into the room. He looked at the clock on the table beside the bed, and cursed. He had wanted to love Giana awake, but it was nearly eight o'clock, and their ship sailed in but an hour.

"Giana," he said against her forehead.

She grumbled in her sleep and buried her face into his chest.

"Come on, laziness, we must hurry." He lightly slapped her hips and unwrapped her arms and legs.

Giana took in the two of them, naked together on a dreadfully rumpled bed, and blushed furiously.

"A little late for that, princess," Alex grinned. He bounded out of bed and stretched vigorously, as if delighting in the suppleness of his muscular body. "If you hurry, you'll have time for a bath. Shall I order one up for you?"

She flushed again as his eyes traveled down her body, "Yes, please," she said in a small voice.

"We'll have our breakfast on board the *Halyon*. Call me if you need any help with your buttons."

He caught her chin between his hands and dropped a light kiss on her lips. "We'll talk about dessert after breakfast," he finished, grinning wickedly. He strode naked from the room, his dressing gown tossed over his arm, whistling a sea ditty whose words, thankfully, Giana didn't know.

Giana was surprised to see the leather-faced, stocky captain of the huge steamship *Halyon* plant himself in front of Alex when they boarded the ship.

"Well, sir," he said in a booming voice, vigorously pumping Alex's hand, "delighted to have you aboard this trip. And this, I take it, is Mrs. Saxton. A most fruitful trip for you, sir. It appears that you've come away with England's finest."

"It was a most ... fruitful trip," Alex said smoothly. "Mrs. Saxton, let me introduce you to my captain, Darrell Duffey, an old salt who can spin an outrageous tale better than any man in the fleet."

"Captain Duffey," Giana said, offering her gloved hand.

"Your stateroom is ready, sir, and we've sobered up the helmsman, poor chap. Got himself caught up with some Irish sailors and was the worse for wear this morning. But he's an American, and they don't come with harder heads. . . ."

As Captain Duffey continued his monologue, Giana looked about the bustling ship. Sailors were high in the rigging setting the sails, while others hoisted cargo crates, fastened down under tarpaulins, belowdecks. She heard Captain Duffey tell Alex there were some fifteen passengers for the voyage to New York.

"You approve of the *Halyon*?" she heard him ask her.

"You did not tell me it was one of your ships, Alex."

"Actually, I bought her during your ... confinement in Cornwall, and rigged her out with my crew. She'll make the crossing in fourteen days, Giana, if we are lucky enough to avoid early-winter storms."

Giana ran her fingers over the sparkling brass railing. "Fourteen days," she said. "I still have trouble believing such speeds."

"The combination of steam and full sails gives us the best of everything. Come, let me show you our stateroom."

Giana had barely time to take in the rich mahogany walls of the stateroom, and the thick carpets be-

neath her feet, before she felt Alex's mouth caressing
her ear, his hands stroking her back.

"It's been a long time, Giana, and I'm starving."

"If you are this hungry much of the time, you'll become fat," she said.

"We'll see which of us becomes fat first."

"Cad!" she said without heat. She wrapped her
arms about his neck and rose on her toes, trying to fit
her body against his, but his sensuous mouth was
still beyond her reach. He gave her a teasing, boyish
grin before sweeping her into his arms and dumping
her unceremoniously onto the bed.

"You have three minutes to get out of those
clothes, Giana, no more."

She was still struggling with her stockings when
Alex, deliciously naked, grabbed her ankles and up-
ended her on the bed. She wondered vaguely as he
rolled down her stockings why his touch should
make her feel so ... urgent. Then he was on top of
her, and she was kissing him, clutching him against
her.

"Don't rape me," he teased her, nibbling her throat.
He pulled her to face him and gently captured her
hand. He closed his fingers over hers and guided her
hand down to feel herself as he caressed her. Her embarrassment quickly faded, and when he loosed her
fingers, she tentatively closed them about his manhood.

"You are so huge, Alex," she said. "I cannot believe
that you don't rip me apart."

His fingers still caressed her. "If you did not want
me, I would hurt you. But you are soft and moist for
me."

Her fingers glided upward, and he moaned. "God,
you little witch, if you don't stop that, we'll soon find
ourselves at an impasse."

Giana felt as though she hadn't a bone in her body when he turned her again, away from him. She turned her head to look at him, but he held her still. He kissed the back of her neck and cupped her breast with his hand beneath her, while he pressed her belly to fit her close against him. His fingers found her again, and she felt him press against her and slowly thrust inside her.

The familiar ache of sheer sensation built within her, and she was wild to reach the pleasure he had given her the previous night. She was writhing against him, locked in her suspended passion, not understanding why he would not give her release. His fingers were tantalizing, feather-light, and she cried out, a jagged, frustrated moan.

"Damn you," she cried.

"It will take me years to slow you down," Alex said against her ear. His fingers scalded her, rhythmically now, his manhood throbbing deep within her, and her last coherent thought was that she would die if he stopped.

Giana shivered as the sheen of perspiration dried in the cool cabin air. She rolled over and pressed herself against his warm body.

"You are superb," she said. "I do not mind that you are so terribly conceited."

"Am I superb enough to be your husband?"

He felt her tense. "You are my husband in name only, Alex. But you are my lover, I will not deny that."

"And do you think you will not want me after our child is born?"

"Probably," she sighed. "But perhaps this passion I feel for you will fade."

"Practice will tell, you know, Giana, and I intend to practice constantly."

She pulled away from him, drawing the velvet coverlet over her. "You must find me very . . . inept," she said bleakly.

"But ever so willing. I am a patient man, in all things."

"Particularly when it comes to your women?"

He cocked a black brow at her. "You already accuse me of infidelity?"

She looked down at her toes. "No, but I will become boringly familiar to you. And I will be too pregnant to share your bed." She shrugged her shoulders. "You are free, after all, and you will likely do just as you please."

He felt his jaw tighten. "I find your blithe cynicism nauseating," he said, unable to keep the anger from his voice. "Don't paint me with your bitter brush."

She whirled about to face him. "Ah, the big stud of Rome is spouting piety! I find your protestations insulting, Alex!"

He rolled off the bed and stood towering over her. She saw vaguely that his member was wet with her.

"Wife or no wife, Miss Van Cleve," he growled, "you continue to rant stupid nonsense at me, and I'll thrash you."

"A stupid man and his threats! The two go together so perfectly. You cannot deny the truth, so you resort to bullying. It becomes you so well, Mr. Saxton!"

"Jesus, I am a fool for standing here listening to you!" He gathered up his clothes and yanked on his trousers.

He was on the point of slamming out of the stateroom when she yelled, "Wait! You cannot leave me, I have no one to help me with my gown!"

"Stay in bed, then," he growled. "You'll likely be

so hot for me when I come back that you'd tear it anyway in your haste to get to me."

"Conceited beast! God, I would never marry you!"

"Take care, ma'am. I might just stop asking you." He turned on his heel and slammed out of the stateroom.

Giana closed her mouth and eyes to let Alex wipe her face with a cool cloth.

"You're sweating like a pig," he said.

"A sow," she snapped, unable to smile at him. "And ladies don't sweat." She watched a half-filled glass of water slide across the tabletop as the *Halyon* careened sharply to starboard in the furrow of a deep trough. In the next moment she was scrambling toward the chamber pot.

Alex turned away from her so she would not see his worried frown. There was no doctor aboard the *Halyon*, and he had not considered what a ferocious Atlantic storm would do to Giana. The storm had raged for nearly three days, and most of the passengers were seasick, but none of them were also pregnant. She had eaten little since it started, and held down nothing as far as he could tell.

"Giana, you must try to eat something," he said, sitting down beside her.

"You must hate me," she moaned. She looked so damned fragile, her complexion pale and her hair lank and shiny with sweat. He had tried to braid it, and left her looking like a little girl playing grown-up. He felt his own stomach lurch at a particularly violent heave of the huge ship.

He was completely unmanned when she whispered, "Please, Alex, don't let the baby die." Tears coursed down her cheeks, and he dashed them away before they ran into her mouth. She wrapped her arms around her stomach and drew her knees up to her chest.

"It's this damned stateroom," he said suddenly, glancing around at all the luxury tilting and heaving around him. "We are getting out of here."

He pulled on several sweaters and his slicker, then bundled Giana up to her eyebrows in warm blankets.

"Are you going to throw me overboard?"

"The fish would likely throw you back. You weigh no more than a guppy. Hush, now. You are going to feel better quite soon."

Alex ignored the aghast expression on Captain Duffey's rain-slapped face when he lurched onto deck, his wife in his arms. He found a spot protected from the slashing rain and wind just outside the wheelhouse and ordered a tired sailor to bring him a chair.

To his relief, he felt Giana relax in his arms within minutes. Alex slipped his hand under the mound of blankets and gently touched her belly.

"Better?"

"Oh yes," she breathed. "I cannot believe it. Alex?"

A sheet of blowing rain whipped around the side of the wheelhouse, and Alex lowered his head to protect her. "Yes?"

"Thank you."

He dropped a light kiss on her brow, and smiled. "You are most welcome, Mrs. Saxton. If we don't get washed overboard, perhaps I have found a cure."

They slept through the morning, their first unbroken sleep in nearly three days. When they awoke, Alex grinned shamelessly at the passengers who lay huddled around them on the deck.

"Quite a honeymoon," he said roughly, delighted to see her color returned. "Never has a man who is not even a husband endured such a sorry excuse for a wife—"

"Who is not even a wife," she finished. "I must look awful." She tried to free her hand from the blankets, but Alex held her still.

"I am getting used to your greenish complexion, Giana. Since you're showing signs of renewed vanity, do you think you could drink some hot broth perhaps? I don't want a wraith on my arm when we arrive in New York."

She blinked, surprised at herself. "I'm starving," she said.

When she had finished the broth, and a piece of bread as well, she slept again, and did not wake until evening. She stretched in Alex's arms, and felt him burrow his hand to her belly.

"No more cramping, Giana? You feel better?"

"Yes, I promise. But how your arms must feel!"

"If you survive, my arms will also, princess." He paused a moment, staring toward the gray, rolling storm clouds. "It occurred to me," he said, "that we have not spoken much of my family."

She dimpled up at him. "Delaney Saxton, sir, I know quite a bit about. My research into your skeletons, you know, before you came to London. He is twenty-eight, and unwed. He is still in California?"

"Yes, indeed. My last letter from him was gleeful. He appears to be gambling on making his fortune in gold, owns two gold mines now, and also has the dubious pleasure of having been drafted into local politics. He was in the thick of things when California was admitted into the union last year as a free state."

"At least England, with all her faults, did away with that nonsense."

"It is true we are fast evolving into two separate nations, shouting at each other through their newspapers. Henry Clay, the senator from Kentucky, staved off a confrontation for at least a while with his compromise last year. I wrote to Delaney that he should stump about the West a bit if he wants to make a name for himself."

"And likely spend all his gold in the process! I look forward to meeting him, Alex, but I shall meet your daughter, Leah, first. And she is truly the dark horse to me."

"She is a charming little girl, I believe, not at all standoffish."

"You are probably a great cuddly bear to her. Does she resemble you?"

"Somewhat, I guess. Our eyes are the same, but for the rest . . ." He shrugged. "I would appreciate your being kind to her, Giana. I have been away a lot in recent years, and she has been left overmuch to her governess."

"That," Giana said firmly, "I do know about. You didn't think I would act like the wicked stepmother, did you?"

"No, but then again, you will not be staying overlong in New York, will you?" She stiffened, but said nothing. "I ask only that for the time we are together, you treat her with smiles and kindness."

"That, Mr. Saxton, you may count on. I haven't been much around children, but she is special, is she not?"

"Yes," he said quietly, "very special."

Giana fidgeted a bit, then blurted out, "Laura must have been special too, Alex."

"That," he said coolly, "is a subject I would as soon leave in the past, where it belongs."

"If you wish."

"You never told me the name of your friend in New York," he said abruptly, wanting to distract her.

"Derry Fairmount, actually, Lattimer. Her husband is Charles Lattimer, a wealthy banker."

A black brow rose. "You mean you know Derry?"

"She was my best friend in school! I gather from your delighted voice that you are well acquainted with her."

"Oh yes. She is a charming girl, but I do not get along well with her husband. Never have."

"The dashing, romantic Charles?"

"Do I hear that familiar note of cynicism creeping into your voice, Giana?"

"Not really. I just hope she is happy."

"Whatever else is true of Charles Lattimer, he seems to have the wit and wherewithal to keep a young wife content."

"There you go again, Mr. Saxton. As if all it takes to make a woman chirpingly happy is to occasionally toss her a bone of affection."

Alex grinned down at her. "Now I know you're feeling more yourself," he teased her. "Shall we continue to bicker?"

"No. Actually, I should like to eat a mammoth dinner."

He hugged her against her chest. "Excellent, Mrs. Saxton. After you've filled your skinny stomach, and my arms have recovered, I'll put you into a huge tub of water, and then into bed."

"That, Mr. Saxton, sounds like a very complicated proposition!"

"Only until the last item, my dear. Then it is simplicity itself."

Chapter 17

The unearthly racket of drayers, hawkers, porters, and sailors filled Giana's ears as the *Halyon* was eased gently into her berth.

"But it looks perfectly civilized, Alex!"

Alex's eyes crinkled into the October sun, taking in the bustling activity on the South Street docks, a sight that always exhilarated him. It felt so damned good to be home again. He turned a lazy smile to Giana. "Surely you did not expect to see the streets lined with log cabins and wild Indians strolling about. That is my building, Saxton & Nielson, the three-story red brick, just across the street. My office is on the third floor, there on the corner. When I get tired of all the mumbling clerks, I have but to look out my windows to restore my good humor. The Saxton shipyards are just down the block."

"It will do quite nicely for my offices, I think, Alex," she said pertly.

Alex cocked a black brow at her. "Actually," he said, "I hadn't thought about that. But I don't suppose it will harm my reputation if my wife appears with her ledgers and skirts on South Street." He grinned widely at her. "You will have to keep your ears covered, though. The language you will hear in this part of the city will burn them off."

"I think you've prepared my ears quite enough, Mr. Saxton."

He smiled down at her only briefly, for he had caught a glimpse of Anesley O'Leary, his personal assistant, waving his tall black hat wildly at them.

"I see that my letter arrived well before us," he said, waving back. "Anesley," he shouted at the tall red-haired man, his deep voice carrying through the melee of orderly chaos. "Bring the carriage around!"

"Anesley O'Leary," Alex continued, "is my assistant. Perhaps I can convince him to lend himself to you. You'll find him industrious, unethical as need be, and a bully boy with his fists. The only problem is that Anesley can't abide the English. But you are, after all, only a woman, and perhaps he will respond to your ... frail helplessness. I gather your intent is to birth our child in the thick of business?"

"Perhaps not in the very thick," she temporized, gazing toward the Irishman on the dock as he waved an open carriage toward the gangplank.

"I do want you to rest a bit, at least for the time being. You're skinny as a fishing pole."

"It warms my silly heart, Mr. Saxton, to know that you would like to keep me sheltered for the next seven months from all the chill winds that blow off the bay."

She drew a smile from him. "You win, Giana. I promise to show you my concern only at night."

Alex waved his thanks to Captain Duffey and guided Giana down the wooden gangplank. They both swayed a moment when they reached the unmoving ground.

Anesley O'Leary was a younger man than she had thought, his serious brown eyes browed with thick streaks of carrot-red hair.

"Good to see you, Anesley," Alex said, shaking his hand. "My wife, Giana Saxton."

"A pleasure, ma'am. Welcome home, sir." He grinned widely. "I should have known better than to think you were bowed with business for the past months."

"I managed to survive both the business and the pleasure, my dear fellow. I trust, Anesley, that the shipyards are still intact?"

"Jake Ransom needs your advice about the mainmast of the *Eastern Star*. Mr. Saxton's foreman at the shipyard," he added for Giana's benefit.

"What seems to be the problem, Mr. O'Leary?" Giana asked.

"The wood, ma'am. Ransom thinks it wasn't properly aged."

"Was it not part of your shipment from the Baltic?"

"Yes, ma'am," Anesley said, blinking at her.

"Sounds to me, Alex," Giana laughed, "like you've been bilked!"

"Well, we will see to it Monday. Have Jake in my office first thing in the morning. Thank you for meeting us, Anesley. I'll see you on Monday, with Jake." Alex helped Giana into the carriage and swung in after her.

"I will likely see you on Monday too, Mr. O'Leary," Giana called back to him.

"I don't think I'll wait for tonight," Alex said. "Making love to you appears to be the only way I can shut your mouth."

She did not answer him, her attention already engaged elsewhere as their carriage pulled onto Broadway.

"Behind you, Giana, is the Battery, and beyond, Brooklyn. We'll head up Broadway, then swing over to Washington Square."

"That is Trinity Church?" Giana called out, pointing toward the tall spire.

"It was finally rebuilt some years ago," Alex said. "Hopefully, you damned British will not gut it again."

When they reached the south end of Washington Square, Giana waved excitedly at a formation of brightly uniformed soldiers marching on the huge green, their bayoneted rifles held at attention.

"Daily exercise," Alex said. "It is the Seventh Regiment performing their drills."

Their carriage skirted the lovely homes that surrounded the square, and turned onto Fifth Avenue. Alex was delighted to hear her draw in her breath.

"So many trees, Alex! And in the middle of the city!"

"It is the only street in all of New York to boast this much greenery."

The homes grew more imposing as the carriage rolled northward. Giana turned a minatory eye to Alex as they drew to a halt in front of a graceful, thick-columned white mansion, with a wide portico, trellised with rosebushes. Bow windows adorned all three floors, and the bright afternoon sun glistened off their sparkling glass.

"Alex, I wasn't expecting a log cabin, but neither was I expecting another Carlton House! It is truly beautiful."

"I would not expect the stepdaughter of an English duke to live in a house beneath her touch. Wait until you see the garden in the back. It's not so impressive now that it's fall, but in the spring it's one of my favorite spots. I do a lot of my work there. I've managed something of a greenhouse in the attic, with wide skylights, but I haven't had as much success here as in my greenhouse in Connecticut. Don't look so ill-used, Giana. You may still find the inside of the house as tasteless as your fondest hope."

A graceful wide staircase swept upward from the central entrance hall, to two diverging hallways at its landing. Solid oak chairs and tables, set beneath paintings of ships and shipyards, lined the foyer, as did three women and one tall, crookedly smiling man with curling gray hair. The women dipped slight curtsies as Alex introduced them to their new mistress: Agnes, the cook, a monstrously wide woman with a wide smile; Bea, the downstairs maid, her Germanic face more restrained and curious; and Ellen, the upstairs maid, a young girl who seemed nervous at meeting her.

"And last, Mrs. Saxton, I would like you to meet Herbert. He keeps the place running smoothly." He added in an aside for Giana's ears, "He is more English than you are, Giana, and the biggest snob in New York. He does marvelous things for my reputation."

"Madam," Herbert said grandly, bowing.

"Thank you for having everything in readiness, Herbert. You may dismiss the staff."

"It was our pleasure, ma'am." He turned and clapped his hands. "You may return to your posts, ladies."

"Where is Leah, Herbert? And Miss Guthrey?"

Herbert lowered his gaze to the parquet floor for an uncomfortable moment. "Miss Leah is, I believe, sir, in the nursery, Miss Guthrey with her."

Giana saw Alex's jaw tighten.

"Miss Guthrey has been in a regular snit, sir, ever since we got your letter . . . about your marriage."

"Oh dear," Giana said, touching her hand to Alex's sleeve. "It must have come as quite a shock. Shall we go to the nursery and see her?"

"No," Alex growled. "Herbert, send Ellen to fetch my daughter down. I will see her in the library in five minutes, Miss Guthrey with her."

"Very good, sir," Herbert said.

Alex ushered her into his library, a dark masculine room with heavy leather furniture, a massive oak desk, and dark burgundy velvet curtains that fell ceiling to floor along one wall. There were a globe, a dictionary open on its stand, and a table stacked with newspapers beside the fireplace.

Giana felt Alex's hands slide up her arms, and she leaned willingly against him. "Your home is beautiful, Alex. You must be very proud of it."

"I suppose I am. Now, you, madam, are looking a trifle peaked." He closed his arms about her slender back. "I'm putting you through too many paces today, I fear."

"I am not a horse, Alex," she giggled, nestling her cheek against his broad shoulder.

"No, you're a stubborn little mule. After you've met my daughter, I'll take you upstairs. We'll have a quiet dinner in our room tonight."

"Wouldn't you prefer to dine with Leah, Alex?"

Before he could reply, there came a scratching knock on the library door. It opened and a tall, attractive woman with honey-blond hair and doe-brown eyes swept in, a thin child peeping from behind her voluminous skirts.

Alex slowly released her. "Miss Guthrey," he said, his voice cold. "Why were you not downstairs?"

Amanda Guthrey eyed the small Englishwoman with great composure. "Leah wasn't feeling well, Mr. Saxton."

"Leah," Alex called. "Come here and meet Giana, your new . . . stepmama."

Giana returned Amanda Guthrey's scrutiny. Alex

had said something to her, she remembered, about blond women. Miss Guthrey was certainly blond, and quite attractive, in a blowsy sort of way, she added to herself not quite truthfully. Her eyes followed Leah as she skipped happily toward her father. The child was ruffled to her eyebrows with a ridiculous array of bows, flounces, and lacy insets. But she had her father's eyes, Giana saw, and her father's firm chin. Her hair was a soft brown, and styled in little sausage ringlets around her thin face, a fashionable style, but one that made her seem too sharp-featured.

Alex dropped to his haunches and drew Leah into his arms. "It's been a long time without you, puss. She is quite pretty, isn't she," he continued, seeing that she was staring toward Giana. "Give me a kiss and we shall talk to her."

Leah gave her father a wet kiss and wrapped her thin arms about his neck. "You will stay home now, won't you, Papa?"

"I'll be hanging about like a heavy rock," Alex assured her. "Her name is Giana, puss. It's a trifle odd, I know, but you'll get used to it. She is rather nice, and most fond of little girls."

"Hello, Leah," Giana said, extending her mittened hand. Leah placed her own small hand in Giana's, and eyed her curiously a moment. "You are not nearly as large as Papa, ma'am. Does he crush your ribs like he does mine when he hugs you? Does he hug you?"

"Occasionally," Giana said, smiling up at him. "He is rather like a huge bear, isn't he?"

Leah was still studying her new stepmama, her dark eyes wide with curiosity. "Is it true that you're English, Giana, and you're very rich?"

"Where did you hear that, puss?" Alex asked his daughter.

"Miss Guthrey told me."

Alex said smoothly, his eyes meeting Miss Guthrey's, "Your governess is well-informed, it appears."

Giana saw Miss Guthrey stiffen. She wondered why. Was it being called a governess that had offended her? How could that be, unless she were something more . . . a mistress, perhaps. Giana shook away her fantasy, and said to Leah, "I am rather tired now, Leah. Tomorrow morning, would you like to have breakfast with your papa and me? We can get acquainted and I will tell you all about our exciting ocean voyage."

"Leah usually breakfasts with me," Amanda Guthrey said.

"Well," Giana said pleasantly, her chin rising a bit, "that was very thoughtful of you. But now that I'm here, Leah will breakfast with her father and me." She ran her fingers over a particularly vile row of yellow lace at the child's throat. "Perhaps, Leah," she continued, "we could go shopping together. Would you like that?"

"Leah is used to a dressmaker coming here to fit her clothes," Miss Guthrey said. "She does not like crowds."

Alex watched, fascinated, as Giana said with all the hauteur of a grande dame, "Perhaps her dressmaker will appreciate my instructing her on what is suitable for a nine-year-old girl with Leah's coloring."

"I like to feed the ducks in the park," Leah said, shyly confiding, unaware that she had stepped innocently into an awkward breach.

"It is also one of my favorite pastimes, Leah," Giana said, "particularly after I've been shopping."

She looked down into Leah's eyes—Alex's eyes—and felt a tug of protectiveness. She had had a Miss Guthrey once, certainly not as pretty or as seemingly possessive as this one, but a governess nonetheless. And she had been so lonely. The child deserved much more, and Giana intended to see that she received it, both from her and from Alex.

"Actually," she confided in a low voice to the child, taking her small hand in hers, "the ocean crossing was vile, and I was embarrassingly ill. I must rest now, Leah, but tomorrow you and I will shop and feed ducks and"—she raised her voice so Alex would hear her—"your father will take us to a very elegant restaurant for lunch and ice cream."

"A fine idea," Alex said easily, bending his dark gaze toward her. "I will make sure your stepmama is in the top of her form tomorrow, puss."

There was a screech behind the teapot.

"How dare he! He is married! And to an English-woman!"

Derry Lattimer set down her fork as she watched her stepdaughter wad up the newspaper in a snit and hurl it to the carpet.

"How could he!" Jennifer raged again, her fist setting the scrambled eggs trembling on her plate.

"How could who do what, Jennifer?" Derry asked, swallowing a tired sigh.

"Mr. Alexander Nicholas Saxton, that's who!" Jennifer spat. "How could he do this to me?"

"I wasn't aware that Mr. Saxton had ever encouraged you, Jennifer," Derry said calmly. "Besides, you know your father doesn't approve of him."

Jennifer waved away her father's opinions.

"Daddy would have come around. He always comes around when it's something I truly want. And now Alex is married, dammit!"

"An Englishwoman? How interesting. Does the paper give her name?"

Jennifer retrieved the wadded society page and smoothed it out. "Mrs. Alexander Saxton, daughter of the Duchess of Graffton, is sailing with her husband on the *Halyon* to New York. The former Miss Georgianna Van Cleve—"

"Giana!" Derry gasped. "Dear heavens, Alex has married Giana Van Cleve! Do you not remember her, Jennifer? She was my best friend at school."

"That flat-chested little snirp?" Jennifer hissed. "Alex wouldn't look at her twice!"

"Four years is a long time, Jennifer," Derry said dryly, "and bosoms do fill out. I'll thank you to moderate your language. Giana Van Cleve is anything but a snirp. Indeed, she is a first-rate businesswoman, her mother's partner in Van Cleve Enterprises. Dear heavens," she said again, sitting back in her chair. "Giana married to Alex. How very odd."

"If they left England . . . goodness, they've arrived by now!" Jennifer bent her full eye on Derry. "What do you mean, how very odd?"

Derry smiled. "From Giana's letters, I had got the impression she never intended to marry. And now the both of us are married to American businessmen."

Jennifer dropped her eyes again to the paper. "It says that Mr. Saxton was in London to negotiate a merger with the Van Cleves. He must have married her to get hold of her money. He probably owns the Van Cleves now."

To her chagrin, Derry burst into gay laughter. "Oh no, Jennifer. Giana is as hardheaded as Alex, and so is her mother. If she married him, it could only mean that she finally fell in love."

"It still doesn't mean he loves her," Jennifer persevered. "He doesn't even like the English, with all their peers and titles. I heard him say once that if you weren't a lord in England, you are best off learning to be a servant. And her steppapa is a duke!"

Aurora Van Cleve married as well, Derry thought. It must have been quite recent, else Giana would have written her about it. And why hadn't Giana written about her own wedding?

"He was only in England for two months! How could she have gotten her coils into him?"

Alex must have swept Giana off her feet to get her to the altar in but two months' time! Derry would not have thought he could do it, though he was a tantalizingly handsome man, the darling of every parent with a daughter of marriageable age in New York.

"Jennifer," she said, striving for patience, "I do not appreciate your insulting my best friend." She glanced down the expanse of breakfast table at her stepdaughter. To the best of her knowledge, Alex Saxton, never hapless, had not so much as glanced twice at Jennifer. It was not, she thought, that Jennifer was ill-looking. Indeed, her hair was a lovely chestnut color and her eyes a brilliant gray. But the man who married Miss Lattimer would likely be driven shortly to drink.

"I want to go shopping, Derry. I will not be outdone by that . . . Englishwoman!"

Jennifer, Derry thought, you are not only outdone, you are undone, the minute you open your mouth. Still, there was a smile of happy anticipation on Derry's face when she escaped to her sitting room. She wondered what Giana thought of the marriage bed, with Alexander Saxton in it.

"Is she your mistress, Alex?"

Alex lowered his shoeless foot to the carpet of the master bedroom and bent an inquiring eye toward Giana.

"Well, is she?"

He was at first tempted to throw his shoe at her, but the rancor in her voice made him smile. Could it be that his counterfeit wife was jealous?

"I assume you're speaking of Miss Guthrey?" he asked smoothly.

"Yes, Miss Amanda Guthrey—very *blond*, I noticed."

He smiled at her wickedly. "Ah, and natural, I am certain of it."

"You insufferable clod! I will not have your mistress living in my house, Alex! Install her elsewhere, if you wish, but you will at least pretend to be my faithful husband while I am your wife."

Her face was charmingly flushed, her eyes darkened with anger. "*Your* house, Giana?" he drawled.

He saw a cynical wariness return to her eyes, and cursed himself for teasing her. "Come here, Giana," he said, patting his thigh.

She said in a distant voice, over her shoulder, "I am sorry, Alex. It is not my place to criticize you . . . or anything you may wish to do or continue doing. It is your house. I am but a temporary . . . boarder."

He rose angrily and strode over to her, one foot still shod. "I was but teasing you, little fool," he said against the back of her head. "I'm no saint and no celibate, but regardless of any pretense, Giana, I will treat you as my wife. I am not one of your lecherous husbands. God knows, I am from Puritan stock, and it is the most monogamous breed in the world."

He glided his hands down her arms and gently turned her about to face him. She stared, as if fascinated, at his unbuttoned shirt.

"I had a mistress before I left New York, I have no reason to be ashamed of that fact. But you may be certain that Lucy knows of my marriage and will expect to see me shortly to end our liaison." He pressed his fingers beneath her chin and forced her face upward. "Do you really believe I would bed my daughter's governess in my own house?"

Giana sighed. "No," she said in a low voice. She raised her hand and dashed it over his forehead. "I do not know why I am being such a harridan. It is just that when I saw the way she looked at you . . ."

"Jealous, princess?"

Giana glared up at him. "Of course not, Alex! Your overweening conceit is showing again."

"My conceit disappears when you are making love to me, Giana. I can be coaxed into bed, if you've a mind for it."

She was silent for a moment, then whispered, "All you have to do is look at me and I want you. It seems I have as much need as any man."

"But only for this man, I hope. Let me take off my other shoe, Giana."

She helped him, giggling, then rose and pressed herself against him. "Please kiss me, Alex."

He did, tangling his hands in her thick hair. He eased her dressing gown off her shoulders, freeing her breasts. He gently stroked her nipple, feeling it harden between his thumb and forefinger. "Your breasts are larger," he said. "Do I hurt you?"

Giana was stroking his thick black hair, trying to arch her back upward to be closer to him. "No," she said softly. "You are always so gentle. I . . . I love for you to touch me."

He let his hand fall to her belly, his eyes following. It seemed incredible to him that his child could be nestled in her womb, so slight and flat as she was. "You are not even a bit round, Giana."

She laughed, her stomach muscles tightening beneath his splayed fingers. "I am not even three months pregnant, Alex. Do you wish me to be an ungainly cow so soon?"

"I shouldn't care," he said, and leaned down to capture her mouth.

Giana did not believe him, of course, but she clasped her arms tightly about his waist and closed her mind against what she knew to be the truth. For a few months, she could let herself enjoy him. It would have to last a lifetime.

It was only later when they sat opposite each other, with their dinner on a small table between them, that she asked him, accusingly, "Why are you being so nice? You were such a ruthless cad in London!"

He grinned at her over his fork of fluffy potatoes. "I am only trying to lull your suspicions to get you to marry me, so I can finally have your fortune and rub your nose in it."

The grin momentarily left his face when he felt a sprinkling of hurled peas hit his cheek. "Must you always be so . . . physical, Mrs. Saxton?" he said, throwing the peas, one by one, back at her.

"Clod," she said.

"Poor Ellen," he mused. "She will wonder what kind of perverted games we play when she sees all the food on the floor tomorrow." Embarrassed color rose to her cheeks, and she slipped out of her chair and scrambled about to pick them up, finishing on her hands and knees at Alex's feet.

"Now, that, Giana, is a tempting position for a woman."

He wished he had not teased her in that way, for her eyes flew to his face, and he knew she was remembering Rome, remembering Madame Lucienne's girls on their knees before the men, pleasuring them with their mouths. She responded to him so naturally, so freely, that he had forgotten all she had seen.

He leaned down and pulled her up into his lap. "I did not mean to embarrass you, princess," he said, forcing lightness into his words. "Forgive me."

"I shouldn't know about that," she muttered against his shoulder. "I shouldn't know about anything." He stroked her back until he felt her relax against him. "I saw too much, Alex. It is hard to forget, sometimes."

"Day by day it will fade, Giana, and you will forget."

She straightened against his arm and gave him a crooked smile. "You will soothe it all away?"

"A husband, even a fake one, is good for something, princess."

Chapter 18

"This is very spacious, Alex, and I love all the light your windows let in."

Alex proffered her a mock bow. "Thank you, ma'am, for your compliment. Not quite as impressive as your mother's throne room, but I survive."

"Jake is here, sir, about the mainmast," said Anesley O'Leary, gazing surreptitiously toward Mrs. Saxton, who seemed in all seriousness to be studying Mr. Saxton's nautical books.

"Show him in, Anesley," Alex said.

Jake Ransom, Alex's foreman at the shipyard, reminded Giana of Lanson. His forearms were the size of her waist and his nose was off center, from one too many brawls in a barroom, from the looks of him.

"Welcome home, sir," Jake Ransom boomed out.

"Good to be back, Jake. My wife, Mrs. Saxton."

"Ma'am." Jake pulled on the shock of brown hair that fell over his forehead.

"Mr. Ransom. I understand the mast on the *Eastern Star* isn't behaving as you expected."

"Ma'am?" Jake regarded the fragile young lady with an uncertain eye.

"Let's sit down, Jake," Alex said smoothly. "Giana, would you care to join us or accompany Anesley on a tour of the building?"

Giana's eyes twinkled at the foreman's obvious

discomfort. "I shall be with Anesley, Alex, if you need me. Oh, Mr. Ransom," she said over her shoulder in the doorway of Alex's office, "it may help to relathe the Baltic lumber, before you dry it in your kiln, of course."

"Huh? Oh, yes, ma'am."

Alex firmly closed the door and turned back to his foreman, a grin on his face. "Well, Jake, have you done what Mrs. Saxton suggested?"

"I wasn't born yesterday, sir!" Jake fell into a brooding silence for a moment. "Well, I didn't think I should do that without your permission, sir."

In Anesley's office outside, Giana heard Alex laugh, and wondered if he was mocking her to his foreman. "I don't particularly care for Mr. Saxton's office, Mr. O'Leary," she said in an overly imperious voice. "The furniture is too heavy and dark. But the windows are nice. Show me what we have at the opposite end of the floor."

"I . . . I don't understand, ma'am." Anesley fidgeted uncomfortably, wishing that Mr. Saxton would appear.

"Why, Mr. O'Leary, I wish an office. As you doubtless know already, Van Cleave and Saxton have merged. I will be directing the Van Cleve interests here in New York, as well as my own business affairs."

A half-hour later, Alex emerged from his office to see a trail of clerks looking numbly at him, hauling ledgers down the stairs to the second floor. He found Giana, a stunned Anesley at her side, directing his employees as they moved desks, chairs, and files out of the large accounting office. He frowned, put out that Giana would commence to take over without even a word to him, and was sorely tempted to take her to task for it.

Giana turned to him, a smudge of dirt on her cheek and a happy smile on her face, then hurried toward him, wiping her dusty hands on her gown. "Oh, Alex, it will be perfect! You needn't worry about your clerks, there is a fine room for them on the second floor. Anesley tells me that we can have the space decorated within a week. I'll go to the furniture warehouse today to select pieces."

Alex pasted a smile on his face. Seeing her obvious excitement, he couldn't bring himself to blister her ears. He mumbled something unintelligible.

"Good heavens!" Giana's eyes darted to a large clock on the wall. "I am supposed to meet Derry for lunch. Please continue directing the workmen, Anesley! I will see you this afternoon, Alex!"

And she was gone in a whirl of taffeta skirts.

"But I like having my clerks on this floor," Alex mumbled under his breath.

"Sir?"

"Nothing, Anesley." He smiled ruefully. "I think the British have landed again."

"I don't know where to begin, Giana! It will take us weeks to catch up!"

Giana regarded the young matron seated opposite her in the large dining room of the Astor Hotel with a fond eye. Her eyes held four more years of life, but Derry was still as lovely as ever.

Derry continued brightly, "For shame, Giana. Married to Alex Saxton, the prize catch of New York!"

"Is he really?" Giana grinned a bit uncomfortably. "A prize catch, that is?"

"Beware, Giana. There are parents and young ladies alike who want to scratch your eyes out! Not to mention my stepdaughter, Jennifer. Lord, what I've had to endure from her ever since she read of your marriage in the newspaper."

"Jennifer has a tendre for Alex?"

"She does, but Alex has never given her the least encouragement," Derry said firmly. "I mention it only to give you fair warning. Jennifer can be the most bothersome creature."

"I'm surprised Jennifer isn't married yet."

"I am more distraught than surprised," Derry said tartly. "She is as you saw her four years ago, only more so."

"Poor Derry!" Giana gave her a sympathetic smile. "At least my stepdaughter is but nine years old."

"A nine-year-old child would do. Would you care to trade?"

"I am afraid I would not have your patience. At least," she added lightly, "you have no need to worry about governesses."

"Jennifer wouldn't mind a tutor, if he spent his days quoting romantic poetry to her, praising her eyebrows!"

The two young ladies laughed gaily, and toasted each other with glasses of white wine.

Giana reached over and clasped Derry's hand. "I am so glad you're here, Derry."

"I am here as always, still a fluttering butterfly with no children to hang on my skirts."

"And so? I am sure Charles is more than delighted simply to have you for his wife."

Derry smiled, but her eyes didn't quite meet Giana's. "Enough about me," she said abruptly. "Tell me how Alex managed to drag you to the altar! The man must have worked wondrously fast."

Only the child nestled in her womb kept Giana from pouring out the whole story to Derry; he would never find out from anyone that he was illegitimate.

"I found, in the end, that he gave me little choice. Alex is very convincing, you know."

"And so handsome! There, I've said it for you. If I did not love Charles, I vow that I would creep into Alex's house and slip into his bedroom!"

"That too," Giana said. "Will you keep a secret, Derry?" she asked, sipping her wine.

"Of course. You can trust me to stay mum."

"I am pregnant."

"But you just got married! That is . . ."

Giana smiled tightly. "Soon all of New York society will be seeing my stomach swell, and counting up the time on their fingertips. I have been pregnant for two months, Derry."

"Oh dear," Derry said ruefully.

"Will you help me, Derry? Things . . . well, they happen, and sometimes don't work out as expected."

"Don't be silly, Giana! We will sail through it together!" She tossed her head. "Who cares if the baby is a couple of months early, besides some spiteful old ladies wagging their moral fingers? Ah, here's our lunch." Derry smiled up at the hovering waiter. "Russian caviar, Giana!"

Giana waited until the waiter was well out of hearing. "Even though it won't be long now, I would just as soon put off the inevitable as long as I can."

"Well, I, for one, am excited." Derry sighed. "How I wish I could give Charles a child. Here you do everything with no effort at all, and I . . . well, I cannot seem do anything as I should."

"Eat you caviar and stop being so silly. Charles is the luckiest man alive to have you. And I didn't want to get pregnant."

"Well, perhaps not so very quickly, but I'm not surprised with a man as . . . well, virile as Alex Saxton."

"And so damned potent," Giana added acidly.

"We never know what we'll find in the cookie jar! Oh dear," she added, trying to stifle a giggle, "that sounded so terribly vulgar!"

"Or who, for that matter!"

"Oh, how my mother would shudder in horror if she could hear us! But surely, Giana, you love Alex. What else really matters?"

"You are doubtless right."

"Of course I am right," Derry said stoutly. "Is Alex excited?"

"Excited? Yes, I suppose he is quite pleased with himself." Giana scooped up a cracker piled with caviar. "I really don't know Alex all that well, Derry," she said after a moment. "Everything happened so quickly, you see."

"Alex is a man who is blessed with his own particular blend of male arrogance and charm. Perhaps you know that he and Charles are rather cool to each other. Why, I don't know. But I count Alex as a friend."

"Enough of me and Alex now, Derry. Tell me what you've been up to."

Derry was quiet for a moment, then smiled into her wineglass. "We entertain quite a bit, all of Charles's business cronies and their wives."

"And there is Jennifer to raise," Giana teased lightly.

"Even Charles commiserates with me about his daughter. How I should enjoy having him all to myself in the evenings!"

"Handsome, elegant Charles." Giana chuckled. "And so urbane. Four and a half years hasn't seemed to dampen your ardor, Derry."

"No, I much enjoy our evenings together, even with Jennifer hanging about."

"And the days?"

"Ah, the days," Derry said. "We were so young," she added unexpectedly.

"Yes, and filled with silly dreams."

"Well, at least you waited for Alex, and didn't marry that wretched fortune hunter!"

"I assure you, Derry, I wasn't waiting for Alex, or any other man, for that matter. I was living my life, and he was suddenly just there."

"You plan to continue in . . . business?"

"Oh yes. In fact, I have taken over an office next to Alex's for myself."

"And what does your handsome husband have to say about that?"

"Why, I didn't ask him. It is my decision, and my time, not his."

"But it is his office building!"

Giana's eyes crinkled in amusement. "True. Of course, knowing Alex, if he doesn't like it, he will tell me soon enough, and punctuated with the most vile expletives."

"Take care, my friend, that he doesn't simply tuck you under his arm and lock you in a closet!"

"Then I would do something painful to him!"

Derry laughed. "What a couple you must make! But you are more than a couple, aren't you, with Leah about."

"She's a precious little girl, and not at all standoffish, just as Alex told me. Her governess, though, is another matter. Very possessive is Miss Guthrey. I fear that she and I will be locking horns more often than I should like."

Derry looked pensive for a moment, then mused. "You know, Giana, when we were girls in Switzerland, you were so very uncertain of yourself. I felt so angry with your mother. But you've accomplished so much now, whereas I . . . well, I haven't done much of anything I can point to with pride. Odd, isn't it?"

"Surely you discuss banking affairs with Charles, Derry? You are so bright and full of ideas."

Derry blushed in pleasure at Giana's compliment. My God, Giana thought angrily, does not her precious husband ever tell her how lucky he considers himself to have her?

"Actually," Derry admitted, "the subject has never come up. When Charles comes home, he wishes to enjoy only conversation about my day, though why, I cannot guess."

Giana fiddled with her wineglass, swirling the white wine about until is sloshed over the edge. "You know, Derry," she said at last, "I have no one here in New York to help me. Certainly I shall hire people, but there is no one I know well enough to share the responsibility with me. Not only must I oversee the Van Cleve interests, I also have every intention of forming a partnership with Cyrus McCormick."

"Cyrus who?"

"McCormick. He is truly a genius. He is now in Chicago and has built a large factory to produce his mechanical reapers. I want to export them to England."

Derry blinked at her.

"I will need funding, of course, if I can make an arrangement with him. But the fact remains that I will end up being frazzled if I don't have someone who is very bright to help me." It wasn't exactly true, for Giana had already determined to take Alex up on his offer of Anesley O'Leary.

"Would you like me to ask Charles if he knows an appropriate man?"

"Man, Derry? No, I was thinking of a woman. You, Derry."

Derry leaned back in her chair, her eyes fastened on Giana's face.

"I can't," Derry said at last.

"Why not?"

"I can't imagine what Charles would say, much less my friends. No, that is not the true reason. I don't know if I can do it, Giana."

"Bosh. Have you forgotten how you helped me with mathematics at Madame Orlie's? Think about it, Derry, 'tis all I ask. I truly need your help. You could select your own hours."

"Oh my," Derry said, drawing a deep breath. "Giana, you come back into my life like a whirlwind!" Derry suddenly raised her hand and waved vigorously. "Waiter! Bring champagne!"

Giana returned to South Street in high spirits. "Is the king receiving?" she gaily asked Anesley when she reached Alex's office.

Anesley smiled, despite himself. "Yes, ma'am. He just finished arguing down the roof with Mr. Blairlock. He won, of course."

"Of course," Giana agreed dryly.

Alex rose when she entered, and stretched. "Well, madam wife, you look like the cat who has just consumed a very large canary."

"Not exactly. I convinced Derry to work with me."

"Good Lord! You have been busy, Giana. First you kick out my clerks, then you hire a wealthy lady as your employee. Will you run for mayor next?"

"If women but had the vote, doubtless your city would be run more efficiently and with less corruption."

"Behold a man who refuses to be drawn. My excited daughter told me the two of you are going to the park to feed the ducks tomorrow morning."

"Yes, just the two of us, I might add. Leah is so adorable, Alex, and she loves you so much. And so very bright. I can see it now, Alex: Saxon & Daughter, Shipbuilders!"

Alex walked around the side of his desk to her, chuckling. "I missed you," he said softly. "At least when I'm with you, I know my business and my person are still safe." He leaned back against his desk and held out his arms to her. Giana snuggled against him without hesitation, and wrapped her arms around his neck.

"Such conduct in an office, sir," she chided him, kissing his chin.

"Haven't you wondered why I have that large sofa over there?"

She locked her hands behind his back and squeezed as hard as she could. But he only laughed. "You can make me suffer, Giana, but not like that." He nudged her face upward with his chin, and kissed her lightly.

"Poor Anesley. But imagine his shock, Alex."

"Then home it is, madam."

"I fear not, Alex. I'm off to the furniture warehouse!"

Chapter 19

Giana set down a cup of strong India tea and joined Derry on the new pale blue brocade sofa. "Take your nose out of all those numbers, Derry, and drink your tea. It is the only civilized thing to do at teatime, you know."

"What? Oh, yes, dear. I've nearly finished with the arrangements Alex made with Mr. Blairlock for the shipyard expansion. He's done marvels, Giana. Van Cleve/Saxton should be in production by early February!"

"Speaking of production," Giana said, her eyes flitting to the clock on her desk, "it's two o'clock and his royal highness is due back from the shipyard." She quickly downed the rest of her tea and rose. "Please carry on, Derry. I hope to be back in the not-too-distant future with good news."

"Good luck Giana," Derry said, smiling as she watched her friend pat her hair into place.

"Is he free, Anesley?" Giana asked a few moments later.

"I'm certain he is for you, Mrs. Saxton."

Giana nodded and entered Alex's office. He was standing with his back to her, staring down onto South Street.

"Good afternoon, sir," she said gaily.

"Ah, Giana, I was just on my way to see you. I believe I have some domestic news that should please you. Miss Guthrey will be leaving tomorrow morning. I have hired a Mrs. Anna Carruthers, an older widow, who will be better suited to you and Leah. I told her you would be able to see her tomorrow."

Giana stiffened a moment at this unexpected bit of news. "Are you telling me, Alex Saxton, that you hired a woman I have never seen as a governess for Leah and dismissed Miss Guthrey, all without a word to me?"

"I believe that is what I said, yes."

The lie was out of her mouth with her next breath. "There was nothing wrong with Miss Guthrey, Alex. We were beginning to deal better together."

He raised an incredulous brow. "Laying it on a bit too thick, Giana. Miss Guthrey was a constant thorn in your side—"

"And you decided to play Sir Galahad and remove the thorn from the helpless, weak little woman!"

"Something like that, I suspect," he said coolly. "If you are worrying about Miss Guthrey's future, you needn't. I gave her a glowing reference."

"You are high-handed, Alex! After all, as the mistress of our house, I'm supposed to make such decisions! You didn't even consult me!"

"Giana, I gave you more than enough time to either settle differences with Miss Guthrey or dismiss her. You did neither. I can see that you do not intend to thank me."

He was in the right, she admitted to herself grudgingly. "Thank you, Alex," she said, and smiled impishly, sticking her tongue out at him. "And now, will you allow me a surprise for you?"

"You've moved my clerks out of the building?"

"Oh no," she assured him, smiling brightly. "I am

going to let you lend me money for my partnership agreement with Mr. McCormick."

"McCormick only arrived in New York yesterday," he observed in a carefully neutral voice. "You have certainly moved quickly on this."

"I saw him this morning, at Astor House. And I signed the agreement. Now, you, Alex, may lend me the necessary funds."

No wonder the thank-you, he thought, wincing. "I would have preferred, Giana," he said aloud, "that you had reviewed your ideas with me before proceeding. What are we talking about in terms of funds?"

Giana was too excited to hear the chill in his voice. "I would have, Alex," she said, "spoken to you, that is, but I've wanted this ever since the exhibition, and the terms we managed are quite handsome. I need about fifty thousand dollars," she finished in a rush.

"You want fifty thousand dollars?" A muscle twitched in his jaw.

"I know it does seem like a rather large sum, but the profits, Alex! We shall make it back within a year, and then you'll be all the richer, what with the interest I'm certain you'll wring out of me. I might even make you a partner," she added, smiling angelically.

"That is something," he said dryly. He suspected his words would fall like water off a duck's back, but he continued in an even voice, "My advice to you, Giana, is to forget any agreement with McCormick at this time. You needn't worry about complications, for your signature on that agreement won't hold up legally."

"Just because I didn't ask for your holy approval, Alex! You're being unreasonable about this. I will not renege on my agreement."

He turned back to her on a grin. "It did sound like

I'm being a dog in the manger. But it really isn't the case at all."

"Then what, Alex? The agreement is straightforward, I assure you. Indeed, in some ways, I fashioned it after the Van Cleve/Saxton merger. He needs capital to expand to fill customer orders I shall doubtless soon have rolling in from England. Surely there is nothing unusual or complicated about that."

"How much time did you spend studying Mr. McCormick's financial situation?"

Giana shrugged impatiently. "He is having some problems with strikes, and some fools are trying to sue him. But that is nothing to be concerned about, surely."

"Mr. McCormick," Alex said slowly, "is up to his bushy eyebrows in lawsuits. Strikes in Chicago have brought production to a standstill. Even with fifty thousand dollars from you, I doubt he can meet your agreement, for first and foremost, he must see to his customers here in America. Back out of the agreement, Giana. Wait a year or so, until you have a clear picture of Mr. McCormick's financial status."

"No," she said, tossing her head. "I think you're poor-spirited, Alex, and too conservative."

"I will not lend you the money, Giana, for the reasons I've given you. I can't risk it now. Too much of my capital is tied up in Van Cleve/Saxton, in the shipyard expansion, as you and your mother so charmingly arranged with me."

"It appears then," Giana said slowly, her eyes fastened on a daguerreotype of Leah on his desk, "that I shall just have to borrow the money elsewhere."

"No banker in his right mind would lend it to you, save perhaps at an exorbitant interest rate or an outrageous collateral holding. But," he said, pausing a brief moment, "there is your mother."

She frowned, and he smiled ruefully. Her mother wasn't any more likely than he to fund this kind of venture.

"Oh damn," Giana said under her breath.

"Let it go for the time being, princess," he said.

"The devil I will," she said, very politely, and left his office.

The carriage rumbled down Broadway and turned smoothly onto Canal Street. Rayburn, Alex thought, a fine lad with the horses, was making it a comfortable ride this evening. He remembered that Giana had not yet met their hosts for the evening, and smiled into the darkness.

"The Archers are New York crème de la crème," he drawled in his finest Virginia accent. "Mr. Hamilton Archer could, I believe, if he weren't such a bloody aristocrat, lock financial horns with Vanderbilt. As it is, he is perfectly content to let his blue blood settle, and, like you, my dear, to be a civilizing influence on us grubbing savages." It took another moment for Alex to realize he was conducting a monologue. Giana was fast asleep.

He shook his head, his lips tightening. He had spoken at length just that afternoon with Dr. Davidson after he had finally convinced Giana to be examined.

"She is a very active young woman," Elvan Davidson had said carefully to him.

Alex had handed him a glass of sherry and firmly closed the library doors. "What you mean to say, Elvan," he finished for him, "is that she is headstrong, won't listen to a word you say, and will continue to run like a racehorse until she is too large and must slow to a fast trot."

Elvan Davidson, a longtime friend, sipped at the fine sherry before meeting Alex's gaze. "She is not what I expected," Elvan said, fiddling with his watch fob. He felt himself blushing, a damnable cross no man of medicine should have to bear, and hastened to add, "Your wife, Alex, unlike any other young wife I've met who is pregnant with her first child, demanded to know every detail of what would happen."

She had probably cross-examined him like a defense witness, Alex thought. "I trust you told her," he said easily.

"Indeed yes," Elvan said. "I cannot imagine anyone refusing your wife anything."

"And that, my dear Elvan, you also found unexpected."

Elvan's blush retreated as he smiled, a disarming smile that his female patients found ever so reassuring, except Mrs. Saxton. If Alex had chosen a young lady as strong-willed as himself, it was none of Elvan's business. And if Mrs. Saxton was nearly four months pregnant, her date of conception the first week of Alex's arrival in London, well, that too was none of his affair. He leaned forward in his leather chair, his voice becoming serious. "You are her husband, Alex, and she will listen to you. Although she is quite healthy, she must rest more. She is too thin at the moment."

He saw Alex's dark eyes narrow. "What are you saying, Elvan?"

"Tie her down, Alex," Elvan said, dropping his watch fob. "Make her rest more, particularly in these early months, and make her eat. For God's sake, Alex, I have heard that besides running this household, she is involved in business!"

"Yes," Alex said, smiling ruefully at the shock in his voice. "She handles all the Van Cleve business for her mother in London, and other business as well.

She has also taken half a floor in my office building, stolen three of my clerks, hired a friend of hers to help her, and spends a great deal of time with my daughter. She seems so full of energy, so very unpregnant, I suppose."

Another thought occurred to him, and he said slowly, "I as well as my wife much enjoy our ... marital relationship. Is there any harm—"

Dr. Davidson cut him off, more to keep the wretched flush from his face than to save his friend any embarrassment. "No," he said shortly. "Your wife also asked me that."

Alex laughed, unable to help himself.

"I might add that she smiled when I reassured her."

"Then you anticipate no problems, Elvan?" he asked finally.

"No. But you should put your foot down, Alex. And I think you should content yourself with two children, no more."

Alex gave him a crooked smile, and Elvan, not understanding, went happily on to other topics.

Hell, Alex thought, gazing down at his Giana's sleeping face, shadowed in the dim carriage, one would be fine, and one child might be all he would ever know with her. He knew she still clung to her resolve to return to England after the birth of their child. Even when she lay panting in his arms, caressing him and holding him as if her world would end if he left her, there was the inevitable wariness in her eyes that made him want to throttle her. He had toyed with the idea of refusing to make love with her, wondering, if he denied her, if she would realize that she needed him, that her body needed him. He couldn't do it, however. He wanted her, his need for her as great as hers for him.

He leaned back against the cushions, wondering at himself. His life had been so damned simple, so uncomplicated before his ill-fated trip to London. Now he was saddled with a woman who seemed to delight in infuriating him, in bickering with him like a stray cat, and yet he was plotting to keep her with him. The truth was, he knew, that he liked to goad her, liked her sense of humor, and he liked having his house run as efficiently as his business. He even enjoyed discussing business problems with her each evening, still surprised, he supposed, that she, a woman, could listen and understand. And he enjoyed waking in the morning to find her curled up against him, her tousled head against his shoulder.

"Giana," he said softly, gently shaking her, "we are at the Archers'."

She grumbled a moment, and stretched like a cat, yawning widely. "Oh dear," she said, shaking away the dregs of sleep and staring out at the well-lit mansion with a line of carriages pulled up in front. "Forgive me, Alex," she said, smiling at him. "I don't know why I was so tired all of a sudden. It must be your rustic New York air."

He would tell her later that he intended to see her rest every afternoon. "We can skip this party, Giana," he said.

"Oh no," she said, straightening her long gloves. "Derry will be here, and Mr. McCormick, and the Waddells, and—"

He held up a mocking hand. "Do not recite the guest list, please."

"And Jennifer," she added on a small frown. "That girl is such a nuisance, Alex. The couple of times I've seen her, she puts Derry to the blush with her jabs at me."

As Alex assisted her from the carriage, she whispered in his ear, "She hates me, sir, because she wants you. Shall I tell her what a marvelous lover you are?"

He looked at her quite seriously, still holding her about the waist. "No," he said quietly. "Tell her what a marvelous husband I am."

Her expressive eyes fell from his face, and he lowered her to the walkway.

"Are you warm enough?" he asked gruffly, after waving Rayburn away. He pulled her thick sable-lined cloak more securely around her shoulders.

"You needn't treat me like Leah, Alex," she said. "Are *you* warm enough?"

"I, my dear, am not pregnant."

The Archer mansion looked like a white-pillared Southern plantation house sprawled over an entire block off Third Avenue. There was even a black butler to greet them and take their wraps. Soon, Alex knew, Giana would be separated from him, the gentlemen of business she assaulted fated not only for her charm but for her endless curiosity about what they did and how they did it. He supposed the women would eye her dubiously, all save Derry, but when she spoke to them, they would probably hold to her every word, for it was now common knowledge that her mother was a duchess. He saw her sizing up the thinly impressive aristocratic-looking Mr. Archer, and said quickly, "If you begin to feel tired, tell me, Giana. We can leave whenever you wish. Promise me."

She cocked her head up at him, a puzzled expression in her eyes. "I feel marvelous, Alex. Are you worried just because I had a pleasant dream in the carriage?"

Alex had no time to reply, for an equally blue-blooded Mrs. Hamilton Archer was bearing down on them, a mammoth ostrich feather, dyed a dazzling orange, swaying among the ringlets on top of her head.

"My dear Mr. Saxton," she drawled, stretching his name out endlessly. "And this is your charming bride. My dear, I have heard the oddest thing. Mr. McCormick—so bearish-looking, you know—has been telling me about your business dealings. I, of course, thought he meant Mr. Saxton, and I confess to an unladylike gasp when he hastened to tell me it was Mrs. Saxton he was dealing with! But don't I go on! Come, my dears, and meet Mr. Archer. He has been talking all evening of the English lady who runs her own businesses!"

"Oh God," Giana murmured, holding tightly to Alex's arm.

"That will teach you to be so unnatural, Giana," he said lightly. "That is one lady I doubt will allow you to get in one word edgewise."

Hamilton Archer gazed down at the lovely creature before him and allowed a tight smile. She was English, he remembered, and of the aristocracy. His eyes fell to her lovely white shoulders and her softly bulging breasts. His smile loosened a bit. The English were eccentric, and the wealthier they were, the more eccentric.

"Alex, my dear fellow! Introduce me to your lovely wife, and then take yourself off!"

Introductions made, Mr. Archer drew Giana's gloved hand to his lips and vowed that he was charmed.

"My husband tells me you are from Virginia, sir," Giana said, gently removing her hand from his. "Do you still own land in the South? Do you grow cotton, perhaps?"

Alex smiled and quietly moved away. Hamilton

Archer would soon be busy pouring out every detail Giana would wish to know.

But Giana, after ensuring that Hamilton Archer had sated himself with viewing her bosom, excused herself, for she had caught sight of Derry, standing, unfortunately, with Jennifer. She accepted a glass of champagne from a passing servant and made her way across the carpeted salon to the massive marble fireplace.

Jennifer watched Giana walk gracefully toward them and muttered under her breath to Derry, "She's finished flirting with Mr. Archer, I see. She doesn't look at all well with that dark green velvet falling off her shoulders."

"I don't believe it is in danger of falling off, do you, Jennifer?"

Giana moderated her greeting and said only, "Good evening, Derry, Jennifer. Is not this a lovely home? The ceilings are so high they are shadowed."

"I prefer Alex's," Jennifer said. "I always feel so comfortable there. Now, if you will excuse me, doubtless my stepmother would like to discuss ... business."

"You will forgive Jennifer, I hope," Derry said, watching Jennifer's retreating back. "She has nourished these die-away airs for Alex, and persists in casting you as the Other Woman. And you are his wife."

"We will both get over it, I trust, Derry."

"I saw you speaking ever so long with Mr. Archer. Whatever did you have to talk about?"

"Cotton, Derry. He owns slaves, you know, but of course I did not argue the politics or the morality of the issue with him. That would have quite floored him, I fear."

"New York will never be the same again, Giana!" Derry laughed.

"Have you seen Mr. McCormick yet this evening, Derry?"

"He's here tonight, of course, but I haven't talked with him myself. I spoke to Charles about the project, though, to ask his advice."

"And what did Charles say?"

"You will find out soon enough, my dear, when you dance with him!"

"I am delighted he will speak with me. It is a risk, admittedly. But, Derry, I have my heart set on it."

The orchestra struck up another waltz as Derry answered, "I know. I believe your husband is about to ask you to dance, Giana, from the way he is looking at you. Never have I seen a man so besotted."

"Alex, besotted?" Giana laughed. "Hardly that, Derry! He is just concerned that I will tire myself out."

"Well, I will keep you with me until he comes, so that you won't. Your waistline still doesn't tell a tale, Giana."

"Thank God for that. Let's have lunch together tomorrow, Derry. For dessert, I promise you some ice cream. Strawberry. I can't seem to get my fill of it lately. Alex is forever complaining."

"Better than pickled onions! Lunch tomorrow, Giana. Here comes Mrs. Vanderbilt with Jennifer. She looks the world like a ocean liner ready to be launched."

Giana giggled, then turned to smile up at Alex.

"My dear?"

She placed her hand on Alex's arm and let him lead her to the dance floor. When she felt his arm around her waist, his fingers lightly caressing her back, she could only stare up at him, wondering how her traitorous body could respond so easily to his slightest touch.

It was as if he guessed her thought, for he smiled intimately down at her and whispered in a mocking drawl, "Don't take me here, please, Giana. The ladies would doubtless be in a snit to see you bear me away to a back room."

"Would they, now, sir," she drawled back, but her voice was breathless.

"You are the most beautiful Englishwoman here tonight."

"The only one, Alex!"

"Oh? I do believe you are right." He pulled her closer and whirled her about the large ballroom. She laughed aloud when he pivoted gracefully away from another couple, carrying her in a wide circle. When the waltz ended and he released her, she looked up at him, disappointment clear in her eyes. "Cannot we dance again?"

He shook his head ruefully. "Were I to keep you with me, love, I should expect a challenge from any number of hopeful gentlemen. Husbands aren't supposed to be so attentive to their wives. We would be thought to be in love, and that would never do, would it?"

Her eyes flew to his face, but his expression was impassive. "No," she said, drawing a deep breath, "that wouldn't do."

It was later in the evening that Charles Lattimer approached her. "How lovely you look this evening, Mrs. Saxton," he said, his blue eyes assessing her upturned face. "The more I see you, the more I have to agree with Derry. You have indeed grown into a lovely woman, although I was charmed by the shy young girl in Geneva."

"And that was a long time ago," Giana said. "You

are too kind, sir. It is your wife who looks lovely to-night. I am a blackamoor and she has the look of an angel."

A fair eyebrow arched upward. "An angel who was so unhappy in her heaven that she fled earth-ward."

"Come, Charles, would you be content with but a harp to strum?"

He shook his head, smiling down at her. "Your logic is terrifying, Giana. But you know," he continued thoughtfully, "I haven't seen her so excited in years. Even my daughter at her sharpest doesn't seem to faze her lately. You know, of course, that all our friends believe that we've both lost our heads."

Giana tossed her head. "It is what you and Derry think that is important, sir. The others, well, they can go to the devil."

"Perhaps, but it does take some getting used to. For instance, I must remember now to ask Derry if she is free before inviting her to lunch."

"Tomorrow is out, sir, I'm afraid."

Charles grinned down at her engagingly. "Do you mind mixing a bit of business with dancing?"

"Not at all, just so long as I can still mind my steps."

"Derry has told me about your proposed partnership with Mr. McCormick. She mentioned that you need in the neighborhood of fifty thousand dollars and your husband refused to lend you the money."

"That is true, Charles."

"That is hardly a household allowance, Mrs. Saxton, but I think I could be interested, if you put up for collateral twice that amount, say, of your twenty-five-percent ownership in Van Cleve/Saxton."

"That is asking a lot, Charles."

He whirled her about before replying, "True, but

the collateral must balance the risk of the investment, which, in this instance, is substantial."

"I should like to think about it, Charles. Could you draw up the papers and send them by tomorrow?"

"Certainly."

"Alex told me no banker would touch my proposal. Are you doing this for Derry?"

"Perhaps in part. Your husband, I'm sure, will not much like this arrangement. But I am a businessman, and if you are willing to take the risk, the loan is a sound one."

"Well, princess," Alex greeted her some minutes later, "I see your eyes are sparkling like sapphires. Have you made so many new conquests tonight?"

"Yes," she said slowly, not quite meeting his gaze. "It has been a most rewarding evening."

She smiled toward Charles Lattimer, who was dancing with Derry.

"Do not treat Lattimer as a conquest, Giana."

"Why don't you like Charles Lattimer, Alex?" she asked curiously.

"It's enough for you to know we both prefer to keep a goodly distance between us."

"My dear Mrs. Saxton!"

She turned to see the comforting figure of Mr. McCormick, standing, as was his habit, on the balls of his feet, with his hands thrust deep into his pockets, weaving slightly as he gazed at her.

"Perhaps you would like to speak to Mr. McCormick alone, Giana," he said. "I will see you later."

How smug of you, Alex, Giana thought. I will not renege on my agreement! She bent a dazzling smile on her future partner and assured him she would have the money by the end of the week.

"Very good, my dear," Mr. McCormick said. "Now, no more business tonight! I have come to claim you for the next dance. Even an old codger like myself likes to be seen occasionally with his lovely business partner on his arm."

Only Herbert, his rheumy eyes heavy with sleep, was waiting to greet them when they arrived home. "Take Mrs. Saxton upstairs for me, Herbert," Alex said to him. "I have a little work to do and will be up soon." He squeezed her hand and strode away from her to his library. "And, Herbert," he called over his shoulder, "take yourself to bed as well. And don't, as I keep telling you, wait up for us anymore."

Alex let himself quietly into their bedroom a half-hour later. To his slack-jawed surprise, Giana was slouched in a deep wing chair beside the fireplace, sound asleep. She was still dressed in her petticoats and undergarments, one slipper lying under her hand in her lap. Her black lashes were like soot against her white cheeks, thick and lush. It angered him that he hadn't followed her up and tucked her in himself. Little fool, why hadn't she asked him to leave sooner?

He walked softly up to her and started to lift her gently into his arms.

"Dammit, Giana!" he suddenly shouted at her.

Giana jerked awake to see Alex's furious face above her. He was shaking her. "Alex?" she said, her voice fuzzy with sleep.

"You promised me, Giana!"

"Promised you what?" she managed, straightening in the chair.

"The corset." He pulled her roughly to her feet, twisted her around, and began jerking at the laces. He pushed and prodded until at last he pulled off the offending corset, and threw it angrily into the fire. "You bloody little fool!" he growled, clasping her shoulders in an iron grip.

"Stop shaking me, you brute! I had to wear it!"

He released her readily, but she saw that his black eyes were smoldering.

The final webs of sleep cleared from her mind and she repeated calmly, "Really, Alex, I had to wear it."

"Why? Why the hell would you do that to my child?"

She sighed, rubbing her arms. "My gown wouldn't fasten without it."

"Then why didn't you wear another damned gown, for God's sake?"

"Must you continue to be foul-mouthed and yell at me?" She stamped her foot, losing her patience. "For your information, Mr. Saxton, it was the only gown I could fit into, and only with my last corset." She looked balefully toward her smoking corset in the fireplace.

"Why didn't you buy another gown?"

She raised her chin. "I . . . I haven't had the time."

He groaned and ran his hand through his hair, ruffling it into spikes. "You're a bloody woman, and you're telling me that you—"

"Yes, I, a bloody woman, haven't had the time. I haven't harmed your precious child, Alex. Now, would you please stop your ranting and let me go to bed?"

"That wasn't the only reason, was it?"

"No. If you would know the entire truth, I did not want people gazing at my waistline!"

"I should beat some sense into you," he said. "So this is how you treat your promises to me? As for what anyone thinks about your pregnancy, I don't give a good goddamn. You are pregnant, dammit, and everyone will know it soon enough."

"Well, I have no more corsets left now, so you needn't worry!"

He was still glaring at her, and she sighed. "Please, Alex, I am so tired."

"You should be, it's the middle of the night." He drew a deep breath and said very calmly, almost gently, "I expect you to stop pretending nothing has happened, Giana, to yourself or to anyone else. You are pregnant with my child and in the role of my wife, and your scurrying about, doubtless working harder than you did in London, will not change it. It must stop, Giana. No more rushing about from morning until midnight. You will get more rest. If you don't care about our child and your own health, I do. You will obey me in this, else I'll lock you in your room."

"I will do just as I please, Alex, and I'll thank you to stop giving me orders!"

"I will cease, Giana, when you stop acting like a stubborn mule and assume the behavior of a reasoning adult."

He was acting as if she were a willful child and he the wise father! She gritted her teeth and flung at him, without thinking, "I will do exactly as I believe right, Alex, with no more smug orders from you! I am not a fool, as you seem to believe, and what's more, I will have my partnership with Mr. McCormick." She paused but a moment, staring up at his set face, and said with exacting calm, "Indeed, I fully intend to accept Charles Lattimer's offer of a loan to do it."

He said slowly, his eyes darkened, "You are telling me that Lattimer offered you the money?"

She nodded, thrusting up her chin.

"And just what collateral does Lattimer demand?"

"Twice the amount of the loan, from my twenty-five-percent ownership of Van Cleve/Saxton."

He shook his head, and his voice was suddenly

weary. "You know that Lattimer and I do not deal
well together. Did it not occur to you that the only
reason he is offering to back you is that he knows
well you will fail and thus he will get to me through
you?"

"That is not true, Alex. He is lending the money
because he believes that the partnership will succeed.
He is, after all, a banker, and a successful one at that.
It has nothing to do with any ridiculous masculine
spat the two of you have nurtured."

Alex said slowly, seeming to select his words very
carefully, "Lattimer and I do not deal well together
for a very simple reason: he was a suitor to my first
wife. Laura's father preferred me as his son-in-law.
Lattimer has never forgiven me for what he believes
was underhanded dealing, in other words, marrying
Laura for her money without caring for her. He
doubtless sees the loan as revenge."

For a moment Giana doubted her judgment. But to
offer her the loan because he was, years ago, in love
with the same woman as Alex, likely believing out of
disappointed spite that Alex was a blackguard,
seemed to her vastly improbable. No, Charles believed in her scheme, and after all, he was Derry's
husband, and thus solicitous of her as well. Only two
proud, stubborn men, she thought, looking away
from Alex toward her smoldering corset in the fireplace, could contrive to act like two dogs in the manger, chewing a bone that should have, years ago,
been decently buried and forgotten.

"Very well," she said coldly, busily untying her
petticoats. "I am going to bed."

Alex only glared at her, knowing full well that
Giana intended to accept the terms Lattimer offered.
Though it angered him all the more, he knew the

story he had told her about him must in truth sound like a tempest in a teapot.

She shrugged her shoulders at him, unaware that the sight of her, disheveled, her hair falling loose down her back, one long tress winding sensuously over her breasts, was fast molding his anger into desire. At his continued silence, she jerked her head up. "If you want to be in a foul mood, Alex, why don't you just sleep downstairs?"

"No," he said harshly, stepping toward her. "I want to sleep with my wife ... and make love to her."

Giana whirled about to face him, standing only in her white chemise, a lacy, quite sheer garment that reached her knees, and left little to his imagination. "I think not, Alex," she said tightly. "I find it difficult to feel any desire for you, much less liking, with your continual disapproval of me."

"That will change quickly enough," he said deliberately, sweeping his eyes over her, "when we're in bed."

"Stop it, Alex! I want nothing to do with you, do you understand? I am not some sort of ... strumpet, here for your blasted pleasure!"

She felt his strong arms close around her, and drove her fist into his belly. He held her immobile against him, and laughed, his breath warm against her temple. "I told you, love, that you should wait until after our child is born. You'll be stronger then and can give me a good drubbing."

"Stop laughing at me!" She tried to wrench away from him, but he merely held her against him with one arm and grasped the top of her chemise and ripped it down her back.

"Are you going to throw it in the fire?" she yelled at him, her voice muffled against his chest. He did not answer her, only lifted her in his arms and dumped her unceremoniously onto the velvet covers of their bed.

"Stubborn, stupid little fool," she heard him mutter to himself as he tugged off his shoes.

When he stood facing her, naked in the midst of his discarded clothes, she gasped, her eyes on his hugely swollen member. "You will not do this, Alex! I will fight you, do you hear? You will not force me!"

She was a fool, she thought, just as she had been in the garden the night of her mother's wedding. She had believed then that he would try to savage her like the men at Madame Lucienne's. He was stretched his full length on top of her, his long muscled legs covering hers, her hands trapped in his above her head.

She stared up into his dark eyes, but inches above her, and tried to steel herself against him. Why would he not be brutal? she thought frantically, trying to free her hands. "You are hurting me, you huge bully," she gritted, wondering if he could see the lie in her eyes.

She was not sure if he did, but in the next instant her body was cool to the air. He had rolled off her and risen. She watched him numbly as he doused the lamps, then felt the bed dip when he lay down again.

Alex lay on his back, his arms pillowing his head, cursing himself for seven kinds of a fool. His frustrated anger had led him to dominate her in the most primitive way imaginable, and the most despicable. There was much he had told her and quite a bit that he hadn't. Damn her. She knew he was right, at least about her acting with blind bravado, denying him and their child. And she knew he didn't want her to leave him, didn't want her to take their child back to

England. How could she be so natural in his bed, share such pleasure with him, and still consider returning to a desolate, spinsterish life after she left him?

"Alex?"

"Yes?" he growled unsteadily.

"Please do not hate me."

His frustration made him say, "Not hate you until after you've taken my child and left me?"

She gave a soft, pained cry, but he hardened himself against her. He turned on his side to face her. "What do you want from me, Giana?"

"I . . . I . . ." He could hear her breathing harshly, her indecision almost palpable in the ragged silence between them. Suddenly she hurled herself against him, and he felt her hands drawing his face to her. He accepted her against him, kissing her deeply, his hands sweeping over her body. He let his fingers probe through the curling hair over her woman's mound. Her delicate flesh was swollen and moist with desire, and the light touch of his fingers made her gasp. So it was no game she was playing with him. He wanted to yell at her to trust him, to forget . . . To forget what? The truth? That many men treated their wives just as she feared he would treat her?

He felt her hand rove downward from his chest, tangling in the thick hair at his groin, until she found him. He jerked as her fingers closed gently about him, and tightly closed his mouth against the groan building in his throat.

There were no more words between them, only the sounds of pleasure as they caressed each other.

When she lay snugly against him, her leg thrown over his groin, her hand curled in the hair on his chest, he found to his surprise that sleep was the furthest thing from his mind. His heart finally

slowed from a climax that had made him want to
yell his possession of her. He would not let her
leave him, not after the birth of their child, not
ever.

Chapter 20

Leah cleared her throat as she opened the London *Times*, Alex's gift to Giana, delivered in bundles nearly every week since Giana's arrival in the Saxton household, and announced her daily tidbit of news to everyone at the breakfast table.

"The most interesting event in London today," she began, "or three weeks ago was the triumphant arrival of"—she stumbled over the odd name—"Kossuth, the leader of the Hungarian revolutionaries. Lord John Russell, the Prime Minister, you know," she added proudly, "to show England's sympathy with the revolutionaries, is offering to pay eight pounds to every Hungarian refugee arriving from Turkey who needs help to pay his passage to America. To us," Leah finished.

"So much violence in Europe," Giana said. "In every country it seems, save America and England."

"Even our country may tear itself apart," Alex said.

"I saw you reading Mrs. Stowe's novel, Mrs. Saxton," Anna Carruthers said.

Giana nodded toward Mrs. Carruthers. She liked Leah's new governess immensely, from the top of her white bun to the toes of her sensible shoes. She was like a comfortable, very kind mother-in-residence.

And Leah liked her. Anna was German, and well-educated.

Alex looked up from his toast. "*Uncle Tom's Cabin?*"

"Yes, indeed," Giana answered.

"My business associate in Atlanta, George Plummer, is irate about the book, needless to say."

"I didn't know you had a business associate in the South, Alex!"

"There is quite a bit you don't know about me yet, Giana," he said quietly.

Giana looked up in surprise at his impassive face, but the brief tension between them was quickly broken by Leah's giggling gasp.

Mrs. Carruthers, aware of the sudden currents at the breakfast table, chided her charge gently, "It is very early for undue levity, Leah."

"But, Mrs. Carruthers," Leah said, raising her head from the obituary section, "this is most unusual! Really!" She ducked her head behind the newspaper and read aloud, " 'William Hodgson, who just died in Newgate prison, is reported to have been one hundred and six years old when he drew his last breath. He was imprisoned for making a revolutionary speech in 1793.' "

"Pigheaded English!" Alex growled.

Giana allowed an amused glance at Alex before bending a bright smile to her stepdaughter. "It was worth hearing two bits of news today, Leah, instead of just one. Imagine, one hundred and six years old!"

"Father's right," Leah murmured aloud, frowning. "It doesn't seem very fair, does it? He only made a silly speech. Think of what he could have done for all those years if he had been free."

"Yes," Mrs. Carruthers said quickly. "Well, in any case, we don't know the content of his speech, do

we, Leah? Now, child, it is time for you to come with
me and learn about the geography of England. We
will study Somerset today, your English step grandmother's birthplace."

Giana started guiltily. She hadn't answered her
mother's latest letter. Well, she would simply appropriate Alex's study and write her of her partnership
with Cyrus McCormick for the export of his mechanical reaper to England. She said to Leah, "I hope you
will meet my mother, Leah. She is ever so fascinating
and lovely."

"Even though she is a damned duchess?" Leah
said innocently, parroting Alex's words.

"Leah!"

"Yes," Giana said, smiling, "she is a duchess and
still fascinating and lovely. And," she added wryly,
"more intelligent than most men."

"But not smarter than Papa," Leah said with all
her child's certainty.

"I would not be so sure, Leah!"

Alex said blandly, "Speaking of duchesses, next
week is Thanksgiving, the celebration of our own il-
lustrious Puritan grandfathers."

"Thanksgiving," Giana repeated. "I have heard of
it. It is a formal celebration, is it not? Every year?"

Alex winked at Leah's excited expression. "It is an
American tradition."

"Puritans—that famous monogamous breed?"

"Ah, yes," Alex said.

"We have apple pies and cider every year," Leah
said.

"Ja, and sweet potatoes," Mrs. Carruthers added, a
smile reaching her pale blue eyes.

"And when does this Thanksgiving event take
place?" Giana asked the table at large.

"Next week," Leah said. "Thursday. Shall we have company this year, Papa?"

Giana gazed at Alex expectantly. "We will see, puss," Alex said, pulling his watch from his pocket and consulting it. "My dear," he said to Giana, "I regret to leave you, but I have promised my charming company to a dreary group of shipbuilders. Unfortunately I won't be home until late."

Giana nodded abstractedly, her brow furrowed in thought. There was curiosity in Alex's eyes when he leaned down to plant a light kiss on her cheek. "Get to sleep early tonight, all right?"

"What? Oh, yes, Alex." She gave him a dazzling smile, to which he cocked a black brow. It was not until they were at the dinner table the following evening that his curiosity was satisfied.

"About Thanksgiving," she began, bending another dazzling smile toward Alex as she toyed with her custard.

"Yes?" he asked cautiously.

"Leah tells me you usually do have guests for Thanksgiving." Her chin rose a bit. "I would like to invite the Lattimers, Alex."

"What a marvelous idea," Anna Carruthers said. "Mrs. Lattimer is such a charming lady."

"I should love to see Derry," Leah added, before she wrinkled her small nose. "Maybe Jennifer won't come."

Alex looked at the three pairs of expectant eyes fastened on him. He knew it must be difficult for Giana, seeing Derry almost daily, to have to forgo her company socially. He couldn't imagine Charles Lattimer wanting to share dinner at his home. Let it be Lattimer to turn down the invitation, he thought. He forced a nod and a belated smile.

"Thank you, Alex!" Giana rose quickly from the table. "I must speak to Agnes about what to cook for this Thanksgiving."

"My dear," Alex said, "Agnes is one of the original survivors of my Puritan grandfathers. She knows exactly what to do, I assure you."

Thus it was, to Alex's chagrin, that the Saxtons greeted their Thanksgiving guests the following Thursday, with the smell of Agnes' turkey and candied sweet potatoes filling the house.

"Lattimer," Alex said curtly by way of greeting.

"Saxton," Charles returned in a bland voice.

Giana and Derry exchanged glances as the two men reluctantly shook hands.

"Jennifer," Giana said, "how delightful you look today! And such a lovely day it is! I was expecting howling winds and snow at the end of November, but instead we have such sun and warmth!"

Jennifer merely nodded in greeting, unable to get a word in through Giana's exuberant chatter.

"We are having suet pies for dessert," Giana continued brightly to Derry.

"No, love," Alex said, "mincemeat pies."

"And the turkey weighs over twenty-five pounds, Derry!" Leah said.

"Then we shall all have to loosen our belts, won't we?"

Thank God for Leah, Giana thought some minutes later over the dinner table. The child chattered happily, and remembered to ask Charles Lattimer politely if he was enjoying Agnes' turkey. He gave her a startled look and a smiling yes.

Jennifer waited until Agnes served the mincemeat pies, topped with vanilla ice cream, before she touched her fingers to Alex's hand and said in a light, caressing voice, "I am delighted to visit your home again, Alex." She gazed a moment about the dining room. "I am pleased that you haven't allowed any changes. But then, of course," she continued, "your ... wife doesn't have time for domestic concerns, does she? And poor Miss Guthrey. Such a *lovely* person. I hear that she had to accept a position with the Waddells."

"How delightful for her," Giana said over her pie à la mode. "I did not realize that you were acquainted with Miss Guthrey, Jennifer."

"I'm glad Anna is here," Leah said stoutly.

Jennifer nodded vaguely. "She was so happy here, I understand. But then again, she is very pretty, is she not?"

"Jennifer!" came Charles Lattimer's forbidding voice.

"How true," Giana said agreeably. "I was dreadfully jealous of her, you know, Jennifer, and couldn't wait to have her removed. I wanted Leah and Alex all to myself."

Jennifer stared at her gape-mouthed.

"I'm sure you understand my feelings," Giana added kindly. "I become quite rabid when any lady regards Alex with a fond eye. The English, you know, Jennifer, are very possessive."

"Is there a petard about?" Derry asked demurely.

"Does everyone have wine?" Giana asked. "Leah, pour yourself some lemonade. I have an announcement to make—and a toast, I trust, is in order."

Alex shot her a suspicious look, but obligingly filled his wineglass.

Giana smiled, raising her glass, and looked directly at Alex. "Alex and I have decided that I should curtail my business activities over the next months and become more a woman of leisure. You see, we are going to have a baby."

Jennifer gasped.

"In May," Giana added, still holding Alex's gaze. He was smiling at her now.

"And I will have a new brother or sister," Leah said happily. "Isn't it marvelous?"

"May," Jennifer repeated, her eyes narrowing.

"Yes, Jennifer," Giana said.

"Congratulations, Saxton," Charles Lattimer said.

"But that means that you and Alex—"

"No matter," Derry said hastily, frowning heavily toward her stepdaughter.

"It does matter," Jennifer persisted, thwacking her wineglass to the table. "It means—"

"Jennifer," Alex said softly, with just a hint of menace, "all it means is that Giana and I found that we cared for each other very quickly. It just took me a while to persuade her to marry me."

"As persuasive the second time as the first," Charles Lattimer muttered into his wineglass, and Alex stiffened.

Derry's eyes flew to Giana, but Giana's smile did not falter. "What a lovely dinner. The baby doesn't at all approve of my tight waistband. Anna, we will excuse you now if you would like to take Leah upstairs. Gentlemen, shall we have coffee in the drawing room?"

There was a moment of stiff silence when Giana rose from the table, like a general, Alex thought.

Giana was the picture of serenity as she distributed cups of coffee. "Sugar, Charles?"

He nodded.

"Do you now own Van Cleve, Alex?" Jennifer asked.

"I fear not," Giana said quickly, seeing Alex's eyes narrow dangerously. "Indeed, Alex refused my dowry. I fear, Jennifer, that I must earn my keep."

"A leopard changing his spots?" Charles Lattimer murmured.

"You find me unattractive, Charles?" Giana said sweetly.

"No, but neither should you be naive."

"Ah," Giana said without pause, "you believe that Alex married me for my money?"

Charles Lattimer started at her bald question.

"You are very rich," Jennifer said boldly, answering for him.

"She won't be if she continues borrowing money from bankers who demand extortionate collateral," Alex said.

"I am a businessman, sir!"

"True," Giana said smoothly. "And with the interest you're charging me, Charles, you will be a richer businessman very soon."

"But that isn't the point," Derry said, her eyes on her husband's face, "is it, Charles?"

Charles Lattimer stared at his young wife. "You forget yourself, Derry! I will thank you not to speak of things you don't understand!"

"No, Charles," she said gently, "it is time that the past is spoken of. Ten years of blind dislike is enough for anyone."

Alex rose abruptly and strode to the fireplace, his eyes resting balefully on Giana's face. "How stupid of me not to have realized that you planned this, my dear."

"Derry, Jennifer, we are leaving!"

"Oh no, Charles," Derry said comfortably. "How odd, Giana, I always thought that women carried grudges to absurd lengths. Men, I was given to understand, exercise more logic, more reason."

"I don't understand," Jennifer began, but she was answered only by a blighting stare from her father.

"Ten years is a dreadfully long time," Giana said quietly. "Charles, Alex wouldn't have married Laura had she been a pauper, any more than you would have. Is it not true that Derry brought you an impressive dowry?"

"That has nothing to do with anything!" Charles snapped. "Derry knows I love her."

"Do I, Charles? If you so firmly believe that Alex married Laura, the girl you were courting, for her money, then why shouldn't I believe the same about you? Why shouldn't Alex believe the same about you?"

"This is quite enough," Alex said firmly. "Lattimer and I would both appreciate our wives minding their own damned business!"

"Why, Alex," Giana said innocently, "if you have married me for my money, and Derry finds herself in the same straits, don't you think it fair that Derry and I decide between us what we must do?"

"Father," Jennifer said, "would never do such a thing!"

"I know, Jennifer," Derry said, smiling toward her tight-lipped husband. "He is an honorable man, albeit a very stubborn one."

"Just as Alex is," Giana added comfortably.

Charles Lattimer turned glittering eyes to Alex. "I know what I know. Laura Nielson would have married me, had it not been for her father."

"I trust, Charles," Derry said quickly, seeing Alex's hands fisted at his sides, "that you cherished no violent emotions toward Laura when you married me. I would hate to believe that I was your second choice."

"Don't be a fool!" Charles fairly shouted at her.

"Didn't my father want you for a son-in-law?"

"Dammit!" Alex exploded. "That is enough! Lattimer, would you care to leave these prying ladies to their gossip?"

"Indeed," Charles said, rising quickly.

"Please don't get too drunk, Alex," Giana called after Alex's retreating back.

Derry and Giana looked at each other for a long moment, and burst into laughter.

"How dare you laugh at my father!" Jennifer cried.

"Oh, Jennifer," Derry said, wiping her eyes, "I am laughing because I am happy."

"As for you," Jennifer spat, turning on Giana, "the only reason Alex married you was that he got you pregnant." "Perhaps," Giana said easily. "Alex is terribly persuasive."

"Jennifer," Derry said firmly, "I am tired of your snitty remarks. Either you mind your manners and your mouth, or you will find yourself without anyone to speak to but the servants. Alex and Giana are married and there's an end to it. Now, get your cloak. We are going home, where, I believe, I shall celebrate with a brandy!"

"Alex, you stink!"

"Brandy," he muttered, pulling off his clothes. He walked unsteadily to the bed and stood for a long moment staring down at Giana. She tried to keep her eyes on his face, but inevitably they fell down his body.

"You are an interfering wife," he remarked.

"I know," she said softly. "Will you forgive me?"

"You apologize? 'Tis unheard of!" he said disagreeably.

"Will you forgive me?" she repeated steadily.

"You're naked," he said, frowning down at her.

Giana patted the bed.

"I should beat the hell out of you," he said, almost as an afterthought. He plopped down beside her on his back, pillowing his spinning head on his arms.

"I hope you can wait until the baby is born." She was quiet a few moments, watching him gaze up at the shadowy ceiling. "Are you going to tell me what happened with Charles Lattimer, Alex?"

He did not look at her, and said in a tired voice, "You mean to ask if we are now fast friends? No, Giana, not that, but perhaps we have reached some understanding. I never before much cared if he thought me a scoundrel." Before Giana could respond, he continued, "You announced your pregnancy to the biggest and the most spiteful mouth in New York."

"As you told me, Alex," she said evenly, "the baby is a fact. If you do not care that people will talk, why should I?"

"You almost announced that you will behave more properly from now on."

"Yes, you were right. I care about the baby's health and my own."

"You gave Jennifer her comeuppance," he said on a smile.

Giana giggled. "Yes, I did it well, didn't I?" She turned on her side toward him and gently caressed the black hair on his chest. "How drunk are you, Mr. Saxton?" she inquired softly.

"Never too drunk," he growled. "You're always easy." He felt her hand glide down to his belly, and stiffened in anticipation.

"Do you think any man could excite me, Alex?"

"No!" he said violently.

"I don't think so either," she agreed. "You are so beautiful, Alex." She rose to her knees above him and leaned down toward his mouth. "Even though you stink of brandy, I want to kiss you."

"You think all will be forgiven if I let you seduce me?"

Giana grinned to herself at the mock irritation in his voice. "No, I'm simply thinking of myself." She rubbed her breasts against his chest, and reached her hand down to grasp him. "Aren't you even a bit interested, Alex?"

"Witch," he muttered.

"I love you to kiss me," she gasped when he released her for a moment.

Alex rolled her on her back and dipped his mouth down to hers again. His hand was gentle on her breast, light against her taut nipples.

"He is growing," he said into her mouth as his fingers caressed over her swelling belly.

Alex raised his face and smiled down into her eyes. "You are beautiful, Giana, save for your feet."

She blinked at him. "My feet? You're drunk, Alex!"

"I didn't want to hurt your feelings before," he said, frowning down the length of her legs, "but the brandy has loosed my tongue. You have flat feet, Giana."

He glided his hand down her leg, pausing a moment to caress the back of her knee, and picked up a foot. "Flat," he pronounced. "At least they're small feet, and don't intrude too much."

"You, Alex Saxton, are a louse!"

Alex grinned shamelessly at her, slipped off the bed, and grumbled, "I need more light. A man likes to see what he's doing."

He moved the lamp close, and resumed his study of her. Giana felt embarrassed color flood her face. "It's only your feet I can find any fault with," he said with satisfaction after a moment. When he covered her again, her legs grew slack and her body opened to him. She cried out his name, her hands tangling in his hair, and tensed beneath him.

"Only your feet," he groaned. He felt her muscles

contract as he thrust inside her, pulling him deeper, and he fell on top of her, moaning his pleasure against her neck.

He fell into a drunken, sated sleep, pressed against her back, his hand lying negligently on her belly.

It has been a very good day, Giana thought to herself, snuggling her hips closer to Alex's belly.

Alex suddenly murmured in a slurred voice, "I did my best to fatten you up today. We'll see Monday if Dr. Davidson thinks you less of a runt."

To Giana's utter chagrin, Alex insisted upon being present when Dr. Davidson visited her. And he was in a devilish mood.

Elvan, aware to the soles of his feet of the scene around him, found that he was blushing again. That Alex should remain simply wasn't done.

"Have you felt the baby move yet, Mrs. Saxton?"

Giana shook her head.

"Nor have I," Alex added.

Elvan cleared his throat. "Are you resting each afternoon, Mrs. Saxton?"

"Yes," she said, "now I do, regularly."

"That is true," Alex said.

"Are you drinking enough milk?" Elvan pursued rather desperately.

"I do not care for milk."

"I pile her toast with *butter*, Elvan."

"Do you, er, have much soreness in your . . . upper body, Mrs. Saxton?"

"You mean," Alex said, "do her breasts hurt?"

"I understood exactly what he meant, Alex!" Giana snapped. "Yes, Dr. Davidson, a bit."

"You can be certain that I am very careful," Alex said.

Elvan ducked his head and laid an uncomfortable

hand over her belly. "The child is certainly growing," he said, as if surprised.

"As I keep telling my wife, Elvan, I am a large man. But you've already told her that, have you not?"

"Yes, I have. I don't think there are twins, Mrs. Saxton."

"Twins!" Giana cried.

"A pity," Alex said. "An American baby and an English baby. That would be quite a tenable solution. Yes, a pity."

Elvan quickly pulled down her nightgown and rose. "You are looking much healthier, Mrs. Saxton, and resting as you should. A first baby is always the most difficult and you must ensure that you are as fit as possible."

"Yes, of course," Giana said.

"I will continue to keep her off her feet," Alex said smoothly.

Chapter 21

"Mr. Saxton is graceful for such a large man," Mrs. Carruthers remarked to Giana as they watched father and daughter glide across the ice on Miller's Pond.

"I should like to be with them," Giana said wistfully. She turned rueful eyes to the governess. "Alex told me he would tie me to a tree if I even looked at a pair of ice skates."

"Mr. Saxton is just being protective of you. He takes good care of you."

"And he likes to have his own way," was Giana's tart reply.

"Leah is a happy child," Mrs. Carruthers continued after a moment. "And I think you are an excellent mother to her, Mrs. Saxton, despite your own youth."

"You are too kind, Anna," Giana said uncomfortably.

"How I look forward to the birth of your child. Babies are such a comfort, and bring new life into a home."

Giana nodded, her eyes on the small jacket Mrs. Carruthers was knitting. For her baby, for Alex's baby.

"I don't know how to knit," she said.

"It is not at all difficult," Mrs. Carruthers said,

looking up from the small sleeve, her clacking needles silent for a moment. "But you are far too busy with more important matters, Mrs. Saxton, to be concerned with this."

"Not really," Giana said pensively. Since she had agreed to spend no more than a couple of hours each morning at the office, there was certainly time in her placid day to learn to knit—or sew altar cloths, if she wished. It struck her forcibly that she was listening to Mrs. Carruthers drone on about how excellent a husband and father Alex was, as if all revolved around him, just as all had revolved around the husbands in Rome. She stared at the small jacket. "It is blue," she said at last.

Mrs. Carruthers nodded, her expression placid. "You will have a son, of that I have no doubt. Mr. Saxton, although he says nothing of it, wants a son, and he, I believe, is a man who contrives to get his own way."

"But I have decided I would prefer a daughter, Mrs. Carruthers."

"Ah, yes, you are two strong people," Mrs. Carruthers said, bending her head to her needles once again. "You are lucky to have found Mr. Saxton. He is a good man, a fair man."

"I didn't find him, Mrs. Carruthers. He found me." Giana sighed.

"But a family man. His family will always come first, I believe, particularly now that he has married you, Mrs. Saxton."

A family man, Giana thought. All the gentlemen in Rome had been family men. She was surprised at herself, surprised at the old cynical wariness that was flooding over her. The faces of the girls at Madame Lucienne's, so worldly wise with understanding of those men and their endless lust for them, rose starkly in her mind. Alex had not made love with her for four nights now. Was he already bored with her, and her passion for him? "Ah, my little Helen," the laughing Elvira had told her once, "a pregnant wife makes us all so happy. Her belly is soon filled with his child, and mine with him!"

She lurched to her feet, startling Mrs. Carruthers.

"Are you feeling unwell, Mrs. Saxton?"

"No, stay here, Anna. I am feeling a bit tired, that is all. When Mr. Saxton wishes to leave, please tell him I have taken a hansom cab home."

She had not been in her bedroom for more than fifteen minutes before Alex burst into the room, his dark brows drawn together in anger.

"What the devil do you mean leaving? Without a word to me?"

Giana gazed down at her clothes strewn on the carpet at her feet, and tightened the sash of her dressing gown. She shrugged. "I did not want you to interrupt your time with Leah," she said calmly. "The child was enjoying herself immensely."

He strode toward her and clasped her shoulders in his hands. "You are my first concern, Giana. I want to know why you blithely left Mrs. Carruthers and hailed a hansom cab."

"I am not a helpless child, Alex! I am perfectly capable of seeing myself home, without your guiding hand!"

"That is not the point," he said grimly. "It was rude of you, and inconsiderate. Mrs. Carruthers thought you were upset about something. What is it?"

Giana felt tears sting her eyes. She tugged furiously at the sash of her dressing gown, striving for calm.

"Well?"

"Mrs. Carruthers is knitting clothes for the baby," she mumbled, her eyes fastened on her toes.

"I know," Alex said calmly, and said nothing more, merely waited.

"And she was singing your praises," she said in a low voice, still not looking at him.

"You disagree?" Giana heard a spark of amusement in his tone, and whipped her head up at him.

"I will not be like those other women, Alex," she blurted out, "sitting about like a lump with nothing to do but sew ... baby clothes, nothing on my mind but what will please my husband!"

"Do you forget so quickly that you are pregnant, Giana?"

"No! How could I? Damn you, Alex, you're just like those precious husbands in Rome! You don't want me anymore!"

"Don't want you?" he repeated slowly, his eyes narrowing in surprise on her upturned face.

"I am no longer a challenge. I am predictable and you are tired of me. And I am getting fat!"

Giana stepped back when Alex strode to her and clasped her dressing gown. She gasped in surprise when he roughly pulled it from her shoulders and ripped open her chemise, baring her swollen breasts. She stood rigidly still as he lightly stroked the column of her throat and caressed her breasts. At his gentle fondling, she felt a familiar churning growing in her belly. She was thinking hazily of the feel of his mouth closing over her breast, when his voice brought her speedily back to earth. "And are you tired of me, Giana? Does it now bore you when I caress you? After all, you now know well what I will do."

"Men are ... different," she said in a taut voice.

"Why?" he asked, whimsically now, his palms lightly caressing her.

"You haven't touched me in four days!"

"Three. It's not because I haven't wanted to." He touched his fingers to the smudged shadows beneath her eyes. "I wanted you to have some much-needed rest. I am not a pig, Giana. I want you healthy. Now, answer me. Why?"

"How can I even think with you doing that?"

He rested his hands on her hips. "Why?" he repeated.

"Men," she said slowly, trying to gather her thoughts, "must have variety. I saw it in Rome. A different girl each time the same man came to Madame Lucienne's. And you, Alex. You were with Margot the first time I saw you. How many other women did you enjoy in but a month's time?"

"Three or four, if I remember correctly," he said coolly. "Many nights I was too tired, my mind too filled with business to be bothered. But if my body needed relief, there was always a willing woman to see to my pleasure."

"Variety," she said. "You do not even bother to lie about it."

"Why should I? I wasn't married, for Laura had died the year before."

"And you aren't married now."

"And I am tired of you, because you are fat and predictable."

"Yes," she said gruffly, raising her chin. "You can be honest with me. You owe me nothing."

"Very well, if it is truly honesty you wish, Giana. Behold honesty, though I doubt you would recognize it if it flattened you."

He closed his hands gently over her breasts, his dark eyes steady on her upturned face. "I want you,

Giana. Your predictability, your openness to me, I find delightful. I am delighted that you enjoy being in my arms, that you enjoy how I touch you. I even enjoy the feel of your rounded belly against me."

He saw a leap of joy in her eyes. Then the shadows of doubt she could not hide. He sighed.

"So much for honesty," he said under his breath.

"Alex, I—"

"Stow it, Giana," he interrupted her gruffly. "I've always been better suited to action." He lowered his mouth to hers, tasting the tart apple cider she had sipped at the park. "Your breasts are so soft against me," he whispered into her mouth.

"I ache," she murmured. "I ache so much I cannot bear it."

"That is honesty I cannot deny," he said, trying to smile. She tangled her hands in his hair as he lowered his head to suckle her breast. He laid his palm against her heart, and felt it racing. "Ache where, Giana? Your breasts or your belly?"

"Both," she managed. "And my legs. They feel boneless."

He stripped off her dressing gown and pulled her ripped chemise over her hips. She stood before him dressed only in her silk stockings, held above her knees by frilly blue garters. His eyes roved upward to her swollen belly, to his child growing in her womb. "You are truly a delicious sight, Giana."

"You must stop tearing off my clothes, Alex," she said, embarrassed at his scrutiny.

"Your damned undergarments are always a nuisance," he said. He closed his hands about her waist and grinned. "The baby is growing, Giana. Not too long ago I could encircle you."

He stepped back from her and began to pull off his clothes, aware that she was watching him. She was fascinated by his body, perhaps as much, he thought, as he was by hers. He looked up at her, and she flushed slightly. "You are a beautiful man, Alex."

"Given your unusual summer in Rome, I shall take that as a compliment." He clasped her hand in his and drew her toward him. When he cupped her buttocks, she pressed her cheek against his shoulder, clutching his broad back, and sighed happily.

"I think I could spend all my time quite satisfactorily like this, Alex." She stood on her tiptoes and rubbed against him, wishing she were taller so she could fit better against him. She felt him tugging the pins from her hair, stroking his fingers through the thick waves that reached nearly to her waist.

"You are toying with me, Alex," she said, and giving him a siren's smile, she slid her hand between them.

"Giana, stop," he groaned suddenly. He closed his hands beneath her hips and lifted her, and she fell forward against him, laughing guilelessly against his throat. He carried her to their bed, gently eased her onto it, and pressed his huge body sensuously over her. Suddenly he raised himself on his elbows, startled eyes flying to her face.

"What is the matter?" she whispered, trying to pull him back against her.

"The baby," he said. "He just kicked me."

Giana giggled. "Please, Alex, promise me you won't tell Dr. Davidson! The poor man would die of his blushes."

But Alex was frowning. "I am too heavy for you now, like this." He saw that she would protest, and added on a grin, "I do not want our child cursing his father before he is even born."

He scooped her in his arms and pulled her onto her side, facing him. "We shall just have to become more inventive, Giana," he said against her mouth. "This isn't so bad, is it?" he gently mocked her, seeing the smoky sheen in her eyes.

She moved provocatively against him, and whispered as he moaned, "No, Alex. I see that you like it quite well."

When at last she was snuggled against him, and he was gently stroking her back to calm her, he felt her arch back to look up at his face. "Will it always be thus?" she managed. "Will you always make me want to die for you?"

"I will always try," he said.

She kissed his chin. "You need to shave," she said. "I should dislike being so hairy," she added thoughtfully. "I should not like putting a razor to my face every day."

"I should dislike your doing it too."

She laughed and snuggled against him, burrowing her face against his chest.

"Princess," he said softly after a moment, "promise me that you will tell me if something distresses you."

"I felt so depressed," she said on a sigh.

"There was no need, as I hope you believe now."

"I suppose you are right," she said, though to his ear she did not sound certain.

He tucked a strand of hair behind her ear, and gazed down into her sleepy face. "I cannot change the laws, Giana."

"No," she said sadly, "no one can. Men will not allow it."

"But we can ignore the laws. They needn't touch us."

She became very still in his arms. He waited for the wariness to shutter her eyes, and realized he was holding himself as still as was she.

She said nothing. "Go to sleep, Giana. We have a couple of hours before dinner."

She heard harsh disappointment in his voice, and felt tears sting her eyes. She was afraid.

Chapter 22

"Do listen, Giana!" Once Leah had secured her stepmama's attention, she read from the *Times*. " 'Lord Palmerston has been dismissed from the Foreign Office after expressing approval of Louis Napoleon's coup detat.' "

"*Coup d'état*," Alex corrected automatically.

"What is that?"

"It means a sudden overthrow of a government," Giana said. "Of course," she added, with all the English disdain of the French, "it is not unexpected in a country like France."

But Leah, having delivered her bit of news, had her head buried again behind the *Times*'s pages.

"Lord Palmerston is an excellent statesman," Alex said.

"Come, Alex," Giana said impatiently, "Lord Russell had no choice. Palmerston has behaved outrageously. What of the supposed apology he snickered to the Austrian General Haynau after the poor man was attacked by employees in a brewery?"

"Haynau is a pig," Alex said firmly. "Lord Palmerston was perfectly justified in his bit of rudeness."

"Who is the painter J.M.W. Turner?" Leah asked suddenly.

"Why, Leah?" Giana asked.

"He died."

"What a pity," Giana said. "He was a dear friend of my mother's. He was a very famous painter, Leah. You remember the Turner paintings in the drawing room, do you not, Alex?"

"Yes," Alex said, but his attention was no longer at the breakfast table, but on a letter he was reading. He raised his face, smiling widely. "Delaney should be here for Christmas," he said.

"Uncle Delaney!" Leah shrieked, slithering from her chair. "Oh, Anna, you will adore my uncle! Giana, he is so funny!" Casting a candid look at her father, Leah continued, "Though he is not nearly so handsome as Papa."

"But he is younger than Papa, is he not, Leah?" Giana asked, giving Alex a droll look.

"He will doubtless improve with age," Alex said. "Now," he continued, rising, "who would like to come with me to cut down our Christmas tree?"

Giana was the one, bundled up to her ears in a heavy fur-lined cloak, who picked out the huge fir tree Alex cut down. They dragged it back to the city tied to a sled behind the carriage. Leah, exhausted from all the excitement, fell asleep in her father's arms. Giana watched Alex gently wipe away the traces of hot chocolate from about Leah's mouth and lightly kiss the child's smooth brow. She felt tears sting her eyes, and quickly turned her head away. It was her pregnancy, she thought, that was making her foolishly sentimental, and a female watering pot. But it had been a day that would remain with her, she knew, a joyous day with so much laughter, one that would never fade from her mind.

"You are very quiet, Giana," Alex said, closing his book to look at her full face as they sat in front of the fireplace in their bedchamber that evening. "Are you tired?"

She started at the concern in his voice, and forced herself to shrug her shoulders. "Of course not, Alex," she said in a falsely bright voice. But his eyes held hers for a moment longer, and the hated, inexplicable tears swam in her eyes again. "I am being foolish," she said, swiping her fingers over her eyes. "It's just that we never had such a Christmas tree," she said shakily. "The past couple of years, Mother had one delivered, delivered like a package, to the back door. The servants decorated it! The damned servants! I always admired it, and duly complimented Lanson and the staff on their efforts, because I was supposed to!" She sobbed, her slender shoulders shaking. "I always hated Christmas!"

Alex watched her silently. He wanted to tell her that if she but stayed with him he would erase all her bitterness. He would make her every Christmas a special time. He waited until she quieted, and asked her gently, "What were your Christmases like when you were Leah's age?"

Giana sniffed loudly, and produced a wan smile. "I got lots of presents. And I used to sneak into the drawing room and help the servants decorate the tree. Mother was so busy, Alex, I understand that now. But a child isn't so understanding. Leah is such a lucky child."

"More lucky this year, I should say. This is her first Christmas with a mother and a father. I much enjoyed today, Giana. You were as excited as Leah."

Her smile became more natural as Alex continued. "We will let the tree soak for a couple of days, then bring it into the drawing room. Mrs. Carruthers is helping Leah make decorations for it."

"That will be marvelous," she said. "Perhaps Anna will show me how to make something."

"I will show you," Alex said on a smile, hearing

the wistful tone in her voice. "I am really quite good at decorating trees."

"As good as you are at growing orchids?"

"Better. If you would like, it is sort of a tradition in this household to have an open house on Christmas Day."

Her eyes sparkled. "Yes, so very much. Should you dislike me inviting the Lattimers?"

His lips twisted ruefully, but he said only, his voice perfectly bland, "No, that would be fine."

"Sometimes you are terribly provoking, Alex Saxton," she said acidly.

"Suffice it to say, princess, that Charles Lattimer will still gobble up your collateral when McCormick lets you down."

"I shan't fight with you about that tonight, Alex."

"Excellent." He patted his thighs. "I think I can still hold you comfortably."

Giana cocked a brow at him, but readily left her chair and settled herself in his lap.

"You know," he said after a moment, "I much enjoy family life. You are treating Leah as if she were your own child."

"I . . . I love her," Giana said.

"Would you love me if I were nine years old?"

His voice was light and teasing, and Giana answered, keeping her voice as light as his, "I can't fight with Leah the way I fight with you."

"I remember thinking once that we were like a couple of stray cats. At least the she-cat is resting as she should now."

"Because you happened to be right about that, Mr. Saxton," she said without heat, settling her face against his throat. "I suppose I was a bit . . . overbearing when I first arrived."

"You suppose?" he repeated in mock surprise.

"You ... well, you've been very kind, Alex."

"Don't let that get around, princess, I would lose my reputation in business." He dropped his hand to her swelling belly and rested it there. "Life is damned odd," he said thoughtfully, more to himself than to Giana.

"Indeed," she said vehemently. "Here I was, perfectly happy, minding my own affairs, and then you, a brazen American, came trooping into my life! And within one short week I lost my virginity, got vilely ill—"

"And became beautifully pregnant," he finished with satisfaction.

"I don't think I'll apologize for being ... overbearing," she said.

He raised a black brow. "Stray cats never apologize," he said.

"Alex, I don't believe it!"

"Merry Christmas, Giana," he said, smiling down at her stunned face.

"You ... you did this for me?" She gazed about the once dismal parlor that had occupied the south corner of the house. The dull dimity curtains, the gray wallpaper, and the odd collection of furniture had vanished. She gaped at the rich blue-and-white carpet, the inset bookshelves, the drawing by Bornet of New York Bay from the Battery hung above the graceful Italian fireplace, the oak desk set at an angle facing the garden windows. On its smooth surface was an ivory-inlaid box filled with pens and pencils. A daguerreotype of her, Leah, Alex, and Mrs. Carruthers standing in front of the jetting Park Fountain in the City Hall Park stood beside the pen box. Two boxes lay on the center of the desk, and she clumsily lifted the lid of one of them. It was exquisite stationery, "Georgiana Van Cleve Saxton" and the address of Alex's office building printed in flowing black script at the top of each sheet. Giana turned slowly. "Why?" she asked helplessly, sweeping her arms about her.

"Why?" An amused black brow winged upward. "Self-preservation, Giana," he said. "You were beginning to take over my library, and I decided you should have one of your own. And with a study of your own, I thought you might stay more at home."

Their eyes met for a moment, and he read her unspoken thought. *But I will not be here! In five months I will never see this room again.*

"The stationery," she said. "It is beautiful." She turned away from his probing gaze to finger the crisp sheets of paper. *Georgiana Van Cleve Saxton.* He had taken nothing from her.

"I thought," he said coolly, "that a woman of your stature should cease using her husband's stationery. I trust everything pleases you."

Giana nodded, unable to meet his eyes. She walked to the bookshelves and gazed at the titles. "Dickens," she said. "I like Dickens."

"There is also the usual complement of Greek philosophers, and modern-day tomes on economics and politics."

"And Jane Austen," she said, pulling down the copy of *Emma,* bound in thick red vellum. "How did you know she is my favorite author, Alex?"

"Your mother wrote me."

She turned slowly to face him. "You have been planning this for some time?"

"I suppose so. The trick was to keep you out of the house when the workmen and decorators were here. Your preoccupation with strawberry ice cream was invaluable, particularly when the fireplace construction ran into the evening hours."

Giana replaced the book on the shelf. "The chair," she said, "it is like yours, only smaller." She had always secretly admired his chair, but of course had teased him about his impressive seat of power.

"Yes."

She picked up the skirt of her dressing gown and ran to him. "Thank you, Alex," she cried, hugging her arms about his back.

He kissed her lightly and smiled over her head at his creation.

"My Christmas present to you is not nearly so impressive," she said shyly, her fingers toying with the buttons of his dressing gown. "In fact, perhaps you won't care for it at all."

"You didn't have to get me anything, Giana," he said roughly.

"You don't like presents, Mr. Saxton?" Her eyes twinkled impishly. "Even a big fierce man is allowed to be excited once in a while."

"I am, nearly every night."

She pulled away from him and waved an admonishing finger. "Stay here, Alex. I'll be back in but a moment."

Alex was still admiring his handiwork when Giana returned, breathless, a large package under her arm.

It was a painting. He could feel the frame through the paper wrapping as he tore away the ribbon.

"It's . . . me," Giana said behind him.

Alex propped the painting up on Giana's desk chair and took several steps back to look at it.

"Mr. Turner painted it," she babbled when he said nothing for several moments. "He was noted for his landscapes, of course, but Mother convinced him to put me in one of them."

Alex stared at Giana's image, smiling at him innocently, her vivid eyes, not quite the right color, he saw, wide with wonder. She was dressed in a dark blue riding habit, standing next to a tall black stallion, her gloved hand holding his reins. Creamy-textured woods and hills filled the background. It was almost the Giana he had seen in Rome. "When was it painted?" he asked quietly.

"The Christmas of 1846."

Before Rome. Six months before Rome.

Yes, he thought, there was innocence and trust on the young girl's face. He realized he would give almost anything to see that look on her face now.

"I had it shipped from London," she said, nearly dancing around him in her anxiety. "I did not know what you would like for Christmas ... you have everything! I thought perhaps ..." Her voice trailed off, for he was eyeing her with a bemused smile.

"You have given me a present beyond anything I could ever imagine," he said. "May I hang your portrait in the—*my*—library?"

She drew a relieved breath. "You ... you really like it, Alex?"

"I like both the younger and older versions of Georgiana Van Cleve." *Did you give me the portrait to remember you by?*

"Come, Giana. I'll wager Leah has already pulled Mrs. Carruthers and poor Delaney out of bed."

In fact they found Leah sitting on Delaney's bed, her legs curled up beneath her, tearing open one of the several presents he had brought her.

"You've come to save me," Delaney moaned, fumbling to place over his eye the monocle Alex had given him as a joke. "Lord, it's only seven-thirty in the morning, a morning I might add after an evening

of grog. Can it be, Alex, that we had such energy and
. . . dedicated greed when we were boys?"

"We had much more," Alex said, grinning. "Remember the Christmas Father gave us hatchets?"

"And poor Mother had a dining table with only
three legs for her Christmas ham! But you were the
elder, all of eight years old, as I remember. I was but
a babe in arms, innocent as the Christ Child."

"Innocent, your monocle!"

Leah shrieked with delight at a gold nugget set in
a delicate petaled flower, which she held dangling
on a slender chain. She flung her arms around
Delaney's neck, hitting him squarely on the nose
with the necklace and dislodging the absurd monocle.

Giana watched Delaney reduce Leah to giggles
again as he replaced the monocle and espied her
with a huge, monster eye. He had arrived two days
before, laden with presents, and when he had rested
his eyes, Alex's eyes, on her face, all the anxiety she
had felt about meeting him had melted away. There
was a gentleness about Delaney, a sensitivity that
banished any feeling of unease in his company. He
delighted in affecting her starchy English accent, the
monocle held in mock snobbery against his eye.

"It appears," he had said, holding her at arm's
length, "that I am to be an uncle twice over."

"If you would get yourself married," Alex had retorted, "I would have the honor of spoiling some
nieces and nephews of my own."

"My dear brother," Delaney had said, his eyes
twinkling just as Alex's did, "there are so many ladies! I simply cannot make up my weak man's mind.
And you have hooked the most beautiful of them
all."

"I am not a fish, sir!" Giana had exclaimed, laughing. "I do hope you don't encourage Alex to grow a beard like yours! He is so dark, he would look like a northern black bear."

Delaney stroked his full light-brown whiskers. "Alex is far too conceited to cover his handsome face," he said in a mocking voice. "And I, Giana, alas, I am cursed with a weak chin."

"Oh, Giana! Look at this!"

Giana gave her attention again to Leah, who had ripped open another of Delaney's presents, a pale green jade lamb about the size of an apple.

"It has a hole in its head," Leah cried, thrusting her thumb into the opening.

"For your pens, my pet," Delaney said. "Now, Leah, would you please spare my modesty? You're quite embarrassing me in front of your stepmama."

Giana got a brief glimpse of hairy brown legs before Alex, laughing, gave an arm to both Leah and Giana and pulled them from Delaney's room.

"California is a continent away, Delaney, and there won't be a railroad all the way to San Francisco for years yet."

Delaney sipped his coffee, casting Giana a droll look over the rim. "Now he will try to convince me to go into business with him."

After the hectic Christmas Day, Giana felt lazily sleepy. It was near midnight, and Leah, dizzy with excitement, had not gone to bed until very late. The three of them, finally left to themselves, sat in decadent ease in the drawing room, facing the beautifully decorated Christmas tree.

"Four years is a long time between visits," Alex pursued. "You left a miserable pauper, and look what has become of you."

"I was lucky," Delaney said simply. "Very lucky."

He said after a long moment, as if he were speaking more to himself than to his brother, "Odd that I always hated Father's shipyard, all the infernal sawdust that filled up my nose. I even refused to take a steamer to San Francisco." He sent a twisted smile to Alex. "I have bought into a shipping line, Alex. The jade lamb came from China, from one of my ships. That and my incursion into politics keep me on the straight and narrow."

"Good God!" Alex exclaimed, grinning. "Delaney wanted to rebel," he said to Giana, "but he needed the lure of adventure to get him off his butt."

"It would appear," Giana said hesitantly, "that you did the right thing. Gold. It has a magic ring." She glanced down at the bracelet around her wrist, a gawdy piece Delaney had explained in his droll way. "The only artisans in California," he had said, "are men who failed to make their fortunes in gold."

Giana dispensed more coffee, then sat back, wishing she could loosen the waist on her gown. "I had forgotten," Delaney said, stirring a cube of sugar into his coffee, "what it is to live among such throngs of people. Do you know that seven years ago there were fewer than fifty people living in San Francisco? Today, with the call of gold, it has swelled to more than fifty thousand. It's still a godawful heap of saloons, tents, and raw-wood houses, but there's an irrepressible vitality to it."

"You sound as if you intend to remain in California brother."

"Indeed I do."

"Oh!" Giana suddenly jumped, her eyes on Alex. "He did it again?"

"Yes, 'twas a vicious kick." She jumped again. "I don't think he likes this tight waistline."

"No," Delaney said, "he is simply his father's son

and wants you to know very early, Giana, that it is he who will rule the roost."

"Well," Alex said, stretching. "I am ruling the roost until he arrives. It's time for you to be in bed, Giana." He held out his hand to her.

"But if I go to bed, Christmas will be over and it will be tomorrow!"

And there won't be another, will there?

"I would invite Delaney into bed with us—more conversation, you know—but even he, a rough-and tumble Californian, might lose his agile tongue in his blushes."

"Alexander Nicholas Saxton!"

"Just like our grandfather," Delaney said. "He'll say and do just as he pleases. He hasn't a sensitive bone in his great body, Giana. You can spare my blushes, Alex, I'm off to bed myself."

Alex found himself watching Giana as she undressed in their bedroom, listening with only half an ear to her chatter. The brief glimpse of her slender thighs heightened his interest, and it was with some chagrin when he leaned over to kiss her that he discovered she was fast asleep. "Be damned," he said, "I don't believe it."

He lightly touched his hand to her belly, and felt a slight movement beneath his splayed fingers. Why, he wondered as he settled himself down for sleep, could nothing ever be easy?

Chapter 23

Giana left Delaney and Derry listening to loud strains of a polka in the vast German Winter Garden, an elegant and elaborately facaded Bowery beer hall.

"I will see you home, Giana," Delaney said readily, reaching for his cloak. She stayed him with a smile, seeing that Derry was glancing wistfully toward the dance floor. "Oh no you don't, Delaney. Derry would surely slay me were I to take her partner!"

She walked out onto the bustling street and breathed in the cold January air, thankful to escape the pounding rhythm of the music. There was a smell of snow in the air, but there looked to be time yet before the swirling clouds gathering overhead blanketed the city in white. She remembered the balloon panorama was on exhibition at Barnum's Museum and waved down a hansom cab bound for Broadway.

She left the cab at the corner of Ann street, paid her entrance money, and spent a delightful hour exploring the museum. Odd, she thought, laughing at herself, how she was fascinated by things mechanical. She stopped at Raffer's cigar store on Fulton to buy Alex a dozen of his favorite Havanas, and dawdled in Brady's daguerreotype gallery, admiring his clear pictures, and bothering the distracted clerk with questions about Mr. Brady's new process. It came as a surprise to her that it was nearly dark when she finally emerged again onto Broadway. She cast a lingering eye toward the D. & W. H. Lee furniture warerooms, but supposed that Alex, immured in his library at home for the afternoon, would worry if she dallied longer. She looked about for a hansom cab, and not seeing one, pulled her thick cloak more tightly around her and walked with a firm step up Broadway. She stopped briefly at the Astor House, with its wide, tree-fronted sidewalk and imposing stone steps, and had passed Barclay Street when she drew to a surprised halt at the sound of shouting voices. She knew she should continue on her way, but in her curiosity, she turned the corner onto Vesey Street.

She found herself in a scene of pandemonium. A mob of roughly dressed men brandishing sticks milled in front of a three-story manufacturing warehouse. She heard them shouting obscenities against its owner, a Mr. Biddle, and threats against his business. She heard a mixture of languages, and a burly man brushed by her, nearly knocking her down. Stern-faced men, some of them drunk, jostled and pressed about her, paying no attention to the pregnant woman pushing her way through their ranks. I've walked into the middle of a protest, she thought, a strike! *You idiot! Why did you leave Delaney and Derry?*

"Hey, little girlie, do you want . . . ?"

She jerked away from the leering man's outstretched arm, closing her mind to his obscene suggestion. She suddenly spotted a hansom cab standing at a curb a block ahead and waved her hand wildly toward the driver. She was panting from exertion when she had at last pushed her way beyond the thick of the crowd, nearly free. It was then she saw a man, dressed as roughly as the workers, running toward her.

"Ger her!" she heard someone yell. "Bring her here!" She looked toward the voice, but she could not see him in the crowd.

Giana felt her blood run cold. She cursed her clumsiness when she tried to run, and screamed when she nearly tripped, grasping frantically at a lamppost to regain her balance.

She heard a man shout her name, but she didn't turn. The cab was just a few yards away. "Wait!" she yelled at the driver. "Please, wait!"

Suddenly a group of workers erupted from an alleyway to her right and surged onto the street, blocking the man who was closing behind her. She heard furious curses, but did not look back. She reached the cab, and shouted up at the driver as she jerked on the door handle, "Quickly, take me to Twenty-fifth Street and Fifth Avenue!"

The driver nodded, as if bored, and slowly raised his hands to click his mare forward.

She leaned her head out the window and saw the man racing toward the cab again. There was another man behind him, but she couldn't make out his face.

"Hurry!" she yelled. "Ten dollars if you will hurry!"

There was an astounding change in the phlegmatic driver. He whipped his mare forward, and her pursuer was hurled backward, cursing at the driver as he fell to the street. Giana was thrown back against the worn leather squabs as the cab careened up the street.

She was trembling, only vaguely aware that he was driving like a maniac up Broadway, ignoring the angry shouts of pedestrians. When they reached the southern edge of Union Square, the cab lurched eastward, barely escaping being toppled over by a careening beer wagon. She held herself in rigid calm until the cab drew up in front of the Saxton mansion, her only thought to get to Alex. She stuffed twenty dollars into the astonished driver's outstretched hand, turned her back to him as he shouted, "Thank you, lady!" and ran awkwardly to the front door.

"Mrs. Saxton!" Herbert gazed aghast at the disheveled mistress of the house. She was pale, her clothing askew, and her bonnet tilted precariously over her left ear.

"Alex ... Mr. Saxton," Giana gasped. "Where is he?"

"In the library, ma'am. He is still meeting with ..."

Giana rushed past him down the long hallway to the library, and without a thought, threw open the doors.

Alex was standing beside the fireplace, his broad shoulders resting against the mantel, examining a sheet of paper. Four men in dark business suits were seated around him. Their heads turned in unison at the unexpected disturbance. She saw surprise in their faces, and then raised eyebrows over narrowed eyes. She stood like a statue, unable to move. She had violated their precious male domain, she thought wildly, interrupted their meeting. A silly female, interrupting them.

She met Alex's eyes, saw him frown and take a hasty step toward her.

"Mrs. Saxton," she heard one of the men say in a voice of impatient surprise.

Words tumbled from her mouth. "I'm sorry ... please, forgive me, please!" She jerked about and ran from the room, slamming the library doors behind her.

Alex handed the paper to Anesley. "You will ex-

cuse me, gentlemen, but I fear our meeting is over."
Even as he spoke, he was picturing Giana's white
face, her mussed appearance, her wide eyes staring
at him. Jesus, what had happened?

He raced up the stairs, taking them two at a time,
waving away Herbert's words from behind him. He
burst into their bedroom and drew to a halt. Giana
was on her hands and knees in front of the fireplace,
her cloak spread around her, staring at the orange
embers.

"Giana," he said, his voice louder and harsher than
he intended. She turned her head to look at him, and
he felt himself start. He saw fear in her eyes. "Dear
God, what happened?"

She stared at him, rigid and mute. He dropped to
his knees beside her and drew her against him.

"It's all right, love," he whispered, stroking his
hands over her back. "You're safe now, Giana. I
promise." He continued speaking softly to her, words
that had little meaning, really, and finally felt her
body ease. With a great sob, she clutched at his arms
and pressed herself against him.

He pulled off her bonnet and stroked her hair, still
crooning senseless words to her, his voice soft and
even over her rasping sobs.

"Come, Giana, tell me what happened. It's all
right, love."

It was some minutes before she raised her tear-
drenched face from his chest. She was trembling violently, still clutching at him as if she were afraid to let
go.

"Two men," she gasped, her voice graveley in her
fear. "I was walking up Broadway, alone. There was
some kind of strike, and a mob of men. I tried to get
through them to a hansom cab. There was a man
running after me! Another man was behind him,

pointing at me. I ... I could only think of getting to you."

Damnation, he thought, holding her crumpled body tightly against him. She had been alone, little fool, and caught in a mob. Strikers, no doubt. Where had Delaney and Derry been? He sat down in front of the fireplace, leaning against his favorite chair, and drew her onto his lap. She curled herself into a small ball and buried her face against his throat. His self-reliant Giana, so fiercely independent, so self-sufficient, was burrowing against him for protection as if her body no longer obeyed her mind.

Giana knew she was being foolish, knew quite well that she was perfectly safe, but her words still spoke themselves, unbidden words. "Please don't leave me, Alex. Don't leave."

To his surprise, he felt his body leap with desire. It was as if she were offering another part of herself for the first time, a hidden, vulnerable part that his body, as well as his mind, wanted for himself. "No," he said softly, "I won't leave you." He studied her pale face, her shuttered eyes, before lowering his head.

She felt his mouth lightly touch hers. She lay passively against his arm, neither encouraging nor pulling away from him as she felt his fingers unhook the fasteners on her cloak, felt it fall from her shoulders. When she felt the heat from the fireplace upon her breasts, she slowly opened her eyes and stared up at him. "You want me," she said stupidly.

"Yes, I want you," he said starkly.

She still lay passively, her arms lying limply at her sides as his hands moved over her. She realized vaguely that something was happening to Alex, something she could not as yet fathom. There was no gentle seduction in his touch, but a fierce possessiveness.

When she lay sprawled on her back, his powerful body pressing against her, her fear mingled crazily with a suddenly awakening desire in her belly and she cried out. She felt his fingers caress her face.

"Look at me, Giana."

She obeyed him, her eyes dark with confusion.

"Tell me you need me."

"I need you," she said. It was the sound of her own voice, speaking those simple words, that made her realize she was willing to do anything, be anything he wished so long as he stayed with her.

"Alex," she whispered harshly, deep in her throat, "love me. Please, love me!"

She cried softly as he moved deep within her, knowing in that instant that she did not want to leave him, ever. His body was a part of hers, melded to her, erasing her fear. She felt herself tensing, felt her body convulsing in the almost painful pleasure. But it was more, much more. A new terror floated like a shroud over her mind. She cried out against it, anguished by its power, yet her body demanded she feel it.

"Giana," Alex moaned, seeing the tears in her eyes, but unable to slow his raging need for her. "Giana!"

Alex felt as though his very soul had been torn from his body. She was his now. Only his. And he loved her, loved her so much that he was afraid. He wanted to shout at her that he wouldn't love her, wouldn't allow her to hurt him. The words trembled on his lips.

"Alex?"

He felt her lips touch his throat.

"Thank you."

For what? "Giana, I . . ." *I love you.* He gently turned her to face him, and smiled at her soft round belly pressed against him. "Giana, did I give you pleasure?" *Inane, stupid ass!*

"I . . ." *My pleasure was incidental.* "Yes," she whispered, "great pleasure."

He started to move away from her, and she clutched at him. "Please, Alex . . ." Suddenly she caught herself, as if she realized he had torn all pretense from her. She heard herself say in a stiff, formal voice, "Forgive me for . . . disturbing you and the other gentlemen."

"Don't be a fool," he nearly roared at her. He saw tears still swimming in her eyes, and buried his face in her tumbled hair. "Forgive me, love. Tell me again what happened."

She did, in pained, disjointed phrases. "It was odd—the second man. I thought I recognized his voice." She shook her head, knowing that she must have been mistaken. "I lost your Havana cigars," she finished stupidly. "I must have dropped them."

He kissed the tip of her nose. "Do you remember what the cab driver looked like?"

"He seemed very disinterested until I offered him ten dollars to hurry." Her eyes narrowed as she tried to picture him in her mind, but she saw only a bearded face and heavy woolen clothes.

"I will find out who the men were, Giana. And you, Mrs. Saxton, will no longer sally forth alone for a stroll. Do you promise?"

"Alex, why would anyone want to hurt me?"

"Likely no one did. It was a strike, a riot, and you were caught in the middle of it. But I will look into it. All right?"

She nodded, and moved slowly from the circle of his arms. "I think I hear Delaney." She reached for her dressing gown, surprised at how normal she sounded.

Alex rolled off the bed and rose. Her traitorous eyes fell to his manhood, glistening with himself and with her.

"Yes," he said shortly, his dark eyes shuttered. *Give me more than your damned lust!* But she had, and he saw it in the sudden hurt in her eyes at his abruptness.

"What is Agnes preparing for dinner tonight?" he asked in an even voice.

The house was quiet. Delaney had left that morning for Washington, with a quick hug for Giana. "I am not such a scurvy fellow as to wear out my welcome," he had teased her. He had shaken his head. "The one time you needed me, and I was dancing a decadent polka."

Leah and Anna were upstairs in the midst of lessons. Alex had left for the shipyard, leaving Giana with some paperwork in her library. But she couldn't seem to concentrate. She was chewing on the end of her pen when Herbert knocked on the partially open door.

"Madam?"

"Yes, Herbert."

"There is a man here, asking to see you. He says he found something you lost."

Giana felt a brief tingling of fear, but she quickly chided herself for being a fool, and rose. "You may show him into the drawing room, Herbert."

The man facing her when she entered was dressed in severe, respectable black. Hes features were plain, his age, she guessed, around forty. She had never seen him before.

"Yes?" she asked pleasantly. "I understand you have something of mine?"

"My name is Chalmers, ma'am," he said. "And, yes, I believe you dropped these yesterday."

He handed her the wooden box of Alex's Havana cigars. Giana's eyes flew to his face. "You were there, Mr. Chalmers?"

"Yes, ma'am. A gentleman asked me to deliver this letter to you, personally."

He handed her a sealed envelope. "If you'll excuse me, Mrs. Saxton."

"Thank you, Mr. Chalmers," she said, forcing her attention from the envelope to nod politely to the man.

She stared at it for some moments, the bold black handwriting leaving her as pale as if the man who had penned her name were standing before her. Randall Bennett's writing was distinctive and elegant, not easily forgotten.

And he was here, in New York.

She tore open the envelope, and spread out the single sheet of paper. "My dear Giana," she read, "as you see, my dear, I am in New York and most anxious to see you again. I would advise you to meet me tomorrow at Luigi's Restaurant on Williams Street at three o'clock, concerning a matter of importance to you. If you do not come, I promise you that both you and your husband will regret it. It would be a grave mistake to inform Mr. Saxton, for reasons I will explain in person. Until tomorrow, my dear." His name was signed with an insolent flourish at the bottom of the page.

Chapter 24

Giana left the hansom cab at Pearl Street and walked the final block to Williams Street quickly, paying no heed to the freezing wind or the light snowflakes that splattered her face. She walked right past Luigi's Restaurant, and had to retrace her steps. She paused a moment before the door to compose herself, and walked, head high, into the restaurant. It was small and dimly lit, and with no more than a dozen tables, each covered with a red-and-white-checkered tablecloth. Her gaze slid past the few people seated at the tables to Randall Bennett, who waved lazily to her from a table at the rear of the room. A fat, aproned man appeared at her side, but she shook her head, pointing toward Randall.

"Mrs. Saxton," he drawled, proffering her a mocking bow.

"Mr. Bennett." He looked the same, she thought, his face still as flawless as a Greek statue's, his body still as lithe and slender.

"So cold, Giana, so cold. And so very pregnant. But I forget my manners. Sit down."

Giana eased herself into a cheap cane chair. "You haven't changed, Randall."

"No? Well, my dear Giana, you have changed, most noticeable. A duke's stepdaughter, living in the colonies. How eccentric of you."

A waiter appeared and Randall ordered a bottle of cheap red wine.

"Improvident as ever, Randall?" she sneered at him, a black brow raised.

"I simply don't believe you worth any more than that, Giana. But I can't get over how very pregnant you look. I trust your husband is out of your bed by now?"

"Randall," she said evenly, "your insults are childish. What do you want?"

"Did you not recognize Chalmers?"

She stared at him. "What do you mean?"

"The strike, my dear. I sent my man after you, but you managed to get away from him. I only wanted to talk to you, you know. The trick has been to get you a letter without your husband knowing of it."

Giana sat back in her chair. "I thought I heard a familiar voice, but I couldn't be sure."

"Then why did you run?"

"I was frightened," she said honestly. "The strikers were a rough group. Then that man you sent after me looked anything but friendly."

"My valet, Chalmers. He's scum, but I find that I cannot afford better at the moment."

The waiter brought their wine and poured two glasses.

"To our . . . reconciliation," Randall said, raising his glass.

"To my walking out of here in five minutes," Giana retorted.

"Still a tart-tongued bitch," Randall said amiably, setting down his glass.

"Randall, I came only because your note was a threat. You will now explain yourself, else I won't wait the five minutes."

"And your dear husband, my dear? I trust you did not tell him of our ... tryst."

"Do you still indulge in trysts, Randall? I find it difficult to believe that seventeen-year-old girls would still be prey to a man of your age."

"Did you tell your husband?" he repeated, his lips drawn in a thin line.

"No, I did not."

"Very wise of you. But then again, you and Mr. Saxton believe that you've been wise in all your ... endeavors, don't you?"

Her fingers whitened about the glass. "You have well under five minutes left, Randall."

Randall Bennett sat back in his chair and smiled widely at her. "You have such *presence*, Giana. Who would ever guess that you and Mr. Saxton are indulging in such an elaborate charade?" He leaned toward her, his eyes narrowing in satisfaction. "You little whore. Did you enjoy spreading your legs for Alex Saxton the first week he was in London?"

There is nothing he can do to us, Giana thought. He knows nothing save that I was pregnant before I was married. "You begin to bore me, Randall," she said calmly. "I might add that my husband doesn't like me to be bored or bothered."

"Very well," he said in a clipped voice. "I find myself in need of funds, Mrs. Saxton, and you, my dear, will provide them. I want ten thousand dollars from you, within the week. You can consider it the dowry I never received."

She gaped at him. "Are you mad?"

"Not at all. Even though I am in somewhat restricted circumstances at the moment, I have access to New York society. They've been rather decent about your obvious pregnancy. But there is something rather unnerving that none of them know, isn't there? I know, Giana. I know that you are not married."

Giana felt herself paling under his watchful gaze. She forced her eyes to the glass of wine.

"Randall," she said quite steadily, "you are talking nonsense. No one would believe you. No one. Now, if you are quite finished . . ."

She made to rise, but his hand shot out to grab her arm. "You think not, Giana? You forget, my dear, that you were once to be my wife, and that I know you and your dear mother quite well. Your supposed marriage with a special license never took place. I checked, out of . . . special interest, you know, but I never really imagined you would perpetrate such an outrageous scheme." He wagged his finger at her. "Poor Mr. Saxton. Having to live with you without even controlling your wealth. What did you and your mother have to pay him for his compliance?"

Whether I give him the ten thousand dollars or not, she thought frantically, he will never leave us in peace. *But if you don't pay him, it will all be over, even before the baby is born.*

She heard his voice, clipped now, and very self-assured. "I will give you two days, Giana, until Friday. You will bring the money here. If you don't, I suggest that you and Mr. Saxton plan to leave New York, for I will make the both of you pariahs. Ah, I see that now you believe me. Friday afternoon, Giana. I will let you buy the wine then, to celebrate."

It was on the tip of her tongue to plead with him, but she knew it wouldn't help. Nothing would help.

"This transaction is between the two of us, Giana. I have nothing against Mr. Saxton, but I will not hesitate to ruin him, if you force me to."

Giana didn't answer him. She slowly rose from her chair and walked silently from the restaurant. The driver of a hansom cab looked hopefully toward her, but she pulled her bonnet tight against the stiff winter wind and walked past him. She felt numb, and very tired. Absurdly, she remembered her old nanny chiding her that a lie is the devil's victory.

She felt the baby move in her womb, and stuffed her hand against her mouth to muffle a ragged sob. She had tried not to think about the time passing, about the time left to her and Alex before she was to return, without him, to London. But she did not want to lose him, now now, not when she was just discovering what they could have together! She paused, blinking at her thought. *You and Alex have nothing more than a brief arrangement. You will leave and he will soon forget you.*

She heard a soft moaning sound, and realized it was coming from her throat. Two days, she thought, I have two days to decide.

"You are quiet, Giana."

She forced a smile to her lips as she looked at Alex. "I am just tired," she said. Her eyes fell from his probing gaze.

He gently touched her shoulder and kneaded her taut muscles. "Come, love. At least you're not too fat yet for me to carry you," he said, easing her into his arms.

"Alex, your back!"

"Say that in another month or so."

He eased her to her feet once they were in their bedroom, but kept her in the circle of his arms. "Won't you tell me what's wrong?"

She felt herself leaning against him, savoring his strength. The truth hovered on her lips, but she slowly shook her head. "It is nothing that concerns you, Alex. Truly."

To her surprised relief, he shrugged his broad shoulders. "Very well, love." He gave her a lustful grin. "Just how tired are you, then?" He turned her slowly in his arms, holding her as close to him as her stomach would allow, and gently nudged back her head, lightly caressing his lips over her mouth. She blocked out Randall Bennett, blocked out everything that was not Alex.

"We must be careful from now on," he said, nibbling her earlobe. "Elvan managed, despite his blushes, to tell me to go easy from now on."

"But you don't hurt me," she whispered. "Really, you are always so gentle, and I ... like what you do."

"Trust me to be imaginative, Giana. In fact, you might try a little creativeness yourself. There is no reason for you to be shy, you know."

"I do," she said, gulping down a knot of embarrassment. "I ... I mean, I have."

He grinned down at her, hugging her tightly to him. "Excellent. I await my tutor's instructions." He turned her gently around and unfastened the buttons at her back.

They slept in the same position they made love, Alex curved around her back, her head upon his outstretched arm, his other hand lightly draped over her belly.

"I love your little butt pressing against my stomach," he whispered against her ear, clear delight in his deep voice.

"You are crazy," she said, her voice still languid from their lovemaking.

Alex felt the baby move against his palm. "Little brute," he said. "Have you thought of any names for our child?"

"Yes," she said. She turned, yelping as she did so,

for her long hair was caught beneath his arm. He arranged her against him, and kissed her rosy lips.

"And?"

Her eyes fell under his intent gaze. He saw so much that it frightened her. She didn't want him to know the power he held over her. But even pressed close against him, she could not still her doubts. She knew he wanted his child, and that to have it, he would have to keep her as well. Everything he had done, since before she could have meant anything to him, was designed to convince her to stay. *Even the stationery.* A sop to gain her confidence, to make her forget.

"Why are you crying?" His voice sounded beguiling and very close.

"I am *not* crying," she said, trying to pull away from him.

"Perhaps," he said with sudden anger, "you are not thinking of our child's name, but of the ship you will take back to England. Is that why you wrote to your mother asking her to come?"

"Nicholas, damn you, Alex. Nicholas!"

He was very still. "It was my father's name."

"Yes, I know, but it is also your second name. Nicholas Van Cleve Saxton."

"So you have decided to give me a son?"

"Yes."

"God knows, whenever you make up your mind to something, there is no changing you, is there?"

"No," she said quietly, "there is no changing ... anything. It is quite beyond either of us."

"We will see," he said. "We will see."

Giana clutched at the leather strap in the cab. She had made a decision, and felt now as if a great weight had lifted from her. After Alex's tenderness to her the night before, she realized she had to tell him about Randall Bennett, to ask for his help.

"Mr. Saxton isn't here?"

Giana's shoulders drooped.

"I'm sorry, ma'am," Jake Ransom, Alex's foreman in the Saxton shipyard, told her. "I think he went off with Clinton Murdock, a business friend from Boston, to the Gem Saloon. Braggin', he was, about the mirror there being larger than anything in Puritan country."

Giana nodded, distracted. She knew of the Gem Saloon, for gentlemen only, of course, an adjunct of the Broadway Theater.

"Then I heard him say something about Dr. Rich's Institute for Physical Education. You know, ma'am, the gymnasium Mr. Saxton visits."

"It's on Crosby Street near Bleecker?"

"Yes, ma'am." Jake Ransom tugged uncomfortably at his ear. "Ladies aren't encouraged to visit, ma'am," he said at last.

"I know," Giana sighed.

"Can I have one of the men take you home, Mrs. Saxton?"

"Yes, Mr. Ransom, you can."

Giana paced back and forth in her bedroom. Mrs. Carruthers had taken Leah to Union Square to feed the ducks. The house seemed as empty and desolate as she felt.

She realized she was dithering about like one of the silly ducks. "This is altogether ridiculous!" she said aloud. She gathered up her skirts and walked purposefully downstairs to Alex's library.

Alex's gun case was locked. She stared at it for a long moment, wondering what to do.

"Would you like something, ma'am?"

"Herbert!" Giana whirled around, flushing guiltily.

"No, thank you," she said more calmly. His rheumy eyes rested a moment on the gun case, but he said nothing. "I just wish to be alone for a while," she said.

When he had left, Giana searched through Alex's desk. At the back of the second drawer, in a small box, she found a ring of keys. She smiled grimly and drew it out. She knew very little about guns, she thought, but she knew enough to scare the wits out of Randall Bennett. Bloody bastard! She would return to the restaurant. Perhaps the proprietor knew Randall's address.

She was sitting on the floor, her skirts spread out about her like a blue silk fan, trying to figure out how to stuff a bullet into the pistol. "Come on, you stupid thing," she muttered, glaring into the barrel.

"Good afternoon, Giana."

The pistol fell to her lap. She raised her eyes at the sound of Alex's perfectly cordial voice.

"You are home," she said stupidly. "I thought you would be later."

"So it would appear. You are having a problem loading the gun?"

"I was just . . . that is, yes, I was!"

Her jaw was thrust out pugnaciously, but Alex appeared only mildly interested. "Would you like me to help you?"

"No," she said, "I shall figure it out."

"As I have told Leah several times, one never looks down the barrel, nor points a gun at anyone. It is odd that I should have to tell you the same things."

"I don't know much about guns," she said, wondering if she were ill-fated. She should have taken the damned pistol and the bullets and locked herself in the water closet. She clasped the gun firmly in her

hand and shook it, her finger closing over the trigger.
"It won't take a bullet," she said.

There was a sudden explosion, and Giana stared at
the gray smoke billowing from the pistol. She flung
it away as if it burned her.

"Oh," she gasped. She saw a large jagged hole in
the back of Alex's desk.

"Sir!"

Herbert flung breathlessly into the library, his face
pale with fright, a wide-eyed Ellen at his heels.

"It is all right, Herbert," Alex said. "Mrs. Saxton
was merely testing the pistol. Leave us."

Alex's heart was pounding so loudly he thought
he would choke. He forced himself to walk slowly to
his desk, lean over, and examine the rent mahogany.

"Good shot," he said. "Right in the middle. I suspect it is irreparable." He looked back at Giana. She
stopped staring at the pistol on the floor beside her
and looked blankly up at him.

"It was already loaded," she said.

He leaned back against his desk and crossed his
arms over his chest. He said quite pleasantly, "Would
you like me to beat you here, or would you prefer we
be more private?"

She gazed up at him, her face as white as her collar. "Is that what a bullet does to a person?"

"Much messier, I assure you. There is a lot of
blood, and a good deal of unpleasant screaming."

She ran her tongue over her parched lips. She
gazed again at the pistol, and physically recoiled
from it. "Oh my God," she whispered, and covered
her face with her hands. "I didn't know . . ."

"Didn't know that you could have killed yourself?
Killed me, or perhaps Herbert?"

He felt his control returning and managed to walk
with a semblance of calm to where she sat on the

floor. He leaned down and picked up the pistol. Carefully he opened the gun case and placed it back into its slot. He took his time relocking the case, and leisurely toyed with the keys. Finally, when he knew he had himself well under control again, he dropped to his knees and pulled Giana's hands from her face. "Come, I'm taking you upstairs."

She nodded, and tried to pull herself to her feet. But she was too clumsy. It suddenly struck her as insanely funny that even if she had managed to load a pistol that was already loaded, she would never have been able to get herself up off the floor. She let out a high-pitched laugh. "You would have found me sitting here playing with your gun," she giggled. "I can't get up, you see." She laughed all the harder, her slender shoulders shaking.

"Giana!" Suddenly her laughter stilled, and tears filled her eyes.

Alex pulled her to her feet, and picked her up in his arms. "How can I beat you if you're crying?" he said. "Stop it. You will not deny me your just punishment."

She buried her face against his throat and wrapped her arms around his neck. "I don't care what you do to me," she said in a low voice.

"Well, I care," he said. "You could have killed yourself quite easily. Besides, thrashing you will calm your nerves, and mine."

When he set her down in their bedroom, she leaned weakly against him for several moments, then drew back, her eyes resting on his grimly set face.

"You will be careful of the baby, won't you, Alex?" she asked in a perfectly serious voice.

"Yes. What the hell are you doing now?"

"I'm taking off my gown," she said in some surprise.

"Forget that for the moment," he growled, running his hand through his hair. "I'm too tired from exercising at the gym . . . and other things."

She looked at him for a long moment, then shrugged. "It appears I must find another way," she said, more to herself than to him.

"I would appreciate it. I wouldn't care to have my wife hung for murdering a scoundrel like Randall Bennett."

Her eyes flew to his face. "How did . . . ?"

"My dear girl," he said patiently, "when I realized you would go out alone, regardless of my wishes, I hired a man to watch over you. I could not be certain your adventure with the strikers was as innocent as I believed. Flobb informed me this morning of your meeting with Mr. Bennett. Now, if you are quite through with your tears and laughter, I would appreciate hearing why you didn't tell me about him."

She sighed deeply. "You always contrive to make me feel like a fool," she said.

"It isn't terribly difficult."

Her eyes darkened with anger. "Excellent," he said, smiling. "I was afraid you had turned into a weak-kneed woman. Sit down, Giana. Your center of gravity has shifted, and I don't want you to lose your balance."

"He threatened to ruin us if I told you," she said after a moment.

"Surely you didn't believe him."

"Of course I did! He hates me for rejecting him four years ago. He knows that we aren't married, and he is threatening to inform the world if I don't pay him ten thousand dollars!"

"Ah," he said, infuriatingly calm.

"His valet was the man chasing me that day." She fell silent, but the quiet was deafening. "I . . . I wanted to threaten him, Alex. I didn't want you to know!"

"But you came to the shipyard to tell me, did you not?"

She nodded. "You weren't there."

"Tell me something, Giana," Alex said thoughtfully. "Why didn't you tell me about this last night? I do have a few more resources available to me than you do.

"Why?" he repeated when her silence lengthened.

"I . . . I was afraid . . . for you. I didn't want him to hurt you."

He gazed at her intently for a long moment, then said evenly, "Well, you can forget the entire incident, and Randall Bennett as well now."

"How can I forget it! Alex, he will do what he threatened! He can make things very uncomfortable for all of us. I don't want you hurt . . . you don't deserve it! He is serious, Alex."

"A man with a broken nose and a cracked jaw has difficulty making himself understood," he said calmly.

"Broken nose?"

"I beat the hell out of Randall Bennett. Most enjoyable," he said as an afterthought. "His valet too."

"How could you? You don't even look . . . messed up!"

He held out his hand and showed her his bruised knuckles. She lightly touched her fingers to the broken skin and felt him flinch slightly. "Why?" she asked.

He smiled sardonically. "If we had been truly married, I would have promised to love, honor, and cherish you."

"But none of that applies to us!"

"I suppose it doesn't," he said slowly, sounding

suddenly tired. "In any case, I told Bennett that if he opened his mouth I would carve his tongue out and force him to eat it. Coming from a savage American, I think such a threat sounded believable. At least he appeared to believe me. He should be returning to hearth and home in England soon."

"I think he is desperate for money," Giana said.

"Scoundrels usually are." He gave her an almost savage smile. "Actually, my love, I know he is on his way to England. A couple of my men escorted him to a departing ship. I did pay his passage. Incidentally, I also sent a letter to your mother. She will keep an eye on Sir Galahad when he arrives in London. Now, Giana, if you don't mind, I think I'll lie down for a while. You scared the hell out of me."

"Do you mind if I join you? My legs still feel rubbery."

"Only if you promise to keep your distance."

Alex was on the point of relaxing when he heard Giana giggle beside him. "I dread knowing what amuses you," he said.

"Randall's beautiful face. Did you really break his nose?"

"You're a bloodthirsty little savage," he said lightly.

Chapter 25

"Derry," Giana shouted, raising her head from the letter, "we've done it! The first thirty reapers are on their way from Chicago to New York, despite the strikes, despite all the wretched lawsuits! My representative in London will be able to fill the orders he's contracted—in two months, at the latest."

"We're not going to lose our skirts?"

Giana grinned. "Indeed not. We're going to buy more skirts!" She danced around her desk, a joyous smile on her face, and threw her arms around a smiling Derry. "I was so afraid," she said, squeezing Derry until she yelped.

"So was I, Giana. So was I." She paused a moment, shaking her head. "I'm not certain if Charles will be pleased or disappointed."

"Well, he certainly will make a goodly amount of interest! Actually, I'm inclined to believe that he'll twit Alex unmercifully for having such an unfeminine wife!"

"At least that is better than those cold silences."

"The Lord be praised for that! The Lord and us, that is." Giana's eyes twinkled merrily. "I must go tell Alex, Derry."

Anesley congratulated her warmly at the news. "Unfortunately, Mrs. Saxton, Mr. Saxton is at the shipyard. He was in a bear of a mood this morning,

ma'am, and went to work it off. Shall I send a clerk
to have him fetched?"

"Oh no, Anesley," Giana said cheerily, "I'll find
him."

"But, Mrs. Saxton . . ." Anesley began, but she
nearly danced out of the office.

A drayer shouted at her to mind where she was
going, and she waved gaily at him, narrowly escaping another oncoming beer wagon in her haste to
cross South Street. Alex would be pleased, he just
had to be! She had won.

She took a deep breath of the winter air, frosty and
clean, as she made her way through the throngs of
people, horses and mules jostling among them. As
she approached the Saxton shipyard, the smell of the
bay, of freshly cut lumber, and the smoky scent of
the iron foundry just to the north greeted her. She
weaved her way through the workers, waving to
some she recognized, nodding happily to anyone
who chanced to look her way.

She was surprised to see Alex in his shirtsleeves,
lashed to the mast of one of the new ships, hammering down a bracing on the rigging. She did not shout
up at him, afraid he might lose his concentration. She
watched him as he worked, the muscles in his back
and his powerful arm flexing with each stroke of the
hammer, and felt a familiar, sharp longing snake
through her. "Damn you, Alex Saxton," she muttered.

The bracing secured, Alex raised a hand to brush
away the sweat stinging his eyes. He was untying
the leather straps that held him safely against the
mast when he chanced to look down. He saw Giana
standing below him, her cloak billowing around her,
her eyes fastened up at him.

Her name formed in his throat and emerged as a

growl. How many times had he told her she wasn't to come here without an escort? It wasn't just the unsavory derelicts who made their home about the fringes of the shipyard, it was simply no place for a woman alone, seven months pregnant. He quickly shimmied down the mast, made his way carefully over the raw planks of the deck, and climbed down the ladder.

He saw her running clumsily toward him, waving a piece of paper in her hand.

"Alex!"

He heard a sudden creaking sound and the rending of wood. He looked up and saw the mainmast weaving in the wind under the heavy rigging. Slowly the mast teetered and split halfway up its mighty stalk. Then, wrapped in its white shroud of sail, it crashed downward.

"Giana!" He watched helplessly as Giana and the men ran from beneath the falling mast. Then it was over. The mast lay near where Giana had stood, one of his men trapped beneath it.

"Stay clear!" he heard Jake Ransom shouting. He stared at Ali Lucino as Jake and several of his men pulled him from beneath the mast.

"It's his leg, Mr. Saxton," Jake shouted. "He's all right!"

Alex rushed to Giana, so relieved that for a moment he could think of nothing to say. He closed his eyes tightly, trying to dispel the image of Giana lying beneath that mast, the life crushed out of her.

"You're all right?" he croaked at last, his hands automatically traveling over her body. "The baby?"

"I'm all right," she said. She gazed over to where Ali was propped up against a tub of tar, holding his broken leg. "That mast broke," she said. "You could have been hurt."

"I?" He threw back his head and laughed hoarsely "I?" he repeated.

Suddenly his laughter died, and his eyes became nearly black. She winced at his tight grip on her arms. "What," he said very deliberately, "are you doing here?"

"I came to tell you the news."

But he didn't hear her. "I told you never, never to come here without an escort, preferably me! Must you always be a pigheaded little fool?"

He was jerked out of his whirlpool rage by Jake Ransom.

"Sir! Is Mrs. Saxton all right?"

"Yes, Jake, she is. See that Ali gets to the doctor. The rest of you—clean up the mess and get back to work!"

"You're hurting me, Alex," Giana said, trying to pull her bruised arm free of his grip.

Alex felt his rage at her mount. It was born of his fear for her, but he would not admit to it. He saw only that once again she had blithely disobeyed him and put her life in danger. His grip tightened. "I'm taking you home. And believe me, madam, you will stay there!"

Giana fell into sullen silence as he pulled her along, barely slowing his stride, not understanding his sudden anger. Once inside a cab, she said with asperity, "For heaven's sake, Alex, you don't need to see me home! I am quite all right! And I don't want to go home. I have some news for you."

"Shut up!"

"How dare you say that to me!"

His arm snaked about her shoulders, and he held his hand threateningly near her mouth. "I said to shut up, but if you won't, I'll do it for you."

Her eyes shot daggers at him, but he turned away

from her and stared straight ahead, ignoring her. He didn't move his arm until the cab pulled up at home.

Alex jumped out, paid the driver, and turned on his heel, leaving Giana staring after him from inside the cab. She wanted to yell names after him, but the cabbie was staring at her, more than interested. She bit her tongue and stomped into the house after him.

Herbert was a different matter. But before she could say anything, Alex whirled on her and barked, "Keep quiet, Giana! Herbert, Mrs. Saxton and I will be in the library. See that we're not disturbed."

He shoved her into the library and slammed the doors closed behind him. His face was white with anger when he turned to face her. "No, don't begin on me, Giana," he said, his voice deadly calm. "You are in the wrong. Would you have had to take Ali's place under that mast to see it? I have told you countless times not to come to the shipyard without me. But you never listen to a word anyone has to say, do you? I am *tired*, Giana, of your stubborn selfishness."

"I didn't mean to be, Alex," she began. "It . . . that is, I was excited, and wanted to see you."

"See me? That's a laugh. You wanted to prove to me that Miss Georgiana Van Cleve does whatever she pleases!" He stared at her whitened face, and his voice was suddenly tired. "I've just been too stubborn to see that you'll never change."

She stood rigid, too hurt to speak, and her silence only further enraged him. It was as if she were baiting him, taunting him with her silence.

"Well?" he growled at her. "Have you nothing to say, madam? Don't you even want to remind me how much you hate me? What a crass brute I am? An American savage?"

"I don't hate you," she whispered, her voice a croak to her own ears.

"Oh, and sure you don't now?" he sneered, drawling in a thick Irish brogue. "Why? Because you still haven't satisfied your lust for me? And such lust you have for such a blue-blooded little English lady! Take your lust, Miss Van Cleve, and choke on it!"

"It isn't ... lust," she said, wishing only that he would stop his cruel taunts. He looked at her as if he hated her. She felt tears swim in her eyes. But his mocking voice stilled them.

"A woman's ultimate weapon? I know you too well to be taken in. What's the matter, Giana? Lost your glib little tongue?"

"Alex, you don't understand," she said, desperate now. "You must listen to me!"

"Listen to you? If I listen to you anymore, I'll go insane. I don't want your damned trust. The only thing I want from you is my child."

"You ... cannot mean that," she gasped. "Please, Alex, don't do this to me, to us!"

He looked at her, then only threw his head back and laughed, laughed until his powerful shoulders were shaking.

Something broke inside of her. She heard herself scream at him, "You are the fool, Alex! You are a stupid, blind beast! I hate you, do you hear? *I hate you!*"

"Your conversation is boring, my love." He sneered at her over his shoulder. "I've heard it all before, remember?"

She stood alone in the middle of the library, the letter from Cyrus McCormick still clutched in her hand. She stared blindly down at it, all her joy, her excitement, turned to cold ashes. There was no one to reassure her, no one to tell her that she had done nothing to turn her husband into an unreasoning brute. She had nothing but her pride. She gathered it about herself like a patchwork cloak and walked slowly upstairs.

Chapter 26

Giana lay watching the dark winter clouds drift by outside her window. Evening was falling, and when the sun rose again, she would board the liner *Star Flight*, bound for Portsmouth. She felt tears sting her eyes, and angrily brushed them away. Stupid woman, she cursed herself. Stupid, weak woman.

She supposed it was the light that woke her, pulling her from a numbed sleep. She slowly opened her eyes and saw Alex sitting in a chair by her bed. He was gazing at her, his face impassive, his long fingers forming a steeple under his chin.

She heard a voice say quite calmly, "How did you get in here?"

"You are awake. I thought the lamp might do the trick." The long fingers began to tap. "I bribed the hotel manager."

"I see," she said wearily. A mass of loose hair was falling over her cheek and she raised her hand to shove it back. "How did you know where I was?"

"Herbert was very upset when you left. He followed you here to the Astor."

"Very enterprising," she said. She felt too tired and too empty to protest. "What are you doing here, Alex? I left you a note. There was no reason for you to come."

"I have come to take you back home, of course. As

for your note, it's been a long time since I've been treated to such drivel."

Giana pulled the cover over her shoulders. The simple movement quelled the moment of anger she felt at his words. "It was not drivel," she said dully.

"Would you like to sit up?"

She ignored him and slowly pulled herself up on the bed.

"I ordered dinner for us here. I trust you have some appetite."

She didn't reply, merely stared straight ahead at a painting of the New York countryside on the opposite wall. A very bad painting, she thought, the sun suspended in the sky like a large orange platter.

"You are not such a coward, Giana," he said deliberately. "You could have had one of my guns loaded and ready to use on me when I returned home."

She turned her head to face him. "Why?" she asked blankly.

She looked so wan, so damned withdrawn. "Do you feel all right?" he barked at her, sitting forward in his chair. To his surprise, she flinched away from him.

"Of course," she said. "I will feel even better on the morrow."

"Ah yes. It is your intention to run away? To return to England, and weather the storm?"

"No. I will go to Cornwall. I do not want my mother or the duke hurt by any scandal."

"Very thoughtful of you." He sneered. "And what about me, Giana?"

"You?" She looked faintly surprised, one elegant brow arched upward. "You made your wishes perfectly clear, Alex. You cannot bear the sight of me. I am but obliging you."

"I didn't want this, dammit, and you know it!" He

rose abruptly from his chair and stood over her. "I have had a perfectly hellish day, and I return home to find that my wife has packed up and walked out on me! Another example of your thoughtlessness. I won't abide any more of it, Giana. After dinner, we are going home."

Giana's fingers curled about the bedcovers as she fought to control her anger at him for his arrogance. She had hoped to ignore him, but instead, she heard herself yell at him, "I am not your wife, and you can go to hell!"

To her surprise, he smiled. "That's better. I wondered how long you could play your spiritless-old-horse act. Come now, tell me what you think of me."

"Stop it! Damn you, Alex Saxton, stop taunting me!"

He sat down beside her, and she wasn't fast enough to move away from him. She felt his fingers gently pushing the clouds of hair from her forehead and close about her face. He leaned down and lightly kissed the tip of her nose. She tried to struggle free of him, but he merely stretched out beside her, and held her firmly against him.

"Let me go," she snarled, bringing her arms up to push at his shoulders. "I know exactly what you think of *me*, Alex. I don't know what game you're playing now, but I refuse to be a part of it."

He pressed his face into her hair. "I have never been so frightened in my life," she heard him say hoarsely.

She stopped struggling. "You, frightened?" she repeated stupidly.

His fingertips roved lightly over her face and sketched the line of her brow. "You could have been killed," he said simply. "All I could see was you ly-

ing beneath that mast. You and the child, both dead."
He drew a deep breath. "I could not have borne that,
Giana."

She stared up at him warily. "I am not demented,
Alex. You were not frightened, you were furious.
And you said . . . awful things to me."

"Yes, I know. But you also know that I am not a
particularly even-tempered man. In fact, I, just like
you, spout the stupidest things when roused."

"Now you accuse me, when it is you who are to
blame!" she said indignantly.

"We are both to blame. In this instance, perhaps it
was I who was the more . . . outrageous. Will you forgive me?"

"You want me to forgive you so I will come home
with you . . . to avoid any scandal?"

"Actually, I hadn't thought about that. No, I want
you to forgive me because I am sorry I hurt you. I
promise to try to keep my godawful temper leashed
in the future."

"You should only make promises, Alex, you have a
modicum of chance of keeping."

"All right. I promise to apologize every time I lose
my temper. Now do you forgive me?"

She stared into his dark eyes. "Does it really . . .
matter to you, Alex?" she asked hesitantly, her voice
a thin whisper.

"Of course it does, Giana," he said, gently kissing
her. "You see, you stubborn little hellion, I love you."
He felt her stiffen, but continued in a soft voice,
"When I came home, somewhat the worse for wear
from brandy, and found you gone, I wanted to beat
the hell out of you and slash my wrists for being
such a maniac."

She stared up at him, as if dazed. "But you can't

love me. You never said so! It was a . . . business deal
you proposed in the first place!"

"That was before . . . before many things." He felt
her wariness, her uncertainty, and said harshly,
"Don't leave, Giana. Come home with me."

The stark emptiness vanished without a trace.
"Yes," she said, smiling up at him. "I will come home
with you, but I shall never understand you." She
turned her face against his throat and breathed in the
male scent of him, so familiar to her now.

"Do you understand yourself?"

"No . . . well, sometimes."

"Did you want to leave me?"

She sighed. "I didn't see any choice. It was you,
not I, who wanted me to go."

He kissed her again, then said slowly, "I would
rather hear you say you trust me than you love me."

She was held speechless for a long moment. He
knew, damn him, he knew! "But we are always arguing," she said, knowing as well as he did that it was
an evasion.

His tongue caressed her parted lips; then he pulled
away from her and rose.

"Where . . . where are you going?" she whispered.

"It is time for our dinner," he said.

She was sipping her second glass of champagne
when he said abruptly, "What were you doing in the
shipyard?"

"I had some very exciting news for you, and if you
had but taken the time to listen to me, you would not
now have to ask me."

"You're pregnant."

"Alex, you wretch! The first thirty reapers are on
their way to New York this very minute!" She lowered her eyes to her plate. "That was why I came to
the shipyard. I was so anxious to tell you that I for-

got you didn't want me to be there. I . . . I didn't think, I suppose."

Alex sat back in his chair, his long fingers fiddling with the stem of his champagne glass. "My wife a successful businesswoman," he mused aloud.

"With good business judgment," she said, raising her chin.

"Yes, that too, it would appear. Would you like to get drunk? To celebrate your success?"

Her tongue caressed her lower lip, an exquisitely sensual gesture that made his body taut with desire. "Can it not be our success, Alex?"

He smiled widely. "Yes," he said, "I should like that. Are we to have a drunken celebration?"

She looked at him uncertainly. He was so damned slippery sometimes, she thought. He had told her that he loved her, yet now he seemed to be playing a game with her. "Yes," she said, disappointment clear in her voice, "if that is what you would like."

Her eyes were on his mouth, and he laughed softly. Her passion for him never ceased to amaze and delight him. He rose from his chair, stretched, and slowly undressed, folding each article of clothing neatly over the back of a chair. When he was naked, he pushed back the chair and smiled down at her from a most immodest pose.

"There is a bruise on your ribs," she said sharply, fear naked in her voice.

"I'll tell you about it—later."

He grinned at her, his eyes flitting from the top of her head to her bare toes, and cocked a wicked eyebrow at her. "Isn't it your turn now, love?"

Giana tossed back her head and looked him squarely in the eye. "Yes," she said, "I suppose it is. You will not embarrass me, Alex Saxton!"

Still, she could not quite meet his eyes when her dressing gown and chemise lay on the floor. She felt his hands close over her arms and draw her gently to him. He pulled her down on his lap. "You have become quite an armful," he said, resting his hand on her belly.

She squirmed slightly against him and pressed her breasts against his chest.

"Have you no control, woman?" he laughed softly. "You are shamefully eager." He kissed her deeply, feeling the violent emotional jumble of the day fade away, leaving a tenderness in its wake, and a burning desire.

He could feel the hammering of her heart against his chest as he lifted her to the bed.

He made love to her gently, with only the sound of her quickening breath and her soft cries filling the silence. When he felt her tense against him, he gloried in it, and buried his own moans of pleasure against her throat.

"I love you, Alex," she cried helplessly, pressing herself against him. "Damn you, I love you!"

He twisted his hands in her hair, and covered her soft mouth with kisses.

"I will take your love," he said, stroking her back gently as she calmed. *Even though you damn me with it.* "It is enough, for now."

She raised passion-drenched eyes to his face. "I am so frightened," she whispered. "I am no longer just myself." *And you want more, much more. You want all of me.*

"Then you know how I feel." He lifted her easily beneath her arms and raised her off him, despite her throaty protests, and smiled crookedly. "Let me tell you what I did today," he said. "Then perhaps you will let me rest awhile."

He settled himself beside her, eased her against his side, and pulled the covers over them. "After I left you, I went to a sailors' bar down on the Battery. The bruise on my ribs is the result of a drunken brawl."

She ran her fingers lightly over the purple bruise. "Was it me you were hitting?"

"No. I am much too mild a man ever to strike a woman."

She quirked an eyebrow. "You, mild, Mr. Saxton?"

"Mild but ... potent," he said blandly.

"Very true," she said impishly, patting her belly. "Your son has been pounding me all day."

"Giana, there is something I want to tell you."

She was alerted instantly to the deep tenor of his voice.

"You remember I told you that Charles Lattimer had wanted to marry Laura?"

"Yes."

"That wasn't quite all of it. You see, love, upon reflection, I think my great anger at you was because of Laura, and my memories of her."

"I don't understand, Alex," she said, cocking her head at him.

He drew a deep breath. "Laura didn't die in a boating accident, Giana. She killed herself."

"Oh, Alex, no!" She felt herself shudder at the pain in his eyes. "But why?" she gasped.

"Her illness became apparent toward the end of our first year of marriage and her pregnancy with Leah. She became ... afraid of everything, afraid of me, afraid of seeing people, afraid of dying in childbirth. After Leah's birth, she slipped into a depression so profound that no one could help her. That is why I bought the house in Connecticut. She lived there for three years with her companion. After the death of her father, she lost all hold on reality and killed herself."

"I'm sorry, Alex," she whispered. She clutched him to her, wanting to erase the memory. "But then I must have brought it all back, all of it, at Thanksgiving! You were so superb . . . you never let on any of it, you never blamed me! It never occurred to me that . . ."

"How could I blame you?" he said, surprise in his voice. "There was no way you could have known. No one knows the truth. I even kept it from her family. They are Quakers, and the truth would have destroyed them."

Giana moaned softly. "I always rush into things . . . I never think."

He drew her to him. "There is no reason for you to blame yourself for any of it. It is over, long over. It is just that you had to know."

They lay quietly for a time, and then he heard her ask in a small voice, "Alex?"

"Hum?"

"Why do you love me?"

He smiled into the darkness. "Because you fake passion in me so well?"

He felt her fingers close over the hair on his chest and tug. He smiled grimly. She had wanted to know why he loved her, and he, agilely enough, had evaded her. How could he explain why when it was simply a feeling, a need that seemed to overshadow everything in his life?

"There is something I would like to hear from you, Giana. I would like you to look me straight in the face and tell me that you want to be my wife and spend your life with me, and damn the unfair laws and damn any men who are unfaithful and harsh with their women."

He heard her draw in her breath sharply. "It is still a matter of trust, isn't it?"

"You must give me time," she whispered at last. She knew she didn't want to lose him, but she could not help her fright. She saw herself at seventeen, so very young, so very trusting, so very foolish. And Rome, a specter that still haunted her, though less now, she realized, so much less since Alex had come into her life.

As she sought for words to explain to him, she heard him say calmly, "There will always be men like Randall Bennett to take advantage of innocence. You were lucky, Giana. I agree with your mother—Rome was preferable to the unhappiness you would have known with him."

She gasped aloud, and her voice shook. "How did you know what I was thinking?"

"If you hadn't been in Rome," he continued, "I never would have fallen in love with the coy little virgin I bought."

"Perhaps you would have loved the girl you met four years later in London."

"That cold woman?"

"I wasn't . . . cold," she said in a small voice.

"You were buried under a foot of snow. I never would have been able to dig my way to you if I hadn't met you in Rome."

"You really believe that, Alex?"

"Yes, I really do."

Giana drew a deep breath. "I know that above all I want to . . . stay with you, Alex. Can I stay, even after the baby is born?"

He was silent for a long moment, knowing that it wasn't enough, but that it wasn't the time to say so.

There is still time, he thought, his jaw tightening, there is always time. He slowly nodded and drew her to him.

"Yes," he said. "I want you to stay." He kissed her temple and listened to her breathing until it slowed and she was asleep on his shoulder.

Chapter 27

It was a glorious day in early April. Delaney, just returned from Washington, strolled beside Giana on the green at Washington Square, matching his stride to hers. She told him about Randall Bennett as they walked, omitting what she thought she must, and dwelling on what Alex had down to him.

Delaney laughed. "You know, Giana, Alex was always beating up whoever dared rub his little brother's nose in the dirt. Thank God he hasn't had to do it since I was ten years old! An honorable man, my brother," he added, squeezing Giana's arm.

"Yes," she said, pulling her eyes from the brightly uniformed regiment practicing on the green. "In all his dealings with me, he has certainly been that."

"I knew once Alex fell in love, he would fall like a mighty oak," Delaney said.

"He loved Laura."

"He was fond of Laura," he said, almost sadly. "Poor girl. He did love her father, dearly. He would have done anything for him. That was really why he kept Laura's suicide from the Nielson family. It was an awful time for him. I am glad he told you about it."

Delaney's eyes twinkled down at her. "But now . . . I have never seen him so content. Never would I have imagined that a pert, mouthy English girl would have gotten under his hide."

"Well, something got under somebody's hide," Giana said, grinning wickedly.

"Spare my blushes, Mrs. Saxton," he chided her severely, "since your husband certainly won't. The man can't keep his hands off you, particularly your stomach."

"Oh, Delaney, I feel like such a cow!"

"Alex told me you were no longer dashing about like a racehorse. But a cow? Really, my dear girl."

Giana suddenly stopped in her tracks. She pressed her hands over her belly and raised shocked eyes to Delaney's face.

"What's the matter?"

"It's a month too soon!" she gasped.

"What do you mean?" Delaney asked, not really wanting to hear the answer.

"My water just broke. Dr. Davidson told me that it happens when labor starts."

Delaney stared down at her, appalled. He knew absolutely nothing about babies and less about having them. "Home," he said, gulping. "Yes, we must get you home!"

Giana felt a sudden tightening in her belly, followed by a wrenching contraction. She yelped, more in fright than in pain, and raised panicked eyes. "The baby!"

"No, don't say it," Delaney said firmly. He hoisted her up into his arms and loped across the green, the eyes of the Seventh Regiment watching his progress. To his heady relief, Alex was at home. He took in the situation at a glance.

"How close are the pains, Delaney?" he barked at his brother.

"I have no idea, Alex." He gingerly placed Giana in his brother's outstretched arms.

Giana winced and clung to Alex's neck. He bellowed orders as he strode up the stairs, Giana in his arms. He nearly dropped her when she suddenly writhed in pain. "I'm sorry," she panted when the contraction eased.

"Don't be a fool. Birthing a child hurts dreadfully."

"Alex." His name was a wisp of a sound. "I am so afraid. It is too soon."

"How the hell can you be afraid? You're with me, remember?"

He fairly ripped the clothes off her, cursing at the knotted ribbon on her chemise. He wondered if he looked as frantic as the ashen-faced Herbert, who had moved with amazing speed to fetch Dr. Davidson.

Alex stayed beside her, gently mopping the sweat from her face. He winced at the fear in her eyes, suddenly hating himself for planting his seed in her womb, for bringing her this pain. "Hang on, love," he said to her. "Elvan will be here soon. Hold my hand."

He almost instantly regretted it, for she dug her fingers like claws into his flesh. When Elvan, red-faced, suddenly appeared in the doorway, Alex vowed to double his fee.

There were no blushes on Elvan's pleasant face. "How close are her pains?" he inquired calmly, pulling off his coat and rolling up his sleeves.

"Continuous, for about ten minutes now."

Elvan nodded, then ignored Alex. He whipped back the sheet and quickly examined her.

"She's a month early," Alex croaked.

"It's just as well," Elvan said, not looking up. "Another month and I would have been worried."

"What can I do?"

"Get out and send me Mrs. Carruthers," Elvan snapped. "Join your brother downstairs. From the look of both of you, you could use some brandy."

"No," Giana gasped. "Don't leave! Please don't leave me."

Alex saw the terror in her eyes, and shook his head at Elvan.

"Very well, then," Elvan snorted. "No, Mrs. Saxton," he said sharply, "don't press down, not yet. Take short breaths. Remember what I told you."

Giana was unaware that Anna Carruthers was now in the room, calmly instructing a trembling Ellen what to do. She was drenched in her own sweat, consumed by a pain she could never have imagined.

She felt Alex's arms about her shoulders, holding her, felt him wipe her forehead with the damp cloth Mrs. Carruthers handed him.

"It won't be long now, Mrs. Saxton," she heard Dr. Davidson say, his voice sounding tired. Long, she thought vaguely. It had already been forever!

For several moments the pain locked out everyone and his words made no sense. It was Alex shaking her that brought her back to a semblance of reason. At a nod from Elvan, Alex said in his most imperious voice, "Push down now, Giana."

She groaned, straining desperately. She let out a scream and lurched upward.

"The baby's coming! Again, Mrs. Saxton, push!"

Alex released his hold on her just in time to see Elvan catch his son. "My God," he said, staring at the mop of black hair. At his son's furious wail, he said again, "My God."

Alex turned back to Giana, a wide smile on his face. He kissed her lightly on her parched mouth.

"Thank you, love. You promised me a son. I should never have doubted you."

Giana smiled weakly and closed her eyes.

"Now will you get out of here, Alex? Damn, if she had waited another month, your son would have been born speaking!"

Alex sat on the edge of the bed, watching Elvan show Giana how to feed their son. When the baby's small mouth suddenly closed around her nipple, she gasped, then smiled, her eyes flying to Alex's face.

"Oh my," she said, "how very odd that feels."

Elvan rose. "Well, you don't need me anymore for the present. I won't ask you to accompany me out the door, Alex. I can see you'd far rather watch your son have his dinner."

"I don't think Giana cares what I do for the moment," Alex said, laughing. He watched her shake aside the thick, plaited braid that lay over her shoulder as she stared down, bemused, at the tiny fingers clutching at her breast. She looked so very lovely, he thought. Who would guess that she had given birth only yesterday. He felt a welling of pride and tenderness so intense that he had to turn away.

"A glass of wine, Elvan?" he asked hoarsely, and led the way to the library.

When he returned to their bedroom, Nicholas was sleeping blissfully in a cradle Alex had hastily bought.

"I expect him to snore any minute," Giana said, pulling her eyes away from her son. "And you, Alex, you look so very pleased with yourself!"

"It is you I am pleased with," he said. He cupped her face between his large hands, dipped his head down, and lightly kissed her. "Thank you for my son."

She felt him trembling slightly, and gently stroked the curling black hair at the back of his neck.

"He is rather nice," she said nervously, breaking the power of the moment. "But he looks not at all like me. It isn't fair, and I did all the work!"

"Ah, but I, my dear, made it all possible. 'One damned time,' if I recall your words correctly." His grin faded and she heard the anxiety in his voice as he added, "Do you feel all right now?"

"Of course. And so flat! Feel, Alex, I'm skinny again."

He forced a smile to his lips, and laid his hand lightly on her belly. "I will see that you stay that way," he said, and she started at the intensity of his voice. It was odd, she thought, but the terrible pain she had endured was fading from her mind more quickly than from Alex's.

Giana looked again at her sleeping son. "Do you like him, Alex?" she asked shyly.

"He's a greedy little begger. Leah approves, but made me promise that I wouldn't ignore her now that I have a son. Silly little chit!"

"We will have to be very careful about that, I expect," Giana said, and yawned.

"Have I bored you already?"

She shook her head, but he saw she was having difficulty remaining awake. "Poor Mother. She missed everything! Nicholas will be a month old, nearly grown, by the time she and the *damned* duke get here," she said, mimicking his voice.

"Perhaps to hear him recite the Declaration of Independence," Alex said. "Go to sleep now, love. I was informed by Elvan that I am not to touch you for a month at least."

She regarded him demurely from beneath her lashes. "We will see," she said.

* * *

"It appears," the duke said, gazing down at the sleeping Nicholas in Aurora's arms, "that your daughter can't tell time."

At Delaney's questioning smile, he added, "I told my wife that babies were like clockwork, yet Giana must needs ignore nature and make poor Alex dash about like a headless chicken."

"Rooster, sir, rooster."

"Ah, indeed, my boy. Forgive me."

"And I'm an uncle, as all you seem to forget," Delaney complained, touching his rough thumb to the baby's chin. "A stubborn chin," he observed. "I don't know whether it's Giana's or yours, Alex."

"Well, since I'm the one who wears the pants in the family," Alex began, only to hear Delaney interrupt him with a laugh.

"Methinks I hear a swishing skirt, brother!"

"How right you are, Delaney," Giana said from the doorway.

Alex looked up, his eyes alight with pleasure. Giana's waist was nearly as small as it used to be, her breasts beautifully swollen with milk for Nicholas. To his bemused surprise, when her eyes met his, she blushed.

As if by magic, Nicholas opened his eyes and gazed up at his grandmother. His small fingers reached for her breast.

"Oh dear," Aurora said ruefully, "I fear it is Giana you need, little one." She rose gracefully and handed Giana her son.

"Don't worry, my love," the duke said, "if it is that kind of attention you want, I will not deny you."

"I'm a mere boy of twenty-eight," Delaney said. "I wonder if I'll have either the interest or the energy when I am a grown man."

"It is the lady, son," the duke said. "Therein lies the secret."

"You are shameless, Damien, utterly shameless!"

Delaney gazed from the duke to his duchess, and sighed deeply. He rose and said, "I think I will go bury my sorrows in a glass of beer. Even Alex pays me no more attention."

"True," Alex said, pulling his eyes from his son, "but can you blame me?"

"I begin to perceive that my destiny lies in California."

"Mayhap even your lady," the duke said.

"I think," Aurora said severely, "that the both of you should keep your tongues in your mouths and leave poor Delaney alone."

"At last I have a champion," Delaney said. "Would you care to join me in my solitude, ma'am?"

"I think that is a fine invitation," Aurora said, flashing an impish smile toward her husband.

"Take Leah, my love. I don't trust brash Americans."

Alex sat quietly watching Giana suckle Nicholas, a sight that always fascinated him. The smile left his lips when he remembered their son was over a month old, and he stared down at his hands, clasped between his knees. It was Giana who had reminded him of the passage of time the night before, when she snuggled against him. He had pulled away from her, telling her in a ragged voice that he wanted Elvan to examine her first, but he knew that was not why he had refused her. He was pulled from his thoughts when Giana said, "I saw Dr. Davidson today."

"Oh?"

"Yes," she said, color mounting her cheeks. She

looked him straight in the eye. "He said I am perfectly well again. Perfectly, Alex."

He felt a leap of desire in his groin, but he sternly repressed it. "That is interesting," he said only, and turned to look out of the window.

Giana blinked in confusion. She knew he wanted her as much as she did him. Why was he being aloof and purposefully obtuse?

Nicholas, glutted, was sleeping soundly in her arms. She dropped a quick kiss on his smooth brow, fastened her gown, and carried him to the nursery to Clare, the new nursery maid. Alex was standing at the window looking down at the street when she returned.

She found herself staring at him, wishing her face were buried in his throat so she could breathe in the scent of him. Her fingers curled at the thought of roving freely over his beautifully formed body, tangling in the thick hair on his chest, and downward, to feel his muscles tense beneath her hand. She felt a shock of desire so powerful that she trembled.

"Alex?" Her voice was a beguiling whisper, but he didn't turn, only drew himself up straight and stiff.

"Yes?" He sounded bored, she thought, stunned. Bored!

"I . . . I don't understand," she said.

He turned slowly from his post at the window and gazed coldly at her. "What don't you understand?" he barked.

"You sound . . . angry. I don't know what I've done to make you feel angry with me."

"I am tired of being the patient, understanding husband, Giana," he said slowly, turning to face her.

Giana shook her head in confusion. "But you are not—"

"That's right. I am not your husband, am I? Well,

my dear, I have discovered that I cannot, will not, continue in my role as your lover. I want marriage. I want all of you, or nothing."

"I love you, Alex," she said at last, her voice shaking. "I have told you I love you many times, but you tell me it is not enough. You want me to trust you, trust you with my very soul." She looked away for a moment. "You . . . want to have the power to destroy me."

"Ah, and your husband would have that power, would he not, Giana?" He cocked his head to one side, and when he spoke, his voice was insolently mocking. "Do I take it, then, that what you want is for me to strip right here? If I touch you, Giana, caress you between your lovely thighs, will I discover that you are already wet for me?"

She flinched at his crudeness, drawing herself up. She gazed at him warily, not knowing what to say.

"Will you pant for me? Make those little mewling sounds in your throat?"

She tossed her head back. "You know that I will," she said.

"And will you whisper that you love me, Giana? And after I've given you pleasure, will you say it again? Give the poor devil his due—is that what you will do?"

She felt her desire dissolve under his mockery, and turned quickly from him, only wanting to escape.

"No, don't run away just yet, my love," he said coldly. "I am not through telling you just what I intend to do."

Unwanted tears were stinging her eyes, and she furiously gulped them back. "I don't understand," she began.

"You don't? Very well, let me explain it to you. You are here as my wife, and I have decided that as your husband, it is time for me to bend you to my will, to show you what it means to be in a man's power. We will begin now. You will take off your clothes. I have not enjoyed a woman's soft body in several months, and since I am not yet bored with you, I prefer you to the other women I will doubtless have in the future. Of course, in a year or so, I might go back to Rome. What was her name, Margot? No, she is too old now, almost your age. I am sure I can find a younger woman, more skilled than you. You, my dear Giana, might as well be my wife, and what man wants to continually make love to a woman he must argue with? A woman he sees every day of his life? A woman whose body is his for the taking whenever he wishes it? But enough. *Take off your clothes!* And be quick about it." He shrugged, and pulled off his waistcoat. "While you are undressing, I will decide in what manner I wish to enjoy you."

"What do you want from me?"

He merely glanced at her impatiently as he unbuttoned his shirt. "I believe I made myself quite clear but a few minutes ago. But since that is beyond you, I see no reason why I should continue to reason with you. I am but fulfilling your expectations, making you thank God that you were never fool enough to trust me, a man." His eyes narrowed dangerously on her pale face, but when he spoke again, his voice was a silky purr. "If you do not strip now, I will take your clothes off for you."

"No!"

"But I will delight in doing it, and there is nothing you can do to prevent me. After all, only a few minutes ago you were hot for me. What's the matter now, my pet? There is never any need to force you, is there?"

He sat down, ignoring her, to pull off his shoes.

Giana turned and ran to the door, but he closed his hand over hers on the doorknob. He grasped the collar of her gown and ripped downward, rending the material to her waist. She twisted frantically against him, but his hands were like cold steel against her bare shoulders.

"I could beat you senseless, Giana, and you could do nothing to stop me. I can do anything I please to you."

She felt him rip away her chemise.

"Ah, what's this? No corset? How convenient." He pulled her roughly against him, crushing her swollen breasts against his naked chest.

"No," she whispered. "There is no corset. I wanted you to make love to me."

She raised her face, willingly pressing herself against him, closing out his hateful words. He gazed down at her and smiled, lightly stroking her back and tangling his fingers in her thick hair. He was all that was gentle and tender when he kissed her. He nuzzled her throat, bending her over his arm to thrust her breasts up to him. She squirmed against him when he brushed his lips over her nipples, and suckled them as did Nicholas. She nearly cried out from the pleasure of it. He eased her up into his arms and carried her to the bed. In another moment he was standing naked beside her, staring down at her.

"Alex," she murmured, and stretched out her arms to him.

Again he smiled. He lay next to her, his fingers following his eyes as they roved over her body. "There are no marks on your belly," he said, gently kneading her. She wanted him to kiss her, but he kept his eyes upon her face, studying her.

"How fortunate," he murmured after a moment,

when he felt her hips move against his fingers. "You could still become a whore if you wished."

"Please, Alex, don't. Please, stop."

He knew she meant him to stop his taunting words, but he rose and moved away from her.

"You asked me to stop? Very well, Giana." He turned his back to her to hide his desire and quickly pulled on his trousers.

She was lying on her back, her legs slightly parted, her eyes wide on his face. "Please do not . . . leave me," she moaned.

He laughed unpleasantly. "Bring yourself to pleasure, Giana. You can do everything else for yourself. You don't need me."

He heard her sobbing softly as he tugged on the rest of his clothes. He found he had prodded the buttons of his shirt into the wrong holes, and cursed softly at his clumsiness. Despite himself, his eyes went to the bed. She was curled up on her side, her knees drawn to her chest, her hair fanned out about her. He pulled the door open, gritted his teeth, and left her. He strode to the nursery down the hall, where he found Clare sewing beside Nicholas' crib.

"Leave us, Clare," he said.

Alex lifted his sleeping son out of his crib, sat down, and cradled him in his arms. Jesus, what had he done? Perhaps too much, perhaps not enough. Would he lose his son because of his refusal to accept what she offered? He traced the tip of his finger lightly over his son's plump cheek, then touched his pink lips. Nicholas began making smacking noises in his sleep, and his small mouth opened to suck his father's finger. Alex felt a shaft of pain. His eyes did not leave his son's face even when he heard a swish of skirts behind him.

"I told you to leave us, Clare," he said, not looking up.

"It is not Clare, Alex."

He raised weary eyes to Giana's face. She was pale, her eyes puffy from her tears. He said tonelessly, "You win, Giana. You can stay, if you like, and we will continue as we have."

Giana fell to her knees beside his chair, her crinoline skirt fanning out about her. "I don't want things to continue as they have," she said quietly, looking briefly at her son's face before she gazed up at Alex. "I cannot bear it."

"I see," he said. Alex rose from the chair, careful not to disturb his son, and laid him gently into his crib. He turned back and took Giana's hands in his. "You know I never wanted to love you," he said. "But it appears I can do nothing about it."

"Would you marry me, Alex?"

He stood very still, his hand tightening about hers.

"I know that I would give my life for you. Since that is true, it seems rather ridiculous of me not to trust you with mine. Please marry me, Alex. I will try very hard to make you happy with me."

"Make me reconciled to my fate?"

"Yes, if fate it is."

He was silent for a moment, as if in deep thought. He said finally, his voice carefully neutral, "Since it has been my ... fate to know you, you have managed to turn my world upside down and backwards. You are not a particularly restful woman, Giana. Just this morning, I found a gray hair in my head. To spend the rest of my miserable life with you is a daunting thought. You will argue with me endlessly, I'm certain, and doubtless you will never be brought to heel."

"Brought to heel! Let me see this gray hair, Alex. I

don't believe you!" She tugged at his head to bring him to her, but he clasped her wrists in his hands and held them against his chest.

"I'll wager you will even refuse to embroider new chair covers for my library."

She leaned against him, pressing her cheek against his hands as they held hers so closely. "Please do not tease me, Alex, until you consent to marry me. I . . . I am frightened."

"You changed your gown," he said.

"You may rip it if you like."

"Only if I agree to marry you," he said very softly, laughter lurking in his voice.

Anna Carruthers suddenly appeared in the nursery doorway. She gazed limpidly at the embracing couple, and a wide smile appeared on her face.

"If you will excuse us, ma'am," Alex said blandly. Without another word, he scooped Giana up in his arms and carried her from the nursery.

"Alex!" she cried between laughter and embarrassment.

When she breathed his name again, it was in passion as he moved deep within her. She had climaxed once before, so quickly, that she hid her face against his shoulder. And she called his name when the rippling sensations built in her again, making her legs tighten about his flanks. He arched his back, a deep moan breaking from his throat, and surged into her wildly. He was still only a moment, then moved against her again, stroking and caressing her until she was crying with the pleasure of it.

"I will marry you," he said when she had quieted.

Giana gazed up at his dark face above hers and smiled. "You will kill me with pleasure before I am forty," she said. "I love you, Alex, dearly, with all my heart. Please, let those words be enough, for there is all the trust you could ever wish in them."

You are late for dinner," the duke said, gazing from Alex to Giana. A slow smile spread over his face. "Well, my boy, if she looked any softer, you could spread her on your bread."

Alex squeezed Giana's hand and said blandly, "She is but a woman, sir, and cannot hide her cream-fed victory over me, a mere mortal man."

"I am leaving for California tomorrow," Delaney said. "If I am scalped by Indians, contrive to remember me."

"I think, Delaney," Aurora said, "that you should come back to England with us for a visit. Perhaps it is there your destiny lies. Who knows?"

"I shall consider it, ma'am. Yes, I shall consider it."

"New York isn't precisely Paris," the duke announced to the table at large.

"True," Giana said. "But New York is so full of life, and people from all over the world, and so free!"

"Bravo, Giana," Alex said, sitting back in his chair.

"Well, my love," the duke continued to Aurora, "I must admit to being most impressed with our colonies. And we are so close now, why the *Sirius* crossed the Atlantic in under two weeks. Of course we would have endured much more to see your dewy-eyed bundle."

"Was I dewy-eyed, Papa?" Leah asked.

"No, you were a wrinkled little red monkey," Delaney said. "I remember it quite well. But your papa decided to keep you."

"Glad I did, puss."

The duke turned his silvery eyes to Delaney. "California, my dear boy. Gad, it seems impossible that you colonists have stretched your hands all the way to the Pacific."

"Only the Pacific could have stopped us, sir," Alex said.

"I had wondered," Delaney said suddenly, "where Giana had got all her beauty. You, ma'am, are a lovely lady, if you will excuse the impertinence of a simple colonist."

"Marriage has improved her," Alex said, grinning at his mother-in-law.

"Hear, Aurora," Damien said. "The lad is most wise."

"For a mere colonist," Giana teased.

"Did I tell you, Alex," the duke said, "about the railroad car Aurora had her fellow design for me? It sports the Arlington crest and runs nearly to our home in the country."

"I would have supposed, sir," Giana teased, "that all your affairs now prosper from my mother's hand."

"What's-his-name seems to smile a lot," Damien said, sipping at the light red French wine, a present from Aurora.

"You do not act like Giana and Father," Leah announced suddenly, seeing the duke lightly caress Aurora's hand.

"Ah, in what way?" Delaney asked blandly.

"Really . . ." Giana shifted uncomfortably in her chair.

"You look at each other so . . . softly! And you're always touching!"

Alex rose slowly from his chair at the head of the dinner table, winked at his daughter, and walked to where Giana sat, her face flushed with embarrassment. He cupped her chin in his hand, forcing her to look up at him. He leaned down and gently kissed her full on the mouth.

"Alex!" she gasped.

"They will simply have to get used to us looking . . . soft, my love."

"The lad needed but a superb example," the duke said.

"Oh my," Leah said, her eyes widening.

"The *lad*," Delaney observed, "hates to be outdone in any arena. Prepare yourself, Giana, to look soft from now on."

"More wine, sir?" Alex asked smoothly.

"Nay, my boy," the duke said, eyeing his wife. "At my age, I need all my wits about me and . . . all my strength."

"Women are demanding, are they not, sir?"

"Dreadfully and charmingly so, lad."

Delaney slouched down in his chair and complained loudly, "As a bachelor, I must protest all this lascivious talk. My ears are burning."

"Ha!" Alex snorted. "If your ears are burning, it's out of sheer jealousy."

"Found out," Delaney mourned.

"Papa, what does 'lascivious' mean?"

"It's very . . . technical talk, Leah," Giana said, casting a reproachful glance at Alex. "All about your uncle's gold mines."

To Giana's surprise, a bottle of champagne appeared at the dinner table.

"What is this?" Alex said.

Aurora laughed. "It is a celebration, I trust. Giana, my love, all will be well now, between you and Alex?"

Giana stared, confounded, from her mother back to Alex.

"You . . . you told her?"

"I think she could tell from your besotted expression."

"Will a draft on my bank do, my boy?"

"Certainly, sir. That will be quite adequate," Alex said politely.

"A draft, sir? What are you talking about?"

"A wager, my dear Giana, a wager. The only one I ever intend to lose to your husband." He raised his champagne glass. "Hear, hear. To Mr. and Mrs. Alexander Saxton!"

"What the devil is he talking about, Alex?"

Alex's eyes were bright with devilry, and his voice was thick with his Irish brogue. "And sure, my dear, you haven't guessed? I am a man who always gets what he wants."

"A thousand pounds," the duke said mournfully. "A thousand pounds I wagered with this American bandit that he wouldn't get you to the altar!"

"Alex! You . . . you . . . !"

" 'You American bandit' will suffice, my love. With a damned English duke for a father-in-law!"

"I think," Delaney said to Leah, "there is a story here that you and I, my child, may never know."

◢▨ TOPAZ

SEARING ROMANCES

TEMPTING FATE by Jaclyn Reding. Beautiful, flame-haired Mara Despenser hated the English under Oliver Cromwell, and she vowed to avenge Ireland and become mistress of Kulhaven Castle again. She would lure the castle's new master, the infamous Hadrian Ross, the bastard Earl of St. Aubyn, into marriage. But even with her lies and lust, Mara was not prepared to find herself wed to a man whose iron will was matched by his irresistible good looks.　(405587—$4.99)

SPRING'S FURY by Denise Domning. Nicola of Ashby swore to kill Gilliam Fitz-Henry—murderer of her father, destroyer of her home—the man who would wed her in a forced match. Amid treachery and tragedy, rival knights and the pain of past wounds, Gilliam knew he must win Nicola's respect. Then, with kisses and hot caresses, he intended to win her heart.　(405218—$4.99)

PIRATE'S ROSE by Janet Lynnford. The Rozalinde Cavendish, independent daughter of England's richest merchant, was taking an impetuous moonlit walk along the turbulent shore when she encountered Lord Christopher Howard, a legendary pirate. Carried aboard his ship, she entered his storm-tossed world and became intimate with his troubled soul. Could their passion burn away the veil shrouding Christopher's secret past and hidden agenda?　(405978—$4.99)

DIAMOND IN DISGUISE by Elizabeth Hewitt. Isobel Leyland knew better than to fall in love with the handsome stranger from America, Adrian Renville. Despite his rugged good looks and his powerful animal magnetism, he was socially inept compared to the polished dandies of English aristocratic society—and a citizen of England's enemy in the War of 1812. How could she trust this man whom she suspected of playing the boor in a mocking masquerade?　(405641—$4.99)

*Prices slightly higher in Canada

Buy them at your local bookstore or use this convenient coupon for ordering.

PENGUIN USA
P.O. Box 999 — Dept. #17109
Bergenfield, New Jersey 07621

Please send me the books I have checked above.
I am enclosing $_____ (please add $2.00 to cover postage and handling). Send check or money order (no cash or C.O.D.'s) or charge by Mastercard or VISA (with a $15.00 minimum). Prices and numbers are subject to change without notice.

Card #_____ Exp. Date _____
Signature_____
Name_____
Address_____
City _____ State _____ Zip Code _____

For faster service when ordering by credit card call **1-800-253-6476**

Allow a minimum of 4-6 weeks for delivery. This offer is subject to change without notice.

WE NEED YOUR HELP

To continue to bring you quality romance
that meets your personal expectations,
we at TOPAZ books want to hear from you.
Help us by filling out this questionnaire, and in exchange
we will give you a **free gift** as a token of our gratitude.

- Is this the first TOPAZ book you've purchased? (circle one)

    YES   NO

    The title and author of this book is: _____

- If this was not the first TOPAZ book you've purchased, how many have you bought in the past year?

    a: 0 - 5   b 6 - 10   c: more than 10   d: more than 20

- How many romances in total did you buy in the past year?

    a: 0 - 5   b: 6 - 10   c: more than 10   d: more than 20 ____

- How would you rate your overall satisfaction with this book?

    a: Excellent   b: Good   c: Fair   d: Poor

What was the main reason you bought this book?

    a: It is a TOPAZ novel, and I know that TOPAZ stands
       for quality romance fiction
    b: I liked the cover
    c: The story-line intrigued me
    d: I love this author
    e: I really liked the setting
    f: I love the cover models
    g: Other: _____

Where did you buy this TOPAZ novel?

    a: Bookstore   b: Airport   c: Warehouse Club
    d: Department Store   e: Supermarket   f: Drugstore
    g: Other: _____

Did you pay the full cover price for this TOPAZ novel? (circle one)

    YES   NO
If you did not, what price did you pay? _____

Who are your favorite TOPAZ authors? (Please list)

How did you first hear about TOPAZ books?

    a: I saw the books in a bookstore
    b: I saw the TOPAZ Man on TV or at a signing
    c: A friend told me about TOPAZ
    d: I saw an advertisement in_____magazine
    e: Other: _____

What type of romance do you generally prefer?

    a: Historical   b: Contemporary
    c: Romantic Suspense   d: Paranormal (time travel,
       futuristic, vampires, ghosts, warlocks, etc.)
    d: Regency   e: Other: _____

What historical settings do you prefer?

    a: England   b: Regency England   c: Scotland
    e: Ireland   f: America   g: Western Americana
    h: American Indian   i: Other: _____

- What type of story do you prefer?

  a: Very sexy   b: Sweet, less explicit
  c: Light and humorous   d: More emotionally intense
  e: Dealing with darker issues   f: Other

- What kind of covers do you prefer?

  a: Illustrating both hero and heroine   b: Hero alone
  c: No people (art only)   d: Other_____

- What other genres do you like to read (circle all that apply)

  Mystery   Medical Thrillers   Science Fiction
  Suspense   Fantasy   Self-help
  Classics   General Fiction   Legal Thrillers
  Historical Fiction

- Who is your favorite author, and why?_____
  _____

- What magazines do you like to read? (circle all that apply)

  a: *People*   b: *Time/Newsweek*
  c: *Entertainment Weekly*   d: *Romantic Times*
  e: *Star*   f: *National Enquirer*
  g: *Cosmopolitan*   h: *Woman's Day*
  i: *Ladies' Home Journal*   j: *Redbook*
  k: Other:_____

- In which region of the United States do you reside?

  a: Northeast   b: Midatlantic   c: South
  d: Midwest   e: Mountain   f: Southwest
  g: Pacific Coast

- What is your age group/sex?   a: Female   b: Male

  a: under 18   b: 19-25   c: 26-30   d: 31-35   e: 56-60
  f: 41-45   g: 46-50   h: 51-55   i: 56-60   j: Over 60

- What is your marital status?

  a: Married   b: Single   c: No longer married

- What is your current level of education?

  a: High school   b: College Degree
  c: Graduate Degree   d: Other: _____

- Do you receive the TOPAZ *Romantic Liaisons* newsletter, a quarterly newsletter with the latest information on Topaz books and authors?

  YES   NO

  If not, would you like to?   YES   NO

  Fill in the address where you would like your free gift to be sent:

  Name: _____
  Address: _____
  City:_____Zip Code: _____

  You should receive your free gift in 6 to 8 weeks.
  Please send the completed survey to:

  Penguin USA•Mass Market
  Dept. TS
  375 Hudson St.
  New York, NY 10014